P9-CQW-756

SOINTULA

*S O I

Bere Point MALCOLM ISLAND

Port MacNeil

VANCOUVER ISLAND

PACIFIC OCEAN

NTULA

BILL GASTON

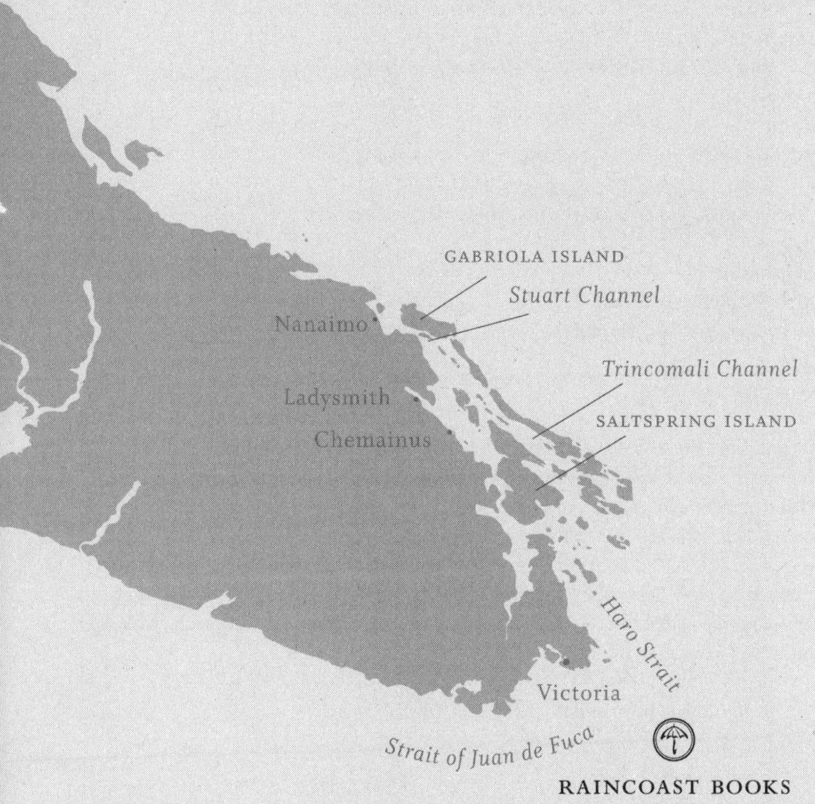

RAINCOAST BOOKS
Vancouver

Raincoast Books acknowledges the ongoing financial support of the Government of Canada through The Canada Council for the Arts and the Book Publishing Industry Development Program (BPIDP); and the Government of British Columbia through the BC Arts Council.

Editor: Lynn Henry
Cover and interior design: Ingrid Paulson

NATIONAL LIBRARY OF CANADA CATALOGUING IN PUBLICATION
Gaston, Bill, 1953–
Sointula / Bill Gaston.
ISBN 1-55192-719-5
I. Title.
PS8563.A76S64 2004 C813'.54 C2004-901965-1

LIBRARY OF CONGRESS CONTROL NUMBER: 2004092410

Raincoast Books
9050 Shaughnessy Street
Vancouver, British Columbia
Canada, V6P 6E5
www.raincoast.com

At Raincoast Books we are committed to protecting the environment and to the responsible use of natural resources. We are acting on this commitment by working with suppliers and printers to phase out our use of paper produced from ancient forests. This book is one step towards that goal. It is printed on 100% ancient-forest-free paper (40% post-consumer recycled), processed chlorine- and acid-free, and supplied by New Leaf paper. It is printed with vegetable-based inks. For further information, visit our website at www.raincoast.com. We are working with Markets Initiative (www.oldgrowthfree.com) on this project.

Printed in Canada by Friesens

10 9 8 7 6 5 4 3 2 1

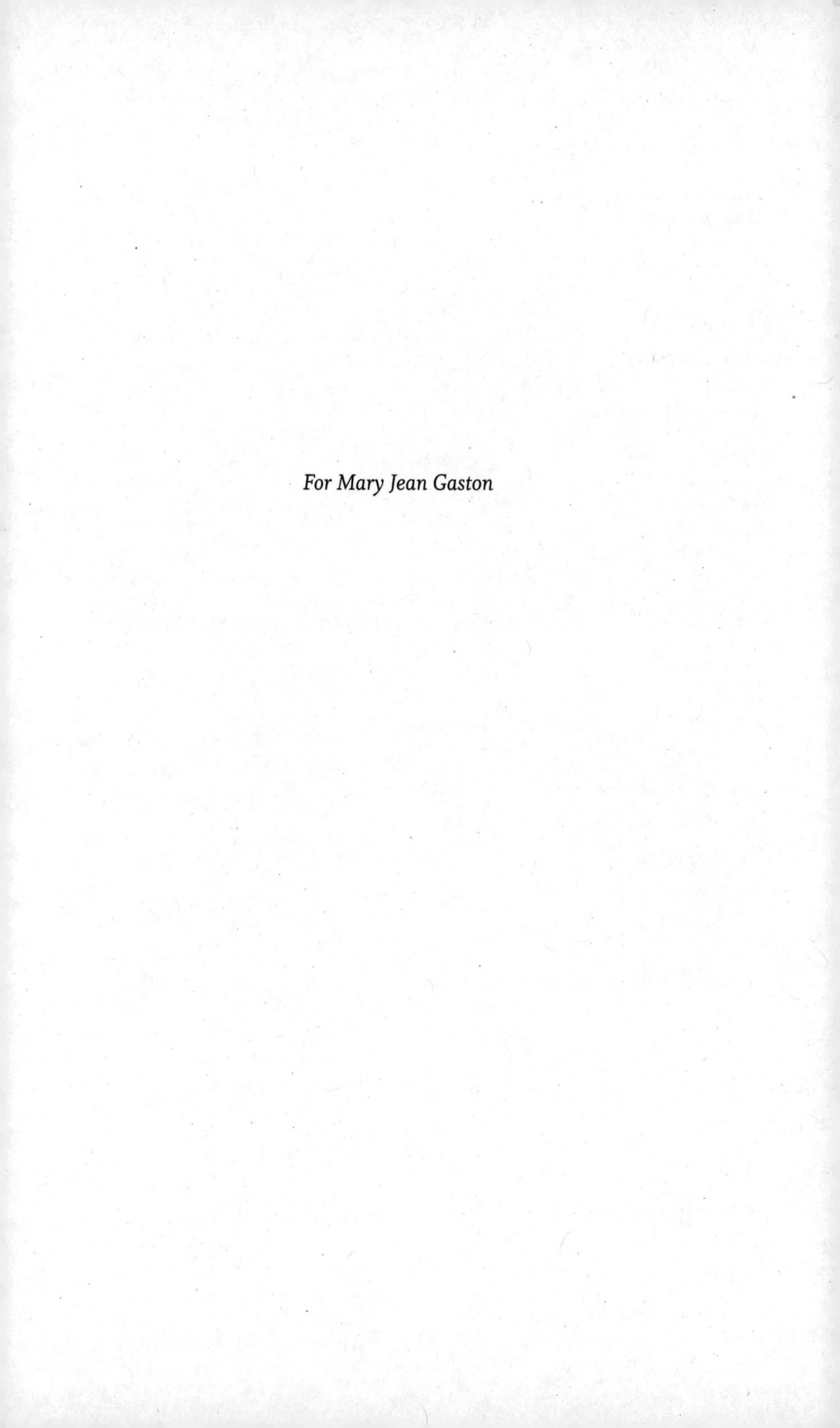

For Mary Jean Gaston

One
SITTING WELL WITH HAIR ON FIRE

The spreading of eagle down on the water is the most ancient and universal symbol of peace and welcome on the northwest coast. In 1774 when the Spanish explorer Juan Perez blundered onto the Queen Charlotte Islands, his ship was circled by two Haida canoes, each with a chief dancing in the bow and spreading eagle down on the water.

— MICHAEL POOLE, *RAGGED ISLANDS*

MALCOLM ISLAND

THE CLOUDY SKY looks like late morning. Tom sits on his log with no idea how long he's had the headphones on. There has been no squeak of whale-talk. Nothing all day. No tiny explosive puff of mist on the horizon, no black fin shocking him awake. A fog bank is coming, swallowing the point.

Staring into the dim north, up Queen Charlotte Strait, Tom lets the soft bass hiss take him over, penetrate him completely. He doesn't know if the headphones give him an electronic version of underwater or if he's hearing the real thing and he's really in it. Whichever, it feels like the ocean has come right into his brain and his blood.

He can sometimes take off on a thought and ride it awhile, like today: this white noise is God's breath he's hearing, it's exactly that. God doesn't breathe like we do, there's no in and out. It's steady, it's in and out at the same time. He rides that one.

He understands this is the noise killer whales hear all the time. He pictures a transient ripping into a blue whale so big you can't see either end of it, just the wall of bluish skin and clouds of blood. The largest being on earth. The orca sleek as enamel paint, a black bullet as thick as a van going thirty-miles-an-hour under water. Imagine water on your face that fast... Both whales were born in this noise, God's white noise, and both learned everything from it. Now one is killing, and one is dying, in breath that goes in and out at the same time.

TOM STANDS AND stretches his spine in the way he thinks he recalls one doctor telling him he should, for circulation. This fog bank is the lifting kind. Overhead Tom can sense, more than see, a threat of blue. They say the sun *burns* fog off. He thinks he's seen that. Well, not seen it. Burning off would be a disappearing, and you don't see that, do you?

No orca at all and he has no sense of any coming. Though he doesn't trust that sort of sense because killer whales always surprise him. He takes his headphones off and turns to consider the wall of trees, wonders if he should slog up to camp and make tea. He notices that, phones off, one ear is cold in the mist while the other he can't feel at all. He's almost used to this.

He once read somewhere that fog can steal your mind. What would that be like? Another disappearing you wouldn't see. It looks like the fog has stolen all the morning light, holds it glowing inside its shape, like a big amoeba lamp the size of a city.

What fog does steal, is all colour. Tom takes in the trees. They are having a hard time looking green.

Orca look unbelievable coming out of such a fog bank, surprising him even more than they do normally. He has seen them come out of fog twice, the first time a massive pod, thirty or more. Your breath catches, your heart stops. They burst through like the true army of heaven. An army of fast and happy devils.

Tom stares into the white glow a moment, inviting it to take him. It looks too innocent. He takes a stance anyway in the beach gravel, shuffling his feet to sink them in and find firmament. He tries to concentrate, but on what he doesn't know. He sees his palms have actually turned out, toward it.

He remembers being a kid in bed, back in Oakville, and hearing that nightly far-off train, how it stole you too, pulled you away if you listened. Where is the closest train to where he's standing now? Hundreds of miles. They never did get one up this way. Only a single road was built this far north and it ends a mile down from this beach at a clearing in the bush. Then a trudge down a trail that, for him and his leg, takes an hour. Today he has to make that trudge, fill his water jugs. When he waits in the clearing it's usually only a few hours before someone happens by to give him a ride to Sointula's gas-station's water hose. He won't forget this chore because the next time he lifts his empty jugs there it will be. Though he already may have lifted them and already forgot. Time dies.

He will also remember to treat himself to a hamburger, or a halibut burger, at the stand.

Or he could just keep going. Someday he will. The road leads anywhere. Take it to the ferry off Malcolm, take it south all day to Victoria, and off Vancouver Island, take it east for a week then dip and you're in New York City, where he went once, as alone as he is now. He was maybe fourteen. Just hitched from Oakville one day. He was kicked out of school that afternoon, why not. He remembers a pool hall in Hamilton, then Niagara Falls, where he heard but didn't see the falls, then over the border and overnight somewhere, there was a girl with him for a while, and then New York, stayed at the Y and got into some fun after Roy sent emergency cash, and the next day two uniforms put him on a bus.

He's standing in the thick of the fog bank and he can't see the tops of the cedars. Can't see the top of the lodgepole snag, with its ghostly face. The Natives were good at spooky. What a name to go by: Kwakwaka'*wak*w. None of them here now. The kids of the socialist Finns turned out to be rednecks — the girl at the burger stand suggested this when he asked why all the Natives lived one island over at Alert Bay. Or maybe he heard wrong.

He can't see the ravens either and their *ploink-ploink*ing comedy clucks come out of the fog like the birds could be anywhere. He likes when they do their scream, the scream of a bad rock-and-roll singer, insincere. Ravens can sound like they're mocking you, but that's impossible to know.

TOM STARTLES AT the sight of her coming his way, using the logs as a path. Some people walk the loud gravel, some the silent driftwood logs. He's a gravel person because of his leg. Though he sometimes forgets and starts on a log.

It's Catherine. He remembers her name is Catherine. Macleod, PhD. He remembers also that he calls her Boss-Lady, and she likes it. She's halfway to him. It looks like she has a pack of some sort; maybe she's brought him some lemons. She's wearing a jacket along with that completely stupid orange vest with its bright yellow ×, the kind highway flag girls wear, or scared hunters. She's too smart to actually believe there's such a thing as safety. People like her work so hard at fooling themselves. And colour like that doesn't fit here, is embarrassing, makes humans not fit, makes him not fit.

He doesn't want to talk to her, even though they'll be talking orca. He sits down on his log, snugs the headphones back on, turns the volume knob up, and turns away.

She's a babe, though, sort of, in that way some pretty women let their hair go totally white young enough that you can still see them as blonde. And he'll have her for his ride to the gas station and burger stand. If he remembers to ask her. If he remembers to lift a water jug. Time dies.

TOM FEELS A TAP on the shoulder. He turns to see who it is. That's right, it's Boss-Lady. Her mouth is open and she's talking to him. The volume on the headphones is way up and, while she talks to him, he simply smiles back at her. Her mouth opens and closes and her eyes are all excited and her cheeks are red, but all he can hear is holy white noise.

When compared to the Danes of Cape Scott, or the Norwegians of Knight Inlet, one can see a certain arrogance in the idealism practiced by those first Sointula Finns. The Finns' arrogance was that of any settlers who publicly announce that they are founding a utopia. In fact it's a two-fold arrogance: on the one hand they claim to know what's wrong in the world, and on the other hand they claim to have a solution.

— DON COTTER, *LOST UTOPIAS*

CADBORO BAY, VICTORIA

LIVING OUTDOORS HAS shown her that the sun is, first of all, wilderness.

Evelyn lies still, the morning too bright in her eyes. She abides the fierce lecture, feeling where religion came from. The wool blanket they gave her wasn't enough last night but it's a furnace now. She rolls out, smelling herself in wafts that follow. She squints into the chiding light. Listens for voices. Then takes her ten hunched paces through the salal bushes, to squat. She hopes she hasn't used the same spot twice. One doesn't want to create a latrine.

Stiff in the knees, Evelyn treads back to her clearing to sit on her blanket and face the sun, which has pulled free of the ocean's rim. She takes a breath and lets it go back out her nostrils, into the morning. She wonders what comes next. No shapes spangle and die, falling off the edge of her vision, like yesterday. Maybe that's over. But she sees Claude's face again and, in surprised coughs, starts to cry.

SHE USES THE SUN like she used to use coffee. With its help she climbs into her senses.

What's serious this morning is, her body craves food badly. Her resolve is still strong but things have gotten physical. Maybe she's more desperate this morning because she's tired. No-sleep tired. Can't even shoo these beach fleas on her ankles, tired.

She stretches stiffly and feels how all night the sand wouldn't conform to her bones. She spent more of last night awake than asleep.

Dizzy, even lying down. She thinks she might have thrown up but sees no evidence in the sand.

Sometime during the night she also felt sick about Roy. Feeling guilty about Roy. She sees her husband as he is this minute, three thousand miles away, at his desk in Oakville City Hall, overlooking that weird blue of his lake, biting into a deli sandwich, an unfocussed stare, worried. Wife incommunicado. What's it been, five days? Six? Roy expecting her home or at least a phone call, an explanation. She's phoned just that once, left a message with bare facts only. All he knows is her "old friend" died and now she's looking for Tommy. And maybe he's seen that she's left her pills on the nightstand.

Isn't that what she's doing? Looking for Tommy?

Evelyn startles at a footfall off to the left but it's only a crow, roughing up a clam shell. Making itself breakfast. She feels her stomach hollow and rumble, as if it wants a chance at that clam.

She can't help but see a Roy entertained by her disappearance. Men like Roy enjoy crisis. He calls it stress but most of him likes it. At the airport he would have waited and waited, hunting her face in the dwindling herd. When she doesn't get off the plane he goes into action. Maybe he called Victoria, maybe he has people hunting her. How did he describe her to them? Middle-aged, middle-height, with middle-length henna hair? "Pretty." "For her age." "Green eyes, flecked with yellow." Despite these eyes Roy used to compare her to the young Elizabeth Taylor. She always saw that as wishful thinking on his part, plus she hated Elizabeth Taylor. But is someone searching Victoria for Elizabeth Taylor?

Other crows have come to scream and stab at the clam and she remembers the party on the beach last night, a young bender, right near her hiding spot because she's farthest from houses. Maybe it's the weekend. Is it graduation time? Female shrieks, male roars. Aside from getting discovered, she isn't worried about a bunch of wealthy teenagers. Cadboro is maybe the toniest Victoria beach. Which is why she came here, figuring it's the last place they'll look for bums to boot out. Last night she came an inch from getting peed on by some kid, it scared him more than her. She can still hear him scrambling away over gravel, hoarse with joy, *Jesus I just pissed on a bag lady.* She doesn't mind being a source of entertainment but she really doesn't want to be found. By some junior drinker lurching out of fire-light to upchuck in private. Imagine, wife of the incumbent Mayor of Oakville, flopped on the sand like a dead seal, revived by a freshet of lemon gin and french fries.

Evelyn startles again, this time at a dog's bark. Dog and owner are a ways down the beach. She'll hide till they pass. Discovery is too raw to bear. Flip a tide-rock with a foot — the way gelatinous life squirts and shrinks and hides, caught without skin.

NO BREEZE YET this morning. The sea is a mirror, which makes for postcard mountains across the strait and an idyllic marina a few hundred yards off, the upside-down masts, the reflected colours so rich you feel them up the nose. Water giving its liquid mood to all. There are the two seals, in their breakfast cruise, heads like lacquered bowling balls. Caddy will be brilliant as Hercules if he decides to show.

Yes — she came here, to this beach, to see Caddy. Claude's sea monster Caddy.

She strips to halter top and khaki shorts. Out of smelling range she is indistinguishable from a tourist, or rich local for that matter. Waterfront-property owner out for her morning walk. Except that this one wants to plunge her head under and come up scrubbing. She wishes she could use soap but public suds are a sure sign of homelessness. But this itch. Pestilence. She must find some soap, and the gumption to bathe at midnight, when only the big-eyed and monstrous cruise the inky water. Octopi, sharks, Caddy. Naked Evelyn Poole. She finds the image monstrously freeing.

In a burst of energy and will she strides down to the water's edge like she owns the place. Well, she does. As much as anyone. As much as the People once did. She is a new native. Off to the right, where the teenage party was, a white sapling of smoke stands perfectly vertical in the air.

EVELYN CATCHES HERSELF chewing beachgrass. She thinks again about what she's doing. Why has she slept here three nights now, why has she put up with this right hip and shoulder so sore from the sand? She's tried flipping onto her back but then her pelvis sticks up, becomes her body's peak, and her back instantly hurts, so it's back to the right hip and shoulder. Never her left. In her left pocket is a metal cigar tube. Which she taps.

And reminds herself she's here because of Tommy. Which makes no sense. Claude told her Tommy is up north watching whales.

No. She remembers: her pills. Went off her pills and hasn't been thinking straight. In fact sometimes feels crazy in the darkest way. Though it is getting better.

But, no, she's sleeping here because Claude slept here. Not exactly here but beaches near downtown. *That's* what she's doing here — joining Claude on the beach, making his last year not seem so awful. From his murmurs — his greasy hot head on the hospital pillow, his eyes open but only maybe seeing her — she learned about his migration to beaches. Waterfront property, he joked. Lost his house, he said. Didn't want to bug his friends, and anyway preferred beaches, even in the winter rains, covered by plastic. And, Evelyn surmised, anesthetized by whatever poison he got his hands on that day.

While he mumbled wisps of memory and dream, she stared at him and marveled at how far an innocent man can fall.

At one point, his head stilled on its pillow and he found her eyes and he said something almost clearly: "Life a little joke, eh?" Then continued his fever, and his falling away.

Is Claude enjoying the punch-line now? Not even the sun knows what's on the other side.

Walking, shading her eyes, staring across at the mountains, she does see her last twenty-five years as a little joke, a quip, a bubble held together only by its surface oil, its swirling colours. It could pop any second. Maybe it already has. Well of course it has: look where she's been sleeping.

Evelyn turns and just makes it back to her clearing to sit hard on the sand. Claude's face. She's crying again. Sitting, crying again. After a time it strikes her that it's become easy. Too easy, a habit. As ignorant as breathing.

NEAR THE MARINA she passes a dead crab before it registers. She turns, spinning on her heel, digging it into the sand. She's noticed these heel-holes of hers up and down the beach, each one a change of mind. An *or*, or a *but*.

The crab's almost full-size. Is it dead, or is it the molted shell of a crab still alive out there underwater, bigger, new shell soft as wax paper? She remembers toeing a similar crab once and saying, *dead crab*, and Claude telling her it was a molted shell. She could see no difference but kept mum. It was Claude's realm.

She toes this corpse, or shell, and understands. Claude's dead. She's only molted. Do the molted cry so much? Probably, they lack shells. But isn't she just playing? Being dramatic? Life truly is unseemly on this beach and she is no further from money than a phone call and she has no reason for being here that would convince anybody, least of all Roy.

The dead crab hurts and hollows her stomach, which can't not see the shell redder from boiling, glossy with butter, a lemon wedge, deep green parsley sprig the diabolical added touch.

Today is a turning point with hunger. Till now she's met the challenge, she's learned to recognize the voices of hunger as not her main voice. Hunger uses the voices of any addiction and she listens to their pleas as she would to toddlers and cheats. She's lost pounds she maybe needed to lose but also some more she didn't. There's loose skin at her waist like an empty money belt. (A downside of Cadboro Bay is that she can't beg. Cops would arrive in minutes. She knows all about paying the kind of property taxes that protect one from the likes of her.) Today, hunger has crept into her main voice. Hunger feels like "I."

So she decides to ask for food. She turns on her heel in front of the group-home. It appears they aren't up yet. Blinds closed to the morning sun, lawn chairs folded up against the stucco. Group homes are often militaristically neat. She volunteered at three of them, teaching lifeskills, the mayor's pretty wife showing how you add tuna and frozen peas to the mac and cheese, call it a casserole.

Her stomach hollows again: steaming macaroni, cheese, whole milk, peas not overcooked but crunchy, tuna on its strong path to the brain and bones, salt, fresh cracked pepper. *Ow.*

There are about twenty waterfront houses here in the middle of the bay. Amid lots of cedar-and-glass is this stucco group home. Boxy, modest, it looks like a big bland nurse. It reminds her of her first Oakville house — the warmth of beige stucco, the old wood inside. Gazing out her sewing-room, she liked how the leaded glass distorted things, jello-like. It made sight innocently less important. When they moved, Roy said the house was too humble.

She's walked past here so often she feels she knows the residents. Two are folded into wheelchairs, one an older Down survivor. Others are more vaguely challenged, but stand and sit uncertain how to do waterfront. Even in bathing suits they seem oddly dressed, though you can't put a finger on how. Evelyn has caught snatches of talk. One man who wears teal shorts often wonders about sandwiches, what kind they'll be having today. One woman, thirtyish and hefty, often asks the others when Mary ("Ma-hee") will come.

It's a brave place for a group home. The neighbours will be nervous about property values. Evelyn sees the group home residents as guardians of the beach. Unsure about why it is they are here — isn't that a lovely contrast to the rest of the human race? Earlier this week, watching the purposeful hordes downtown, Evelyn saw mass mental illness.

She knows the residents aren't less complicated than she is herself, but as a group they do resemble a vegetable garden. Unlike flowers and their confident way they face the sun, these folks face in random directions. A lopsided pepper, a lolling squash, a beet pointing its purple worry down. They are too humble to have questions about the sun.

But if they did, they'd ask Rolf. He's blond, ice-blue eyed, and certain, so Evelyn calls him Rolf. He either owns the house or works there. Sitting in his chair, with flicks of the wrist or small asides he conducts their lives for them. So it seems from Evelyn's glances up. One doesn't want to be caught staring at the wounded.

Rolf rarely moves from his chair. Steady amidst their uncertainty. He reminds her of something the older Tibetan woman said to her on the steps of the Oakville Art Gallery, that good meditation is like keeping your seat though your hair is on fire. In any event, Rolf will see her and won't judge. He's used to handing sandwiches to the badly molted.

She returns to her end of the beach. It's hot now and actually she *is* starving. She checks that nobody's watching, steps into her bushes, takes up her jug and guzzles it down, to fill her stomach. A hostile *woof* scares her, and now a low-growling dog follows its nose into her clearing. Evelyn is instantly unafraid because it's small and old. The look in its eyes accuses her of trespass. Then fraud. They stare for a few moments and she shouts, *Go!* just as a man shouts *Come*! from beyond the bushes, and with a final chastising *woof* the dog goes, or comes, and she's left shaking her head at coincidence.

Emerging from the bushes, Evelyn poses briefly as a disappointed berry-picker. Then scans for Caddy, semi-famous sea monster. She heads back down the beach and passes again in front of the group home, still no one about. In a walkway between it and the next house a lady clicks up in heels. Before going indoors she shoots the group home a nose-up, but what Evelyn notices is her hat. A big Sunday hat. So today is Sunday and Rolf may have taken his charges to church. Group homes excel at field trips that are free.

Nine or ten strollers enjoy the beach. Maybe one of these days she'll run into an old friend — what are the chances? She did grow up a few miles away. Would she recognize a forty-five-year-old from high school? Even less likely that they would recognize her. But, these beach strollers: two she recognizes from her several days here. Which means they recognize her. She dreads the day that she is deemed approachable. "So," the homeowner will ask, "which is yours?" And

Evelyn will lie, “That peach rancher up the hill,” pointing at the house belonging to the homeowner’s bridge partner Iris.

WADING ALONG, she finds the muddy shallows near the marina to be the warmest, so she takes her plunge, her bath, soaplessly kneading her skull. Only drying off in the sun does she feel what still clings to her. Already she feels itchy again. She considers the water’s thick colour and riper smell, and suffers the image of boaters flushing their holding tanks. There are far more clams here too, little shit-eaters squirting up her calves as she treads their mud and hard lumpy backs.

Tribes in these waters dubbed themselves The Clam-Eaters. A description neither idealistic nor humble. Accurate. What are we? Be accurate: Hurriers. Planet-eaters. If the sun is our fierce king, the ocean is our vast queen. Our queen is prone and receptive and look what we are doing to her.

She needs to find a beach where she can eat the clams. She needs something to dig with and a pot. But now from her bath she will probably get swimmers-ear, which she had once as a child. Screaming and a round of antibiotics. From here it’s a two-hour walk downtown to a street clinic that tends the penniless. Will she be screaming when she finds it? Is pain her next challenge? She’s never been good at it. There’s a normal hospital only a mile from here. Maybe it was rash to lose her ID.

Can something be both rash and necessary?

She told Roy that her old friend died and that now she has to find Tommy and that’s all she told him, cryptic message into the phone. She hung up, turned away, left the building, let the airporter drive off with her luggage. She spent her remaining cash on a taxi, which dropped her at the oceanfront south of downtown. “Away from this smell” was her first direction to the driver. As she walked the shoreline she could feel her empty seat flying to Toronto and this left her breathless. That first night she sat up till dawn on a bench so she could have the ocean’s clean breeze on her face and not smell that smell. That’s it — *smell* is why she’s here on this beach.

She had just signed Claude's death papers (his next-of-kin sister okayed long distance that she do so) and was riding the hospital elevator with a well-dressed man. His cologne was sharp in her nose and suddenly, *here is* Claude's death-face again, fresh, horrific. Then in the corridor a woman wore some kind of bold scent and, *here is* Claude's face, sharper than nightmare.

Outside in the crowds it continued, and Evelyn understood that there must be a chemical in people's perfumes common to the shampoo or soap the hospital had used to wash Claude. Leaning in to kiss him or whisper in his ear, she'd smelled it, an inhuman smell, it raked inside her sinuses. Now, passing scented people, she kept smelling it, and smelling it meant *seeing* him at the last breath, his muscles slack, face falling bloodless, cheeks yellow and grey, whiskers growing out of yellow and grey. Eyes empty as tin.

So it was smell that drove her to the ocean, where she could hold her face up in the breeze. A few times she tried moving back to the city, perhaps even to find a hotel. Until she left her cards and ID somewhere. But even when unscented, the streets and the people were hard to take, their complications, their weird desires coming off them like rays. The kids, they were now so cool that *nothing* mattered except being cool. This is also what drove her off the streets — all these kids trying to act like Tommy.

And there was the newspaper story, *Rocket Fights For Life*. A hockey icon was back east in a coma. A coincidence: Claude has just lost his own fight and here's Rocket Richard, Claude's all-time hero, so much so that when Claude spoke of him he struggled to find words. Richard was maybe Claude's biggest tie to a hard Quebec childhood. Evelyn could vaguely picture Richard in his red uniform, his big glaring eyes. How did this headline writer know The Rocket was *fighting for his life*? Here was an icon with one more easy lie circling him. She would give the seventy-three cents in her pocket to read the headline *Rocket Confused and Frightened*. This constant lying drove her down to the beach as well.

Roy will get an explanation when she phones him. He deserves that much. But, so far, she has nothing to tell him that he could hear.

Roy could not conceive of this style of camping, of her destitute on purpose, hunting a sandwich.

And she should be getting off this beach. Isn't that what she should do? Go find Tommy? It's what she promised Claude. She taps the cigar tube in her pocket, tries to picture herself delivering this father to that son.

She's now in water up to her knees, the tide having risen while she's wondered at endless things. Returning to the clearing she sits, drawing in the sand with a stick, crying only a little and hardly noticing. She draws a cartoon Caddy, giving him a smile then erasing it for a neutral mouth, a straight line.

She first heard the name "Caddy" downtown. The young fellow was stuttering, raving to his fellow panhandlers about a sea monster and two sightings this spring. They should all hitch to Cadboro Bay with a camera, there would be "like total money" in a picture of it. Instead the kids pooled their change for hard lemonade and Evelyn ended up in her nook in the library. Could this be the same creature Claude used to swear he had seen? She read that seventy years ago the creature got the diminutive "Caddy" from Cadborosaurus, after being spotted in Cadboro Bay by someone respectable, a city councillor. Similar creatures had been seen by many others up and down the coast. Native petroglyphs showed a likeness also described by sailors and fishermen: head like a camel, two knobby horns, a stringy sort of mane. Those who saw the animal up close exclaimed on its eyes, which were huge and — a word she read more than once —"kind." Evelyn suspects large eyes indicate a hunter of the lightless depths more than they do "kindness." Nonetheless, witnesses, already out on the limb of public ridicule, felt compelled to say these eyes were not just "kind" but also "calm"and — most remarkably —"calming."

Claude had no name for his monster. Recalling the times she heard him tell his story, she remembers how no one really listened. He was working mid-coast on a tug, going two miles-per-hour for days. "I dunno what in hell it is," is how he'd finish, "but *ow*, I know it is *some*thing." She hears his "ow" so clearly. Maybe a mispronounced "wow," or "woah," he said it all the time. It could mean amazement. Or wariness. Or that he understood. Last week, when he said it from his hospital bed, it could have meant all of those things.

Claude is in her pocket, ashes in a tube. *Ow.*

Evelyn scans the distant group home again and, finally, there they are on the lawn. The two wheelchair fellows, the big woman who says "Ma-hee." Rolf, she can see his head, blond and steady. She gets up, dizzy for a moment, then locates her hair brush. She will be frank with Rolf: I have no food. I will not be a bother tomorrow. And, *I'm not like this.*

Brushing her hair she casts a long look over her shoulder for Caddy, a romantic tic she's enjoyed for some time now. She realizes she actually thinks she will see him. She wants mostly to see those eyes. To get that close, she'll have to be in a boat. A boat seems right in any case. To search for Caddy, then find a beach with edible clams. Where the People once lived.

HAIR TIGHT TO her skull, scalp-itch brushed dull for now, she makes her way down the beach. She has brought along her things — blanket rolled around sweater, water jug, knife, brush — because if all goes well she will ask if she can wash everything, maybe even ask for a bath. Rolf might even ask her what kind of sandwich she prefers. She will say tuna, and cheese, with lots of greens. She won't refuse his offer of two.

The beach is now a scatter of children, dogs, bright plastic toys. Twenty years ago it would have been the Ontario lakeshore, her and Tommy. She remembers giving him empty yogurt tubs and serving spoons and him eyeing other kids' red, blue or yellow plastic. She can't remember *Roy* and Tommy at the beach. Roy is out grinning as he cuts a ribbon. No, untrue, twenty years ago he wasn't His Worship, wasn't even yet an alderman. Evelyn remembers when he was first elected, when at their victory barbeque she asked, "Would Your Worship like a dill on the side?" He chuckled politely, but his eyes told her that the office wasn't to be mocked. This is another reason she's here, walking up to a stranger for a sandwich.

But if she phoned, Roy would come. If she even said the word "Victoria" he'd be here tomorrow and would search in desperation. He has no way of knowing that, if he found her, he would have to sit and listen, and his worry would take a whole new turn. He is a good man and a good man only, and this is also why she is here.

She feels weaker the closer she gets to her sandwich. Her stomach has turned to face her and she knows that from now on it won't leave her alone.

She's twenty steps from the group home when snarling and screaming breaks out. It's hard to separate the two sounds, both coming from a savage place. A girl of six or seven, and a dog. There is blood, and a father's screams, louder than the girl's.

The dog is being kicked by more than one adult but it won't let go of the girl. A piece of fried chicken is trampled in the sand; maybe it had a role in the attack. The dog, squat and muscled, is grey, almost a mauve. It might be a pit bull but she's never been clear on that breed. The dog has the girl deep at the armpit. There is much blood. Beaten around the head, the dog flattens its ears and squints. It looks ancient and reptilian in its clamping down.

The group home residents edge the seawall fence, mewing, moaning. The big woman's chest heaves. Not leaving his chair, Rolf watches and speaks calmly to someone.

Evelyn bangs open their gate and leaps the stairs — why hasn't Rolf run for the phone? She shouts at him, "*911! C'mon!*" and still Rolf doesn't move, even when she stands over him and yells and points at his glass patio doors. The sounds he makes are wispy and muddled, and only now does she see he's been talking all along to no one but himself. His ice-blue eyes reveal confusion less earthly than that of his housemates. On his arms are scabs from what appear to be burns. She catches a whiff of his cologne.

Back on the sand she walks moderately fast, away from the screaming. There's nothing to do, and she doesn't want to know. By now more than one homeowner has gone inside to call. Often it's best to calmly remove oneself.

When she sees the boat she spins on her heel and heads for it but doesn't hurry. It's inflatable. Unlike a child's yellow-and-blue kind, this boat is mostly olive, with a camouflage pattern resembling a frog, and larger. Nearing it, she can see it's made from canvas. Two plastic oars splay up, antic little wings.

The feeling in her chest is one of moving forward, not away from. Evelyn throws her blanket roll in, tows the boat to knee depth. The water is icy, focusing her itchy head. Behind in the near distance the screams and shouts rise and fall as if hell has a rhythm. Water runs off her legs as she clambers in and when she falls to a sit her bottom is wet. She kicks aside a telescopic fishing rod and what looks wondrously like a nylon day-pack of lunch. Rowing takes a few moments to remember and then her boat moves well. She entertains for less than a second that this could be the little girl's boat — it simply can't be because if it was, Evelyn would have to die.

If she's being dramatic, only the sun is watching. It's maybe five minutes before she hears deep male shouts aimed her way, but they're faint and she's almost around the point and into an excellent current.

After days of waiting for favourable weather,
more than thirty canoes set out, some of them
fifty-footers, six-and-a-half feet across the beam.
Before embarking, Collison knelt on the beach,
commending his family to the care of the Almighty.
The Haidas took more tangible precautions,
exchanging their children and other relatives to
bind the party together in common interest.

— MICHAEL POOLE, *RAGGED ISLANDS*

VICTORIA

IN THE BRIGHT HALLS behind him, some woman exits the hospital speaking clearly to no one about a smell.

Seated at her desk, which also looks made of linoleum, the nurse proffers a vial of Demerol tablets. Barely conscious, wobbly on his feet, Peter Gore reaches. He feels infantile and violated — minutes ago he was ordered to vacate his cot and leave the hospital. Before dropping the vial into his palm, making him wait, the nurse meets his eye and says, "One now for pain, one every six hours as needed." Her bovine drone-of-spirit threatening to re-anaesthetize him as he stands, Gore accepts the vial and clutches it. The pain has been fading but you do as they say.

The attending physician walks in, flips open his chart, over his glasses meets Gore's eye, repeats himself with authority and some malice: "*Get it done.*" He turns on his heel and heads back into the emergency catacombs to attend to the next ailing slab. Gore knows that to these people he was never a person but a troublesome and now ambulatory gallbladder.

These Canadian doctors, tough buggers. Gore gets the wall clock in focus: 6:30 a.m. He has spent six hours in his curtain-cubicle passing gallstones, kneeling in his little backless gown, pounding his fist on his pillow, retching their watery lemonade. He's slept one hour, if the pastel swirl they'd induced by injecting morphia into his meat could be called sleep.

"Please, can you call me a taxi?"

"There's a phone in the concourse."

Snubbed by the busy bovine, Peter seeks a "concourse." He finds no quarter in his change. He is hating this nurse, and Victoria. But the phone she directed him to turns out to be a direct line to a taxi company, free. Peter Gore decides to forgive, and to begin again.

HE FIGHTS off sleep in the cab's back seat, its warm somnambulant leather. *Get it done.* Yes, sir. I've been meaning to, sir. The doctor actually raised his voice after Peter whimpered that his gallbladder had been having-at him a few years now. In his wincing agonies it was impossible to explain that his is a well-trained, perfectly controllable bladder; that as a biologist he understands its squeezings of bile and jostling stones; that the hotel's chicken curry had been made with cream reduction and that he'd ignorantly wolfed it, though he hadn't even been hungry, what with lunchtime pizza still swollen down there. Mostly he'd wanted to accuse the doctor of living in and thereby condoning a city whose two-hundred-fifty-dollar hotel wouldn't let you sleep in its bed because its forty-dollar meal landed you in hospital.

So, what a waste, staying at the Empress. So much for the symbolic start of his trip. He had checked into its opulence, turned on the bath with its floridly wrought faucet and knobs, watched the languid Victorian steam rise, and vowed: One night of posh, then tomorrow I start roughing it. He did the hotel's "high tea" (pouring it all on top of his swelling pizza, and being charged thirty-six-fifty for the ritual), went for a stroll along the inner harbour, rented one of those tiny motor scooters upon which he scooted the celebrated waterfront routes with other tourists, the writer-in-him feeling embarrassed if not debased to be part of this string of obese Americans zooming topsy on underlarge farting toys — and then returned to swallow that curry. Then he lay back to watch some telly, and in the midst of a *West Wing* rerun began his two hours of gut-pain pacing before he headed off to hospital. Now the taxi meter is clicking close to ten dollars, he hasn't slept in his expensive bed, a doctor has shouted at him for wanting to hang on to one of his organs, he is about to head into the B.C. wilderness, and he has three hours — until checkout time — for a nap.

He pays the cabby and turns to face the ivied magnificence of the hotel, which he in some sense owns for a few more hours, but he can't lift his eyes from the white carriage horse poised there imitating a postcard. Shifting, slightly, the heft of one buttock, it moves a hoof, widens its stance, raises its tail. It is clear what it is going to do. It does, and Gore can't not stare as the stuff just sort of *falls* out, all thickly tumbling disorder, to land and steam on the pavement. Mushy monstrous gallstones. The four-legged white gallbladder — muscular, healthy, successful — lifts its head and whinnies relief. Gore feels his own head lift in a near-whinny of congratulations. The horse's driver, wearing a vest and top hat and a look more interrogative than scornful, seems to consider Peter Gore something of a perv.

Deciding not to claim that as a biologist he should be expected to watch exactly these events, Peter ignores his accuser and dares a look up at the Empress and its ivy, the edifice chiding him, as he knew it would, as he approaches the hole of her mouth — she a colossal and heartless mother, her imperial mood backed by the weight of the British Empire. He takes out his vial, swallows another Demerol, climbs the broad stone steps, enters Mum's maw, attracts the attention of the crisp young woman behind the counter, and asks that she schedule a wake-up call at checkout time, and that she let it ring and ring, ten or twenty minutes if necessary, because he is at present drugged.

GORE NAPS FITFULLY but is undiscouraged, for he has prepared for Vancouver Island and for the writing of his book. He spent years, in both Ann Arbor and then Spokane. He read Franz Boas and Jack Hodgins and Roderick Haig-Brown. *Klee Wyck* and *Burning Water* and *Lost Utopias*. And a gem called *Ragged Islands*, wherein a moody fellow is dropped way north then *canoes* the dangerous ocean coastline home. *Canoes*. Through interlibrary loans he secured material on Northwest Indian lore, Kwakiutl art, settlers' histories, and no end of tracts on saving the Pacific rainforest, et cetera. But what stirs him now and confirms his quest to explore this island, and write his own book, is one he got hold of in a bookstore here yesterday and is halfway through: *Cougar Annie's Garden.*

Cougar Annie, dead now, is one of those creatures who lives a life too improbable to be a Hollywood movie. Possibly related to English royalty; living in Vancouver circa the Twenties; in order to save her husband from that city's opium dens she moves them to the remotest spot possible, the west coast of Vancouver Island. Nothing there but a few Natives and a semi-annual mail steamer. There she hacked and cleared acres of virgin wilderness (her first husband was useless there, too — Peter suspects he had a hidden opium source), bore eleven children, vegetables, and fields of flowers. She got so good at flowers that she started a mail-order business sending hybrid bulbs and seeds around the world. Along the way she kept her children and successive husbands safe by plugging perhaps a hundred mountain lions, and one infers that she plugged one or more of her useless husbands as well.

Who could imagine. Cleared a rainforest, shot man-eating cats, raised a mob of children, and got famous for flowers. She was in all likelihood a Presbyterian biddy whose glare could force tulips out of barren ground — but who could imagine. And it wasn't that long ago. She was still kicking when the western world had seen Dada, and the Dalai Lama. Her garden still exists, is becoming some kind of park. Gore has planned a visit. He thinks perhaps an overland hike.

While his book would be no mere portrait of this land, while it would be his personal dance with the living and the now, nature would have its place. In fact one couldn't escape it: look out any window and see rainforest brambles inching into the city's cracks. Wake up any morning and find a thorned arm across your throat, blackberry ugly.

One couldn't escape certain island features. Beauty, sure. But take fear. Here is an island steeped in fear. One isn't talking just cougars or bears, or red-tide poisoned clams; one isn't talking the mood-funeral of endless rain and isolation. One is talking Indians' fear of other Indians. It is Gore's favourite story, this. How, here in the south, the

Salish lived with one eye cocked for black war-canoe prows slicing in from north's horizon. Unlike tanks or jets, these machines were silent. If you weren't watching, the Haida raiders were suddenly in your face and you were dead, or a slave.

He planned to visit Cortes Island to see the battlements one writer had called "pathetic." Low, earthen walls — little ditches basically — were the only defences of a peace-loving people. No match for Haida bravery, whose favourite meal was others' weakness. Lacking anything resembling fear of death, the Haida would beach their craft and trot up the sand to kill whichever man hadn't fled into the forest. Then rape and pillage, as per raiders anywhere, and steal women and children to bear north to the Queen Charlotte Islands as slaves. Their genius — Gore's favourite part — lay in their technique of numbing, for all time, the minds of their captives. Huddled in bilge water, the newly enslaved women and children would, over endless paddling days, have little to look at except, inches away, the severed heads of their husbands, fathers, uncles, and brothers as they knocked and rolled on the curved floor, sightless, slackly apologetic for their failure not only to protect, but to live.

Gore loves this story because it grates so nicely against other opinions about the Island Aboriginals, which is that they were "the most complex culture in the history of the world ever to flourish without resorting to agriculture." Gore admires the writer's somewhat arrogant use of the word "resorting." And heads knocking in the bilge is complex indeed.

More modern fears abound here as well. Vancouver Islanders live in constant fear of the Big Quake. (Hidden in the seabottom hereabouts lies fault-line cleavage that renders San Andreas a trouser wrinkle.) Aside from the Big One, some islanders still fear cougars and bears, but more pragmatically they fear the hordes from Toronto and Wisconsin, who keep arriving not in war canoes but moving vans, with nary a pathetic ditch to stop them.

All of which adds to the main fear, which is the thesis of his book: *there is nowhere on the planet left to go.*

His book will be called *The Rim*. Perhaps with subtitle: *A Journey Round the Last Island*. The Natives of the Island had a description of the best storytellers, which was that while speaking they could cast a spell that made the sun move slower in the sky. Peter Gore wants to write a book that makes the sun move slower in the sky.

MID-AFTERNOON, Gore feels more evicted than checked out. He sits in a café called The Dock. A clean but well-scuffed place. An ancient warehouse it seems. Tea, unmilked, and toast, unbuttered, with strawberry jam. A cheap café. His squandering is past. He has not many hundreds of dollars to get him around this island. It is an amazing fact — a sad one if you dwell on it — how a man can work steadily at a job he hardly likes, eschew expensive cars and draining addictions, and after twenty-five years have no cash to show for it. He couldn't blame Gail, though she got the house, because she got more mortgage than equity. No, he couldn't blame Gail for anything, though he tried. She remained at least as sad as he was, which proved the severance was fair. It was just a sad business all around.

He owned almost nothing. The day they formally split and he signed the rental agreement on his tiny new apartment, it took him five minutes to move in. He finished by hanging a new Dali poster, Dali reminding him of his university days. He did twenty push-ups, put a six-pack in the fridge and a can of soup on the stove, and turned on the used TV. He lacked a remote control; the golf tournament was fine. Forty-eight-year-old teenager, he proceeded to make a leisurely mess of himself and his apartment.

He can no longer remember why he had decided not to work longer and save up more for this project (not to mention his life), which would allow him to go the gentlemanly rather than the vagabond route. He suspects he had good, romantic reasons. The *book*'s the thing. Whatever comforts or internal organs that suffer will do so in service to *the book*.

He sees he is almost asleep, in a nose-down hover over his untouched toast. He takes a sip of tea. Sleep is what he needs. Cheap motel with thin curtains drawn, telly on low for company, gallbladder outrageously free of pain. He'd managed an hour of stupor in the Empress before getting the tinkling call and the ornate boot. The pain is gone, though he feels a lingering rawness at his liver. He has his vial of pills at the ready but he must stay alert for any fat attempting to enter his mouth. No chicken-wing platters at whenever a.m.

His café sits across the street from the Salvation Army, not far from the second-hand store where he traded in his suitcases for a nylon backpack-and-frame, the old chiseller charging him five dollars for the exchange. Judging from the café's clientele, and the passersby on the street, this is a rough part of town. Just to get into the café he had to manoeuvre past a well-dressed bag lady, an apprentice, perhaps, who blocked the doorway, crying and turning on her heel, unable to decide whether to come or go, even as he loomed in front of her with intentions that couldn't be clearer. "Excuse me," he said, and it took her a while to see him, whereupon she spoke an embarrassed, "*I'm* sorry," her teary eyes rather pretty and so possibly sane that, on second thought, you doubted all you had just seen.

His book doesn't begin in this café, he doesn't think. As if to challenge this assessment, outside in the rain a young ragged man catches his eye, turns only barely away, and spits. Maybe it's the Demerol, but everything about this man spitting seems excellent. Mythical, or part of a gritty TV documentary. The spitting goes with the town's general unfriendliness, also fine. Why had he assumed the rim of the world would be friendly?

An insight about Victoria rises with his teacup steam to become words. He will ask the waitress for a pencil and get this down: the mean people of Victoria are ready for a leader in the same way Italy and Germany once were. Peter stifles a giggle, and doing so he understands he's been giggling, in spasms, all day.

Everything is fine, inside and out. Outside, the rain and the spit, gusts of wind plishing it against the window in one's face: one can imagine oneself seated at the prow of a ship heading west into a gale. Inside, these sagging customers, their lips glossy with mayonnaise;

these old wooden walls enduring the hangings of poster art. But these walls had seen worse, you could assume sprays of immigrant blood, or salmon blood, or the sticky smudge of opium smoke, or — No, let's not get romantic here. More likely it was racks of bagged rice, or shoes. Ancient utility has its own romance.

Drug-rosy or not, Peter Gore knows he is still happy with the knowledge that his whole life has been but preparation for what he is doing at this moment. His life when summed up in a paragraph attests to it: Restless boyhood in East Sussex, listless youth in London and a bit west in Land's End before emigrating radically west to New Jersey, then westward again to Michigan to teach high school biology in Ann Arbor for eighteen years; add in, then take out one sweet then sour marriage, then westward ho for two final years teaching and golden (well, silver, or bronze) handshake at age fifty in Spokane, Washington. In any event, his life has trod a constant path west. Always west. Vancouver Island is the farthest west a body can go. Hop a boat from here *farther* west and somewhere at sea you sail through the looking glass and you are *east*. So Vancouver Island is it. Where all young men stopped going west, *but only because they had to*. Everyman's wanderlust *stymied*.

It's a place begging for its frustrating story to be told. *The Rim*. By Peter Gore. Modelled after, though not derivative of, Paul Theroux's meandering the perimeter of Britain. Its style will be participatory, like much contemporary travel writing, like Theroux's, like Hunter Thompson's, though less selfish than the former and less clownish than the latter. It will be as funny as O'Hanlon. As poetic, as full of white space, as Chatwin. It will be all of these styles, but mostly his own. He rather fancies himself a machine-gunning hyperbolist. In fact, his style will coin a new literary term: *Gorey*.

"Would you like more hot water for your tea?"

Twenty and with an eyebrow ring, but incongruously dressed in the café's starchy mauve dress, the waitress stands ready with a white plastic electric kettle, its cord dangling to the floor. Fat white duck, long rat tail.

"Please. And some lemon?"

She glugs water into his empty cup. Then, absurdly, points to his tea bag, indicating that he should now return it to the water. Peter picks up his soggy bag.

"Have you — Excuse me —" The waitress stops and turns to him. "— Have you, you and your friends, say, have you ever travelled to the west coast of the island?"

She drains her face of expression to assess him a moment. "Vancouver Island?"

Gore nods.

"You mean, like, to Long Beach?"

"Yes, that's on the west coast, I believe?"

"Yeah."

"And so you've been there."

"Well, like, partied there. It's a spring break place."

"Did you get there by boat?"

Her face gains life as he is deemed a helpless tourist.

"There's like a major highway that goes there? It's about five hours' drive, though. From here."

"Aha." He sees her try to turn away. "Were you born on Vancouver Island?" Her look drains wary again. "It's okay. I'm writing a book. Interviewing people."

"We moved here when I was ten. I'm from Toronto?"

"Aha."

"I've been to England," she adds, helpfully.

"Well. So have I," he says, waggling his brows, a well-used joke, and she smiles back, irony the métier of anyone under thirty it seems, even Canadians. Who was it who said, When tradition dies, irony enters? He recalls once being fed up and announcing it to his class. So it was him who said it.

He's hoped that coming up to Canada would somehow erase his accent, but of course it hasn't. Twenty-five years in America, and citizenship, hasn't. Hasn't even scuffed it much it seems. In their last argument over the phone, Gail's response to his declaring his love for Spokane and "the American West," was a scoffed, "You still sound like you're just off the boat, Cowboy." His retort to himself was the childish, Who wants to sound American anyway? To be honest he really hadn't been trying to lose anything. He still caught himself about to say "toe-may-toe" but switching mid-word to "toe-mah-toe," the second syllable like a sigh of relief at having escaped American brutality. Face it, they are barking dogs. Teaching his yapping teenagers, he could hear his voice in elegant bas-relief to their noise. If Americans simply enunciated properly they couldn't help but speak the Queen's English. Alabama's "Imo git me a gun," was a tongue-dead "I am going to get myself a gun." Please give us a break. *Imo* equals *I, am, going, to*?

"Sir? You have to put the bag in the water for it to be tea?"

Peter registers that he has failed to hit the target; the bag lies on the table some inches from the saucer; he's been sipping hot water. He plops it in, and she fills it again.

The waitress has been thinking hard for him. "Okay. *Tony's* from here. Tony's the owner. You could talk to him?"

"Could you ask Tony if I might please speak with him?"

"He's, like, golfing today?"

"Aha. Well, thank you. Long Beach then. Five hours by car."

"Depending on pit stops!" She gives him a naughty smile as she spins away.

Gail never really understood. Early on in their relationship he told her of his boyhood affinity for the American Wild West and naturally she found it quaint, that presumptive American view that of course any English dainty-lad would adore their dusty west. But she didn't get it, as demonstrated by her first birthday gift to him: a collector's plate of Gary Cooper. In a colourized still photo from one of his lamer films, one whose title he didn't bother to remember, Cooper stands all fearless with his sheriff's badge and points his six-gun at unseen evil. The unabashed corn of the thing wasn't the problem. The problem was that Gail didn't understand that the essence of the rugged west wasn't its lawmakers but its law*breakers*. It was the nasty *lack* of rules that seduced the urban English child. It took no leap of imagination to see that this promise of lawlessness is what brought him to Vancouver Island.

And this small city of Victoria is symbolically just right. Look at it: trying to be more English than England. You can buy "sweets," can ride a double-decker, can take high tea at the Empress: give us all a ripping break, please. The island is even named after an Englisher, Captain George, who came to map it, in that English urge to tame, to prune all the loose green in the garden. Yes, the English fled west and ended right here, and Peter Gore has arrived to record the pressurized stories hissing from their stall. Everywhere, stories to be plucked like berries. Of people precariously perched planet-edge. Of a shotgun marriage between man and wilderness. For instance: even the Empress Hotel, for all its delusions of civility, had but ten years ago seen a cougar captured in its underground parking garage. A mountain lion in a five-star hotel? If that isn't a portrait of lawlessness, Gore doesn't know what is.

He loves this place. He *loves* it. What other *city*, anywhere, has *lions roaming its downtown*? Apparently the island's northern half also sports wolverines. *Wolverines*. That weasel beast of legend, fifty pounds of hairy gristle that *chases grizzlies off their kill*. Apparently they honk or whistle or *scream*, they make some kind of horrid sound like —

"Sorry. Here." The waitress is at his side, proffering a silver beaker.

"Sorry?"

"Did you just ask for cream or something?"

"*God* no." Though hadn't he asked for lemon? Long ago?

"Oh. I thought you... Okay."

"Sorry." So he's been talking out loud to himself. There's another fellow staring.

"Hello," Peter says, lifting his hand in friendly wave to the old fellow. The man, who may be part Chinese, or Native, looks away.

Gore nudges his packsack with his foot to feel it safe. His laptop, state-of-the-art and afforded by a cheque from Gail, is wrapped in a used Cowichan sweater and takes up more than half the space in the pack. Solar battery charger, enough memory to fight the next war. When he first uses it, he will thank her and ease his guilt. Though she did say in her letter that it felt like "spending money on a stain." She didn't mean him, he doesn't think, but rather the tainted last few years of their marriage. Though it did feel a bit like being bought off. Anyway: she still has a job and he doesn't. Or, rather, his new job — author — will take some time to generate a paycheque.

In the meantime, despite the strain on his money, despite the gall bladder setback, there is no need to panic (not that panic is possible while holding Demerol's pearly hand) because he has it all planned. In his pack is his map of Vancouver Island. Yesterday, at the wooden sign at Beacon Hill Park proclaiming "Mile O," proffering his new Pentax, he asked a tourist couple to take his picture beside the sign. His book might include writer-in-action photos. But, smiling, hearing the click of the shutter, noticing all around him the groups of old ladies tired and snippy from over-tourism, he felt nothing like an intrepid travel writer. He then and there vowed to flee anything touristy. Instead he would penetrate the island's living meat. Locate the locals. Report on their fish breath, their cougar eyes, their loggers' busted bones. Retrieving his Pentax from the tourist, Gore threw his twenty-page itinerary into a trash can. Taking out his map of the island, standing, he wrote on its back a new plan of attack.

He removes this map now and spreads it on the table, smoothing the island down and admiring its ragged cigar shape. He flips it over. Written in magic marker, in the bold calligraphy of spontaneous decision, are his Main Goals:

One. Speak to the Nootka.

The Nootka, on the island's extreme west coast, greeted Captain George Vancouver. While Europe's conquering of American Indians began in the east and moved west, it also began west, in Nootka Sound, but didn't move east, because the Nootka massacred the next ship that arrived. Gore reminds himself that in Canada "reservations" are "reserves," and Indians refer to themselves as "First Nations Peoples."

Two. Interview squatters.

There is a tradition hereabouts, he's read, of squatting in the wilds. No doubt this has to do with the mild climate, as well as a terrain that makes it difficult to be found. Interestingly, there is also a tradition of squatting in the deepest bowels of London.

Three. Visit a logging camp.

Interview these salt-of-the-earth British Columbians. Speak with those who are raping paradise in order to buy a satellite dish. Find out if they know they are pawns of corporate evil, and that all profit flies south.

Four. Infiltrate a cult. Visit the old compound of Brother Twelve.

Vancouver Island, he's read, has attracted charismatic gurus forever. Brother Twelve, about whose powers historians still couldn't agree, was but one cult leader in this area early in the century, purportedly healing people and amassing great wealth. He disappeared with much gold. The goal will be to find a contemporary cult, perhaps a coven, and befriend them.

Five. Whales.

A maritime culture has turned from slaughter to shepherding. Viewing whales-on-the-hoof is a main altar in the church of environmentalism.

These five goals make a fine framework, and Gore stares at his book's skeleton for a dreary length of time before he notices the waitress rushing by him with her fat white duck, its rat tail dragging sibilance on the linoleum, but comically loud, likely amplified echoes of Demerol, which wouldn't be too bad a recreational drug were it not for the paralysis and the stupidity. Plus, at his core something wheedles like an infant.

"Excuse me."

"More hot water?"

"I was *hoping* you could direct me to a bar, or tavern, but one with some character. Perhaps one where Natives gather? First Nations Indians?"

She studies him anew. He sees that her outfit is not mauve at all, but extremely brown.

"Across the street," she says, pointing through the window; or maybe she didn't speak at all and he is supplying the voice to her finger's pointing. Something in her manner of walking away makes him want to explain to her — so he does — that because he is a teacher of biology, all his life he has never not been studying *her*. In the study of a plant rooting minutely for its water; in the study of phototaxis — sorry, Miss, an involuntary moving toward light — in larvae; in any animal eating *anything*; in all the myriad other fleshy styles of effort — all right, let's just call it *life* — none of it signals anything but *dissatisfaction*. And the whole swelling mess peaks in evolution's greatest vehicle of want: *us*.

The waitress hasn't stayed and he feels, not unpleasantly, alone. He quickly wants to phone Gail but knows he won't. His journey has just now, just this moment, begun. Across the street, through the rain, the tavern's dark entrance looks like the most ominous mouth. Tonight there will be stories from a bar. He will buy drinks and hear proud lies and, likely, bitterness at having lost utopia. He will dare ask about the residential schools. He will endeavour to stymie his accent and hope that his listeners will have forgotten that their conquerors were the English. And then tomorrow he will find himself in their wilderness of land and spirit.

"Welcome, tribe!" he said. "That you have come quickly, following my word, for it would not be good if you were infected in the way my son is, for his body is scabby. He has a bad sickness. Therefore I wish that we leave him, and that we go far away, all of us, with our women and our children." Then they left, and the boy was there alone.

The boy made a fire on the ground. He cried pitifully... and he scratched his body, and the boils came off his body. He scratched his body a second time. Then his stomach began to move. His stomach began to swell. Then he scratched again, and a hand came out and showed itself on his stomach... Then his heart became strong, and he did not scratch. Then the hand came out farther out of his stomach, and the boy looked, and watched it coming. Then a boy jumped out of his stomach, and now there was not one scab on the body of the child.

— FRANZ BOAS, *KWAKIUTL TALES*

MALCOLM ISLAND

THIS TOM POOLE is a tough one. Dr. Catherine Macleod watches him start down the bank, planting his good foot into the gravel hard and, she thinks, angrily. She has said nothing provocative and her instructions were simple: move the hydrophone. She said please.

She hates, and loves, coming out here to Malcolm Island, to Sointula, for her data. It's a two-day trip from Vancouver, but it gets her out of the office. Though Tom works for free she could have refused him employment on these grounds alone, his refusal to link up and send data through e-mail, or even fax, or even, unbelievably, mail. He'd communicated an "If you want it, come and get it," with a shrug, and with those eyes, and she has no clue now why she agreed. He's tough. But it does revive her, coming up here. Places as wild as this are rarely accessible by road and short hike, and it is wild in ways she can't identify, in ways that take her beyond science. She feels something troubling in the shadows and, strangely, even in the light that casts them. Though beautiful here, it feels threatening.

From above, she watches Tom descend. The crimped arm he holds against his body. The bad leg he drags then swings, drags then swings, generally getting it a bit in front of him. Thus he moves down the gravel bank, which is still wet though the tide retreated hours ago. On this shore nothing dries, except maybe the very tops of rocks. Malcolm Island is so cold. Today's rain is only beginning. She wonders, if Tom picked up his head to see, would he notice the approaching clouds, the wind bringing them down Queen Charlotte Strait? She wonders if, like her, he finds it hard to believe it is the first day of summer.

His long unwashed hair wouldn't look much different wet. A mane of stringy metal. His scalp must itch. A whip of kelp has become wrapped around his boot and he stops his descent to kick at it, and kick at it, which throws another loop around. Kicking, he states — with patience and, almost, affection — fuck *off*. He kicks some more, laughing, but with abrasion in it now, and a set to his face, as if something is about to give.

"Use your hands," she calls, nervous, though she is older, almost double his twenty-five. And his boss.

He stops kicking. For a moment he doesn't move at all. Then, smiling, he looks up at her. Holding her eye, with all the time in the world, he says, "Why not." Then reaches down to simply undrape the kelp.

He continues his climb down. His route follows a black cable, insulated wire thick as a thumb. Below the gravel slope lies the mud flat, still under water but visible in the troughs of smallish breaking waves. Clamped to a length of padded rebar planted in the mud, peeking up like a small periscope, is the hydrophone mike. His job is to pull up the rebar and mike and move it fifty yards to the left. She has explained to him that she needs it elsewhere, in a spot still near to but more distant from the whale rub. She has made today's journey mostly because of this extreme low tide. She won't see him again in weeks.

Tom reaches the mud and slogs to the black metal shaft. Wavelets crest over his boot tops, flood in. She could consult her charts and learn the exact temperature of this water in this bay on this day of the year, but she knows it is ice and sees that he does not care. He did not ask why she wanted the hydrophone moved but she explained it anyway. She wants him as involved as possible. Earlier at his campsite, in past the first line of trees, out of the wind, he made them camp coffee (grounds boiled in a pot; as you sip, you filter with your front teeth) while she explained.

She never knew when he was listening. He apparently does listen, though, because he has been doing a good enough job, all orca visits properly recorded, cassettes labelled with date, time, tide. Corresponding notebook entry with pod ID if he knows it, otherwise numbers, sex, and behaviours: rubbing, feeding, breaching. Residents, transients. Aggressive behaviour, play. Any calves. He takes photos — artful, many of them — when he can. He has also noted peripheral sounds he (correctly) suspects are white-sided dolphins, though he has not been asked to do this. At times he has even noted the marine traffic as picked up by the hydrophone, his irritation showing through. *Three big tugs today*, he once wrote, *and a freighter too fucking close*.

They sat upwind of his fire, beside his little tent and water jugs, on facing deadfall logs. Trees towered around them, in the wind some trees croaking low at the base, or squeaking way up high. She gripped her hot coffee with her sweatered wrists and noted the state of his little tent: blue nylon faded to a ghostly colour, fire-char smudges at the entrance from his hands. She felt an absurd sexual tug, no doubt from memories of younger days and small tents hidden in nooks. But, also, here she was alone with an isolated man, handsome (under the dirt), confident, too confident, despite his injuries. She saw herself as he might: white hair framing a face that is still pretty and nearly unlined. He cared not a whit for her, of course. He was of another world, not just his age but utterly out-of-society, and he looked it, wearing that filthy cable-knit sweater, like every fisherman and hermit around here. In any case, there was a woman. According to a circulated e-mail, a "Cal" had pestered the office to the tune of making them promise that anyone visiting him had to bring him fresh vegetables for his health.

Knowing his history she didn't trust him, of course. In fact when she parked to begin her hike in she phoned the office once more to tell them exactly where she was and for how long and with whom. Rechecking his name on her clipboard, she had paused and wondered again how much of the story was true.

Sometimes wind dipped from directly above to blast the cedar smoke randomly, often in their eyes. Weather, here, was really nothing other than chaos in the sky. Once today, when she checked on the roiling clouds above them and then looked back down, she encountered a sudden bold shaft of sunlight-through-the-mist, right behind the young man. Her reaction to it made him turn and look too. It was something out of Emily Carr, one of those heavenly angled beams that gave gothic cathedral glory to a forest, triggering awe and hope and conversion. It could be stupifyingly beautiful here. But not for long.

Though she explained her problem at length, nothing appeared to register. Tom didn't nod; he jotted nothing down. His eyes, which met hers directly and settled there, were clear but showed nothing at work behind. It was some sort of refraction she couldn't see past. He was nothing like her eager grad students in their camps along Robson Bight. If it was drugs he was still into, well, who wasn't into a bit of that up in this neck of the woods? Though she doubted he could be growing it here, out on this freezing shore. Anyway, as long as he was doing his job. Apparently he'd been more into the selling than the using. At the office she'd heard the phrase "gangland hit." Imagine. And here she was talking to him. But any hard loner up here had a storied past that was probably only one-quarter true: up here there was little to do but embroider stories.

She couldn't see any visible wound. She had heard the story of the beet juice on his face but didn't know whether to believe that either, and knew him not nearly well enough to ask. Thinking beets, she remembered the broccoli and carrots in her day pack. She leaned to rummage through, lifted them out, met his eye and smiled, and placed them beside his two water jugs. By way of acknowledgement he stared at them for an oddly long time, wiggled his behind on the log as if scratching its depths, and then sipped, distracted, at his coffee. When she began talking again he interrupted her and asked if by any chance she had brought any lemons.

She wondered what his response would be if she offered to cook something for him. He was very much the angry child. He wanted mothering, that one. Wanted in the sense of lacked.

"Anyway, I need the mike moved so *they* won't hurt themselves on it when they come in to rub," she said clearly, sipping the ridiculously strong coffee. The wind was building, almost on schedule. Trees groaned rhythmically now and the canopy far above them hissed. She had to speak louder. "*Not* because they'll hurt the mike."

At the Institute, concern-for-equipment had been the assumption. According to the tapes the hydrophone had twice been bumped by an orca on its way in to rub on the underwater gravel slope, and she'd exclaimed that she had better get the hydrophone moved. Yes, they're expensive, was the nodding comment, and she had to stifle her anger while responding that *that* was not the point at all. She saw one of the sessional instructors biting his smile down. To him, how was it possible that a multi-tonned creature could hurt itself on a small padded microphone when its desire to begin with was to pound itself against a wall of rocks? She explained that its getting hurt was not the point either. The point was that hydrophones were not a part of the orcas' world. It was that hydrophones were as alien as, down south, the fleet of whale-watching boats chasing them all day while they tried to feed, mate, play, rest, or — who knows — *philosophize*. The point was that she did not want her hydrophone to be the straw that broke any whale's behavioural back. It was that she wanted to be *purely* invisible to them, as should they all.

Spitting coffee grounds from her teeth, she explained this to this young man who gave her nothing in return. She had no idea what he thought of her reasons for moving the hydrophone, reasons which made others in the field accuse her of religiosity.

"So, what do you think? You think moving it's a good idea?"

"Why not."

That had been it from the quiet, odd, purportedly criminal fellow who, knee-deep now in waves and spindrift, tugs the rebar out of the tidal flat. A young man on a disability pension who is, in essence, volunteering. A young man who, in his data books, has twice made her deeply curious. She almost missed both entries buried among the dates and tides and weather. He'd written, and who knows why: *The big auntie came in at me fast and so straight her fin looked like a needle. She's the kind who will change me.* The other time, and Catherine suspects it refers to the same female: *Her black is exactly the colour of the black hiding in the middle of tar.*

Shamans had a variety of responsibilities, including interpreting events, ensuring successful foraging or warring expeditions, and curing people when the cause of the illness was unknown or the symptoms were not responding to ordinary treatments. A common diagnosis by a shaman was soul loss — when a person's soul had left the body. As a cure, a shaman could visit the spirit world to retrieve the soul.

— ROBERT J. MUCKLE,
THE FIRST NATIONS OF BRITISH COLUMBIA

HARO STRAIT

SHE KNOWS HOW her craft — an outsized bagel with a floor — looks out here in open water. To worrying stares from pleasure boaters Evelyn throws a relaxed wave to show she is happy where she is. Which is way out in the middle, halfway to San Juan Island. If anyone is looking for her it's not where they'd look. The tide and breeze take her north. Her breaks from rowing don't seem to slow her pace much.

She takes stock of her new possessions and wonders about the boat's owner. His lunch, which she ate during the first hour, was an array of finicky tidbits. Greek olives, two kinds of paté, a handful of champagne crackers. A Baggie of dried mango pieces, another of candied ginger, another of wasabi peas. She wanted bread. A casserole.

She has a life jacket. A collapsible fishing rod. She remembers enough about fishing with Claude to see that what's in the small tackle box is useless: mostly trout lures, split-shot sinkers the size of peppercorns, and line too thin to haul much from these deeps. Maybe the man, or woman, didn't care about fishing and was looking for a reason to drift in the sunshine.

Drinking water is her one worry. Other than getting caught. But what could they do? (Besides give her water!) I'm sorry, my old boyfriend died, I'm not handling it well, I'm "deeply disturbed," here's your boat back, call my husband please, Oakville City Hall, he'll tell you not to yell at me. He'll tell you *how exactly* not to yell at me.

The day has been long and she's exhausted from the bones out. She radiates her hot exhaustion to the sea and the sea doesn't complain but simply cools it for her, finds it not a burden at all. Seagulls soar in from surprise angles, so graceful and angel-coloured it's easy to forget they're hunting flesh, and garbage. Eyeing Evelyn-on-a-bagel. Her other worry is too many visitations from Claude's face. She is helpless to protect herself from this face so afraid of death.

She lolls her head back on the cushiony rubber, wills her muscles to melt one by one, an exercise she recalls from yoga, another of her West Coast selves abandoned decades ago. She is the languid lady on an English pond, being rowed about by her stiff Oxford beau. She lets a hand fall, palm up, to trail in and be cooled by the water. Holly Hunter does this at the end of *The Piano*, before she steps into the uncoiling rope and tries to die.

Sunset, the sky's blue has flexed from misty to royal. She should not sleep. She should worry about this witless drift, north. The sky above, offering itself so profoundly, is both the question and the answer. She can hardly look.

ON THE PHONE, a sitcom's nasal voice: "Evelyn Poole? This is Royal Jubilee Hospital in Victoria, British Columbia? We are contacting you to inform you that Claude Longpre has asked for you and that Mr. Longpre is —" The woman is so emotionless that Evelyn has to interrupt to ask if Claude is sick. Still a thrill to hear his name, though the woman pronounces it wrong, rhyming it with plod rather than load. "We're afraid that Mr. Longpre is dying and he has asked for you."

Evelyn has no time to think. A flight west is handy, non-stop, serendipitous. Her own voice is flat as she lies to Roy about an old girlfriend. She stuffs a shirt and change of underwear into a bookbag, calls a cab, shares deceitfully soulful eye contact with Roy, and flies to Victoria expecting to bury Claude, not watch him die. On the plane she feels the guilt of having lied to Roy: why has she lied?

Flying, sipping tomato juice and melting ice, she allows memories of Claude to come, at first the rosy and false, those memories of memories. Then come the real thing: memories that hurt. Their intensely pleasant trips together. She recalls Claude giving her a gift picked up off the sand — a clean bird bone — his liquid eyes pleased with themselves and instructive. The kind growl of his voice.

As they bank over the low mountains of southern Vancouver Island, silhouetted black against an orange sunset, looking like its own empty island nation, a tourist-woman behind her calls out almost in fear, "There's nothing *down* there." As if this is some sort of truth, it wakes Evelyn up, it triggers in her a double horror: the *fact* of the airplane's roar, the *fact* of Claude's dying. Evelyn begins to hyperventilate. Only now does she realize she has left her pills on the nightstand and that she is overdue.

She makes it to the hospital, finds Mr. Claude Longpre's room. She walks in and he is awake, looking at her. Something like a smile, irony in his eyes. His eyes. She finds his hand.

"Hi."

It's all she says, and he isn't talking. But here he is. It's Claude. Twenty-five years didn't happen. Yes, it did — look at his face. But, *his eyes*. She looks into his eyes, feels how well they know each other and always have. That twenty-five years is gone in a finger snap makes her feel utterly sane, or insane, she can't decide. His eyes keep her impossibly between these two possibilities. She doesn't know if she's feeling the lack of her pills, or the truth.

She minutely shakes his hand, says it again, softer. "Hi."

Then comes the warp of going off her pills, a hard-growing neon that glares within the time she will spend at the hospital. Claude's face, and the septic smells, the tube dripping clean fluid in and the tube draining brown fluid out. Claude's eyes, bright with fear, race in an unmoving body. *His eyes*. He knows and he is a terrified little boy. Here at last, the only real nightmare, the one he's worked hard his whole life pretending would never come.

She has to go out into the hall to ask a nurse to give him morphine. "Is there pain?" the nurse asks. "He's afraid," Evelyn tells her, but this moves the nurse not a bit. Nor does it when Evelyn cries. Only when she goes pretty much hysterical does the nurse agree to consult a doctor. Unbelievably, the nurse is angry and won't look at her when she comes to shoot a syringe of morphine into Claude's tube. He is soon more peaceful, more able to drift, perhaps in a grand boat he never owned. Evelyn asks herself if she just denied Claude an alert death but, no, she has seen that panic is nothing like alertness. Panic is less alert than morphine.

Imagine, not seeing such fear as pain.. Imagine not responding to a little boy's panic.

Evelyn's awful neon grows through night and then dawn and then noon. Claude suffers the worst kinds of chaos. Some of his talk makes sense, some doesn't, at least not on this earth. She rarely takes her eyes from his face. As she sits with him, waiting until he doesn't take that next breath, she sees some things that are instructive — how all people are still frightened children no matter how they've learned to act — and other things that are so horrific she will be unable to think of them or remember them, even seconds later.

And she learns some things about her precious pills. For one, these spikings of heart are unlike anything she's had in years. While painful, they are *appropriate*. Claude is dying and despite how he treated her it is right that his moans burn her heart. Two, she is angry at the pills for letting her not ever visit this man, despite his several humble letters and then more lately the entreaties from his friends who brought him in after his first stroke. God, she can feel his yearning through the clench of his hand. Even in the last hours there can be yearning. In one letter he said simply that she is the only woman he ever loved. She didn't believe him then but she believes him now.

Angry at her pills, she decides to stop. They are a strong antidepressant but she feels there is more to them than just that. Roy seems to approve of her taking them, or at least he isn't eager to talk about her going off, and for this she no longer trusts him in some fundamental way.

THOUGH SHE HEARD no passing boat, a sudden wake rolls under and her rubber bronco bucks. She lets her head loll in rhythm to an enjoyable sloshing. She knows better than to blame her dilemma (floating in a bagel, directionless except for thirst) on going off her pills. However rough this past week (at one point her brain felt like itchy spaghetti being twirled by a fork), she does feel saner now. Clearer, anyway. Somewhat. Hallucinations have mostly stopped.

But why steal a boat to drift in? The reasons are in her body, there are no words. Or: you're a child and your cat is lost. You can either sit waiting in the living room or you can go searching. The living room feels all wrong. An urge fills your body. You can't *not* go search the forest, no matter how dark and cold, no matter that you know searching is useless. You don't know where your cat is but you sure can't sit still.

Evelyn's not even sure *what* her cat is.

She leans out over the water and looks in. In the shadow of the boat's rubber wall there is no reflection of sky and she can see deeply. Down there is an unlikely place for a cat. The water is so clear it's impossible to know how deep she is seeing. What looks to be a three-inch fish an arm's reach away, is it actually a three-*foot* fish way down deep? Is that tiny white round thing she thinks she can grab actually a deep jellyfish the size of a hubcap? If she sees a little brown wormy thing, might it not be hundred-foot Caddy five-hundred feet down?

She lies back, dizzy. Lets her Holly Hunter hand remain trailing in coolness. She knows this feeling on her hand exactly, from rare sleepy-hot summer days as a girl on an air mattress, in a cove not that far from here. Her sexy baby-blue suit that turned her tan to gold. She felt exactly this cool hand that July she was sixteen and the man who is now ashes in a tube in her pocket came up from under to kiss a foot, then the other, then nibbled a toe for fun, then licked the back of a knee, which got to her, and she flipped over, and her baby-blue suit was off before he'd towed her to shore.

These reasons in her body have put her Oakville life on hold. On probation. Maybe she is trying to understand her past. She used to live here but she never *understood* it. She used to go boating with — Claude. She's in one now and she's floating north to Tommy, his eyes flashing like fishing lures. Tommy, I have something to tell you. And, Tom, I have a question. Did you really buy him a house? Claude said you bought him a house. Claude looked me in the eye, laughing or crying, I couldn't tell, and he said, "Bastard bought me a house, eh?" He seemed to believe what he said and the idea swam in his eyes until he lost consciousness again. What else did he say about Tommy? There was other stuff. He's injured, "*dey got him bad,*" but now he is better, "*he okay, he gonna be fine.*"

Her attention is suddenly in her cool hand as, too vividly, she pictures a real Caddy coming fresh and big-eyed from the depths, *ow*, bringing its wet, icy mane to her touch. Bug-eyed, teeth, panting like a dog. Evelyn sits up and continues rowing.

BOTH KNEES AUDIBLY creak when she unbends them. She stomps, scuffs noise into the sand, marvels at her teetering body and what are called sea legs. This beach she remembers is John's or Jim's Island. She had to land because it is almost dark and a wind came up. She had toyed with the notion of drifting through the night. Her decision to come ashore felt like a decision not to die.

But it's a dangerous and shitty beach. She can tell from the uppermost logs that tides go right to the base of the sand cliff, so if tonight's tide goes to extremes she will sit up on a log till morning. And there's no trickling stream to drink from. And no underbrush; passing boats will see her bagel, camouflage colours or not. It's lousy for other reasons, too: she can see the lights of Sidney, and these lights sharpen her thirst. And Claude took her crabbing out this way as well — she suffers a memory of his hands pulling thin blue rope.

But she is free of that smell, and the headlines. No one is fighting for their life within miles. Except the gooey and the shelled who, thankfully, die under rocks and sand.

The wind rises out of the dark. She pokes about the larger drift-logs looking for a nook. At least there are no houses on this beach. Scanning the houselessness, she gets peevish about Roy even now, even here. As if he is at her shoulder, both a comfort and irritant, agreeing how nice it is that the beach has no houses, but he says "homes." It is one of the small things she hates about him but has never told him. Buying their first house, Roy, like the realtors they toured with, took to calling houses "homes." "Remember," he'd still say, "that one home, that vacant grey one, we decided not to buy?" It always struck her that realtors using words like this was their most obvious crummy manipulation: at a "house" you eyed cement cracks and iffy tile, while at a "home" you were already in your cozy slippers, and it saddened her that Roy had been such an easy recruit. Roy, there is no such thing as a vacant grey home. She'd drive by half-done housing developments and see the gold lettering, Deluxe Homes, and feel Roy to be part of the conspiracy.

Evelyn finds her nook. The log is half as thick as she is tall and is embedded at an angle, one end hovering slightly over the sand. She can dig down enough to get herself and her rubber raft under. Like a dog — no, a fox — she'll simply dig a hole. Dig a home.

EVELYN SITS ON her folded blanket watching, through clouds, the moon set. It touches the horizon. Before she knows it, there is only a half moon. Time could horrify her if she let it. Now the moon is a sliver. And now the moon is dead.

Everyone wants to leave wherever they are. They want to leave whether they know it or not. Claude built a wall of agony not to leave, but left anyway. People leave but don't know how they did it. Somehow Evelyn's blasted through the peche-melba wall of her kitchen. She was almost content there. *Almost content* is what she left.

She is feeling more herself tonight because she is feeling more *of* herself. It almost feels like she has rowed the pills out of her muscles.

She hasn't found a new room yet, not unless these mountains and water and sky make one. You could call this big place a room. Evelyn's place. Her retirement home. The floor and ceiling and colour-scheme keep changing, so she'll never have to redecorate. She needn't move at all because her room moves for her.

Self-conscious of her joking, she taps her pocket. Then takes comfort in the first sob, which feels earned.

THREE DAYS AFTER he died. Evelyn misses the service itself, finds the church just as people are emerging. She wonders if Tommy has heard and is here, but somehow she can tell he hasn't and isn't. In the parking lot, Claude's sister has the urn, and friends take turns holding it. More than one does the whoops-almost-dropped-it routine, with a "Sorry Claude." Evelyn is surprised at the number, maybe thirty. He'd made an impression. Mostly guys, all ages. It's hard to know his lifestyle by the look of them. Noon, a few smell of booze already, or still, working-class bums, guys who might straighten out enough to get another two months on the tugs. Then a handful of the ex-hippie kind, still with the extra hair and well-made cotton clothes, and those permanently wild eyes that now fight mostly with age, their issues forgotten. A few could be musicians, probably are: Claude could always be counted on to belt out a tune at two in the morning, and real musicians got a kick out of his Québécois bravado. A bunch more look like businessmen. The scatter of women who appear to be alone all wear a similar look; maybe it's custodial, and Evelyn decides not to think any more about that.

She smells cologne, and his face is everywhere. She stays well off to the side. One guy who'd come by the hospital nods to her. Someone holds out and shakes a box of good cigars, the kind encased in matte silver tubes. A younger, street type, thorn tattoos around his neck, accepts his cigar and asks deadpan, "Claude have a baby?" and other men snicker without smiling, nodding that, yes, Claude has had a baby, let's have a cigar. Boy or girl, they wonder. "Who's the mama?" brings some raunch and cackle and a few men glance at Evelyn. (All but the sister pronounce his name to rhyme with plod, so somewhere along the line he gave up correcting. She remembers his little explanation, given with a smirk, "No. I rhyme with *load*.")

Claude's sister doesn't look disturbed by the carrying on. Evelyn knows they rarely saw each other. Dominique. Maybe fifty-five, a decade older than Evelyn. Dominique looks like she's been cozy with a bottle herself. Heavily made up, she is at the age where it should look desperate, but she pulls it off. Something about being French, and how confidence alone is beauty. Evelyn can see Claude in her full claim on life. Dominique doesn't "have much ingleesh," but she is game to joust with the fellows. Evelyn accepts a silver tube, gives away its cigar and asks Dominique for some of Claude's ashes. Silenced for a moment, everyone watches the exchange, they watch Evelyn dig into the canister then pour a stream of granular ash from her cupped, tipped hand. She doesn't spill much, gets the tube mostly full, caps it. When the guy with the thorn tattoo wonders dryly whether Claude will enjoy his new life as a dildo, damned if Dominique doesn't laugh louder than any of them.

Here, on Jim's or John's Island, the wind has cleared the night sky. It has also dried Evelyn's face. She looks up to the stars but they say nothing. Where is Claude now? Other than ashes in her pocket, other than tears in her eyes? What of him still exists in this room, this ludicrously big room? When she smells that smell and sees him, is that him, or is it her? What about memories? Of him looking ninety, not fifty-nine. He looked fifty years older than her, not fifteen. His awful yellow face, all slack. His body sudden pale meat, a compliance so unlike him. Eyes thick and empty as bone.

What were Claude's exact words about Tommy? Smiling as he said it, trying to be gentle with her.

THIS MORNING, she has to move fast, find a room that includes fresh water. She knows Sidney Island, that next one over, has a marine park where boaters anchor and go ashore. There's a campground. Her rowing muscles are sore but it feels okay to be back in her little boat. Approaching Sidney Island and Sidney Spit, a shallow ribbon of white sand a mile long, she knows she's zoomed past decades before but has never set foot.

The scatter of anchored pleasure boaters watches her row up in her bagel. She has developed a technique whereby she lies almost flat back with splayed knees up. It must look quite leisurely. Missing is her martini glass to raise to them.

Dragging her ship up the sand in among the drift logs, she feels weak. She doesn't care if anyone here has been alerted and she is caught. Her room would merely change. She feels how thirst squeezes all of you, every cell probably, and creates its own panic. A note more shrill than hunger's. Up past the logs, down the path, halfway to the outhouses, Evelyn finds a freshly painted red hand pump. She works and works its squeaking arm, bends to its bounteous hole. The gush is cold and clean. Grunting like some kind of animal she gulps and laps at this very best of life's things. Bent over she can't swallow fast enough so she falls to her knees. The boaters and campers will soon stop staring.

SHE SPENDS THE day hunting things and it proves to be a pleasant, Robinson-Crusoe time. Sometimes she keeps a certain-shaped stone, sometimes she drops it. Sometimes she knows what she needs. She abandons one hiking stick for another that has a growth shaped like an ear. The ear is slightly larger than human size, and head-high. She fancies it will hear danger ahead. Carrying it, she finds she can relax a little.

She has flipped her boat over, propped it as a roof, and built walls with driftwood. For water she has found in the tide logs an old yellow pail missing its handle. Over in the campground she found a chip of soap and in the heat of the afternoon washed her hair in the warm lagoon. This evening she surreptitiously followed a family on their butter-clam hunt, spied on their modest success, and now takes over their patch of muddy gravel when they move on. Using a flat rock the size of her hand, she scrapes and unearths enough clams to require her to use her T-shirt as a pouch to carry them. On the way back to her camp she borrows matches from a smoking hiker and, despite the glaring red NO FIRES signs, on her sandy doorstep she starts one. Picturing Claude's hands, on flat rocks she lines the clams half in, half out of the fire. When they open, it smells like heaven's secret kitchen. Tawny meat pouches sizzle in their own broth. They are sandy to chew, but she feels the protein go right where it's needed. Despite her best efforts, she eats them all too quickly.

She ruminates, picking clam shreds from her teeth with a cedar splinter. When she was a child, anything like an Easter egg hunt gave her her deepest contentment. She recalls hunting wild mushrooms with her woodsy Uncle Matthew, near Chilliwack. Also a family trip to the Maritimes and fiddlehead picking on the shore of a muddy river in spring flood. She could have stayed stooped all day, flipping debris with a foot to reveal vivid green fiddleheads, food for later, but most of all, a prize for now. Pluck, pluck, drop them in the bag, head already up scanning for more. Hunting. It was always best when it was food (once, her mother wondered about dandelion greens in a salad and Evelyn was already out the door to hunt some), but it could be anything. On holiday, mention of arrowheads in the vicinity would have her kicking dirt and stones with a foot, and she'd do it until called in. Birds' nests, bottles in the ditch, four-leaf clovers. Dimes in the grunge under parking meters. Once, at Guelph, a false alarm made someone flick an untied baggy of hashish chunks out a dorm window and Evelyn was out there on hands and knees searching the lawn, softly breathing, deeply content finding a pellet and deeply content anticipating another; she didn't even smoke the stuff. But food was best: fishing, with Claude, she'd hold and stare at her rod, hours would pass, and Claude might even get a little jealous.

The clams have her full and tired. She wonders if she will like anything better than going out hunting clams, every day. She declares herself a born-again hunter-gatherer, dips a finger into the cooked amber juice in a shell, and touches it to her forehead.

THAT DAY THEY launched his aluminum boat in Egmont and trolled north up a wide inlet, the antique engine putting miraculously, Evelyn feeling safe to head into the wilds because Claude had pretty much built that engine himself. She would have been twenty, which would make Claude thirty-five.

Claude has made a big show of packing only the fishing rods, a frying pan, butter, and a lemon. That and his bottle of bourbon. They troll long enough to catch a salmon, which Claude throws back for being too large to eat all at once, and they troll some more until they catch a small one, which he keeps. Then he jigs a small ling cod off the edge of a kelp bed. After this they zoom up to a wide, gravel bay, for butter clams, which they toss in the bottom of the boat alongside the two fish. They are in a week of perfect weather, and Claude takes belts of bourbon and expounds on the puffy clouds, the gnarled arbutus, the seal they scare into a dive —"Evelyn! Paradise!"— still with that accent, though he'd run away from Quebec almost twenty years before. He removes his shirt in the sun. He is completely without fat. His muscles stand out as defined as bones, and Evelyn sees veins, faintly green, that link and feed them. Sometimes, when they make love, the hardness of his muscle does almost feel like bone.

From the gravel bay they zoom for an hour and come to Princess Louisa Inlet, the entrance to which they miss once because it's a camouflaged chink between two cliffs. Going through the narrow channel they battle a tidal rip replete with sudden whirlpools and standing waves, but Evelyn still isn't scared, because Claude is laughing and shouting. Inside, she can't believe where they are. The mile-long inlet feels smaller for being surrounded on all sides by sheer mountains. Cliff-faces fall right to the water at a dark slant that continues under forever. "Ow, *twenty-tree waterfall!*" Claude shouts over the engine, pointing willy-nilly all around, his long hair blowing, and indeed there are waterfalls sluicing white off the cliffs everywhere you look. He points straight ahead, yells "*Chatterbox Fall*," and there lies their destination, a roar of white water entering the far end of the inlet. They ground the boat on a tiny crescent of beach in a tangle of fallen logs. The beach is mostly oysters, in places a foot thick. Claude gathers and arranges some wet wood, sucks a mouthful of gas from the tank hose, spits it on the pyre and lights it, *whoosh*. He rinses his mouth with salt water and chases both with bourbon. A lone yacht penetrates the inlet and cruises slowly through, and then they are alone again.

Claude plucks salal berries, which he tosses into sizzling butter and ling. He lights a joint, "for da taste bud," but Evelyn shakes her head. The salmon he simply guts and skewers with three sharpened alder saplings propped in rocks so it leans over the fire. His fingers moving deftly, Claude shows her how to arrange the oysters and butter clams —"Put dere ass-end in da fire, eh?"— as he nudges their hinged side into the coals.

He drizzles lemon over the crisping salmon skin, he splashes bourbon into the sizzling cod and butter and berries. The oysters and clams open by themselves, a kind of offering-up, a declaration that they are perfect, now.

They can hardly stand letting the gorgeous food cool enough as they eat with just mouth and hands. They moan eating, Claude's rising to shouts of "Paradise!" and "Evelyn!" Always louder and more French when he drinks, and today he has cause to be loud. It is the best meal Evelyn has ever eaten. She cuts her fullness with sips of bourbon and does at last reach for her one small toke, and as soon as the food is done and another yacht has left, their clothes are off and the lifejackets under her bum and shoulders, Claude as deft and loud over her as he'd been over his food. She doesn't feel it when she cuts her calf on an oyster. When they are done, as if it's connected to their lovemaking, Claude points across the inlet at the highest cliff. That rockface, he explains, Salish boys were made to climb to pass into manhood. Evelyn nods dumbly as Claude adds that, attached to their body, roped to bone spikes piercing the skin of their back, was a twenty-pound boulder. If they fell, when they hit water, "Dey go down fast, eh? Dey drown a mile deep." Claude shakes his head at the empty cliff face with wonderment and what looks like envy.

Claude, whom friends dubbed Mister Natural. Man of appetites, who loved what came in through his senses, loving most the green and the wild and the fast. Claude whose appetites grew roots in his flesh, became addictions. Whose seasonal work in the forest and on water afforded him long winters in the chemical wilds of city streets, where his lovely energy was bled and bled.

EVELYN RECKONS TODAY must be a Monday because yesterday the boaters sailed and campers left on the water taxi. Alone again, she suffers some animal nervousness before she can feel in her gut that *alone* is fine, that indeed it might be best. With people around she always in some sense had her head down, her eyes averted. While this was fine for hunting good flotsam in the logs (to her Crusoe stash she'd added three mismatched socks, a fine rubber glove, a length of fishing line stout enough for jigging, a Legion 145 coffee cup, plus more bits of rope than she'd ever use), this eyes-to-the-ground bearing felt more crab-like than dignified.

Scanning her beach, Evelyn sees for the first time the lovely contour of the spit, how the grand forces of wind and water caused this mile-long reach of sand to curl, like a perfect eagle's talon. She sees its gradations of colour, its many shades between beige and bone. Taking this first heads-up walk along the talon's top, kicking into it with her feet, she understands what she is walking on: a huge midden, a mile-long mound of pulverized shell left here by the Clam Eaters.

And now, looking back toward her little shelter, she sees her first ghost.

She's been preparing for it. Before this morning she has begun to know about them, having sensed them, but until now hasn't seen one. Preparing has lessened her fear, and she knows that this is why she's being allowed to see. This law she feels in her body: when fear leaves, something better floods in to fill it.

Mostly, Evelyn has learned about ghosts from Joe, her crow. Joe has been hanging around since she set up camp, hopping ever closer for crumbs and for bits of clam adhering to shell. Last night he was two feet from trusting food from her hand. She speaks to him. *Joe, just come and get it. Joe, I'm stripping for a swim, avert your eyes.*

Once as she came up from her swim, dripping, and lay down to dry, she told him — he was perched impatiently on a log five feet from her — *Joe? Lunch is in an hour*. She laid her head back then picked it up again to see what he was doing, but he was gone. This sense of *no-crow* felt as rich as Joe had himself, his absence as palpable as his presence, and Evelyn recognized then that she'd been sensing *absences* all over this beach, and beaches before this one. She also understood that it's this trick, this *inversion*, that gives ghosts their energy, and us our fear. Seconds into his death, Claude's hospital room had been full of both.

This first ghost is standing over Evelyn's firepit. She looks about twenty, and is one of the People who use to live here, though her clothes are maybe from the 1920s. She gazes Evelyn's way but Evelyn can't tell if they're meeting eyes. She can sense a personality. The woman shakes her head once, one distinct motion. Then walks away, past the logs, up the sand, disappearing over the midden mound to the head of the spit and into the forest.

Evelyn is not at all afraid. What had the ghost shaken her head at? The fire? The empty clamshells? Yesterday a tourist wandered by and asked Evelyn about the clams she was cooking, saying the usual about red tide and July not having an "R."

Having seen the ghost, Evelyn has a quick string of wonderments but no answers: Is a ghost in a state of undying hunger? Would she ever be one? Is she much different from one now?

AT LOW TIDE the mud flat at the base of the spit is like a Serengeti for birds. Alone, naked, Evelyn sits drying from her swim, watching the hundreds of shorebirds forage. It's seagulls mostly, and easily a dozen great blue herons. She sees the birds as feathered casings of protein. Under the mud is the root crop of fishy meat that the birds are hoping to convert into their own. To make it into themselves is their main lot in life. The clams, of course, have their own conversion going; when the tide comes in they filter the water ceaselessly, making anything usable into themselves. Until a starfish creeps along and lies upon the clam, boring into it and making it into itself. It is the oddest marriage. Everlasting, but utterly egotistical.

Evelyn wonders if hunger isn't just ultimate ego.

Suddenly all the gulls rise as one and a gangly second later the herons do, too. What has scared them? A shadow runs the ground past her and now she sees the eagle gliding in.

You learn things by sitting and watching. She has just learned that eagles attack and eat gulls and herons. Otherwise why would all these birds abandon their killing field? Evelyn watches the bald eagle closely. She's seen her share but still they spark her, like rainbows or roadside deer or a quarter on the sidewalk. What is it about an eagle? Its white head is a kind of beacon, so clean. Such fierce glamour.

When Claude stared at her she could see him as a hawk...

The eagle lands and begins to pull at something half-buried in the sand. The seagulls begin to land, and then the herons. Soon they have all landed again. Some have landed rather close to the eagle. In fact, some have sidled over to within a few feet, then two feet. They don't look concerned about this creature that just made them panic. Evelyn sees how awkward the eagle is on land, how it walks almost painfully on its balled talons, on knuckles. If it tried to lurch and peck it would likely fall over. The gulls around it are much more mobile, nimble kids around an arthritic grouch.

So: eagles are dangerous only from the air. Evelyn sees the lesson here. It's almost a truism, if that's the word. Or fabulistic. The sleeping bully. Samson shorn.

No, it's exactly this: what you can see can't hurt you.

EVEN EARLY ON in their marriage Roy didn't seem interested in her recent past, one Evie herself laughed off as "degraded," and sometimes mocked by saying, "I wonder where those brain cells went?" if she dropped a dish. Respectable now, she liked to remind him that she hadn't always been. Not that she'd been wild compared to some friends, but compared to Roy there was no question. He still didn't drink beyond a single glass of wine to toast with. Once, shortly after Tommy was born, at an impromptu stag of sorts he cheerfully drank until he became dizzy and threw up, an event he would recall without embarrassment, saying he "tried drinking on for size and it didn't fit." (He never did have a recognizable accent but the slick little expressions like these labelled him forever an American.) He would announce, apropos of any discussion of drugs, how he would "like to try smoking up, just the once, gain some context." In their social circle the opportunity never arose, and of course he never asked Tommy for some, but he could be so stubbornly liberal.

In one way his past was far wilder than her own. Her crazy times sounded merely typical alongside Roy's teenage years, which he'd sometimes mock as his "lost years." Evelyn could not conceive of such conviction. Central headquarters in Utah told you where to live and you simply went. But never alone, always with your partner, even sleeping, even leaving the bathroom door open when you peed, because headquarters decreed that "alone" was bad. You might do something sexual to yourself. She could not conceive of Mormon teenagers, their hormones abnormally explosive by being so clamped. She could only shake her head at Roy's stories. How they all wore long underwear under those suits, even in the desert heat, always long underwear — clean, white, somewhat stylized like the Hasidic brand — and when they took a shower they would stick a leg out of the curtain and keep touching that underwear with a religious toe. The idea was that they were never to be actually naked. Evelyn wondered how they hid the vibrating horniness under their underwear and suit-and-tie as they knocked on countless housewife doors in their dutiful, cheerful rounds to save all humans from themselves. She imagined their fundamental sperminess rising up to their hearts and heads and being literally channelled into horny-as-hell, hot-breathing love of God. When she posed these musings to Roy he more or less nodded his agreement that, yes, that pretty much describes how it was. In any case, Roy's young-Mormon tales left in the dust her ubiquitous stories of drinking too much or spending stoned afternoons in trees and what have you.

IN FOG, IT CAN turn so cold here. Wet wind pesters the face and neck and there's the taste of brine, the fishiness of tides. This taste is everywhere, all the time. The soul of this place is its taste. She sees herself, one of the People, standing here, a thousand years ago, the fishy water taste not only outside but inside, exuding from her flesh. She steeps in fish and salt and wind. Brine is how she feels and how she thinks. Her urine is flat compared to the salt of her thoughts. Her tears are brine and brine-thoughts are what cause them. Her breath is sharp with fermented salmon egg, her crotch rusty with blood. She dips a hand. Red is shocking in this grey place, is not a natural colour here, though people are walking bags of it, always ripe and ready to reveal. It is too cold to clean herself with a swim today so she does not want to and anyway she does not care. She is about to dig the morning's clams but she is peevish. Her period is flowing full so why do this chore, why bother with food at all?

PARADISE STARTS TO grate. Well, it hasn't been paradise. It's been a possible life.

This morning she watched the dock as a uniformed man climbed out of a deeply rumbling boat. Not a half-hour later, just long enough for her to be ratted out by campers perhaps, she is confronted at her shelter by a park ranger who tells her, "You *will* be fined if you light another fire," and also that there is a red tide warning in effect, that all of Washington state is closed, the red tide's headed north, that a single bad clam could kill her, and that she has to camp at an assigned site. The ranger is thirty-five and blond and would not have been alone at the prom. He is comfortable with his power, in the sense that he needs it and has it. Speaking, he scans the horizon for threats to nature. He doesn't want to look at her. Evelyn can actually feel the weight of her greasy hair. Maybe her nose is burnt, maybe it's a red clown nose. She looks away, too. After a minute he turns tail and leaves.

You will be fined. A ban is in effect. Evelyn knows so intimately these government types who rely on the passive voice. Mistakes were made. It's like their breathing has become measured and planned. Roy cruises through the living room, sees her camped on the couch for what he considers too long a time to be healthy, and he announces, for the two of them, "There is nothing to fear but fear itself," a nice little passive-voice ditty, and maybe even true. In any case gentler than the more honest, "You really should get up off your ass." Most of Roy's wisdoms tend to be passive and float in the air. He was doing her dishes for her once and she poked her head in, and he said, "The most overused word in our language is 'I.'" Roy could get to you, he really could. She imagines him the most passive voice in city hall.

DECIDING NOT TO KILL herself with seafood, she has stolen from three campsites now and some people have stared at her hard. No one can prove a thing because the food is gone almost as soon as it's in her hand. Her diet hasn't been half bad. Folks who do the near-wilderness are often those who eat trail mix and fruit and tofu. She feels light and strong. In fact, two food episodes make her consider health food as a lifestyle. The first involved a pound-and-a-half of Polish coil and the second a mega-bag of cheddar Doritos. Both were the only food that day and both were followed by a heavy stomach, enforced but restless sleep, and unpleasantness in the outhouse.

The outhouse is fine by Evelyn, one concession to indoor living she gladly makes. Once, sitting inside it, she hears laughter outside, and murmurings, and realizes that she has been caught singing. She tries to remember what, and suspects it was a tuneless hum.

She's happy to break any rule for the sake of comfort. She still lights her fires. The campers still eye her for this. Perhaps out of jealousy. They can't be so stupid as to think she'd start a forest fire, which is the only possible reason for the ban. It has rained every second day, and her pathetic little flame flickers mid-talon, a half mile away from the nearest tree. The ban is passive-voiced ignorance. Some weeks ago someone like Roy leaned over some clerk's shoulder in some office and had him type something like: All Parks No Fires. If the Roy-person would only come here he'd see that you couldn't start a forest fire with gasoline. But then the edict would have to be Some Parks No Fires, which was simply too complicated a thing.

This morning's little fire is pitchy and smells. It occurs to her that bureaucracy has no smell. Which is why it has taken us over with no struggle. We didn't smell it coming.

Her fire smokes brazenly and now here comes a fellow camper, meandering over from one of the proper sites. The woman looks forty, wears hiking boots, khaki shorts. Evelyn has seen her two near-teen girls and husband tag along with her on the approved trails.

"Excuse me," the woman asks, all smiles but stopping ten metres away. She has a forest-green Celtic knot tattoo on a shoulder, showing-for-summer while hidden-for-office. "But are we allowed fires?"

This, on a beach sporting red signs, from a woman who would have studied pamphlets in advance. Evelyn would prefer a blunt, "Put your fire out."

"I'm sorry. I'm cold."

The woman's mouth smiles anew, though her eyes don't change. "Well, it says 'no fires.' They're pretty dangerous."

Instead of asking the woman why she lied in asking if fires were allowed when she knew they weren't, instead of pointing out the wet, smoking wood and the forest a wet five-minute walk away; instead of explaining that she hasn't cooked her two stolen eggs yet or that the woman is an officious pest, Evelyn surprises herself by asking in the Montreal Jewish voice Claude might have used in a similar fix, "What, you don't want to be cremated?"

Deaf with anger the woman goes off and Evelyn feels what just happened. Something has shifted. It wasn't quite enjoyment, but she was *wanting* that argument. So she's in Tommy's realm.

Though with Tommy, there would be a fire inches from that woman's tent tonight.

THE WAY TOMMY always takes conversations to a painful point. In the car, Roy tries to engage their bored seven-year-old, doing him the favour of including him.

"What would *you* rather be, Thomas, the elephant or the eagle?" Roy and Evie have been playing lightheartedly with the notion of reincarnation. Evie chose elephant, Roy eagle.

"What would *you* rather be," comes the drole sass from the back seat, "an elephant's *dick* or an elephant's *butt*?"

Roy will normally reprimand, or ignore. This time he decides to play seven-year-old.

"I'd rather be an elephant's butt. That way you could *see* everything. If you were all tucked away, if you were an elephant's d—"

"You could *pee* on everything."

"Well, I guess that's true."

"If you were his butt you could *poop* on everything, kill everything with your giant elephant *poo*. If you were his *dick*—"

"That's enough."

"—you could *pee* all over the *poo* and flood all the towns—"

"That's *enough*."

"— and kill everyone. If you were an eagle you could *poo* from way up and get them in their *mouths*."

"*Tom*."

"And you could *shit*."

Tommy can never not have the last word, even if it means severe punishment, which it used to. Now Roy simply quits, for Tommy will only keep interrupting, upping the nastiness. Roy's shoulders are stiff with Mormon patience, his eyes hollow with dismay. Evie wonders if Roy has registered the play on words, the logic leapfrogging in a way that could have been admirable. They are used to it, and even if smart it points always the wrong way, the worst way. They have discussed consulting a professional.

WAKING ON ANOTHER nameless morning, she finds the air shockingly cold. It's a clear, still dawn but she can't get warm and she panics, flaps her arms with a desperation that has to do with survival. How can this be June? It might even be July. She shoves a careful teepee of twigs together, lights and tends it with worry, adding strips of bark only when they're needed, then timing the finger-thick, then arm-thick wood. At last she quits hunching stiffly over it and settles back, the heat relaxing her whole front. Hot front, cold back, so she flips herself like meat on a stick. She only now becomes aware of the rising noise of bees, like nothing she's heard anywhere. Maybe it is because she's alone, or because there are no other sounds, but she swears that if someone were here with her they would have to shout to be heard over the bees.

She flips herself back to her front. Then it happens.

Bathed in the bee-sound she stares dumbly at her fire, its flames grasping up and up. A hummingbird, a creature she hasn't seen in perhaps years, thrums close to her face and stops there, scaring her. She startles and — it flies into the fire. All in a fatal second: it buzzes to an inch over the flame and drops weakly in. It makes no noise, dying.

She doesn't breathe. As fast as it drops she sees there is no rescue. It is already charcoal grey. Even the ruby throat, made of sequins. She suffers its brief sizzle, its peanut-body almost already gone. As soon as feelings come she feels dirty. She is a hulking destructive presence here. She feels this in her body, which suddenly feels far too big. It's the symbol stuff of teenage poetry — death of little bird the corny summing-up of human rape of nature — but here the symbol is. The hummingbird *was* nothing but nature most vulnerable. It *is* dead because of her. Maybe the bird had never seen fire before and here was a fantastic flower.

She breathes carefully. She is now wide awake and again very unsure of her reason for being here. For sitting on her log and for continuing to. Her heart has taken on something of the speed of the bird's. If she were schizophrenic, or religious, she might make something out of this. It might have changed her life. Maybe it has, a little bit. Well, it's changed her morning. She'll see about tonight, and tomorrow. She's already thinking of a small ceremony in its honour, after her mind's cleared.

For now the hummingbird is another ghost she's added to this place. Will it be sensed as a whisper? A wasp at her neck?

THEY LOST CONTROL OF him long ago, if they ever had it. It's a school night, two in the morning and Tommy comes crashing in drunk. Usually he is calculating and won't let himself get sloppy, but tonight for some reason he didn't care. A problem with a girl, or cop, or deal, or drug trip, or any combination of these, has sent him thrashing home. He doesn't care about her and Roy's anger, never has. *Fine, I'll leave*, murmured from day one with utter non-caring. Leaving would be an inconvenience: his bed gets made, the fridge is filled. Tonight from their bed they hear him going through the fridge, stuffing his hole, which is how he eats, impatiently filling a cavity. They hear a bang and a smash. Putting a hand on Roy's arm, keeping him in bed, she strides to the kitchen. From the hall she hears his proud, sloppy, *I got the fucker*, and a low chuckle. She flicks on the fluorescent and Tommy is caught under it, hunched at the fridge door. He squints dully at her like an animal who's decided not to bite her because there is no need. At his feet a broken jar of mustard. Some has splashed on his jeans, the yellow super-real against the blue. He's got a package of sandwich ham and several slices in his mouth hang out and flap as he chews. He smiles for her now, exaggerating the flapping slices. Then, holding her eye, he does exactly what will make her crazy: he steps calmly into the biggest gob of mustard and lets his stocking foot rest there. He says through the ham, "*You* clean it up."

It's almost funny. The joke between them is that he knows she expects him to always say the very worst thing. Here in the kitchen, even now, something like charisma flirts with something like a mother's love, but they are both tired of it.

He's fifteen. He'll be gone the morning after his next birthday.

POISON CLAMS. The poisonous eyes of campers, their moods wafting over to infect her. This afternoon, dragging her rubber raft up the beach, it snagged on something and is losing air. She can't find the leak, nor could she fix it if she did. So the signs are everywhere. Evelyn decides to leave this beach. She can still travel if she stops rowing to blow air in it every two minutes or so. But how stupid is that, life jacket or not.

She studies the couple climbing out of their double kayak. White as a new microwave. She's watched how, to get in, you steady it with a paddle, stab both feet in then slide them forward and plant your bum. She eyes the tarp they use to cover it before starting up the beach for their hike. What a fine tent that tarp will make. The couple seal their kayak's fate when they walk past her and glance at her with suspicion. Fear attracts dogs, suspicion attracts thieves.

It's harder than it looks. She is almost spastic in her paddling, in her gut-clutches for balance. Twice she almost tips, but Evelyn does leave Sidney Island. She is also slowed by her crying. It begins at the sight of all the footprints in the sand. She sees that they are portraits of time, the brutality of time. They all contain the ghosts of feet, the feet of parents and children, and none of them will step those steps again. It doesn't help that many of those footprints are hers.

Soon she can paddle more leisurely, because she's around the point and the couple can't see her now, and by tonight she'll be on one of any number of small islands, hidden. If she stops at all. She sees that, with a kayak, you can travel fast. You could hunt with whales, at night.

While watching the two hikers disappear, she'd considered guilt for a moment only. It wasn't just that they eyed her with suspicion.

Nor was it that, judging from their high-tech gear, they were yuppies, their kayak and all else insured to the hilt. Nor was it that she left her well-loved bagel for them in the kayak's place. No, Evelyn sees that guilt is glue on your hull that slows you down. And if you are going to take Claude up to Tommy, you are entering their realm, and you should practise the world as they know it.

Anyway her boat is so gleaming white and swift that guilt can't keep up. She takes to the paddling. It's more a rock-the-hips, as on a bike, than a keep-it-steady, as in a canoe. She heads for an island whose name she doesn't know. The sea is green jello and she's a white-hot knife.

It fits that Tommy ended up on this coast and that it is here she will find him. All her men are here. Claude is ashes in her pocket and his face a constant. Roy is here too, his worry glued to her back.

Roy. Tommy. Claude. All her men. How very alike Tommy and Claude are. But even Tommy and Roy are the same in their core, their look while watching TV the same, the hungry male distracted for a time. Distracted from the race, the one with no beginning or end, one they don't see themselves but which sets them so clearly apart from her. (In Roy's line of work it's even called a race.) She can get excited for them in this race of theirs, but it's excitement for them, not for the race. A character of Toni Morrison's, one of the old wise ones, said to her daughter something like, "Any man is just a man." Like any sweet sentence, it is just true.

She notices on an upstroke, clinging to her inner wrist, a result of her success at jigging. She sees she hasn't washed in a while, not even her hands. It's a flat bit of organ on her, maybe liver. Dried almost black. This morning before setting off she could have had a dip but did not.

She knows this didn't start in Victoria. When did she start letting herself go? She can't locate when. "Letting go" had started as ambiguously as grey hair. Maybe it was on a Thursday night, Roy watching one of the TV shows he said helped him stay in touch. With *your subjects*, she might joke, and he might smile. One show was *Friends*, so slick and happy-breasted. Another was *ER*, which she couldn't bear even hearing from the next room. Sick and dying children, the show banking on vicarious horror. Another was *The Simpsons* — yes, once while watching *The Simpsons* with Roy she understood she was "letting herself go." The cartoon's knowing cynicism matched her own mood as, out of habit, she began stroking Roy's neck — their weekly signal. She realized she hadn't showered or worn makeup for days, save for the residue from the last time. There was a *Simpsons'* flavour to a dirty woman petting a clean mayor. She may have imagined it but when Roy didn't rise to the occasion, though not uncommon these days, it seemed a rebuke, as close as he might ever come to using the words, "You're letting yourself go."

He would eventually ask her, more than once, "Is everything okay?" She would assure him, "Yes," and once, a tease, "Why do you ask?" And he said, "Just wondering," or, another time, "You haven't seemed yourself lately." She liked to leave it alone. Talking about it felt like more *of* it.

Heather next door dared ask about Tommy and the empty-nest syndrome and this only got Evie laughing. "Didn't you notice," she asked Heather, who did get the joke, "that when he moved out all my hair turned black?"

Was she depressed? She wasn't lying in bed all day, or drinking, or on medication (yet), or addicted to shopping, and this set her apart from many of her friends and neighbours. It felt less like depression than it did like relaxing, less like fatigue than it did like settling. It felt less like sadness than it felt like humour, though maybe a gallows kind.

She did sometimes ask, What's the point of it all? But she could ask this neutrally and scan the menu of possibilities, knowing she would never make a choice. It felt only sane to judge those who continued to buy new makeup and the latest cars because, falling so easily into line, obviously they were the ones who had given up. One small wisdom she heard somewhere, or maybe made up for herself, she waved like garlic at the fangs of many a mood: if you still have a sense of humour you're probably okay.

She dropped her volunteer posts one after another. Roy was concerned and she wasn't. Then he was concerned *because* she wasn't. The arts board, the parks committee, all her "mayor's wife stuff." Roy said his concern had nothing to do with appearances and she almost believed him. She lasted longest at the group home teaching life skills — odd, because this job was the most painful. There were moments there of forgetful happiness — shouts of *Survivor*'s on! *Survivor*'s on! — or group jigsaw puzzles, all the residents' heads bowed, focused, content, the soft snap of a piece correctly placed, Evie careful to hide how much she helped. But these were ripples on their gloomful deep knowledge that they were different and their difference was ugly, and their whole life would be so. Evie could take only so much sadness and she said goodbye to that job, too.

At one point two or three years ago, again maybe a Thursday night, she felt clear and sharp and she decided to confront Roy. The idea was that Oakville sometimes felt like poison. Helpless to change her life, she was keeping her emotional distance from it. She was ready to announce this. She chickened out and stroked his neck instead, and he rose to this occasion, maybe sensing something precarious in the stroke. She knew she couldn't follow through with the whole truth, that good and dutiful Roy was earnestly immersed in poison. More than that — he was its mayor. It didn't matter that he had morals, that fairness was his credo. Tapped into webs of power, he was tainted to the core. He was mayor of Great Lakes pollution, mayor of Nike, mayor of global warming. He was mayor of downsizing and Prozac and sitcoms.

So Evie chickened out. That evening, Roy on top of her and as always careful on his elbows, she began to cry. Roy stopped and his plaintive, almost knowing, "What's wrong?" got from her the single, hinged, plaintive sound: *Tommy*.

She knew then why she had quit the group home and everything else. Since she had failed to help her boy, every failure to help anyone else kindled the same misery.

SHE HAUNTS THE ferry ramp on Mayne Island. A place she can beg, borrow, and steal. Begging is easy because she disguises it. A pristine Gulf Island, a woman her age, alone? She wears stolen Gortex hip huggers. "Excuse me, but I've had my money stolen. This is most embarrassing but could you spare..." The "most" adding a touch of class. It is generally no trouble getting the day's hamburger money in one ferry lineup, though somehow lots of people do see through her and turn away as if she were sixteen and scoring change on a city street. Maybe if she worked on her hair, maybe some of yesterday is still on her face, perhaps she should swim more.

Across Active Pass is Galiano Island. In its tiny village is a bookstore which, though she's been told by the owner not to return, she visits frequently, treating it like she does libraries. That is, she selects a book and sits and reads it. At first the owner, a woman Evelyn's age, was very pleasant. She was herself "a refugee from southern Ontario" who had "found a piece of heaven here." Evelyn's third morning in the store the woman's questions turned markedly personal, perhaps as a result of Evelyn's hygiene, or her naps, or her constant helping herself to the free coffee and, one morning, to many doughnuts and the whole plate of English cucumber. "May I ask where you're staying?" kinds of questions. Which led to her not allowing Evelyn further entry, but not before Evelyn stole a handy book: *Wild Food in British Columbia*. All along, she could have been eating those limpets, which aren't affected by red tide.

She makes use of her new book this afternoon. Drifting at a fair clip through a kelp bed in Active Pass she jigs a fish off the bottom. At first it feels like something big-shouldered, and the idea of bringing it aboard scares her. But she is starving, and soon feels that much of the weight was the current and length of line. She brings to the side a brown fish about a foot-and-a-half long, flapping listlessly now. She takes note of its coloration and character. Pinning it on the fibreglass in front of her she manages to hit it enough times with the paddle edge to kill it. Then, almost embarrassed as she watches her hands' hurry, she knifes it open to expose the flesh. She gouges a ragged chunk out and eats it.

She thinks of it as sushi. It's pleasantly sort of crunchy and it's fresh, of course, and so mild it's almost tasteless, like the best white fish is supposed to be. Lemon would completely cover its taste. Chewing, she decides next time to try to hunt and dig up some wild ginger; she thinks Claude impressed her by doing that once. Her new book depicts several kinds. She might conceivably steal some soy sauce from a campground here. She should have saved some wasabi peas.

But she doesn't know what kind of fish this is, which unsettles her. Minutes ago this torn-up creature had that proper bullet-form of a basic fish. Its skin glows wonderfully in the sun. From a certain angle it flashes a colour she's never seen.

Locating the book with her feet and drawing it to her, she thumbs through *Wild Food in British Columbia*, staining it, appropriately, with blood and scales. She learns she's eating a kelp greenling, also known as a tom cod. She can smile: *Tom* cod. But, named, the fish feels lessened. A general creature, not this magical individual. Its skin glints *iridescent brown*, which she'd have thought impossible were she not seeing it in her hand. Its smells slightly sour, reminds her of dandelions.

Bobbing in the rip, understanding that she's just caught, killed and eaten a raw fish while sitting L-shaped in a kayak, she knows she is no longer insane. She has, though, begun seeing too clearly. Her problem will lie in digesting what she sees.

She feels best on the water like this. Claude's face doesn't visit here as much because, on the water, which he loved so much, his face is finely ever-present.

But she should turn north.

Pictographs are often painted over one another. Some were probably created to record events and identify territory. Much of the art is thought to be the work of shamans attempting to influence supernatural beings or individuals on vision quests. The simplicity of designs and the practice of painting one pictograph over another suggest that at many rock art sites the process rather than the final product was the most important aspect.

— ROBERT J. MUCKLE,
THE FIRST NATIONS OF BRITISH COLUMBIA

STRAIT OF JUAN DE FUCA SHORE

SITTING ON A BEACH LOG, bent over his laptop, Peter Gore mumbles his compelling sentence over and over to himself so he won't forget it while he tries and fails to get the solar battery thingie to work. The sky here on Sombrio Beach is overcast — debatable whether to call it 'fog' or 'low cloud' should he ever have opportunity to type these words — but there is enough light. He can't get past the *Install* prompt on his screen. He's plugged the thing in, what needs installing? He knows that the solar gizmo, a black Darth-Vaderish plasti-metal appendage, falls under the *Hardware* category, but forays into the *Help* catacombs get him nowhere. Micha, his computer-whiz neighbour, had demonstrated the thing for him. Plugged it in, tapped a key and had it humming nicely, feeding off the Spokane sun streaming in the window.

Here on the log, Gore's typing becomes finger- then knuckle-punches and he resists the urge to slap the computer hard, jar its carburetor. He has watched its regular battery decharge coyly, still able while dying to chide his stupidity with its blinking red weasel-eye. He wants to boot it, literally. Azimov's future has come, machines win. His book is dead before it took a first breath. He feels foolish because he *is* a fool. He is Van Gogh reaching his remote hamlet in the south of France, setting up easel and brushes but lacking paint. Gore recalls the romantic notion he'd had back in Spokane, of arriving at a beach much like this one and waiting for the urge of art to crack open his machine and devirginize it.

Sure enough, what triggered today's labour was the imperative of the single sentence that rose out of his first glimpse of this place. After his long hike from the main highway — mercifully downhill; let gravity take a hangover by the hand — he walked through a dark grove of ferns and cedar to emerge onto a truly splendid vista. Across perhaps ten miles of water, the snow-capped Olympic Mountains of Washington State waited for tourists' jaws to slacken and their cameras to come out. The sea, glassy-smooth, swelled with rollers which gently lifted then lowered whole kelp beds before tastefully rattling a shore composed of smooth stones uniformly the size, Gore decided, of ostrich eggs. Providing a canopy for the beach were the lower boughs of one-hundred foot trees. Gore consulted his handbook — Western Hemlock. To the highwater mark, storms had delivered a dense playground of blond logs, some with the girth of sports cars. A lovely stream exited the forest to provide thirsty, hungover humans with clean water. (Gore had knelt, cupped his hands and drank a cure.) No bugs, no trash. Nothing, as far as the eye could see in any direction, man-made. An eagle off in the sky. The sentence that sat him down at his computer and in the end made him feel only impotently thumbish, was: *There exist places so perfect that people don't matter at all.*

Now as he abandons his computer, restuffs it in his pack, jamming sock-balls and T-shirts around it, he abandons the sentence as well. He'd been abandoning it bit by bit. Its first clause was the first to sour: what began as a decent bit of drumbeat, the alliteration of "places so perfect" soon sounded only cute. Then the stirring notion of the word "perfect" eased back into the vacant cliche that it was. You don't *say* perfect, you *convey* it with a killer image. There was not one image in the entire sentence. Why struggle to fire up one's computer when one is only imageless? At this question, urgency ebbed and hangover rose.

Another tactic would be to leave the perfection implied — "There are places where people don't matter at all." But, while mysterious, it emphasized too much the second clause, that people are essentially tripe, and this wasn't the best message to confer upon one's readership in one's opening line. This rudeness was the sentence's final betrayal, and Gore flicked it onto his life's pile of imperfect sentences.

It dawned on him why the sentence had arisen in the first place — he'd been hating people all morning. Hitch-hiking, he'd earned only amused glances and several open jeers as cars passed him by. Then the bus driver laughed in his face when asked if Sombrio Beach had a cheap but clean motel. The two trashy passengers, one of whom smelled like a walking haggis, the other of whom despite glowering pimples remained haughty and judgmental, wouldn't engage in cheerful conversation, which is what a hangover needs in order to avoid itself. Then a tongue-pierced guy and girl sitting on their packs on the highway shoulder merely hooked cool thumbs back past their ears, toward a dirt trail, when asked directions to Sombrio beach.

Computer stowed again, Peter Gore stands with his pack and gazes left up the beach, then pivots to gaze right. Then out to sea, as if he might choose there. Then behind him, to the path that leads cruelly back uphill to the highway. What seemed such a nice, profound little sentence when it first trotted up and sat musing in his ear was all along only dim-witted, porous, and born of peevishness.

The honest sentence would have gone: *I'm free of you bastards, here are some trees.*

HE KNOWS HE ISN'T good with solitude. But solitude isn't what he's here for. In any case, Gore soon finds himself one hundred yards down the beach, next to a tidy little tent and beach-fire. Walking past this fire and a display of food, Gore has simply stepped over and said, "Hi."

They've answered, but the fellow named Bill doesn't look at his brother named Bob as he rummages stiffly in a box and asks Bob how it's possible that they have only the one can of pinto beans. The question sounds rooted in earlier dispute and blame. Gore has watched while into the large pot Bill has deposited a heap of diced tomatoes, two fistsful of chorizo sausage, a quartered red onion, some mushroom caps, a squeeze of lemon, a squat habenero pepper, and the one can of beans. Bill is deft, and adds pinches and dashes

Gore doesn't follow. The stew begins to bubble over the fire; already it smells rich and good.

"Do you fellows like *whisky*?" Gore taps his pack. "I have some whisky."

Bob winces as if to say that whisky is dangerous, and Bill doesn't respond at all. They are both perhaps approaching forty. Bob is robust and muscular and the more animated of the two. Bill has a premature hunch and is overtly gay. They'd introduced themselves as brothers, but a little, Peter suspects, too quickly. In fact they'd introduced themselves as "Bobby" and "Billy," using cartoonish American accents, though they'd already said they were from Victoria. From "Billy's" quivering lip and side-glance to "Bobby," Gore can see the accent is a wee joke at the dim Englishman's expense, scare him with two good ol' boys. He finds it funnier that he is more American than they are.

"Anyway, please — *please* — just help yourselves. I have more than this one bottle."

He withdraws from his pack and opens one of his tubes of plastic cups. It is perhaps laughable that he has more cups than clothes, but he'd deemed the cups necessary, a means of getting locals to speak, for presumably not all Canadians liked to suck on the end of a communal bottle. Into one of the three cups he's placed on the log beside him, Peter pours an instructive drink, takes a taster's sip and, as if he's never had Jamieson's before, nods appreciation. He caps and places the whisky in a handy ball of unearthed, bleached roots. The huge root-ball rises out of the beach behind the log on which he sits, backing him like the gnarliest of halos. It has so many handy crotches it could be a wine-rack.

"I *do* want to be rid of this whisky before I tackle the West Coast Trail."

"*You're* doing the Trail?"

Gore sees Bob scan his body while asking this and he hears incredulity in the question.

"Yes." He pauses. "Why?"

"Well, it's a toughie. When's your reservation?"

Gore snickers at the wit: hiking-trail-as-Hilton. Bob responds with a look that makes his stomach fall. It hadn't been wit at all. He must consult his *Tourist Guide to Vancouver Island*. He really should have studied it more, but the first word of its title had put him off, had put him in the spirit of winging it. History, facts, lore — this he had studied. Ask him what vegetation backed Bill 'n' Bob's campsite: salal, blackberry, Western Hemlock, and there is a red cedar. Ask him about the Natives hereabouts: Coast Salish, peaceful, not much art; fifty or so miles north began the Nootka, whalers, not so peaceful, art that looked simple and mean like voodoo. Don't ask about reservations for the West Coast Trial which, he remembers now, attracted people from around the world, so much so they had "*limited its access*."

Gore doesn't care about that now. There are other trails, non-tourist trails. He needs some of their stew. They can't not offer him some, though he notes with a feeling of deep social clumsiness Bill setting out two lone plates and two lone forks. Gore discreetly scans the tide-line flotsam for a flat, fork-shaped stick of some sort.

"So. You lads come here often?"

He should not be blamed for having brought no food. When one unfolds one's map of Vancouver Island and locates on it a dot named Sombrio Beach, how can one not assume a restaurant or two? Motels, a resort? Any place earning a *dot on a map*, for god's sake, should at least have *some*thing unnatural. It is cause for a letter of complaint to the Tourism Bureau, outlining for them in hair-splitting fashion that, while no doubt worthy as a *destination*, Sombrio Beach in no way warrants a *dot*.

"It seems you two have mastered one-pot cuisine."

Half-way here, on the bus, Peter Gore had already suffered intimations of foolishness. Recalling why he had chosen the Sombrio dot in the first place, that it had to do with one of his six goals, "interviewing squatters," he'd consulted his guidebook to re-read the paragraph describing it: "... a secret spot known mostly to locals, and squatters who over the years erected structures in the surrounding woods, some with bedrooms and lofts. Some had tree houses. Some commuted to work in Victoria, lived at the Beach for years until, under pressure from local taxpayers, the government evicted them and demolished the structures. Still there are rumours of hardy individuals living deeper in the forest ..."

Bouncing on his bus seat, romanced by this Eden of squatting, certain words leapt out: demolished, evicted. It dawned on him that the article was all in past tense. And that, along with no taxes and no law — Gore closed the book at this point, hungry already — there would be no grocery store.

Savory wafts of stew make him shift his bum on the log and rattle his running shoes in the rocks, which are smaller at this end of the beach, uniformly about the size — Peter decides — of eagle eggs. The glassy mounds of water have never stopped rolling themselves onto the beach, the sound — if one tore one's attention from the smell of stew — of a planet exhaling through a single fleshy gill flap. Or it's the sound of a big sleeping god's rhythmic dreaming of dessert. Gore tells himself to remember one of these images.

He sees his whisky cup is empty. He had vowed to save his spirits to loosen the tongues of interview subjects but, when one's plans are dashed, perhaps one should drink. Alcohol is one way to settle chaos and make it seem like an itinerary.

"Apparently," he announces, swallowing whisky and clearing his throat, "there was some sort of *commune* here at this spot? Where all was shared? A sort of, 'what's mine is yours' sort of —"

"I don't know if it was quite that," Bob says, peering into the stew. "But yeah. It was a scene. Over that way —" He waves his hand at a meadow-like indentation in the trees down the beach, "— you can see some of it. They carved stumps and made some pretty wild faces and stuff."

"I think they enjoyed their 'chemistry'," Bill adds.

"A*ha*."

"There's still some old floors," Bob continues, "that are good places to put your tent." He eyes Peter's small pack with suspicion. "But watch out for old outhouse pits."

"Aha. *Yes*."

"Well, no," Bill is disagreeing, shaking his head, "they'd be *utterly* benign by now."

Bob eyes Bill a moment. "They're still giant holes to fall into? And I dunno, *Billy*, you still see some very *non-benign* types wandering around. Who sure *look* like they live here."

"A little mossy on the north side, are they?" Peter offers with a smile.

"Shrubbies," says Bob.

"Shrubbies?"

"'Shrubbies' is what they call them on Hornby Island. All sorts of burn-outs just living hidden in the weeds."

"Shrubbies!"

"They come out and steal coolers," says Bill, sternly. "On Hornby they found a cooler graveyard."

"Go shrubbies!" says Gore, and Bill gives him a tilted-head look.

"It was quite the scene here, though," Bob says. "I was here once. Maybe two decades ago."

Bill grimaces. "*Please* don't speak in decades."

"They had a doctor—I think even a dentist. Some people specialized in getting clams or whatever, some were carpenters. Some just, you know, 'decorated,' played music, or—"

"Or were 'decorations themselves'," says Bill, looking sideways and up.

"Burn-outs kept landing here and I guess it got bad-druggy and fell apart. But they had a nice barter thing happening for a while."

"Tambourines long into the night," Bill says, still mocking.

"*Indeed*," Gore agrees, though he has stopped liking Bill.

"No," says Bob. "It was nice."

"I just remember hating being smiled at for no reason," says Bill.

"Indeed," Gore gets in quickly. "The *smiling*. But speaking of bartering, I seem to be in a position of lots of *whisky*, and very little food. Actually, *no* food. So, lads, I was wondering..."

Bill and Bob glance at each other. Bob shrugs "sure," though Bill looks longer at Bob, as if to say, first you forget the cans of beans and here you are giving away the one we have.

"So," says Gore, hoisting the whisky high into the sky and waggling it, "please. *Ease* my conscience. *Guzzle* away."

Bob half-heartedly reaches for a cup, but Bill turns his back on them both to make lots of noise withdrawing from their cooler an expensive-looking bottle of white wine. Then searches furiously for the corkscrew.

GORE STRIDES A requisite distance from the stew-fire in order to pee. The stew proved extremely necessary — though he is now burping chorizo and onion — not just for survival but because all the whisky sips had gathered and gone public just as he'd begun eating. He wasn't used to drinking in quantity, or to hard liquor at all. First came the wave of unearned jolliness, next the not-giving-a-damn what he said — a noble enough condition with friends, but precarious with strangers, especially when one is a mother hen named Bill.

It was the bull kelp joke that severed ties with Bill. Gore really shouldn't have said it, given their probable sexuality. There he was blissfully wolfing his first bowl of stew, shrugging off Bill's horror by saying how in Spokane everyone ate with their hands, just like this, slurp, slurp. He added, wagging a brown but instructive finger at Bill, "Utensils are for the weak." The food released his body's clench and allowed his eyes to do some actual seeing, and when he saw the glossy twenty-foot whip of bull kelp lying almost at his feet he couldn't not joke about it. Again, liquor had him jolly and there was no time to preface his joke with explanations. Like, he him*self* had outgrown scatology, he really had. Like, the English are condemned to eternal bathroom humour *precisely* because, as a race, they are terrified of the bathroom and what is revealed there and, as with death, it must be wrestled down with mockery.

He probably chose the southern accent to get back at them for the "Billy" and the "Bobby." There he was, pointing with bean-stew finger at the slick kelp whip with its cockoid, baseball-size bulb at the end, suggesting, "This'n is *so* slippery-lookin, y'all could swaller *that* end, an' yer *buddy* reach up yer ass to get 'er an' you wouldn't feel a *thang*. *Billy*-Bob."

Bob smirked, but Bill stared blankly at him and said, "Go away."

So he has and, done peeing, Gore stoops shyly into the uphill reach of a wave to rinse his beany hands. He decides to give Bill a break and have a look-see in the old commune clearing. He is full-to-bursting and his gall bladder could use some exercise. The chorizos aren't moving much. He taps the vial of Demerol in his side-pocket to hear its soothing rattle.

Back on the ostrich-egg rocks with a hundred or so yards to go, turning his ankles on three steps in succession, he understands that, whatever the past inhabitants' love of 'chemistry,' it likely didn't include hard liquor, at least not when they had to walk anywhere. It is odd to walk and be made to stare only at one's feet and choose where to put them next, a claustrophobia of not-being-allowed-to-look-up. Especially in this place of ocean trees eagles, etcetera. This place of beauty where people no longer matter. He stops, teetering, a skull-sized rock under each foot, to check if there are still eagles in his sky. One soars in duo-toned elegance up over his right shoulder. He nods and looks down again to aim his feet at more rocks.

So what did the people here do? They did what all people do—work long enough to feed and house themselves, and then find entertainment. Which would have been rustic and noble, carved, so to speak, out of the forest itself. You could imagine a fire and a ring of musicians around it playing bamboo flutes and stringed curly-root things. Kids keeping time banging something hard against something clangy. You could imagine quiet conversations on the expected subjects: I sense from the tilt of your chakras that tomorrow you will smile from a deeper place, at which time the elders of Mu will send a message. No—they were likely educated, and talked quantum physics, or the degraded society from which they fled. They probably played chess, for god's sake. No—they played Go.

Most likely their work took up all their time. Finding food, keeping warm, keeping clean. Though maybe—in fact probably—their work *was* their fun. The Marxist ideal. Why else would you come here and stay here? No bosses overseeing as you pick berries, dig clams, bathe in the sea, stoke bonfires, build tree houses, piss where you stand and yodel when you want: it was more vacation than lifestyle.

Gore locates a path into the shaded clearing. In here it is cool and oxygenated, the air of a vast healthy cave. He steps onto a platform of what once were floorboards, rows of weeds eager through the cracks. The boards are flat, milled somehow. Maybe this was the dentist's house. Jaunty ferns and salal has overtaken the clearing, but he can see the carnage of eviction: broken timbers, dirty plastic sheeting buried in mud, a dented pot, shredded blue rope hanging from tree limbs. Trickling through the clearing, a creek cannot be heard over the surf. Someone has dug a body-sized pool and lined it with rocks. Ten feet upstream, two flat sluice-boards, old and algae-covered, provide a trickle just right for filling bottles and pots, or for kneeling and slurping.

He spots, up a slope in the shadows of a secondary clearing, the oddest face. Gore jumps from the platform and climbs to it. In a grand cedar stump, its girth that of a church organ, someone has chainsawed the image of a ham-smiling Tiki god. Its eyes are crossed — more in defiance than goofiness, though Gore does not know how this effect has been achieved — and years of candles melted on top have created a head of garish multicoloured hair. All is mossy and sooty and weathered, lending it somewhat the demeanor of archeological ruin. Though he does spot some wax-dribbles which look suspiciously new.

Gore wanders the clearing, discovering side-paths that head off into the mysterious dark of the deeper forest. He smiles ironically at the sudden understanding that his archeological snoopings have to do with a group of flower children who squatted here for maybe a decade, rather than with the Native culture which lived and died here for thousands of years. But it is ironic too that both were wiped out by the same white machine.

Gore climbs the platform again and sits. He sits still, trying to imagine himself a Native, or a squatter for that matter, taking a rest from what he did all day. It is too quiet and he is soon bored, and he is certain that these people — Natives and hippies — got bored too.

In the short time he's spent here he's already noticed how entertaining a raven's croak can get. Sitting knobbly cross-legged on these floorboards, he senses the famous winter rain, and bone chill surrounded by monotony. He intuits how lonely the people here were. Gail once called him the loneliest man she'd ever met. Gail and her gift of exaggeration. Though for some reason, likely self-pity — or even more likely whisky and a need for drama — he thinks she might have been right. He recalls the sensation of having made his students laugh, the room erupting, and he up front making wry eye contact with a few. Here, there are no students to make laugh. There is no television to snap on, no phone to pick up. Maybe you learn to live with the silence, learn to enjoy your own inner chatter. He does know that, if they both lived here, out of necessity he and brother-Billy would either become friends or kill each other trying.

Gore sits on the floorboards. The light is falling but otherwise there is no time. Certainly there is no hurry. Another raven's croak would be most welcome.

The loudest thing, over-crowing the waves on the rocks, has been the heavy voice of a constant question. Not the luxurious, What is the meaning of life?, but the much more pressing, *What do I do now*?

Because this is precisely what Peter Gore has been asking himself his whole life, since before he could remember. Asking it now he suffers, for the first time, the answer: I am doing it. My plans have come to pass. I have researched. I have retired. I have left Spokane. I have left her. I am exactly where I took great pains to be. Here I am.

Now what?

He will write his book, of course. It will be both his work and his play.

At this notion Gore feels a presence, and his hair stands on end. For some reason he thinks: *cougar*. He recalls in his reading how the Natives say that your hair-on-end means a "ghost cat" is watching you. Or was that *stalking you*?

Gore feels his body go clammy and his stomach — though full of stew — hollow. This is crazy, he thinks. There are people on the beach, there are trails, there's a highway not far from here. He is perfectly safe. Indeed, he recalls reading how attacks are few — the number 'ten' comes up, though he can't remember if that's per century, or year. Attacks, or deaths. He does recall that, in cougar territory, one's children should stay close and make no jerky movements. He also recalls that, of all animals, the cougar is the only one not included on Native totem poles. They hated cougars. They thought them evil. These notions do not comfort Gore, having just realized that sitting down he has the stature of a child. Struggling to be graceful rather than jerky, he stands and, doing so, his spine suffers the terror of a footfall in brush behind him. His hair jumps so thoroughly it lifts the flesh beneath it.

"Hello."

Gore turns to the female voice. His gasping 'hello' sounds nothing like the word, so he adds, "You startled me."

She says nothing but smiles as she turns and squats (sometimes that word is so evocative) with her bucket at the sluice-boards. She has waist-length blonde hair, somewhat greasy, and wears a colour-drained ankle-length skirt and yellow halter top. She is pretty in a mature, square-jawed way. Gore has a notion that she hasn't worn underwear in years. Barefoot, she entered the clearing from the woods.

"So," he clears his throat, "that water is clean to drink, then?"

It's a lame ice-breaker. She doesn't look at him to say, "It's clean."

She is making him desperately lonely. He wishes he could offer her some whisky, but he has left his pack back at Bill and Bob's.

"Have you lived here long?"

She stands with full water bucket and turns to him. In her tanned face, her blue eyes are rich with their own light, and haunting from having gazed distances. So severe is her look that he thinks she must be on some weird drug, or one of the fiercer brands of meditation. Whatever the case, she has assessed him and he feels like a mosquito, his whole face an unwelcome probe.

"I don't," she says while turning away. She disappears between two bushes and begins her walk home.

He has had an encounter with a shrubbie.

IT GROWS quickly cool. The sun has dropped into the sea, leaving a purple sky over a thin horizon-line of orange. On his walk back to Bill and Bob's, Gore keeps to water's edge, as far as possible from the woods, its cougars and feral women. He has made a potential discovery for his book, though: It is possible that this most westerly of western places breeds a basic unfriendliness.

It even made sense. Who would expect a bunch of people — the *go west* song in their blood stalled by land's end — to be friendly? You could see it on the map: the entire west coast of North America delineated by a wall of water, a geography of frustration. You can imagine ants piling up at a shore, shoving, milling, getting on top of each other. Add to this the tectonic fault lines under everyone's feet, keeping nervous systems hopped up and owly.

Which is precisely how he feels approaching Bill and Bob's fire. He has no place to sleep but, no matter how much he drinks, will not stoop to begging his way into their tent. He sees two younger men have joined them. The four face each other in a square. One of the two — they are in their twenties, and Gore hears now that they are German — waves an angry hand in a most unGerman way. All four stand rigidly and the air is flexed. He imagines himself Hunter Thompson arriving and pulling a honking huge gun out, for no reason other than to contribute.

He has no clue what the argument is about. And, in what happens next, the ocean itself appears to be supplying the gun.

"What exactly again was stolen?" Bill asks of the Germans.

"Our *stove*," the taller one recites, "our two *ponchos*, and all of our *food*. But it is the *stove* we care about *only*. All we want is the *stove*."

"If we had it," Bob tells him, peeved, "we'd give it to you. We don't have your stove."

"It was *hanging right from here*." He points at an overhanging branch.

"What did it look like again?" asks Bill.

"It is *compact*," says the taller German, shaping his hands as if to a pineapple. "*It cost one hundred thirty dollars American*."

"We didn't *take* your stove," says Bob.

Gore has noticed movement behind the four men, something coming at them from out of the sea. From its shape, and awkward lurching, he thinks "seal." But then sees it is a large bird. A loon. The white belly, the black back, the spots. It's very large, this close up. What is it doing, so close? Aside from being pleasantly spooky, loons are famously shy. Gore has raised his arm to point it out when he registers its feeble gait, and in its climb up the rocks it tumbles onto its face. He sees that it has no feet. Just stubs. Broken-off drumsticks. Raw bone ends. Its mouth is half-open.

"We must, only, know where our stove is. *Please*."

"Fellows—" Gore frantically waggles his finger at the footless bird that sits, mouth open and staring, not six feet behind them, "—take a look at this."

No one hears him. Bob repeats, almost in sing-song, "We *got* here, *about* noon, *set* up our tent, there was *nothing here*."

The other German, eyes half-lidded, adds in monotone and understatement, "Yes, and so we are wondering where is it..."

"Guys, look behind you."

Only the taller German takes a quick look behind him, registers the loon, turns away from it and re-enters the argument.

Gore is angry. He stabs at the loon with his finger. How would a German know that loons don't leave the water, don't come close, are supposed to have big webbed feet, and don't sit and stare at you with their mouth open?

A shark must have risen to it. Maybe a sea lion. Look at it. The silent agony. A mammal would be shrieking. Look at its eyes—nothing. Loons lack muscles to contort their face.

"Here—" Bob has one German by the elbow, guiding him toward their tent. "—Look everywhere. Search everything. We didn't damn take it. Let's get this over with."

The young man bends and peeks into the brothers' food box, shifts aside a few bags. He lifts the box and looks under it. He peers under the log against which the box rests.

"Bob," Gore pleads, getting Bob to look. He stabs eagerly at the loon. They both look where he is stabbing, but the bird has vanished. Bob gives Gore the briefest questioning stare.

Now the German has dipped his head into their tent, then stops, and withdraws sighing, apparently feeling silly.

"Well," he says, timid now. "It has been taken by *some*one."

It is almost comic how first Bill, then Bob, and then both Germans, turn to look at Gore.

"Let's see," Peter Gore says, not angry yet, still shaken by the loon. "I did take a *walk*. Are you missing your *walk*?"

He strides over and opens his pack to display its meager contents. Though they try to stop him, he empties the entire pack. As he does so, he hears their story. Though camped fifty yards up the beach, they (the Germans also introduce themselves as brothers, and Gore snickers at this, it must be some kind of Sombrio code) had followed their camping manual's "bear safety" (the Germans pronounce this as one word) instructions to bundle everything to do with food and hang it from a branch some distance away. They'd done so this morning and had just returned from their day-long hike to the "famous-caves." Upon their return, Bill and Bob's camp was set up under said branch and their bearsafety bundle was nowhere in sight. The stove, bought in Germany, was a high-tech marvel that burned tiny amounts of regular gas-station gas. The five of them reach the sad, nodding conclusion that a local thief must have witnessed them setting off for a hike, watched them round the corner, and made off with their stuff.

"*Scoundrel*," mutters the taller German, who has been introduced as Veit, pronounced "fight." The other is Hans.

Bill asks if they are hungry — they are, very — and he prepares them some food with the dismissive shouldery bluster of a Jewish mother. Gore, petulant, refuses to eat any, though he is growing hungry again. Gall bladders, he has learned, should not be called upon to perform just before bed. Instead, he offers whisky, and while the other four sip carefully from his cups, he downs two medicinal doses, back-to-back. It is cold now and he lacks shelter. Whisky will be his lonesome home, yessiree, twang twang.

Once relaxed, the Germans ask him if he is related to "this robot who lost the election in Florida." Gore supposes his name must sit funny with foreigners, who note literal meanings; perhaps especially so with Germans, considering their past penchant for eviscerating villages. Perhaps he will ask them. But he is glad his namesake didn't win the presidency. Imagine suffering through with the name Clinton or Bush. And had he been president, Al Gore was destined for endless gaffes and boners; his blank face was a petri dish for idiot sincerity. Thank God the Texan prick won.

As the evening wears on into night and the fire dwindles, conversation has leveled off into anecdotes of camping in various countries' most beautiful spots. Sombrio is being held up for comparison. Gore has long since stopped talking, having ceased communication when a simple word melted in a slur. He finds himself lying on his side on the sand, lost in thought. He is less on the sand than in it, for with his free hand, the one not holding the bottle-neck, he has been casually scooping sand over his legs and up against his torso.

His thoughts have gone raggedly everywhere. One refrain is that this place is full of tricks, perhaps omens. It is time to quit this part of the island, start again somewhere else. This place is tainted, haunted, off-key, cursed. Bearsafe but peoplebad. For a coastline so beautiful, why is it that, according to the map, its several hundred miles has only three scant villages? Best begin again on the eastern side, with its towns, roads, motels. Grocery stores. Buy a little tent and some food and a pot of his own. Try those little feeder islands — Saltspring, for instance, was described as "charming." So, beat a simple retreat and in no way feel a failure. There are reasons why people don't live somewhere and why they do live somewhere else. He had come to a foulbeautiful place.

He hears fire snapping, he catches whiffs of story, tales of a canoe portage, a hail storm, a view from atop some mountain, a bear walking through a campsite. He will not contribute his own tale, yesterday's whale watching excursion, for it is touristy and the writer-in-him feels once more debased. He paid seventy dollars to don a red survival suit and climb, with twenty Americans, British and Japanese, into a high-powered zodiac and zoom for an hour to the American San Juan Islands, where that day's orcas were. The shoreline mansions — wall-to-wall and with American flags prominently flapping, for July Fourth neared — squatted as spectators to a depressing scene. Perhaps thirty vessels, some almost the size of ships, ringed a pod of six of the small whales. Engines droned, people shouted and pointed, cameras automatically wound, endless sodas tipped under the successful summer sun. The boat-ring — in essence a big growling noose — moved everywhere the whales did. It dawned on Gore that these whales, pressed to come up for air, would never during daylight be free of them. Feeling tourist-stupid from the outset when at the dock the first thing their guide said was, "Orcas are not fish," he now felt a part of *boatloads* of stupidity, and wanted to let the whales be. Their black looked pallid, more like grey, and though he knew it might be Demerol residue he thought he could sense their fatigue, almost a resigned lolling. When one large orca stood on its tail to lift its bulk a third out of the water and calmly take them in, Gore felt judged. He actually looked down. Back at the dock and free of his survival suit, Gore was on the highway with his thumb out in minutes. He had an almost physical notion that sad whales had chased him off the sea.

Now, only his head, arms and chest not covered in sand, he savours the style his book will take — ironic, gonzo, life-as-travel. He pictures himself a broken loon half-buried here by wind and tide, drying up and rotting already. The word 'intrepid' morphs on its own to 'insipid' and he can smile at this. As he can smile at tonight's symbol, which might be a silly and perfect chapter title: "Two Germans and a Legless Loon."

The flames are dead. Smoke rises in silence. The Germans are gone, Bill and Bob are in their little tent. Apparently all are brothers indeed, for when Bill and Bob mentioned their father's recent death, Veit and Hans spoke of their dead mother. Smashed is Gore's fantasy of a gay wilderness-beach and his journey into a new sexuality, his book recounting his oblique seduction at the hands of four "brothers." Gore chuckles, bouncing minutely in his press of sand. Even if he and Gail had problems in this regard, he is nothing if not chastely heterosexual. Though homogeneity might be easier at this stage of life, the thought of kissing a man makes his penis retreat. You would know way too much about each other. Embarrassing is what it would be. Imaging that kind of sex, and then remembering his and Gail's kind, he sees that, under the surface, he's been thinking about her far too much. He recalls, too clearly, what turned out to be their final time, another failed attempt at using their bodies as a bridge.

Trying to pass out, to get comfy in sand that is as cold as the night air, he remembers how Gail scratched his back almost nightly, this gesture her way of punctuating another day of their sad marriage. No matter how bad the day had gone, she gave him his scratch. They both knew it was replacement for the sex she couldn't (though he maintained *wouldn't*) give. Still, the scratch was something he grew to expect, and to need before he could sleep, and he would lie on his side and wait for it. He suspected she needed it too, needed to give something—and therein lay their difference—perhaps to ease some sort of guilt, or perhaps simply because she was kind. He never did come upon a gesture to give her in return, and soon forgot to try. But under this open black sky, beside the sleeping-god surf, amidst four scattered men half-drowned in his whisky, he does want someone to scratch his back now. He's always understood that anyone of intelligence must maintain at least a flirtation with sadness—but sometimes sadness is just too easy.

He hears one of the brothers snoring gently through their thin nylon wall, which he can reach out and touch if he needs to.

Occasionally, all the members of a pod will line up abreast and make very slow, shallow dives or lie almost still on the surface, moving and breathing as a single animal, in perfect synchronization. They will hold this pattern for an hour or more, apparently in a state close to sleep. Once common in the strait, these resting lines, as they're called, have not been seen for at least five years.

— MICHAEL POOLE, *RAGGED ISLANDS*

BERE POINT, MALCOLM ISLAND

THE ONLY HUMAN sounds here are the visceral thuddings of ocean-going tugs out in the sound, or the odd water taxi bringing loggers to Port MacNeil, or the nasal drone of seaplanes or, way up, the ethereal rush of a jet. But hours pass between any of these. When the salal flowers, bees appear and their drone is ceaseless. Otherwise, aside from the croaking of ravens and trilling of eagles, the noise here is wind in treetops, waves on gravel and, today, the hiss of rain which, to this young man in certain moods, sounds like massed voices of gossip.

As Tom appears between two monolithic cedars and steps limping into his clearing it begins to rain harder. Though bare-headed he doesn't hunch against it and his pace to his tent doesn't change. When he treads on a clear plastic bag beside his water jugs, he stops and stares at it for what seems a more than adequate time to register its contents. What the bag contains is broccoli well past its prime; the stalks are pale, almost grey, and the florets yellow. His gaze now moves to the fire-ring, in which, scattered throughout the char, are the gnawed stubs of what used to be a dozen or so carrots.

Tom is reminded that he is hungry. Boss-Lady — Catherine MacLeod, PhD — brought those carrots here. He wishes he had some more. When was she coming next? Usually Boss-Lady shows up to take away three or four cassette tapes, and a notebook. And film rolls. He slowly fumbles with the flap on the outer pocket of his day pack, lifts it, peers inside. Only one finished cassette. She won't be here again until he's finished making a couple more.

His face shows concentration as his bad hand moves up, wobbles as it changes direction, and taps on the end pocket of his day pack. There are no exposed rolls of film. Which means that either she's recently taken some with her, or he's had no cause to take pictures. No — there's that rotten broccoli in the bag. Boss-Lady came and went some time ago now.

Tom continues his stare as a phone begins to ring. It is an incongruous electronic warble here at Bere Point, with no road, not even a dirt one, for over a mile, and with no electricity for ten more. There has never even been a permanent human dwelling near here, what with ancient nomadic people choosing to winter on the sheltered eastern side of the island. From Bere Point in clear weather you can see the small island which owns a sheltered nook called God's Pocket, the last place to run from a gale until the Queen Charlotte Islands, which you could also see from Bere Point were it not for the curve of the earth and a couple hundred miles of fog.

The phone had stopped ringing, but now it begins again. Tom turns to his tent at the second ring, pulls a bag of clothes out and finds the cell phone in it by the tenth. He drops the bag on the wet ground, pushes the button and places the phone to his left ear and says, "What." He waits several moments, then smiles and switches the phone to his right ear.

"No, I'm here," he says. "I'm here."

He listens. His smile drops, then rises again.

"No it isn't *bugged*. Was there a click? I had it on my, on my deaf side." He listens. He coughs a laugh but doesn't smile. His speech is at times vaguely slurred, but it's a defect indistinguishable from speech that is simply very casual. "Yeah. Just a bullet in the way."

He listens again but appears to fall instantly bored. He stares off into the woods. It looks like he could easily let the phone just drop away.

"Maybe it *is* bugged. How do we know if it is or isn't? It's your fucking phone. I don't *care* if it's bugged. I'm not doing anything."

His voice is blandly angry now, an edgy monotone.

"Why not. I don't give a. I'm just waiting for whales. I'm waiting for whales. I wait for whales. I saw seven yesterday. Seven orca. Seven in the group. They call them 'K21.' I call them 'the Germans'."

He listens, impatiently tapping his foot. He side-steps to the plastic bags and starts kicking at the one holding grey broccoli until it begins to shred.

"Well, I think it is. Why not. Whales are cool, fuck off."

He stops kicking and listens. He notices it has stopped raining and he stares up into the trees, blinking hard when an eye is hit by one of the large drops falling from the canopy of branches.

"Yeah, it's up working again. Boss-Lady came by and we set it up again down the beach. I hear everything. Engines too. Loud as shit. Tugs are like — No, *tugs*. Tugs you can feel in your bones. Your armpits and crotch throb sort of like woofers. Sort of cool."

He kicks the bag with a purpose now, directing it towards his black fire pit.

"I'll hear it. If it's even a small freighter I'll hear it."

He listens.

"I don't know, ten miles, fifteen miles. Maybe more."

He listens.

"What is it, coke?"

He nods.

"Okay, whatever, I'm not in it, I'm just here."

He listens impatiently.

"Whatever. See you next week or whenever. Hey — bring me some ... Get Cal to bring me a lemon and some carrots. Put Cal on ... Well go get her ... Okay whatever, I won't."

He waits, hears a voice. One side of his face changes, animated with some subtle humourous shtick.

"Hi. That's right, carrots an' lemons. Don't bring me any fucking *vegetables*."

A kick lands the bag in the middle of the pit.

"Sorry. 'Proper hello.' Bring yourself, too."

The bag begins to crease and shrink, having landed on coals apparently hidden in the heart of the wet, black ash.

"I mean *other* vegetables. Just the lemon and some carrots. Or maybe a cucumber, the kind you can just eat."

The bag starts to smoke and stinks harshly of plastic, which, like the ringing phone, does not fit this place.

"*That kind you don't have to fucking peel.*"

It appears as though the phone might soon be punched, or thrown.

"No, tell him I don't need a gun." His expression doesn't change. Then, forgetting he's talking on a phone, he shakes his head at something, then shrugs while saying nothing more.

Abruptly he smiles. Seeing into the future, his eyes gain a feral shape and light.

"Okay, Cal, tart out, *don't* come."

One eyebrow is up.

"Only if you want. But remember the — Yeah. And a lemon. And a sixpack. Sleeman's. Not the red shit, the Honey Brown." He pauses, listens, smiles. "And your blue underwear. Your baby-blue underwear."

What he hears makes him laugh grandly. He rocks back on his heels and the size of his laughter seems to fit the trees and forest.

"That's right. That's all you ever have to remember. Baby blue."

A hummingbird zips past his head. It looks like he's ignored it entirely but then he flinches, far too late, when the bird is already gone, way off in the trees. The clearing is as silent and empty as before. It's like he's flinched at nothing.

One morning the women were wailing in the house while the men were out fishing. Since many people had died, the sound of wailing was heard in every house. Suddenly a voice was heard louder than all the wails of the women:

"I was supposed to go aboard the canoe of he who had me for his princess, but now I have empty orbits in my house, only holes in my house, I who was to go aboard the canoe of he who had me for his princess."

The women ceased wailing when they heard this song, for it was strange to them. They tried to find out where the song came from. Finally they discovered on the floor of the house a skull which was singing. It must have rolled down from a tree, and fallen right into the house.

— FRANZ BOAS, *KWAKIUTL TALES*

SALTSPRING ISLAND

HUMBLED BY MANY kinds of hunger, Evelyn beaches the kayak in darkness and struggles out, getting wet to the knees. Her legs already weak and frigid from this long day, the cold water feels like she's stepping into possible sickness.

She lifts the bow high so not to scrape it on rocks she can't see. It's odd that she can't see the kayak either, though she can still smell it. Three days ago, finding a half can of black marine paint in the dock-shed she sneaked into on Pender Island, she painted its top. Now it's white only below the water line. The kayak feels permanently hidden.

She feels with her feet, crunching barnacles. They are alive but this doesn't nudge her. She knows their cool, scrambled-egg insides — twice now she has tried, and failed, to eat some. Raw egg that tastes like sour fish.

Up in some sand past the high tide mark she drops the boat, finds a log, sits and catches her breath. She shuts her eyes hard, steeping them in a more total darkness, to give herself the vision of a cat. There is no moon. She will be stringing her tarp by feel.

She has doubled back to this shoreline campground she saw an hour ago. It was a decision her body made on its own, her arms suddenly stroking backwards, starting the kayak's slow turn — her body's need for other bodies tonight, for their campfires, voices. This is Saltspring, she knows. She's been here too, in that other life. It's the first time since Claude's death that she's felt drawn to people.

She wonders if she's coming out of it, whatever it is. Wonders if this marks the start of a return to Oakville.

She whispers to herself, "herd mammal," and opens her eyes, and can see.

WITHIN THE BUTTRESSING roots of an immense tree she finds a flat spot. A bat swoops a welcome, or a warning. She is tired of reading signs. A bat is a bat is a bat. Her last tin of sardines and single rice cake she eats standing, in the dark. Eating food you can't see could be depressing but she calls it entertaining. Fingers tooling in flesh and oil. And it's like she's fueling up for a party.

Murmurs and pot-clatter come from random distances. Nothing of drunk teenagers. She has seen no road and guesses this to be a hike-in campground. Lanterns are scattered thinly in the trees. Perhaps a hundred yards away, a child cries. Three, four years old. A boy, she thinks. Over-tired. Actually, sick. She feels in the pleading bend of his cries how she ached in those years.

She wants to lie down too, roll herself up, eschew the campground's promise and fall instead into its safety. These huge trees, safe from loggers, stand confident for it, and she could easily lie dreamless at their feet. But she has to dispose of this sardine tin, bait for racoons. And she wants to move her legs. When the moment of decision comes, she will or will not check out that fire she saw near the beach. You mammal, you.

SHE ALMOST DOESN'T sit down with them, something ridiculous almost spins her on her heel, away: approaching the fire she glances down at her jean cutoffs to check for overt stains and sees that her cigar tube — sees that Claude — has shifted in her front pocket and looks just like a penis angling down her leg.

But Evelyn continues walking forward, feels herself smile, says a soft hello, hears jovial responses, sits.

She sees them register her helpless clothes, her hair. Notes their appraisal: she is alone at a time of life when she shouldn't be. She is careful to sit apart for she knows she smells. But in the fire-circle everyone is automatically friendly. Their being here at all proves this, doesn't it?

Sagging, she sighs. She's no longer in a kayak. She's sitting with people, ordinary people. Maybe it's the novelty of people, but the chiaroscuro of firelight throbbing on faces is almost hallucinogenic. She tries not to stare as she gleans:

Francis and Shelley own a bookstore in Vancouver. They are approaching goofy with their red wine, celebrating their store's closing, another casualty, they say, to the chain stores. Turning failure into adventure they will lease a shop in Gastown, sell candles and curios, maybe books in a corner nook. Otherwise almost pretty, Shelley has a willful growth, a sort of mole, riding the outside of her nostril: it's the size and shape and colour of a baked bean.

Jack and Jean, Chicago, forties — about Evelyn's age, in any case — are on an easy, paunchy cycle through the Gulf Islands. They no doubt pedal slow, taking in the smell of pine, the squirrel husking a nut. They sit gently shoulder-to-shoulder waiting for someone to say something funny, whereupon they both laugh generously. Even their laughter has a Chicago near-drawl.

Then Jordan, maybe twenty. He sits across from her so she sees him only through dips of flame. He plays a guitar blanket-soft, with occasional crystalline notes. He seems to be trying for the best background music he can, in service to them. Shelley has asked him where Bree is, or maybe it was Free, and he says, "In the tent being alone." Jordan smiles but looks sad saying it.

Francis and Shelley have their wine, Jack and Jean a six of those fruity coolers, and Jordan a wineskin on a cord. She has nothing, and she declines when Francis lifts the wine to her and apologizes naughtily that they are drinking straight from the bottle.

When asked about herself, Evelyn doesn't mention her mode of travel, though she stole her kayak many days and islands away. Nor does she tell them that, other than two elderly ghosts a few days ago, they are the first people she has spoken to in maybe a week. She tries not to sound evasive. Camping, one is allowed brevity. She tells them she is on walkabout. Francis and Shelley nod understanding, Jack and Jean laugh like she has told a joke, and she thinks she hears Jordan's fingers shift into something softer for her. Evelyn is content in their company. She can do this. They have relaxed past small talk. They spend minutes describing for each other what they see in the fire, agreeing how the cedar, compared to the alder, breaks down into patterns of glowing rectangles. Shelley, her dark bean not at all ugly, announces her self-amazed discovery that Haida art had to have been born of staring at burning cedar, because just look at the shapes of those embers.

Someone says "Eden." Cars are a mile away at the gravel parking lot. Electricity further away still. From where they sit they can see nothing but a flashing buoy. More sea monsters out there than lights, Evelyn says. She adds that she imagines them calm, and Jack and Jean laugh at this. Evelyn is hungry already and wonders if tomorrow she will be comfortable enough with any of them to ask for food. Or if she will simply steal again. It is almost too easy. Campers go for hikes and smack in the middle of the picnic table leave their cooler as an offering. Bright red or blue, like a target. A training ground for infant thieves.

As easy as taking that meal off Claude's tray. The delivery of a meal was absurd, there was no way the man would be eating again — and so it was her first thievery. Cold roast beef and mashed potatoes and broccoli. Apple juice. Some kind of flan dessert, which she licked clean. It was not more than an hour after licking the plastic flan dish that Claude —

Evelyn startles on her log. Perhaps she gasped. They watch her. She has remembered something she'd forgotten about Claude in the hospital room. Seeing Claude die — an instant softer than a breath, but harder than a mirror — she knew that for the first time in her life she was seeing something impossible to doubt. In that moment of no next breath and dead face, there are no layers of possibility. Absolutely no question that what you are seeing is true. And that you won't know such truth again until you die yourself.

In the meantime you are left with Claude's partial truth. Or mysterious truth.

Ya took it out on him, eh?

A SHORT MAN peeks into Claude's room. Claude is deeply asleep, or perhaps at this point he's in a coma. The man asks, "How's he doin'?" He comes and stands beside her.

Evelyn doesn't know what to tell him. They never do exchange names. He tells her he was here once before, the day they brought him in. Evelyn keeps glancing at him, wondering what's so familiar, and then she knows it's because he's an aged version of one of the Monkees, the drummer. Micky. She can't not see him as Micky. Though dressed in jeans and leather jacket, he looks and feels wealthy. He smells like he's just eaten Thai food. It might *be* Micky. She bears in mind she's going off her pills.

From the way he talks it's clear he and Claude are friends. He isn't in a hurry and what with Claude unconscious they settle in and talk, positioning their chairs to face the patient, like he's their entertainment. Mostly they talk about Claude, Micky answering Evelyn's questions. It turns out that Micky met Claude's son Tom, on several occasions, but not for over a year now, and not since Tom was hurt.

"You heard about that?" Micky looks at her sideways from his chair. He hasn't asked her who she is or why she's asking questions about Claude's son.

"And he's better now," Evelyn says, nodding to herself. Because Claude had said Tommy was *doin' great*.

"Well it's a territorial business, you just don't come to town all new and, you know, *loud*," says Micky. When Evelyn has no question for him he continues. "And Tommy, I don't think, wasn't exactly good at keeping quiet. I mean, even *I* knew about it. Which is ridiculous!" He laughs fondly at the notion of a fellow like himself knowing Tommy's business. "I mean, do you know Tommy?"

"More or less."

"Well then you know he makes enemies and someone who makes enemies shouldn't be so, I don't know, public?"

Micky goes on to speculate that if Tom's enemies hadn't stopped him then the police would have, because he was equally visible to them — having no job and spending lots of money.

"What did Tom spend his money on?"

"Well, Claude's house, for one. Ever go there?"

"No."

"First he sets Claude up with this, this *place*," Micky says, looking at her significantly. His voice is rather deep, and Evelyn remembers now that Monkee Micky's was squeaky and sassy, so this can't be him.

"Little place up Pandora, I think he even paid off the whole thing, and he gives Claude the main floor and he 'borrows' the basement suite. It's big, though, not really a 'basement' — you know, garden entrance and all that." Micky smiles fondly when he says, "Claude had an *address*."

Evelyn sees Micky in a new light — he looks a little crazy and though he has wrinkles he's closer to forty than sixty.

"Tommy just sort of went for the big money. Didn't care."

She wonders at this. Claude, who distrusted success of any kind. Even of hippies, in whose number he would continue to proudly include himself. "I have no problem wit' guys who *wannabe* Gandalf," she remembers him saying, only half joking, "it's assholes who *are* Gandalf that bug me." Claude and his cult of non-ambition, a cult he stayed true to. Its tenets were friendliness, ignoring others' rough edges, and good times. That huge pleasure resulted in equally huge pain was a natural law recognized and joked about by all. A cult of celebrating who and where you happened to be, its rituals of booze and drugs breaking out at any time.

"It was great, Claude's house, really fun, but that's what I mean about going public. You can imagine the scene. I mean you can walk there from downtown. And Tommy was hardly ever around so Claude sort of took the downstairs over too, I mean his friends did, I mean a band kept their *gear* set up there. All of Claude's drums too. You can imagine. Then those two guys dying there the same month — you hear about that one?"

Evelyn shakes her head no.

"Two ODs. I heard it was bad drugs, or drugs that were 'too good,' however that works. Nothing to do with Claude or Tommy but anyway the cops closed it all down. I don't know how, legally. Found some of Tom's stuff, I think. Or said there was faulty wiring, who knows. But they boarded Claude's place up and then there was Tom's thing right around then too and that was the start of this." Micky nods at Claude on the bed. "Both things. You could almost hear Claude saying to himself, '*Ow*, time to check out.'"

"Ow…"

"'Ow,' that's right. Old Claude."

"He had drums?"

Micky glances at her as if assessing all he's said and wondering if he's said too much.

"His hand-drums. Bongos, tombas. He collects them. Well, *plays* them, actually. Wore out some collector's items." Micky laughs at this. "He got really good. I taped him a few times. It's how we met."

Evelyn's look gets him to explain that he teaches musicology, something called world percussion, at the university. As if they both need time to digest information, they stare at Claude for a long silent moment. Evelyn can remember Claude aimlessly but frantically slapping rhythms onto his thighs. At first she had thought it showing off, but it was one of his ways of evading boredom. Yes, he was really good at evading boredom.

Evelyn asks about Claude's career on the tugs and Micky shrugs and suggests Claude didn't seem to have to work much. Micky shakes his head and adds that Tom had a new sports car, and a jeep after he cracked up the first one. That sort of thing. If Tom came home to a party he would order in a whole swack of good food. So there was money around.

"Lots of which he put into his blood stream," says Micky, with a jerk of the head toward Claude. He catches Evelyn's eye and adds, "Not laying blame but, I mean, you could say that Tom's money hurried Claude along this particular path here."

"Did you see them together?"

"Oh yeah." Micky visibly searches his memory and looks doubtful. Evelyn can see now that of course he is a partier too.

"What were they like together?"

"I dunno. They laughed a lot. All I remember is they laughed a lot." He stares at Claude for a longer moment. "Course our man here likes to laugh."

"He does."

Evelyn has been given whole new realms of imagination. *They laughed a lot*. She tries to picture it. Their mouths are open. Neither one expects a thing from the other. Claude doesn't make a single demand, certainly not of the heart, so Tommy feels nothing chasing him. Both are free of the bonds that come with being related. She can see both of them mocking the expected roles, Claude saying sternly, "Call me Dad or I'll — I'll *spank* you." She hears Tommy demand the twenty birthday presents he is owed. "I want them *all* you old prick." Something like that. Nothing serious, ever. She wishes she could have seen them both laughing, though she doubts she would have laughed herself.

"But —" Micky nods at Claude again. "He really does like Tom. You could see it. He hit it really hard after he heard about Tom. I mean, they say Claude was living on the *street*. Then when Tommy got out and —"

"Tom was in prison?"

"The hospital. And went way up island there, I think it's Alert Bay or somewhere there, and Claude kept wanting to go up and visit but I mean there's no way. I mean, look at him. Said he was gonna get a boat and go surprise him, but there's no way."

"And Tom's better now?"

Micky looks at her before answering, and answers in a way that tells her he's shutting his information down. "I guess so."

Micky leaves soon after this and doesn't return, though in less than a week they will nod to each other outside the funeral home, and Micky will turn away and light his cigar.

THE FIRE-CIRCLE is newly alert with silence and Evelyn wonders if she's said something aloud. She doesn't think so. No, it's that they can hear someone coming, their heads are turning, someone is approaching their fire, proudly percussive on the beach gravel. A man arrives out of the darkness, lit orange in the firelight. He is swinging a full bottle. Weak at the shoulders, he is shaped like a long pear.

"Here comes the whisky," is how he announces himself, but Evelyn sees him more articulately announced by the others: Jack and Jean glance at each other, Francis whispers "not again," and Shelley's face gives up, muscles in it gone, a social death. Her bean looks ugly again. Jordan plays his guitar noticeably louder.

The man sits next to her on the log, so she gets a clear side view. Late forties, he has a new untended beard, wire-rim glasses, a bookish quality and a smile that never goes away. She thinks she's seen him before.

"*Peter* Gore," he says to her, turning to offer his hand, proper as can be. He has an English accent, and speaks with exaggerated stresses.

"Evelyn."

He is already looking at the rest of them, smiling. They appear to be waiting.

"Okay," Gore says. "After last *night*, which still *hurts*, I expect you to *help* me with this." He waggles the bottle at them. "This is *too* much to ask of *one man*."

He has come with clear plastic cups. Evelyn alone accepts some. Gore happily glugs it into her cup until she thinks to say stop.

"This *thing* in the *paper* today. *My* my." He shakes his head, pausing so someone can ask him to share the story, though no one does.

"This fellow in *St Louis*? He was spotted walking in a *park*, missing one of his *feet*? Fresh stump, blood pouring out, walking on the *bone*. Just walking. Out for a *stroll*."

After a sip, Evelyn holds the cup to her face and watches the fire through it. The light is tawny, alive — the colour, she thinks, of a hunting cougar. Peter Gore is easy to suss. Travelling alone, he can't stay alone, and when with people he won't let talk fall below the colourful.

"At a park *bench* they found the *foot*, and an *ax*." Gore waits. "Can you *imagine*?"

No one can, and Peter Gore goes on to wonder "just how solid the delusions of the insane must get." He dismisses as pedestrian the "*voices* telling me to kill my *family*" stories, and lists some of his favorites, one a man who "electric drilled his head numerous *times* — when was he *satisfied*? "— and another who sewed a chicken —" the *saran*-wrapped kind, the standard Safeway *chicken* "— onto his belly, then lived routinely until it began to rot and he was discovered.

"How solid is *that*?" Peter shakes his head as he drinks but the cup doesn't move with his mouth and whisky trickles into his beard. Evelyn thinks he looks unpracticed at drinking.

Jordan is playing chords now, "Proud Mary" it sounds like. Peter smiles at everyone in turn. He waits a polite time then turns to Jack and Jean.

"Where you biking *tomorrow*?"

"We thought we'd go up to Quadra Island," Jack says. He turns to Jean and she nods.

"*Wow* now that is a long haul. You are *properly* ambitious."

"Taking a bus," says Jean. She places her empty in a brown paper bag and folds its mouth up tight, suggesting they will soon leave the fire ring.

"It takes bikes," explains Jack. "There's a rack on the front."

Evelyn doubts she will ever grow so solid that she will sew a chicken to herself. But she has a too solid sense of the night around them. Behind her is a pressure that is nothing but emptiness. It is being yelled at by the tiny inferno of their fire, which keeps them focused and unafraid. Huddled early humans, drawn to a fire's heart while not necessarily liking each other. Why else are they sitting here? Why else is she at this campground? Her voyage having no solid direction other than *away*.

"*You're* giving the angels their share." Peter is speaking to her.

"I'm what?"

"The *angels'* share."

"The angels share?"

"Of *course* they do."

Gore grins at what they learn is his pun. He explains "the angels' share," an Irish phrase describing alcohol that is allowed to evaporate.

"As in *cooking*. As in good whisky that gets *ignored*." Peter points to her glass and laughs, but not sarcastically.

Spirit to the spirits, Evelyn thinks. She feels Claude as a spirit, one that hasn't had much practice at it yet.

Peter Gore takes a break from his noise to lean back for a glance straight up. Evelyn sees him as a boy, a young hopeful boy who has no clue what is in store. His glance, almost a salute, lasts only a second but is so humble a look that Evelyn realizes he shares her lack of direction. Also that he is kind. She likes him despite what she has read on the others' faces.

Gore looks up again, smiles and takes a big sniff.

"Ahh — ya hafta stop," he says in American, "and grab them roses."

No one save Evelyn laughs. She knows his joke included the thorns. She empties her cup, and asks Peter for more. And more, when he fills it only a quarter full.

"*I'm* sorry," says Gore, delighted. "But did you just call me a *mammal*?"

SHE CAN QUIET a man like this. He wants only entertainment, only spectacle. He lacks eyes to find it for himself, to see what she can in the fire: faces suffering every possible mood. He can't hear the tiny marimba of pebbles in waves, or the silence as its aching measure. Can't parse the accents of smoke, or smell the low tide as a charnel ground of clams, the non-stop enormity of this. He is handicapped in ways that invite anger. He needs only distraction, like any boy.

She could sleep with him, but she won't. Another possible mood. Or maybe if she drinks down this full heft of whisky.

"I want to show you something really cool," she says suddenly, to Peter alone. He turns to her, instantly shy, mouth slightly open. What she's done affects everyone. Jordan's hand falters in its strumming. The fire crackles loudly. It is as if someone has offered a wedding cake to the barking dog; someone has invited the clown to come with them into the bathroom. It is pleasing, while watching him gather his whisky and get clumsily up (why is it the nervous English rise so clumsily?), to know that the others have no grasp of her now, none, and only see the two of them crudely pairing off.

"Come on." She leads the way, steps into the darkness towards the water. She slows. "Lots of rocks. If you're drunk, hold on to my sweater."

"*Wait* then. Maybe *you* should hold on to *mine*."

"I'm not drunk."

"Then you're a *spooky* little thing, *aren't* you."

The wilderness, all routines left behind, is a stage upon which you must invent yourself. She remembers the first time she camped with Claude. She was sixteen. They fished; she read, and gathered. Their last day, a camper van pulled into the next site and out stepped a family of three — father, mother, son Evelyn's age. The boy glanced her way furtively, once. She was taken by their activity, all done in silence. The father, red-faced, set up their world in seconds: cooler, containers, cleansers lined up on picnic table. The mother untied a rake from the van's roof to clear the site of twigs. The boy shook out, then re-folded, sleeping bags. The mother set up two chairs, sat alertly in one and opened a book, tucking her book-mark in her shirt pocket. The boy, never gazing at the forest around him, sat with his book and pocketed his book-mark too.

She understood this family when the father began his chopping. Neither mother nor son watched him as he stretched, touched his toes, then took from his back pocket two white gloves. From a stiffly-tied canvas wrap he removed an ax.

"What wit' da glove?"Claude whispered to her, eagerly watching too. Bourbon on his careless breath.

Evie saw her own site for the first time — its scatter of plates and kindling, her cairns of shells. Two fishing poles still baited with ragged, dry herring, a sloppy X leaning against the tent.

The white-gloved father chopped and stacked a week's firewood. He focused only on his work, though he did look over, sharply, when the mother asked something of the son. And from the way the three gathered tensely to commence a hike — the father de-gloving and wrapping his ax; mother and son bookmarking in unison and standing — Evelyn saw that though the wilderness meant you had to reinvent how you did things, some ways were less sane than others.

Tonight, almost three decades later and in wilderness once more, as she foot-feels through beach rocks with Peter, Evelyn feels freedom's invitation, the same wide-openness in front of her. She can invent herself. No, she must — every moment, here she will be. No matter what new facet of honesty, or ruse, appears she will be surprised by her own unfolding.

"Well," says Peter, fingertips violently tickling in the water, creating flashes of light, "I've never *seen* this."

Evelyn stands beside him, smelling the sea, its brew of ice and vegetation. She doesn't remember why phosphorescence comes out in certain places on certain nights. She does know it is alive, some kind of plankton that gleams when it moves, hence the comet-trail behind a paddle or a hand. Once at night while Claude cleaned fish, she saw a seal or salmon streak past the dock, a ten-foot flash. She can hardly imagine the wake of a killer whale. Or a still bigger whale, passing below her kayak: under her, the sea becoming a sun.

"I know a good one," she says, and taps his shoulder. "You're the man. You bring that." She points to a white, skull-sized boulder.

To their right, barely visible, a rock bluff rises from the beach. Evelyn begins to climb. She hears Gore unearth the boulder and huff up behind.

"Ka*boosh*," she calls back, her only explanation.

"I'll follow you anywhere," he whispers. "You little *spook*."

She enjoys his timing.

She is just drunk enough to take extra care. They climb the twenty feet to the top and settle side-by-side. Back behind them they can just make out the campfire, but can hear no voices. Peter points out a distant ship, a cruise ship judging from the stacked strings of lights.

"Alaska," she guesses.

"Look how *bright* it is," says Peter, who's caught his breath. "The *noise* in there." He stares. He winds up. "They might as well be in a *casino*. Platters of *crab louie*. They're packed into a great bloody *stereo*." He sounds genuinely sad. "You can *see* the god-damned *conga* line … grey heads *queuing* up, all smiley and *daring* …"

She hears a clink on the rock as Peter opens his whisky. Somehow this superb Englishman has ascended with a boulder and a bottle both. She accepts another drink, though she shouldn't. She lacks water for a thirst later in the night.

"It's Marilyn, right?"

"Evelyn." She likes that he's comfortable with having forgotten her name. He's asked her none of the usual. His selfishness is pure and harmless. He's a man she could tell everything to.

"I'm writing a travel book on the area," Peter announces. It's all he says. It's as though he's reminding himself.

"Will I be in it?"

He does a cockney, "Depends, dunnit?" She imagines his smile. He takes a noisy gulp.

Evelyn moves to stand. "We should get this rock in the water." The climb down will get harder with each sip. "Give it a heave."

"No no. You do the honours. I insist."

She takes the boulder in both hands. Together they edge towards the brink. In front of her she can see nothing. Neither rocks nor water. The phosphorescence will be good.

He steps quickly behind her, scaring her. She feels him slide two fingers into her empty belt loops. He pulls, anchoring her against him. She can feel the bottle he has tucked down the front of his shirt.

"How's that?"

In answer, she brings the boulder to chest-level. She pauses, taking it all in. She doesn't breathe. In front of her: absolutely nothing. Into it she heaves the rock. Her lurch surprises Peter Gore and she easily takes him with her over the edge. She grazes something on the way down and then they hit hard and are in the water, flailing, gasping through clenched teeth. The sea freezes and is bright with churning fire. Evelyn has no sense of where to swim, then she sees what she trusts is the campfire, not the ship. She hopes Peter can swim.

They are on the beach and it's like only a second has passed.

"*Jesus*!" Gore is striding in a circle. "*What just happened*?"

"I hurt my leg."

"You — you *jumped*. You pulled me *in*."

She has worked her hand under her denim shorts. On her hip she can feel the cut, and the blood more slippery than water.

"You could have *killed* us." He circumnavigates her, crunching gravel. "You're *mad*. I'm *leaving*."

"I hurt my leg."

"That was *insane*."

Stinging salt lets her feel it perfectly. The cut is long and narrow.

"*Why did you do that*?"

"Shh. You'll wake people up." She tries to remember whether or not she jumped. She doubts that she did.

Peter Gore stomps off, hissing to himself. She thinks he is leaving, but hears him double back. To get at the wound she begins to struggle out of her shorts. She checks her pocket, feels Claude still in there. She wonders if he enjoyed the ride too. Did your stomach go up into your throat, Claude?

"Okay, so is it *broken*? Can you *move* it?"

She remembers the boulder pulling her with it. She recalls a feeling of no resistance. She hadn't jumped.. She'd done exactly nothing.

"I didn't jump."

"Right. Can you move it?"

"It's only cut."

She is out of her shorts and he is kneeling over her, rigid with anger. Her underwear gleams white. She wonders if it's alive with phosphorescence.

"I *think* I can see it. It's black. Is it right here?" He touches near the cut.

"Yes."

"Can you walk then?"

"I think I'll just relax here." She smiles, speaks carefully. "It's such a nice night."

"*Oh* but you're quite the spook."

"Peter?"

"What."

"Do you have your whisky?"

"*Jesus*."

He removes his bottle from his shirt, opens it and takes a gulp. He holds it to her hand.

"No. Could you pour some in the cut?"

She hears him hiss something about "bloody western movie" as burning liquid splashes onto her hip and pelvis. The glugs become gligs and the bottle is empty.

"*There*. Are you coming along?"

"No. Thanks. You go. I'll hang out here a while."

"Fine."

"Goodnight."

Gore crunches off and she can no longer hear him once he reaches the grass.

Silence is immediately the biggest thing. She lies still, breathing softly into it. She can hear her breath and, when she tries, her blood's drumming rush. Pain is the sharpest facet of herself. The burn of the whisky pins her to the sand, focuses the night.

In no time at all she finds that her mind has wandered. To tomorrow's paddling — can she? — and now once more to Claude. She knows his death, vastly confused, was nothing like this. She is simply lying on a beach with pain the size of a small bright carrot.

Still, the night grows so much wider for it. Her breath stops at an understanding: *away* will move as fast as she paddles into it. And: a pain as clear as this one can distract her from such notions.

With a finger she flicks the cut, freshening it.

SHE MIGHT have slept. The full moon has risen bright and hard over the beach and the sight of it makes her colder. She should get herself to her blanket and tarp. The cut on her thigh spikes when she shifts. She picks up her head to see herself. The gash has clotted black. Her legs are splayed. Underwear stained with blood and liquor, body covered in grit, smudge. A thick waft of alcohol catches in her nose. She lets her head fall back.

Footsteps on the beach. They are soft, and remain soft as they keep coming, until they are just above her, where they stop. It could be Peter Gore, concerned and wondering whether to wake her. She imagines Jordan, the guitar player. She senses curiosity and a kindness. It could be anyone. She shouldn't assume human. What a sight she must be, sprawled this rough under the moon. Whoever it is can smell the whisky rising from her and she feels generous with this entertainment.

Two

THE RIM

"Mother!" Mink said again, "I want very much to marry this Frog-Woman."—"But won't you get tired of her when she begins to croak?" said Mother.—"That is what I like," said Mink.

— FRANZ BOAS, *KWAKIUTL TALES*

SALTSPRING ISLAND

WHEN SHE APPEARS this morning, Peter Gore knows he will always have her to blame for interrupting his book.

Poised with pen over paper (the computer actually got swatted this morning, to no avail), he is about to wax poetic about marine phosphorescence and the glory of swimming at midnight when she comes out of the woods and startles him. It seems that this morning Evelyn (or Eve — Gore likes thinking of her as Eve because she's something of an apple-bearer, something cute but rather nasty) has come by to beg a meal. Not beg exactly, but her timing is such that he suspects she's been watching him from the bushes. Having trouble with his first sentence, he's just opened a box of fruity granola bars and, like a calm but expectant dog, here she is at his side. Gore eats one bar and Eve eventually eats five, which is the rest of the box. It is a silent breakfast. Smalltalk sticks in his throat around her, and Eve's mouth focusses simply on its mash.

Plus, he is hungover. He's disappointed with himself to be hungover for already the second time on his trip when his usual rate is once a decade. Some writers quite famously manage to drink-and-write, but his dislike of pain is such that he long ago decided he wouldn't be one of them.

Considering last night, it surprises him that Eve appears altogether well-mannered. She's no shrubbie after all. She's even rather proper. Keeps a cupped hand at her mouth to catch crumbs and peeks apologetically at him while doing so. She even looks decent, her black hair trying to burst into curls but tied back, the morning sun on her smooth skin. She has changed into a faded blue T-shirt and black gor-tex shorts, and looks to be in terrific shape. In brief glances his way, her green eyes betray an impossible mix of utter knowing and dizzy innocence. She is really very pretty in daylight. Plus their cliff-plunge has, in effect, washed her. The bird has had her thrashing little bath.

She is stoically not limping much. He hasn't asked after her wound because he doesn't want to speak of last night. Despite her claim to the contrary, she jumped. Gore hates to have to consider that she might still be dangerous.

She has interrupted not only his writing. His plan had involved lying back down to tempt more sleep. But box of breakfast done, Eve begins to talk, responding uberly to his polite question, "So, what brings *you* to Saltspring?" While not quite her entire life story, what follows is a spew — clearly she has been long alone — that includes her flight here to BC where she grew up; an old friend's death; a hubby back east; an odd decision to just stay here, "living off the land," which included some suspiciously baglady-like behaviour in Victoria; her journey via rubber dinghy and now kayak; and a plan to visit her wayward son, one involving a haphazard, nil-equipped, two-hundred-mile paddle north. She doubts that her son, one Tom, wants to see her. She isn't even certain he is there, and "there" means miles of coastline, where he's watching whales. And — at this point Gore begins to question the story's truth — Tom might be wearing a disguise, one that involves beet juice.

Listening, Gore thumbs through maps and such. For some time now he has been tapping a finger on a dot named Sointula. He takes a breath and leaps into her tale.

"Excuse me. *Excuse* me. But why — please — *why* would your son be camped in the wilderness, wearing a, 'a disguise'? Seems a *little* redundant?"

"Well," Evelyn begins, glancing down. Gore sees that she might stop her story, might turn away and go back into the woods. But she continues, first giving him the most sincere look. Her eyes glint tears. She is standing rather erectly, arms at her sides, facing him. Gore is disarmed and a believer again.

"I might have heard wrong. It was ... unclear. I got it from Claude — my friend who died. Actually he was my lover. My long lost lover. I'm still in shock, you know, I really am. I never saw anyone die before. And I don't think it was all that nice a death. He couldn't, he couldn't stop *moving*." And here Eve has to move, herself. She shakes her head minutely, gasps, and then turns a half-circle on her heel, a response to inner horrors. And now Gore thinks he has seen her before.

"Well, I'm sorry."

"He was out of it and I couldn't hear him well, so I don't know what's true."

"Quite."

"No, I know it's *true* — I just don't know what I heard right."

"Understood."

"Anyway, the thing is, Tommy was involved in drugs, the business end of drugs, and for a while he was hiding, someone wanted to hurt him. *Did* hurt him, enough to land him in the hospital. I don't know if he's still wearing a disguise."

"Seems a little late, now." To which Gore adds, "Sorry," should she think he'd been lightly joking about it, which in fact he had. About a hurt son, good god. "*Beet* juice. My."

"I'm embarrassed that I ... I'm not embarrassed, I'm *sad* I don't know all the details. Tommy left ten years ago and I lost contact. We had a falling out."

"Ah."

Two ravens fly over, squawking harshly at each other, almost as if to supply a portrait of what this family spat might have looked like. Gore finds ravens creepy. He notes that their respective squawks are entirely different from one another's. Tit for tat, one croaks, the other shrieks.

"Actually, we had a falling out when he fell out of me. He was difficult. He didn't like the world."

Some humour, good. Though her eyes are closing and she looks to be considering another spin. There's no guarantee that she isn't bottomlessly daft.

"So your friend Claude was in contact with him, then."

"I think Tommy managed to keep him consistently off the wagon."

"Aha."

"I think they were able to get high together about a million times before Claude died."

"Tommy must be sad that Claude is gone."

"I don't think he knows yet."

"Ah. You want to find him and tell him that —"

"That's right. That his father's dead."

Her story continues while he makes coffee. Searching for matches, he explains to her how he traded in his excellent camera in order to purchase this tent and sleeping bag and camp stove, and while explaining this he knows that one motive is to make clear that he has little money. He feels like he's just eluded a sidewalk panhandler, striding past with change balled in a fist so it doesn't jangle his cheapness.

But she appears not to be hunting his money. She talks away, her story drifting from the main drama to the details, which flesh her out for him. He is happy to hear she taught handicapped youth, which places her somewhat in his sphere, all youth being handicapped by definition. Then she worked in an art gallery. And on a hospital committee. She is otherwise a housewife. At this detail she grows a little too angry and hisses, almost to herself, "I'm almost *old*, it's almost *over*. I'm done with the *bullshit*, I really am." Once he caught her staring at herself, at her arms and then her legs, perhaps at what she was wearing, and then she looked up, somewhat stunned, to tell Gore, "I'm not *like* this." Sometimes she stops midsentence and apropos of nothing adds something like, "Claude and I were here, on *this island*. You hit the booze store, you buy a loaf of bread, you catch the ferry. Not even a tent. Can you believe we just *did* that?" Wanting to say that she still appears to be just doing it, Gore is warned by her eyes rimming tearful, and a possible spin.

Mostly it's details, it's gabbing, and Gore begins to feel like her girlfriend. He wants to put a stop to this feeling because, let's face it, that's precisely what it had come to with Gail. On her second cup of coffee Eve is talking too quickly and non-stop. Much of the detail involves comparisons between her life in Ontario and here on the west coast, including, "You wouldn't know it to look at me, but I've made dinner for the mayors of Buffalo and Detroit, and their wives, at my house." She laughs a little too crazily adding, "And I hated it. I didn't know it at the time. I'm sorry but I fucking *hated* it." To which he mumbles, "Politicians, yes," and she fires back, "No! They were *nice*. That's what I'm *saying*."

What is she saying? She is tired of having a role, tired of the caged life? Peter can understand all of that. Perhaps he does understand what she's saying. What he can't understand is what she's doing.

"Well now —" Gore knows that with his emerging logic and his proffered map he might get himself in trouble, perhaps of the financial kind. "Here there's a *highway* all the way up Vancouver Island. Then a *ferry* over to Sointula. Why don't you just, you know, take a *bus*?"

"I'm not sure."

"Well, what if — what if you find out that, that..."

"Tommy."

"That Tommy's back in *Victoria*. Turn your *boat* around and paddle *back*?"

She doesn't answer, and Gore jerks his head to the side, which arouses fresh head-hurt. He decides not to help her any more. He also decides to stop drinking. But he understands that at least part of his headache comes from having just made the fatal calculation, one he always comes to after spending time with a woman, that she is more attractive to him than he is to her. It also registers now that a raven has for some minutes been tossing a grotesque sound their way, a *blooo-ip*! that resonates like a water drop in a huge cave.

"Thing is," she smiles gamely, "I don't know if I really want to find him."

"Ah." Though she seems to think she has made a joke, she looks headed for tears or anger.

"There's a reason he left."

"There *would* be, wouldn't there."

"You'd have to meet my son to know what I mean."

"Real *case*, is he?"

Eve stares off. Pain is so palpable on her face that Gore can see it as a map — no, a receptacle, a *garbage* receptacle — of this son's misadventures. Gore doesn't like what he sees of this Tom fellow.

"I guess I'm in no hurry. To go any particular direction."

"Surely that's not a bad thing?"

"Claude dying sort of... threw me."

"Well, it would. Give yourself time."

"I feel like I'm surrounded by men. Including him — Claude. A man everywhere I turn. Every direction I go."

Though he, too, is a man, Gore does not feel included in her complaint. The notion of "girlfriend" has crept back into the campsite and he doesn't like it.

"So you say you were a *street* person in Victoria?"

"I don't know. I had access to money." Evelyn stares off into the trees. "Just tired of all the bullshit..."

"*Had* access?"

"Well, I guess I've left my husband."

"Ah."

"For the time being."

"Does he —" Being her girlfriend is an easy enough role. "Tell me it's none of my business, but does your husband know that Tommy isn't, isn't — shall we say — 'his'?"

She doesn't look at him. It takes her some time to venture, "Probably."

"I see." Though he doesn't. He is picturing her in good clothes, standing in a fine room, backed by a wall of books, most of which she's read. She is buffeted by urban conversation. Her fingers are light on the stem of a wineglass containing, he decides, a deeply tasteful red. What is easiest to see is that she doesn't care about any of it.

"You're still sort of *doing* it, aren't you."

"Doing what?"

Standing in the morning sun, sad, she is really quite lovely. When feeling sorry for themselves most people buy food or go otherwise indulgent. Eve has chosen the opposite way. It strikes him as funny that all the hair-shirt monks, all the contorting fakirs and self-flagellators are actually a common enough species — they feel bad and try to feel better by feeling even worse.

"Peter?"

"Yes?"

Hers can be a dark little smile. She uses irony sparingly, this one. Has it for dessert. She is looking at him, beautifully eye to eye, for what might be the first time. "I just realized. *I'm* on vacation."

EVE'S INVITATION to join her on her "paddle north" comes out full-blown, as if it's been percolating. Or as if she's indeed decided to be eighteen again and anything is possible and everything makes sense. His protestations are easily countered. He moans that he's never paddled a kayak — she claims it's easier than riding a bike. He offers that she's on vital family business — she tells him he doesn't have to meet Tommy if he doesn't want to. When he smiles coyly and says, "But we hardly know each other," she shrugs, doesn't smile and says simply that if they don't get along she'll drop him off near a road.

Saying yes, he sees he is excited in two distinct ways. A phoney part of him, an academic side perhaps, announces to itself that taking to the sea will prove to be just the adventure he needs to both inspire and inform his book. A more honest part of him instantly pictures sex with her, spontaneous dirty campsite fucking. Perhaps because he's never in his life done any. Hearing her invitation, he can only stare blankly at her while both excitements vie for attention in his head like two pots being banged. The noise ceases, snuffed just as loudly by the knowing face of Gail. Good god, Gail, go away. You have no *right*.

In any case, Evelyn disappears back into the dark woods to gather her things and Peter breaks down his camp. They are to meet on a beach "over there," in the direction Eve pointed. For the first time she seemed a little shy of him, as she pointed and as she went off. Not gone twenty yards, she trotted back to ask him if he ever wore any scent. His stuttered, "Do you, um, *want* me to?" she took to be a joke, because she didn't respond and simply trotted off again.

Of course sex is not *necessarily* in the cards. You simply can't tell these days, it's as simple as that. Not to use as an example his unfortunate last few years with Gail, but it seems that nowadays women often seek only friendship from men — they sometimes even assume it. As if it were a natural thing. If you could believe television, young men and women are falling into cheerful, platonic, prime-time friendship all over the place. If this was to be the case with Evelyn, well, that was fine. Because, if he steadies himself, if he steps back from the erection-like fever that has taken him over, including the muscles of his face, he has to admit that her invitation has made him rather glad. To be asked. To be asked to accompany her. Despite all lingering questions about this somewhat spooky woman, she is certainly an *interesting* creature and it seems that she — that she likes him.

AN HOUR LATER Gore finds the beach from which they are to launch their adventure. He sees that their impossibly skinny vessel has a white bottom and a black top, with two small holes in it, holes which remind him of empty eye sockets, holes where presumably they will insert themselves and sit. He sees that either she owns nothing or else it is already stashed in the kayak — which still wouldn't account for much. Their craft looks constructed to hold nothing but paddlers' legs.

Eve has a fire going and tends it on her haunches. She looks practiced. The fire is ringed by flat rocks, and on these rocks is a tight necklace of clams. They face outward — at least what he thinks of as their faces, all their unsmiling mouths — while their asses are getting burned. Even as he watches, some of the clams begin to open. It looks at first like they might speak, but then they grow very, very tired. And now their saliva is bubbling away and they are still. They smell rather good.

Gore doesn't ask why they are having lunch not two hours after breakfast. He makes himself useful by spreading his map on a boulder. He makes calculations. Using the width of his thumb to represent approximately fifteen miles, he stamps their course to Malcolm Island. He tells Eve that, paddling ten miles a day, it will take them exactly a month.

"It'll be nothing like that out there," is all she says.

HEADING INTO A one-foot chop only yards from the beach, Gore sees that she is right. Against this wind they move grudgingly. Rounding the tip of Saltspring they enter a tidal current that sweeps them sideways and at a speed that makes him hold his breath. Clearly, *against* such a current they wouldn't move at all, except perhaps backwards.

They paddle into and through a horrid smell like burning plastic, and both admit they have no clue what it could be. Otherwise they don't speak much at all and Gore fears their conversational pace might be set for the trip. He was ready to call the trip off if she chided or mocked his admittedly clumsy "getting into the boat," but she laughed only sympathetically as he bruised his leg bones on fibreglass. He tried to be charmingly self-effacing but he felt anything but sexy in his clamberings, especially since his rival Claude, though dead, had apparently been capable of carving a canoe with a jackknife then catching King salmon over the side with his sharp French teeth, etcetera. Nor did it help Gore's physical efficiency when Eve, not caring if he watched or not, stripped out of her gortex shorts, which she said rubbed against her injured leg. And now, underway, with her in the back paddling hard, it was simply too easy for Gore to imagine that he was being chased by a rough-breathing woman in panties.

Their craft functions more like a torpedo than a boat. He thinks they are too low in the water but is reluctant to say so. He tells himself that these things are supposedly unsinkable, that the Eskimos who invented them paddle in water so cold it kills them in seconds if they capsize. But surely their boat is overloaded with all of his stuff. Tent, computer, sleeping bag, air mattress, two whisky bottles, food. All of it stuffed up in the bow at his feet. He can rearrange sardine cans with his toes. His backpack and frame, bungeed onto the deck in front of him, is already sopping. Eve indeed owned nothing. Before setting off, she took him back to a campsite and, shrubbie-like, with him a reluctant shrubbie-accomplice, plucked a collapsible water container from a picnic table. Looking in no way guilty she hustled it away and filled it at a pump. They stuffed it in her crab trap and bungeed the mess onto the deck too. They are top-heavy and hick. What with his floppy hat and stained pink dress shirt, and the lumberjack checked shirt she wears as a coat, they look like ocean-going Beverly Hillbillies in search of Gilligan's Island.

A few power-boats have droned past in the distance but now all is quiet. Too quiet. Large puffy — cumulus? — clouds billow overhead, and somehow it's strange that they don't make a grand noise. Gore understands that the ocean has a distinct smell, rather indescribable, but if one sought adjectives, as he will have to for his book, one would be "living," and another "dead." In the distant vista, at which they point, sit grey islands and mysterious water. He can feel breeze on the backs of his ears. To their left is the constant shore of Vancouver Island and its immense forest backdrop. Gore decides that, what with the distance to shore, what with the wind, and what with the fathomless depth beneath, Nature feels far too Sizable. Their paddles' dipping and the boat's progress is unnervingly silent, and only when they overtake seaweed or a floating stick does he see how swift they are. Yet so Sizable is Nature that they are moving not at all. He feels quite swallowed. And his big toe has begun inexplicably to hurt like hell.

Apropos of nothing except wanting to change his own subject — that is, drowning — Gore is on the verge of asking Eve about famous

Vancouver Island people. He has a theory that you can understand a place by its celebrities. In a pamphlet about Vancouver he read that its famous folk included Michael J. Fox, Brian Adams and Douglas Coupland. Asking the Empress desk clerk, he ascertained Vancouver Island's celebrities to be Atom Egoyan, Nellie Furtado, Diana Krall, David Foster and Pamela Anderson, though two parts of her came from somewhere else. Gore's theory holds that the island's entertainers are plainly weirder than the more mainstream Vancouverites. Foster is the fly in this theory's ointment, but Gore decided that, with music so sweet, the man obviously hides demons.

But somehow this simple kayak, and Sizable Nature, makes his theory feel lame and the subject of famous people altogether cheap, so Gore keeps mum.

They do eventually speak. What Eve says is not at all cheap. In fact it's dire, which might be cheap's oblique opposite, and Gore hopes that their conversation is not the model for many conversations to come. What happens is, Eve suddenly stops stroking. Puzzled, Gore follows suit. Eve gazes intently around her.

"Humans," she proclaims, "are superfluous." She says this while gazing at Sizable Nature all around them, and Gore has a chill — she is about to tip them on purpose and end both their journeys here and now.

He won't plead with her not to. Instead he offers, "That's like saying, 'gangrene's superfluous to a leg wound'." He likes that. He adds, "How *is* your leg, by the way?"

"So you agree."

"No, I don't 'agree.' I 'more than agree'."

"That we're superfluous?"

"No. That we're a fucking *pestilence*."

"So you agree."

"No. I *more than agree*."

They paddle again for a time, saying nothing. Gore wonders if Eve is having second thoughts about him and he tells himself that he doesn't care.

"Peter?"

"Eve."

"No, *please* don't call me Eve. I *hate* Eve."

"Apologies."

"I think for us to have a good time talking to each other, you might have to relax a little bit with your words. I don't want to feel like I'm in some kind of contest."

Gore isn't sure he likes Eve deciding on rules for conducting their conversations. Or their relationship. She has to understand he feels girlish enough up here in the bow, following orders and only semi-useful, what with her *manning* the stern, steering, making the nautical decisions. Her sitting back there in her panties now seems wanton and thoughtlessly teasing.

"Certainly we can still have our little *debates*." He waits for her to respond. She doesn't. "I mean, there's not a lot to *do* during the day."

Though he soon sees he is wrong. They are doing it. It is called "paddling." Though in its ceaselessness "paddling" doesn't describe it fully; there are many versions, all of which start with "s". When he is bored or angry it is called "slicing," or "slashing," as in *slicing* or *slashing into this bitch ocean's skin*. Or "smacking," as in *smacking* the water and getting Eve — Evelyn — *wet*. Or "stroking," as in, *At last*, I seem to have fallen into a *rhythm*, it's actually quite mindlessly *pleasant*, something of a *physical relationship* with that creature *behind* me, dare I say something not unlike the mindlessly pleasant physical rhythm of *sex* except that this nautical as opposed to naughty version takes far — *far* — too long.

ANOTHER DISAGREEMENT follows not long after.

"I don't believe it's *en route*, but I really would like to check out D'Arcy Island." He waits a moment. "Have you heard about D'Arcy Island?" Eve's shoulders have seized.

"It's not *en route*," she says.

"So you know of it?"

"I slept there one night last week."

"It was the leper colony, true?"

Eve says nothing at all.

"Wasn't it the leper colony?"

"Yes."

"Was it worth the visit?"

Eve pauses before saying, "You don't know what you're talking about."

"Sorry?"

"I went there by accident. I didn't sleep at all. It's horrible there."

"In what way?"

"*It's a leper colony.*"

"Yes, yes, I understand that. Indeed it *was*. Chinese immigrants. Quarantined. All men. All died there. The last one, I believe, in 1915. I think I read that you can still see the grave markers of one or two of—"

"I wouldn't go back within a mile of that place."

"Why?"

"Because you will never feel so—Peter, it's a *leper colony*."

"Ah." Alright. He will concede. One-upmanship of the sensitive.

THAT EVENING Gore begins to think that Evelyn Poole is a witch. The leper colony isn't what did it; intuiting bad vibes at a leper colony could have been anybody's boast. Nor is it what he saw her do to her leg wound, which was now a black scab. What she did was stand there, ready her pointer-finger, and *stab* it. Then harder, so that she gasped and bit her lip. People have their own relationship with pain and he didn't want to pry.

The true witchiness was yet to come. They had beached the kayak for the night and had just finished setting up camp. He did raise an eyebrow when she wandered into the near woods and said a few soft words to someone or something he couldn't see, but he shook this off as residue from her flower child days, an "I-talk-to-trees" kind of showiness.

Despite all this he proudly displayed his talent for erecting his tent, aware that the glaring size of it—that is, small—promoted images of the two of them shmushed together in the darkness. Gauging poles and fashioning knots, Gore fell silent with this image, as did Eve, who went to wash her face and arms in the salt water. Wanting to demonstrate for her that fresh water is more pleasant on the skin than salt, Gore went instead to their water container and slopped some onto his hands. She turned to this noise and didn't quite yell but was severe with him, informing him that they hadn't passed a creek for miles and who knew where their next source of water would be. Feeling somewhat emasculated, Gore seated himself on a stump with his laptop on his lap and a plastic cup of Irish at his side.

Here he perched rather Hemingwayesque, sipping, today having moved his feast to another island. He doubts he'd done this to strike a pose, though perhaps he had. But he also had to get weight off his big toe, which throbbed sharply — what an odd boating injury. But, pose or not, sitting at his computer made him restless. He couldn't help thinking that, were this machine not dead, he would have something excellent to type into it. He considered asking if she knew anything about solar-powered battery chargers, but didn't know if he could stand it if she did. She had caught him taking a bath in their drinking water. True, he should pay more attention. Roughing it demanded a certain alertness. Eve had had this woodsman Claude as a teacher and apparently she'd retained a lot. But there was no reason why he couldn't contribute.

"How's it coming?" Eve hunched at a mound of smoking twigs, blowing into its base.

"It?"

"Your travel book."

"Ah."

It is here Gore begins to think of Eve in witchy terms, for as he ums and ahs an excuse, as he delineates the book's basic intent and even gives her a verbal taste of its Gorey style, she gets the fire going. When it's roaring high and bright she plucks from his backpack his neatly folded map, and tosses it in.

"Sorry," she adds, and looks at him, eyebrows innocently up.

Gore stares at her, not at the extra-leaping fire. Then stares at the freshly eviscerated map-pocket of his backpack. Her timing wouldn't have, *couldn't* have, been deliberate. For one, she doesn't, *couldn't*, know that he's written nothing, and that the six-point plan is, was, written in magic marker on the back of that map.

Gore leans at the fire, one arm feebly up, heat on its skin. He thinks he can see the outline of islands in the fragile sheets of ash.

"Really. Sorry," she repeats. "I should have asked. I owe you a map."

"'You should have *asked*?' Well what do you think I would have *said*?"

He's not sure that he shouldn't be afraid of her. She did push him off a cliff. No matter that the book's six main points are safe in his brain's keep. It is the sheer uncanny symbolism of her act that's unnerving. Witch-like, she has done it whether she knows it or not.

"It's just — I don't want to know where we are. I kind of knew this was Kuper Island, and I wanted to check on the map, and it hit me that if I knew this was Kuper it would wreck any chance I had of really seeing it. Where we are." She shakes her head. "I'm not explaining it."

"Would you like something else from my belongings to add to your fire? I have a nice *down vest that might burn*."

"Sorry."

"I thought you wanted to find your son."

Here she ponders him a condescending second. "Well, we just go north." To his blank look she adds. "We know it's north by keeping Vancouver Island to our left." And then, "It's impossible to get lost."

"Rivers then. Fresh water. My map showed where all the *rivers* are. No: *Were*." He looks at his feet and upbraids her softly. "You've burnt all the rivers."

"Sorry." Map ash lifts and scatters in a gust, and now she ever-so-femininely adds a fresh log to the fire, securing the ash. "But isn't it better not to know? If you didn't know that's Irish whisky you're gulping, wouldn't you taste it more carefully? Like it was the first time?"

"I see your point but—"

"As soon as I learn a name, half my questions are gone."

"Well, that's a shame."

"I don't want to know that this ground I'm on is called 'Kuper,' because if I do I also know the reserve is that way through the woods, and the next island over is Thetis, and it has a store, where we could buy Campbell's mushroom soup, which I know the taste of just by reading the stupid..." She adds a barely audible, "And all that stuff."

"Reserve? We're near an Indian reserve?"

"We're on one. This whole island's a reserve."

Gore clicks his laptop shut and stands. "Won't they mind? That we're here?"

"I don't know. Teenagers might. If they're political. I don't think these guys are all that political. Claude used to—"

"'Political?' Meaning they 'hate whites'?"

"—buy fish from them off-season and run it to restaurants in town. I was here with him once. He got caught eventually and they took his boat."

"*Indians took his boat*?"

Evelyn laughs.

"*What*?"

"Fisheries did. Cops. Peter, relax. They're just people. And look—it doesn't look like anybody ever comes here. They're all watching Monday Night Football on their satellite dishes. Or *Survivor*. They're all watching *Survivor*."

Gore ignores Eve to scan the surrounding forest. He goes to the tent and pours himself more whisky. A raven—or perhaps a crouching enraged teenager—has begun making the oddest oink-like sounds somewhere over there from the heart of darkness.

IN A FIT of machismo he decides to go out in the kayak himself before night falls and get them some crab for dinner. Actually it was her idea, the crab. His manly fit involved only the failed jigging of fish, but Eve suggests he try for some crab while he's out there. He complains of no bait while in fact he apparently owns seven cans of it, a sardine tin with a few holes punched into it being a favourite bait of Claude's.

He is proud, learning while doing, following her occasional instructions. After baiting the trap and securing it on the deck (he sits in Eve's spot in the stern) he paddles out. He keeps to within swimming distance of shore but he finds he is confident, even alone, though his muscles are dismayed to find themselves back aboard. He lets the trap down on its rope that ends with a little orange float. Then he jigs for fish — arm motion not unlike hoisting endless celebratory pints — all without tipping. Or rather, you sort of do tip, wobbling on purpose but in rhythm, much as when you stand up to pedal a bike. The fish aren't biting (actually the line is fatally tangled with the lure when he pulls it in) so it is a wondrous fine thing that the trap has crab in it — six. He lifts the trap and its skittering mess onto the deck and gets to shore using only one arm. Three crabs are too small, says Eve, and she shoos them off the beach with a foot. Gore gets water ready in his pot. When it is near boiling and he suggests she throw one in — the pot is big enough for but one at a time — she tells him the most efficient plus most humane way is to kill them first and then cook only the legs and claws, which is all you eat anyway. After some sober contemplation and a large cup of whisky, Gore pins one crab with a stick, takes up his hatchet, and smashes it in half. *Crashes* it in half, "crash" being perfectly onomatopoeic. He *munches* it in quarters, and *cricks* the legs off. He *crashes, munches* and *cricks* the other two, and *bubbles* them all in the pot for ten minutes. They taste wonderful; he has caught, killed and cooked them, and eventually he and Eve are full. Such rich meat, and so healthful, so non gall-bladdery. Some lemon in butter would've been fine, but. At the Empress Hotel, one Dungeness crab cost forty-six dollars.

Gore sits on his Hemingway stump picking crab from his teeth with a cedar sliver. It takes him another cup of whisky to regain the gut-dropping image of the two of them together in that tent, very soon now. He stands and creeps closer to her, where he leans against a tree, cocking a knee, which takes the weight off his bad toe. Swirling his cubeless drink, it is rather like he were leaning on a mantel at a soiree. He has tried to tempt her with a whisky and she has refused any. He watches her squat at the fire with a pot, emptying two cans of his soup into it. He turns down her offer of soup. She eats directly from the pot. She eats . . . wonderfully. Her eyes are . . . deep with firelight. Look at her rather small hand grip the pot handle, which is about the width of—

Eventually she has eaten it all. It was beef noodle.

He can admit to himself that he is nervous. It has been years. He could probably calculate exactly how many years but he knows it's been more than five. Perhaps seven. Which is over two millennia of days, and remarkable when you think of it. Him, a warm-blooded male animal. *Married* male animal, at least until two years ago. Speaking of marriage, he has been half-listening as Eve relates tidbits about her own spouse, one Roy, who sounds a decent enough chap. A refugee from a severe Mormon background, about which Eve supplies colourful details — long underwear they never took off, getting partnered with a total (and fanatical, that's a given) stranger and shipped off to anywhere they told you, going door-to-door to experience the joy of the suburban damned slamming them in your face, etc. Not your typical coming-of-age. Roy's path turned to civic politics when — Eve's conjecture —"organization became his new religion." Married for twenty-five years. Son Tommy ran away ten years ago, but that was that whole other story.

"You say he's a *mayor*? Remarkable." In firelight, her face is so smooth. Tawny milk.

"Oakville isn't big but, yes, Roy's the mayor."

"A Mormon. They're the polygamous ones, no?" Her bottom is a perfectly slim pear.

"I don't think it's allowed any more."

"Well, I always *wondered*," Gore ventures, shifting his shoulder between ridges of bark, "about the *math*. If for instance you had the successful *bull*-Mormons, as it were, each with, let us say, *five* wives apiece, all things being equal that would leave four lonely Mormon lads with, pardon the expression, nowhere to *put* it."

He instantly regrets his raciness, though Eve shows no hint of censure on her face. She is clearly no prude. Clearly *experienced*. He has concluded that, aside from the *natural* nervousness at not knowing Evelyn all that well, his *sexual* nervousness has mostly to do with his fear of performance, not in the sense of "forgetting how" so much as "arriving too fast." Seven years. God. God bless him, every one. Amazing he hasn't exploded here, standing. Amazing he can speak.

"Evelyn. You're looking, um, rather tired."

At this she smiles and nods and stretches languorously for him, and for a second he thinks he might explode as feared. But she puts an end to all nervousness, and to this night's hopes, by extracting from the kayak a tarp, and blanket. The tarp goes up in a minute as if by magic — a bit of string and two overhanging branches — and it's all he can do to swirl his drink.

WHAT THEY REALLY need, she says, is a good sharpening stone. She is hunkered down and scraping away with her big ugly knife on one of the flatter stones that ring their fire. The knife is chipped and dirty and sequined with fish scales.

All morning he has been anxious to get going, get moving. His toe hurts like hell now, and the sky threatens rain. Or maybe it's because he doesn't want any Natives finding them here. He knows they can't out-paddle the weather, nor can he out-run his hurting toe, nor would the Natives "do much to them," presumably, other than wish them good morning or at worst ask them to leave. Still, he wants to move.

Maybe he wants to leave this spot because he isn't entirely sure that last night Eve didn't hear him through the thin wall of his tent. He hadn't been able to wait and had gone at himself upon hearing her very first deep breaths. He became aware of no more deep breaths, but by then he didn't care. It took longer than usual, becoming an interesting battle of wills between the pleasure of his penis and the agony of his toe. He couldn't keep his glossy sleeping bag from making its insistent *swishings*. Not that he wanted to make public noise, but nor was he ashamed of his nightly habit. In such circumstances as these — that is, a woman choosing not to join him in sex — masturbation was his right. Use it or lose it. He'd been using it in this way for seven years straight. Not nightly but nearly.

And he'd enjoyed it with Eve last night. She had aroused him at the fire, and then in bed this excitement continued. To masturbate in the proximity of a woman who was not Gail. He pauses to again watch Evelyn sharpen her knife on the stones, and he feels somewhat grateful. The way she squats on her haunches, the way she moves her blade back and forth like that, the simple glazed look in her eyes — he could get excited all over again.

Still, he hopes she didn't hear him, and he wants to go.

Yet the travel writer in him regrets leaving this campsite, this island, so quickly. He is embarrassed he hasn't yet spoken to any Natives. He should damn well tramp through these woods and find some dwellings and bang on doors and engage in some meaty conversation. Redmond O'Hanlon, for godsake, paddled remote Amazon headwaters and engaged Natives who lacked English to speak with, let alone doors to bang on, and who might spear him for any number of noble reasons. So where were Peter Gore's guts? The night in that bar in Victoria he had tried, a little. Two fellows wouldn't speak to him, one woman actually changed seats. A younger sort with a bitter face answered his questions with, "Ask Henry," indicating the man beside him (who had to be his father) who was drunk and giggly and refused, despite the din, to speak above the faintest whisper. Well, a bar was the wrong place to expect anything but irreverence.

But according to the lightbulb that went off in his head last night, maybe the Natives here no longer mattered. That is, their relatives — the ones still in Asia, whose ancestors had waved knowingly at the foolish braves crossing the land bridge at Alaska several aeons ago — had watched over the centuries as their wanderlust brethren of North America got massacred by both Europeans and smallpox. Recently these more patient Asians had simply picked up and moved, and succeeded where their ancestors had failed. No land-bridge for them, they came over the pole by jumbo jet. Gore had been surprised in his day-trip through Vancouver, where instead of a bunch of pasty-faced Brits like himself he encountered far more Chinese than he had ever seen in one spot. Plus, his research informed him that many Vietnamese had successfully resettled hereabouts; newspaper scannings told him that they controlled much of the region's famous marijuana —"BC bud"— so strong it trades ounce for ounce with cocaine and is British Columbia's number one cash crop, surpassing logging, fishing and mining combined.

In any case, Gore surmised, the Asians here had done it, they had won. The early foray of Natives, with their colourful disguises, drums and such, had been a sort of fact-finding probe.

And here is Eve, sharpening her knife, acting out her gone-native role. Fingertips of both hands spread flat along the blade, scritch scritch, it's like she's *scrubbing* it on the rock, an archetypal, streamside, National Geographic, bare-breasted endeavor, except that she isn't doing laundry and he can't see her breasts.

"Are you planning to amputate my toe?"

She glances up and smiles for him. She can look so wonderfully pretty. And he's not once seen her try to.

"I mean, would you *please* amputate my toe."

BY LATE AFTERNOON of this second day he is too tired to speak, and the whole affair feels pointless. He no longer registers "Beautiful British Columbia" because the trees on the bank go by so slowly, there are but four varieties, and the appearance of each lovely arbutus seems timed and regular. Floating kelp bulbs shine identically in the sun. Each seal she insists on pointing out to him apparently knows how long it takes him to turn and squint and find it, and he is given only the teasing ripples of an event-just-passed. The occasional boat wake arouses more fear than excitement as they ride it out, their forced cooperation in a balancing act reminding him of near-fatal perchings on others' bicycle bars. He no longer knows why he is here, toe throbbing, paddling north. He feels kidnapped, not so much by her but by his silly attraction to her.

No, not so silly. He is on vacation — well, working vacation — so why not take advantage of that universal biological trait that conjoins transience with lust? That is, when our species hits the road it wants to get laid by strangers. Sure, it's a trait more common to the younger, backpacking set, but then so is lust altogether. (He does still have his suspicions about Gail, a certain wistfulness in her look after returning from more than one conference.) In any case, the trait is simply the physical expression of a gene pool's need to expand beyond any given valley or hamlet, thus ensuring enhanced survival and a reduction of slit-eyed banjo-players as neighbours. But the crucial point is that Gore has never enjoyed, first hand, the workings of this fine trait.

"What are you thinking about? You're hardly paddling." This coming half-amused, half-censuring, from behind.

"High school biology. I can't seem to let it go."

"Why not just rest a minute."

"Excellent. Thank you."

"I was being, you know..."

"*Good* one. Touché." It's a disadvantage not being able to see her from his seat. A face is necessary to catch humour as dry as hers.

"You know I haven't seen one herring ball? Anywhere? All my days on the water?"

"'*Herring* ball.'"

"It's when salmon or something scare a school of herring to the surface and they all splash at once. It looks like torrential rain but in one small spot, like the size of a car. Gulls are wheeling overhead, screaming and crazy. It used to be Claude's great joy, to see one."

"*Really*." Claude apparently being an easily entertained —

"No, it means salmon are feeding. It also means there's something to feed on. You used to see lots of them. I don't know if this means the salmon are gone, or the herring."

She is beginning to sound somewhat the environmentalist. What did that old salt tell him, that day on the Victoria dock? They've clear-cut the ocean bottom worse than the mountains?

Only no one's yelling because they can't see the damage? Something like that. The old salt looked too much the old salt, and the dock was writhing with tourists, so the guy was likely a university professor, or working for Greenpeace, this dock a long soapbox.

"Well, *we've* had our luck. That was a *fine* lunch. I remain *amazed*. You caught those in, what, all of two minutes?"

When she brought out her handline around lunch he readied himself for at least an hour's patience, but there she was hauling up a tight line a minute later. Then again. Impressively, she filleted them on deck with her newly sharpened knife. Though it looked like she might just keep going and eat it raw — indeed, she tasted some — to his relief they beached on the north tip of what she was reluctantly certain was Kuper and she cooked them. A quick fire, one pan, the fillets fried in Gore's olive oil and sprinkled with a bit of his salt.

"Those were just rock cod," she says."They're easy if you know where."

"Still."

"In fact we used to try to avoid them."

"Really."

"Notice they're mostly head?"

"And you say those *spines* were *poisonous*?"

"Well, like a bee sting. Does that qualify as poisonous?"

"I'd say somewhere between '*haz*ardous' and 'poisonous'."

"What you really want is ling. We'll get some tonight if we're near a kelp bed."

There is dry blood on the front of her shirt and her hands could use a better washing, up to the elbows. Actually, continue that wash up and into the armpits, please. This cessation of paddling has turned the boat and he is downbreeze and her "natural odour" flirts briefly with his nose. He thinks he can smell today's fish and also butcherings of yore.

Gore begins to paddle unilaterally as combined thoughts of smell, aboriginal kidnap and wanton lust with a stranger lead to a memory of a passage from a book, the gist of which had been shadowing him. He loved that book. It was an early bit of research he'd done for this trip and it was years since he'd read it, but he'd read it twice. The White Slaves of Chief Maquinna. A wonderful story. And true, the journal of one John Jewitt. In Nootka Sound, not too far north of the spot he'd been attacked by the two Germans and the legless loon. A ship, the *Boston*, was attacked and its sailors massacred. Two survivors were kept as slaves. For three years Jewitt kept a journal using a split feather and ink from the juice of berries or his own blood. God it was romantic, and the lingo so wonderful — *all foodstuffs drenched in a ubiquitous whale rendering to which they referred as 'train oil,' and to which the European palette was decidedly unaccustomed*. After two years, Jewitt was asked to take in marriage a young princess. Now, all along in his journal Jewitt had waxed most clearly about this tribe's habit of eating almost nothing but decayed fish — indeed, their idea of a celebratory dessert was a scoop of the fish eggs putrefying in a wooden tub — and that one endeavored to keep upwind of them. (Though he did mention that they bathed daily, often twice daily, whereas he and his English mate took to the water only on Sundays after their prayers, and not at all during winter. So, one asks, who smelled like what?) Still, Gore can't shake a persistant image of Jewitt on his wedding night with his bride — Mrs. Jewitt, sixteen, smiling shyly, waiting demurely if not coyly for him, quite lovely, and quite encased in her aura of stink, that of an oyster that had died and liquified some weeks ago.

When John Jewitt was rescued, his princess was pregnant with his child. Perhaps a pair of cedar nose-plugs had been the solution.

Gore doesn't think he is being overly English in thinking this way.

But *damn* if this kayaking isn't a most efficient generator of human smell. Here he is on his wanton-lust vacation and both he and the object of his lust possess neither bathing facilities nor the gumption to jump into the icy water and yet they are both *exercising to the limit*, all day. Their respective stinks are now full-bodied, if not dominant parts of their personalities. Oh yes, and let's top it off with the spectre of their respective nether zones, shall we? Yes — as the upper body flails freely away, let's picture their dank sexual parts down there encased in an airless fibreglass tube, churning darkly, an endless chafing of hair and membrane, a hidden marine cess, a crucible for a brand new and quite remarkable stink, to be unleashed at the onset — if it ever onsets — of shared nakedness. Great. Could he bear her smell? Could he bear sharing his own?

"Yes, how's that toe?" Eve asks from the back.

He may have moaned aloud. Not about the toe, though it burns him steadily.

"It's awful."

"I've been thinking about it. I've seen how you drink. But what have you been eating? What did you eat, say, the night before we left?"

Gore realizes what she's on about. He thinks back to what it was he ate.

"I ate two cans of sardines the night before we left."

"And drank whisky."

"And some whisky, yes."

"And last night you ate crab, and this morning it's even worse?"

"Yes."

"You have gout, Peter."

"You suppose?"

"It's gout. You have to drink way more water. And no more shellfish."

He feels their speed pick up as Eve begins paddling as well. He knows she is right. What else but gout attacks your big toe?

"You say water?"

"Lots of water. Avoid — I think I remember it right — your sardines and your shellfish. I don't think the whisky's great either."

Gore feels belittled because Evelyn is a witness. Out here in the wilds he has been attacked and injured by nothing but *food*. His gall bladder, and now gout. Behind him, he can feel Eve seeing him as a jowly poof who lifts his pinky as he slurps down more sauce, one footsie resting on a plush velvet stool. He hates this more than the toe-pain. And — what is there left for him to *eat*? Living off the ocean, he cannot fucking *eat seafood*.

Eve catches him off guard with a question.

"What about you, Peter, you ever been married?"

"I'm not sure," he answers, though in his snideness he feels his betrayal.

"How do you mean that."

"Let's just say that when it turns poorly, and stays that way for a long time, and then ends bad, you can't help but question if it was *ever* good at all. Ever a *marriage* at all."

Eve goes silent and they paddle through their private thoughts, Gore not unhappy for perhaps causing her to view her own marriage anew. This fellow Claude's death seems to have kindled all sorts of idealized memories, which is to be expected but of course it has made poor Roy pale in comparison, as indeed it makes *him* very pale as well. He should just relax and enjoy this entire strange journey. He begins to do just that. He tells Eve about the Pig War of 1850, a lark that happened not miles from here. He describes how the beaches where Natives built their villages needed to be sloped just right for their canoes to launch; he tells her why, in these waters, the oldest skulls have the smallest teeth. He engages her in some banter about Claude seeing his sea monsters, then teases her about Mormons and their polygamous ways. When, out of the blue —

"You think you and I will end up married, there, Peter?"

And then —

Whop.

Eve is a witch and she has conjured a coincidence of dramatic proportions to illustrate his shock: right there, a seal has emerged with a long fish in its mouth to shake it, slap it — *whop* — against the water like a dog would shake a rat.

He is doubly shocked, and he can't read her. What did she just say? He is excited and he has to tamp it down. "*Aha. Good* one."

They paddle no more than three strokes before Eve almost shouts, almost angrily, "Think we'll fuck under the stars tonight, there, Peter?"

He doesn't break rhythm. His face burns. He tells her, steadily and clearly, "I think you may have to be nicer to me."

Cedar was to the Coast as buffalo was to the Plains. The bark, stripped to its fibres and woven, made soft, warm clothing. Thicker strands made baskets of all shapes and sizes. The straight grain of the wood was perfect for planking — fifty, sixty feet long if needed — for their long houses. Smaller planks were steamed and made into bent-wood boxes, so well-crafted they were sought as objets d'art *in Paris and elsewhere. Out of whole trees were fashioned sea-going canoes, holding up to two dozen people in comfort. Pre-contact, before iron tools were acquired, huge cedars were burnt down with a carefully controlled fire.*

— DON COTTER, *LOST UTOPIAS*

MALCOLM ISLAND

IT IS LATE EVENING when Cal arrives at his campsite. All he says is, "Hey Cal," and it isn't clear to her if he even looked up.

From her manner of glancing around to get her bearings as she gets comfortable on her portion of log beside him, it appears that she will be spending the night. Which is surprising because it looks frankly wrong, if only on esthetic grounds. Though she is very attractive, it is her simple cleanliness which, in this place and especially compared to him, becomes the most striking thing about her. Her blonde hair is freshly washed, a reminder of what shampooed hair looks like. Tom's is so heavy with grease it rides close to his head, save where he has scratched at his scalp and created fissures in the gloss.

Her blue jeans are new and end mid-calf with little slits up the sides, a style made for the urban beach. Above her expensive sneakers, bright white socks daintily fold down on themselves and magically stay that way as she bends over logs, picking up bits of trash to toss into his smoldering fire. Even in this custodial mode she looks fresh and innocent. Even when she pinches up from her purse the plastic bag that holds a single stuffed sock (which, from its shape and apparent weight, is clearly a handgun) and passes it to Tom, she manages to convey an innocence that might in fact be showy.

She has also brought him, also in plastic bags, bulk carrots and three English cucumbers, the kind you don't have to peel. These he dropped carelessly inside the tent flap out of sight, just as he does now with the gun. Perhaps drops it in the same pile. She has also brought a small cooler which, when he opens it, makes him scrunch his brow and open his mouth to say something. It contains a cooked, still-warm chicken, which she declares to be free range and organic. He appears to have expected something else. Other than the "Hey Cal," all he has said to her so far is, "I missed the pod last night," and, now, "If we hurry and eat and stuff, maybe we can see them tonight."

Her quick-hooded eyes and half-smile suggests she's heard more than an invitation to eat. From the way she touches Tom's arm it is clear that they have sex casually, in the sense that it's no longer novel, nor even perhaps all that frequent any more. Despite his body's obvious damage, from his bearing one assumes he still can.

Within an hour they emerge from the tent. Cal opens the cooler and sets out paper plates she's brought. The evening is overcast and blowy. This is not the monochrome grey ceiling of the winters here but rather an ugly loitering of mongrel clouds, no pattern to them, and the wind comes from different directions and something like spit flies in your face though your shoulders are hunched and you thought you were turned away.

Tom's mood is evidently an extension of the weather. When he does speak it is quick and clipped, functional. Her mood is so unlike the weather it's a kind of proof that she can't have been here long.

She has just closed the cooler. He looks vaguely angry as she steps out of the clearing and into the woods to pee. He nudges the cooler with his foot and looks uncertain, eyeing briefly the spot where she'd disappeared. He sees a Sleeman's bottle cap in the dirt and remembers his thirst and his command, and he is outraged that she has not brought him the sixpack. Jesus, and where's the lemon, all he really wanted was a lemon. He waits for her to return. He is going to tell her to fucking get in her car and go get him some. As he waits for her to reappear from deep in the bushes — why doesn't she just piss at the edge of the clearing like he does? — his face contorts with the emotion, and the style, of what he will say to her. When she does appear, flicking glances behind her because she can't rest with the thought of cougars, his face is contorted and his mouth even begins to open, but then — nothing. In his eyes there's basic surprise as nothing comes out, except a simple, "*Fuck*," like a cough. Face still rigid, teeth bared a little, his eyes search for what has his gut on fire like this but they already seem to know they won't be finding anything. Even when she asks him what's wrong. She asks him sweetly, and he begins to wonder if it was even about her.

THEY HOLD HANDS to walk the fifty yards through trees to the steep gravel beach. Though it's him who walks slowly and with a severe limp, he is guiding her.

The instant they emerge from the trees his head is up and scanning the horizon for a blow. He does not have to look at the logs he begins to clamber over; doesn't have to glance down at the recorder to know what buttons to press. Another fire smoulders here at his watching-site. A few feet from the fire, under a garbage bag pinned down with rocks, lies the tape recorder, transducer, and headphones, and the camera. He simply leaves the equipment here, there being no people, let alone thieves, for miles.

They gaze out over the water and its pattern of waves — the black tips of which could be a million fins, says Cal, as a whining complaint. He tells her to watch only for *difference* amidst the pattern of waves. Otherwise he ignores her and snugs on the headphones. He can hear the engine of one thudding tug, miles away, as well as the faint, tinny zipping of a runabout, a few miles distant as well. Hearing these he wonders what size boat will be coming here with the shipment, and how they'll unload stuff. A zodiac? It's apparently a drugs-for-drugs sort of arrangement, pot for coke, pound for pound, which is truly amazing, he's never heard of such a thing. But the coke will have been stepped on, and who knows how much, so it's maybe a less-than-brilliant deal. And does Mckay even know that there's no road? He can't remember if he's told Mckay there's no road. Mckay needs to be told this: there's no fucking road. He should tell Cal to remember this for him, but he doesn't want her knowing anything, anything at all. But who gives a shit. He smiles to picture Mckay and a couple of paunchy hippies pissed off and humping big square parcels of dope through the swampy trail to the parking lot, back and forth. Yelling at him that there's no fucking road.

"*Tommy*, it was *only a log, with a bird on it*," Cal is telling him, laughing. She has him by the good arm and is yelling through the white noise of the headphones.

"Don't call me Tommy."

Cal falls into the brief pout she uses too much and which, he thinks, is beneath her. Though it occurs to him that lately she's been using it more like a trick, almost like an ornament, and doesn't mean it to be taken seriously.

"Well, what do you want me to call you?"

"Don't call me anything."

He sort of means it and she knows he sort of means it but he's smiling and she has to smile too.

He hopes the whole drop doesn't take much time. He's irritated by being made to think about it at all. He wants only this, this in front of him: this big grey sea and the chance of black whales, any second. Any second.

After a half-hour, no orca sounds. He isn't particularly drawn to their chit-chat — a treble gibberish, an alien code. In fact it almost nauseates him if he lets it: something so meaty and muscular and the size of a van making mouse squeaks like that. But hearing them does mean he might soon be seeing them. He takes off the phones and hands them to Cal, instructing her to let him know if she hears "squeaks or shrieks or whistles. Or *clicks*."

She puts on the phones, takes them off, adjusts the headband sizing, puts them on again. She too looks out to sea, but with not much sense of what it is she's watching for, other than a big, black fin, or a spout of water the likes of which she remembers from cartoons, the kind shaped like a bird bath that picks up a whole rowboat filled with scared cartoon animals. She wishes she could talk to Tom but he won't let her. She's still mad at him for the name thing. He can be such an asshole. Look at him: his face is all ready for whales. It's windy right in his eyes and he won't even blink.

HE LETS HIS EYES literally rest on the horizon, the line where water meets sky. It's something he's learned to do — place the gaze on the horizon line, which sort of holds his vision up and makes it less tiring. What he's really watching is the big grey mass below the line. He watches for nothing except a tiny change in pattern. Because that's what orcas are best at. That's what they do. They follow no pattern of their own and they break everyone else's pattern too, even the weather's, even the ocean's.

Speaking of patterns, he grabs the knob of bone beside his knee, his "extra kneecap" he thinks he's always called it. He knows he broke his leg as a kid, and had to stop running track in school. He's not sure but he thinks he remembers two, maybe three trophies on his bookcase in his bedroom. Also a bunch of ribbons thumb-tacked to the wall. He thinks he once knocked the head off one of the trophies by whacking it on the edge of his desk. He doesn't know why he would have done that, but he remembers the grainy texture of the broken-open metal at the neck. It was grainy, sandy, and the colour of charcoal. In any case his knob of bone has that deep ache that announces a big dump of rain. Now he wonders if this knob might actually be a birth deformity, not just from the smooth look of it but because it feels like something he's always had, like his feet. Anyway, it tells him it's going to rain tonight. It's going to rain like shit. With Cal here, the tent is going to feel very small.

He's tempted to impress her with his powers of prediction. He did once before with a sudden gale and she got almost excited and thought he was a nature wizard or something. He says nothing because he wishes she wasn't here. Her little socks, little sockettes, are so white they don't belong here. They need some dirt on them. She's bouncing her knees together, she's bored and she's pretending not to be.

Sometimes, like now, her face is frightening to him. Normally so cute, so easy on the eyes, sometimes she's a surprise he can't look at. He described it to his main doctor once (Dr Haspray? Dr Hesketh?) and the doctor wrote it down simply as "a visual impairment that comes and goes." (Tom always demanded to hear what he wrote down.) The doctor more or less shrugged, and repeated that the bullet had not touched his optic nerve. (Tom suspected right away that criminals don't get examined as carefully as other people.) So though he tried, he knew he didn't succeed in describing the "visual impairment" to this doctor or to anyone else. Even for himself it's hard to put into words. Mostly, it's that ordinary things become distorted. Usually it happens if he looks at something hard, and with appreciation. Ironically, when he wants to enjoy something. A grand sunset, for instance, might distort, its colours becoming somehow hollow, or *empty* of itself, in a sense the vacuuming opposite of themselves, though the orange is still orange. Or a face will become an instant caricature, though nothing obvious changes. It's a weird inversion, like seeing through to something's secret uncaring essence, something's glistening functioning guts. Imagine a loving mother turning suddenly into a transparent *machine* of love. It gives you a weird feeling. You have to look away.

Sometimes it happens even with memories — maybe, Tom thinks, because memories are what he looks hardest at. Even when it's something small, and he doesn't give a shit. Like the trophies, and the rough, dark metal at the severed neck. Or like his parents playing cards. He can't see their faces, just their arms and torsos sitting across from each other. It's early in the morning and he may have just come in from the night, and there they are, pretending not to notice him at all. In the room it feels like meaningless, almost threatening space, like the chill of a dark and empty classroom. Listening to his parents' conversation as they play cards, it's like they're both alone and playing solitaire, murmured words sounding no different than if they were talking to themselves. Maybe that's what marriage was, he probably thought at the time, because that's what he thinks now, and he had to get the thought from somewhere. When he tries to see either of his parents' card-playing faces the image inverts like crazy and he can't do it and he feels a little ill. He remembers his mother had sharp features, good looking like his own, and he remembers that once, before the bullet, old Claude told him, *Yer mum's sexy as can be, eh?* not knowing, or maybe knowing, that you don't say such things to sons. But Tom mostly hates these slivers of memories because their brief flashing illuminates mostly the huge *void* of memory, making him aware of all he can't remember. Once Dr Hesketh, or Haspray (maybe because doctors can say such things to criminals) shrugged and with a shameless smile told him to relax because memory isn't all it's cracked up to be.

In any case, Cal's tiny cute features are a little gruesome and sinister today and he wishes she'd leave. It's better with Boss-Lady, who at least has a few things to say about whales, and who doesn't think it's strange to want to see them. Cal sitting there so straight, her perky little face, all eager to look his way if he so much as moves. She knows every guy in every bar in Nanaimo and has been around the block a thousand times and yet here she is way out in the middle of nowhere where no one's watching and nothing matters and she's still playing cute and playing dumb. It was okay earlier in the tent but that's over. He has no idea how long she plans to stay. She didn't bring much food.

Whales are never over.

You never know when they'll come. Their arrival is never the same. For as long as they stay, everything they do is unexpected. They dive out of sight and might reappear in a leaping explosion two seconds later. Or they might not. Or a single roll so calm that it's coy. Then they're underwater again. They don't come up. They don't come up. And they don't come up. By the time you understand they won't be coming up, they are already miles away.

So you never know when they've left.

Before Europeans brought metal, Natives had an ingenious method of obtaining a single plank from a large cedar, in a manner that the tree survived! A man climbed to the desired height and with his sharp stone gouged a notch a few inches in. Then he pounded the stone down into a growing crack. Over time — due to swaying wind, and the weight of the stone itself — the stone worked itself down and the plank began to fall away from the tree. The process could take several years per plank, but if the band had many planks in process, it was a case of checking the forest to see which planks were ready to be carried back to the village.

One can only imagine this kind of patient husbandry in contrast to the mood of the Sointula Finns when they landed. The first group arrived in December, 1901, cold, hungry, staring up at an impenetrable wall of massive trees. The thirty-thousand acre Malcolm Island had been described in the government literature as agricultural land.

— DON COTTER, *LOST UTOPIAS*

STUART CHANNEL

FOG DISGORGES A YACHT, which overtakes and passes their kayak. A monstrous kitchen appliance, too-white fibreglass and chrome. In a fog-held world, nature quietly pure, here comes a fat plastic condo. An outsize American flag hangs off its wide-ass end, which rumbles and farts and bubbles.

The flag's colours are perfectly unnatural. She tells Peter that the planet's most powerful flag is also its weirdest and Peter doesn't respond. She can see through the smoked windows a clutch of heads in the main lounge watching TV. The heads are too large to be those of children. Look at where on the planet they are, then look at them, clustered intent on the pap-signal from home. Or maybe just bored, maybe they've been cruising forever. She can forgive them that.

The thought that they might be gathered at the tube, stricken by another September 11, breaks Evelyn's rhythm. *Ow*, she doesn't want to entertain that. But — there's no need to. If a bomb went off somewhere, no one here need know it. This place she paddles is beyond terrorism. Unless you're talking bears terrorized by chainsaws. Or salmon squeezed big-eyed in a net.

Evelyn stops paddling again, to marvel at how a brain moves its pictures so seamlessly, so randomly. Jetliners exploding into New York towers, to the eyelidlessness of fish. In seconds. Brain a crystal ball rolling out of control in head-oil.

She knows she's really just been coveting the yacht's bathroom. Clean, has hot water, mirrors, a massage shower-head. She hates this boat for bringing such a bathroom within feet of her then floating it away.

Peter waves to the rich old retired fellow in the captain's hat, steering from up atop the flying bridge, who waves back. She thinks Peter betrays a wistful look as the big flag flaps past. He looks always on the verge of timid hysteria. He's still stung from being caught posing with his computer, typing nothing. She called him "Jimmy Olsen, cub reporter," then had to explain what it meant.

Trying to be considerate, the yacht's skipper slowed the craft to exactly the speed where its stern dug in and sent the biggest wake. The first waves reach them and Peter goes so rigid he makes the waves dangerous. She tells him to roll with them but he can't.

She's been on Oakville boats as big, knows the people. She knows their success at money. The proper hair, the right scotch, the understated charisma, the passing on the third glass of wine. She's seen that too much about respectability is fear. We learn to tie our laces not because we might fall but because people will laugh if we don't know how. She hates the boat because it is a mirror.

Tom has no respectability because he has no fear because he has no respect.

"Tom" was the wrong label for him, for a boy all edges and thorns. "Tom," a brown tranquility. Sacred Om. A boy that Evelyn can feel and see with her bones — eyes aglint, smile not attached to anything inside, arms shooting out *instantly* for what they want — a boy whose hard heart she tried not to see when he was seconds from her womb, this boy should have been given a name more fitting, onomatopoeic: Spike. Hurt. Hitler.

"You're laughing," says Gore. "Yes, these waves are big. So it's *gallows* humour? You're 'laughing in the face of death'?"

"Sort of." The wake is quickly gone, the water calm, yet Peter is still rigid and dangerous.

Peter Gore has an interesting name himself.

It's comforting to think of Tom as an Adolph. To see him as a genetic result, as nature's black tendril. Tom as something beyond her input or control. No blame. In fact, Roy (now there's a name) often tried to ease her grief by saying exactly that. "*You* did not make him this way." It was most comforting of all when he said, "He did not make himself this way either."

Peter has asked her something about Americans and pigs.

"What?"

He is beginning to irritate her. Waking up on Kuper this morning, having survived their first night together, Peter was skitterish and wanted to leave the island at once, afraid to be on Indian land. Evelyn was only happy to linger and sharpen her knife, worn too dull to do a good job on fish. The granite fire-ring stones worked. Being back in the kayak felt lovely to Evelyn but not to Peter, who hurt all over but mostly his toe, and he didn't like hearing from her that he has gout. He felt instructed, and now he is instructing her back. The mood in the kayak is tilted and unaware. It's like they could be any two co-workers in any office tower in Toronto, too busy over nothing on any afternoon in history.

"Do you know the other war between the U.S. and Canada? *Not* your proud little War of 1812?"

"No."

"You grew up in Victoria and haven't heard of the Pig War of 1859?"

"Nope." Though she thinks she might have.

"It took place on San Juan Island." Gore waves in the direction he mistakenly believes San Juan Island to lie. "The pig belonged to an English farmer there."

"San Juan is American."

"It wasn't anything yet. There were American settlers too and one of them shot the English pig. An argument ensued. U.S. troops arrived. Then two British warships. The dispute became one of where the American-Canadian border should lie. The German Emperor was called in to arbitrate. The American was fined for shooting the pig, and almost starting a war, but, you're right, the Americans won the island. Though Victoria lies *south* of it, I believe." Peter declares that "Americans in these waters deserve a chapter all their own," and Evelyn realizes he is talking about his book.

Peter calls a stylized halt to the paddling by raising a hand. This same hand he turns slowly around to show her his blister, at which he raises his eyebrows. She tells him, "Good work," which turns him back around and he digs in with more gusto than he's shown all day.

"I just love this," he announces after a few pulls. "Don't you?"

"Yes," she says, not clear what he means by 'this.'

"You were so lucky to *grow up* here."

"Yes."

She's not sure if "here" means the west coast, or this wilderness, or what. She grew up in a small city. She noticed nature if a sunset backed it or if it shone with rare snow. The sea was important for its beaches, lying on the sand with friends, thumbing down the elastic on your bottoms to check your diff. If "here" means wilderness, means out on the water with no houses in sight, it means Claude. For three summers, and often throughout the year, it's what they did.

That "here" reminds Evelyn mostly of sex.

She paddles on, talking herself out of regret at having invited Peter along. It's necessary for mental health — she explains to herself — to spend at least part of each day talking to someone besides yourself, someone outside your own skin. Good to focus on another. Good to have someone to tend to. Or fend off. Actually his crush on her makes him more manageable.

THE DRIZZLE ON her face isn't as bad as the icy drips falling down her neck. She is again cold in the bones. She looks up to gauge the sky: the ceiling of cloud slides over them, slowly, from the west. Further west are breaks of blue. In an hour or two it will be sunny and she will be warm. What is more lovely than those coming jewels of blue?

"Jeez," Peter wheedles. "It's *July*."

Peter will flinch in a sudden wind because he hasn't seen the dark line on the water approaching. On the beach he sets up to bask in the sun, unaware that a tree's shadow will be on him in minutes. He relies on a word in a calendar—'July'—and doesn't look up. He can't see this place. Claude thought people like him didn't deserve to be here.

He's been whining about quitting early to find a place to camp. He doesn't see all that blue approaching from the west. Because of this, she's too angry to tell him.

"Peter."

"Yes?"

"Why do we hate stupid people?"

She sees him think fast, not wondering why she asked. He only wants to impress her with an answer and part of this means not taking too long finding one.

"Um," he says. "One *suspects* it's biologically rooted. In any *herd* species, survival means the *culling* of weaker members." He chuckles. "Which for humans would include the *stupid*. The imbecilic. The *dull*. Socially, we do quite heartlessly *stomp* them. Um. Look at children?"

It's awful, knowing you can hate someone for being weaker than you. Knowing doesn't change it. She suspects she's normal enough in this. She also suspects it isn't good to think of a husband in these terms.

She remembers a small party to host the Mayor of Oshawa, Richard, and his wife, Melissa. Oshawa and Oakville shared an industry—automobiles—and a giant neighbour—Toronto. More than once that evening Evie would hear the mayors compare their cities' relationship to Toronto with Canada's to the States.

She was out on the deck with Roy, setting the table. Richard and Melissa stood in the door holding drinks. An Atlantic salmon sizzled on the gas grill, guarded by Tommy, ten, his spatula up and ready. Sometimes, if asked, he would help. It did mean, though, that he would turn the fish only when *he* thought it was time.

It began to sprinkle. Roy closed his eyes, smiled his long-suffering smile.

"And here I am putting down the last fork!" Roy lifted said fork and shook it at the heavens, then quickly began gathering up plates. Doing so, he stayed hunched. He yelled at Evie as though from the chaos of a thunderous downpour. "*We're moving in! It's raining! Find the wing to the dining-room table!*"

"What?"

"The *wing*! The insert! To the dining-room table!"

Roy dashed in with his load and came back for more — salt shakers, corn handles — dropping some onto the deck. He wasn't suffering. He enjoyed crisis.

Evie looked up. The sky was mottled with clouds, what Tommy called "a Simpsons sky" after the opening to the cartoon. Over their heads was one large but lone dark cloud. The rain came harder now but the cloud had already almost passed over. From the direction it had come — and the source of the rest of the evening's weather — was nothing but blue patches and harmless fluffy white.

"Roy, no," Evie said, putting a hand on his arm, "it's going to stop."

Roy still didn't look up. He looked at her instead. So Evie pointed.

Roy squinted up, his gaze travelling mindlessly, his face getting rained on. He looked at her in puzzlement, but this time also with impatience, as if Evie were claiming psychic powers in a time of need and haste.

"It's *raining*!" Roy bent to pick up his dropped things.

"It won't be in a few minutes. Look, over there, that's what'll be over us soon."

Roy humoured her with another bobble-headed glance at the sky, not just a host but a mayor in a hurry, almost angry now, looking but not seeing, even when shown, as uncomprehending as an ox, and Evie wanted to butcher him for the crime of stupidity.

Roy rushed in with his load. Evie caught Tommy smiling. Obliquely, almost sympathetically, as he prodded his fish on the barbeque. He lost interest, the look passed, but the dark knowing in his eyes had been clear: this sort of thing happened to him all the time.

They ate their salmon and corn cobs in the diningroom while out in the evening sun birds sang revivified morning-chirps, and Evie was careful to say nothing. Roy hadn't noticed, was busy trading arcane quips with Richard. The running joke was what could they tax next? Oxygen! Birthdays! Both men pleased with themselves and each other. It's great to decompress, they kept saying. When Melissa asked that the blind be pulled because the sun was right in her face, and Roy rose to do it, all lit up by the sun but still not seeing, still trading wit with the other mayor, Evie's stomach caught a little, the feeling of a ball being nudged at the top of the stairs.

THE FOG AND CLOUDS lift but her mood doesn't. Now that she's farther north of it, the brown haze to the southeast is a thick and obvious dome. Vancouver's air, a city-version of obvious stupidity. She's heard it called The Big Toke. From here she can see that during her past weeks on the water she's been paddling in it, living in it. What is the reach of that hellish air, sixty miles? Back with Claude there was no bad air, or none that you could see, even when the surrounding mills were going. The mills have mostly stopped because there are no longer enough trees to feed them.

No herring balls. No Caddy, as yet. Ghosts glum and scattered.

North. Maybe Tommy's found himself a clean world.

PADDLING, IT SOMETIMES helps to talk. What she tells Peter about Roy's past pleases Peter greatly. But it makes her queasy, his eager mocking of her husband, like he's besting a rival. He mocks the long underwear, the "marketing strategy of rapping on doors," polygamy. She tries to end it:

"Mormons are okay. For extremists they're fairly gentle."

"*Fairly gentle* with six *wives*?" He does his Brit timing, his self-happy "um" deep in the throat. "It's not 'gentle.' It's '*tired*'."

Peter has to stop paddling whenever he speaks and she digs in to compensate, keeping up speed to exit the tidal suck of this channel. Not many of Peter's quips need answers. She tries to imagine amiable, diplomatic Roy with more than one woman: 'I'm sorry, Rachel, tonight you see it's Sarah's turn. It's what we all decided after praying-for-guidance. But' — Roy's racy joke — 'hold that thought! Now if you wives come to some other agreement, it's six of one, half dozen of another to me.' Good god, how does one get sexy with something like that? Evelyn pictures a style of female fervor that begins with a sober pinching up of a crinoline hem, then softly clenched teeth, which, when it builds in shameful breathing, will be excused as God's will.

God's will: there are worse ways of viewing sex.

They paddle across the head of a small bay with its inviting, crescent-shaped beach. It looks tropical, the way trees hang over the sand like a canopy. It's some distance, but Evelyn sees what might be a clutch of ghosts in the shadows behind those boulders. There's the ghost of a smoky fire. They might be smoking fish.

"Well, you *know*," Peter declares, arguing with her although she is fairly sure she hasn't spoken, "there *won't* have been an Indian village there. Nice as it looks."

"Why do you say that?"

"There's no *stream*. No *water*. The two requirements for establishing a village —"

"Maybe there's a creek. A spring just in the woods."

"— or even a seasonal *camp*, are, one, *water*, and two, the slope of the beach. The slope of the beach had to be good for launching a canoe in any manner of tide."

"Is that one the wrong slope?"

"Do you *know* —" He pauses to give her time to consider all that she might not. "— From evidence from *skulls* here in the Pacific Northwest, they ate so many *clams*, with so much *sand* in them, that their teeth *wore down*?"

"I didn't know that." She does know that grit of chewing one.

"To *nubbins*. You tell the age at death by the teeth. It's inverted. The old ones have the *little teeth*."

They leave sight of the beach behind and Evelyn is relieved.

"How many clams have you eaten since you started your trip, Peter?"

"I had a chowder in Victoria. Quite good."

"How many clams have you dug?"

"None. As yet. Why?"

Because you *read* instead of *do*, she wants to say, mimicking him. It also bothers her that this is stuff she should have known, history which should be required of all travellers to this place.

"Maybe we should dig some."

"I *thought* you said there was a *red tide*."

She remembers something Claude did that disgusted her at the time. "You smash open a live clam and rub your lips with it. If your lips don't tingle, the clams are safe." She thinks for a moment, remembers more. "Avoid the butter clams. They hold the poison longer. Mussels are safest. They live in faster water and get rid of it quick."

"Well, it's *mussels* then, isn't it."

Off to the left, a sea lion has been watching them but she is tired of pointing such things out to Peter, so paralyzed is he with his paddling. Point out a loon and he goes stiff to turn and almost capsizes them. This sea lion's a biggie, head like a dented old paint can, and she doesn't want Peter frightened. But they get closer and now he does see it. He stops paddling and stares at the ripples it leaves submerging.

"You *actually* believe your Claude saw a sea monster?"

"Not 'clod.' Claude. He saw something. Twice." They went over this last night.

"But you say this chap enjoyed all manner of *drugs* and such."

"He was an expert. He knew what was the drugs and what wasn't the drugs."

"It's impossible. Dinosaurs are *reptiles* and reptiles breathe *air* and these *Caddies* don't seem to be coming up for great lungsful of *oxygen* now *do* they."

"Who knows."

In one library book, an impatient author put it simply. We believe in giant squid, which reach eighty feet long. No one's ever seen one, even a big dead one, but we find their huge beaks in whales' stomachs and their suction wounds on whales' skin, and their numbers are calculated at one to two hundred thousand in the Atlantic alone. We've never seen an atom either.

"Knobs on its head, a mane of seaweed..." Peter snorts, besting another rival. But keeps watching the spot where the sea lion went down.

Evelyn recalls how Claude would falter trying to describe what he saw, once in the early morning through the steam of his coffee, and once near midnight under a full moon. He said they were identical and could have been the same individual, though the sightings were years and a hundred miles apart. Even when asked, Claude rarely told the story, but if he did he'd stare into himself, especially when recalling the one at midnight. Hearing his words, Evelyn could see it too: no more than twenty feet away, a moose-like head standing out of the water on an impossibly long neck, maybe five, maybe six feet, big eyes which see you too, the moonlight bright on sleek dark skin, then one huffing breath, inquisitive, a holding itself in vibrant fear, an immense panicked splash when Claude hisses for his friends to come see. Claude took to bringing a camera with him after that.

Evelyn tries to get Peter to talk about his recently failed marriage, but he won't say much. Instead, as usual, he talks obliquely about sex.

"Do you *know*, the Indians here were polygamous too?" Peter stops paddling to say this.

"I guess I didn't know that."

"Just the chiefs and next-in-*command* types. Basically, the bullies. Those who *could*."

"I didn't know that."

"Isn't it oddly coincidental to be talking about *Mormon* polygamy while navigating polygamous *waters*?"

She has to stop him.

"So you think you and I will end up getting married, there, Peter?"

He is stricken. And with perfect timing, a seal killing a ling cod gives it a good whack very close by.

Whop.

Peter, who hasn't noticed this seal till now, looks overwhelmed.

"*Aha. Good* one," he says gamely. He's once again stiff with his horny fear of her. She hasn't known what to do about it besides have some fun, though she feels guilty. It's not fair: he jokes about sex with his scaredy-cat innuendo, and when she jokes back he gets all in a knot. Torture of the English. Well, why not.

"Think we'll fuck under the stars tonight, there, Peter?"

Her cruelty surprises her too. With one foul word she feels the distance she puts on Oakville. Re-inventing herself with a sentence.

His paddle pauses, then dips gently in the small waves. His arms have gone almost limp while his neck reddens. He mumbles something into the wind.

"What?"

He turns, wobbling but too angry to be afraid. "I think you have to be nicer to me."

He turns back and continues paddling, still gently. His neck still red.

Cloud the length of the horizon is approaching from the west. It could be a wet night.

"Sorry. I was just fooling around."

"We are not amused."

"Sorry."

He accepts this without comment and paddles. He could have been amused. He could have been. Watching his straight back, she sees a posture shaped entirely by emotion. Soon his paddling gains strength.

"Here I was under the *illusion* you were of breeding. You held dinnah pahties."

Humour, good, but how easily he can be hurt. Her tease has stained the day. She tries to throw a prank into the mix, but knocking his dumb hat off with her paddle is a near-disaster.

Her strength around him feels cheaply won. She sees how someone's vulnerability is the door to hate and love both. At an open wound, you can do either of those two things.

"I used to be fun."

His answering tells her she said it aloud.

"Well, um. I think you still are. I'm having unspeakable fun."

"I guess I mean —"

"No, I *am*. I'm having an *adventure*. How often does one have an *adventure* at my age? *Share* an adventure?"

"I think I meant more, 'It used to be fun, being me.'"

"Ah."

"Wasn't too clear there."

"Well, so what do you think happened? I gather you don't mind me prying since you, um, 'brought it up.'"

"Just stuff. Too much stuff. Over the years. A big cloud formed. Isn't it like that for you?"

"Ah, well, yes I think—"

"It's too many *questions*."

"And too few answers. Quite."

"*No* answers. At all. Do you have any answers, Peter?"

"None. *Ask me my name*."

"No, seriously."

"Absolutely none. In fact I have less than you. I have a large *negative* number of answers."

"You win again."

"I always win."

Evelyn doesn't continue the back-and-forth, and Peter respects this instantly and allows silence between them. While always eager to talk, in his respecting her silence Peter reminds her of the shy letter writer who, if a single answering doesn't arrive, will stop too.

HE LIKES HER again. But how long will it last, this sojourn with a man she hardly knows? He's in her kayak not because she needs a man. She wants him to understand this. She needs protection, not from bears and other men, but from herself. From this non-stop talk with herself. From this ragged coastline of a voice. This suffocating conversation. This one that doesn't stop. *This* one. It's like an argument that has no point, and where will it endlessly take her? Peter is a lonely man and he would know something of this voice. Maybe he's with her for the same reason. Any two heads being better than one: even playground scorn from the second head keeps the first from the most obvious errors. Someone to tell you if you're crazy, for instance. That's the key: if she can keep this stranger in her kayak and carry on a conversation, it means she's not entirely crazy.

"Want to hear my story about sex under the stars, Peter?"

SHE IS NINETEEN, Claude is thirty-four and more alive than anyone she knows. She is so in love with him it's vertiginous, a cliff edge. If he shoves, she'll die. This couldn't be more clear.

The shove comes mid-summer when she learns his exhausting month of tree planting also included the inexhaustible planting of someone named Mary Beth. Turning devastated to friends, she suffers more cliffs because these friends now have more tales to tell about Claude. A flight from endless pain, off she goes to Ontario, under the guise of pre-veterinarian studies at Guelph. She comes home summers and does see him. Fiery reconciliations and camping trips where they can't get enough of each other, where they make love in the tent and then in the mud on the way to the water to cool themselves off from making love.

It's now only obvious that Claude owns no urge to monogamy. Evelyn, studying her biology, learns to see him as a force of nature, as primal appetite in human form. Any animal eats when he is hungry. Certainly there's nothing wrong with this, no sin in living honestly. Wait, wake up, there is lots wrong. He hurts people, and his appetites include not just sex but booze and drugs beyond imagining. And the thrill of stolen boats, dealing dope and illegal salmon, and who knows what else? He came back so utterly tanned, refreshed and happy from his holiday in Europe, spent sailboating smuggled Moroccan beads to England.

Bent over her slides of sectioned organs, formaldehyde burning her nose, she realizes that the spectacle of Claude's animal appetite might be what got her interested in biology in the first place. Him splitting the white belly of a sockeye, the blood welling black. Pressing the gloss of a coho's eyeball and knowing from its give how many hours it's been dead. The same touch marks sex with him. A man so open to flesh, to guts, lets her open completely: stomach to stomach they are both slit fish, their organs bouncing and sliding together in helpless gory hunger. She knows he loves her as desperately as she loves him. But he's an animal, he has no memory. He loves whoever's in his boat.

She's human. Though he keeps a hooked finger in her guts she puts distance between them. In any case, it's all he'll let her do.

Age twenty-two, in her final year, she meets a political science grad student from the States. Since leaving Claude, each morning she meditates again, and a new simple-heartedness lets her *see* Roy. Roy Poole, twenty-six, is as unilaterally decent as Claude Longpre is not.

Roy is worldly in that he appears to have survived warfare of the psychological kind. If he ever had much personality he's shed it, and this success lends the quietest power. Which is nothing, really, but a wholesomeness. Simplicity its subtle pinnacle. He enjoys seeing himself as a naked foot-soldier in Truth's humble army. This, and his effort of never trying to be sexy, is somehow, at the time, sexy. He has given deep thought to both past and future. He has a measured humour but is capable of fun. His high voice she hears as insistent, and confident. He is American enough that he calls her Evie, for good and always. So much for her famous west coast, Evie realizes she's never met anyone who truly cares about people. He has dropped religion for humanism but the fervor is still there. It's a foreign concept and Evie can't even begin to do it, not really. Roy's compassion for his species appears to be genuine. It's not very grandiose: local politics will be his tool. Evie sees Roy Poole as a model of human sanity. After a year they find themselves living together and engaged. She doesn't write to Claude about the impending marriage because she doesn't want what happens next.

Having instincts for these things, Claude shows up in Guelph the very evening Roy has gone off to his bachelor party. (It's a party Claude will question all night, as if concerned for Roy: "What kind of stag is it, eh? De main guy don' drink?") He has a wad of cash and a rented car; they drive to Toronto and hit the funkiest bars, Claude drinking cognac. She cries but Claude doesn't, he's stern with her. Like an older brother he asks questions about Roy and gets mad at what he sees to be deficiencies. He's irritated with Toronto in general and she sees a new side of him, the Quebecois who hates Anglos. No fighter, he seems to be trying to pick one. They buy wine and wander into a Don Valley ravine. It is a crisp, wolfish, full moon night, the kind where shadows are bright black and emotions come off a person and can be read in the air. She resists — her only battle is with herself — and their sex is violent. She has one leg out of her jeans is all. It hurts when her underwear is ripped clean off. She cries through it, for several reasons.

The next day at nine in the morning she comes home looking like hell. As sober and alert as he will be every morning for the next twenty-five years, Roy asks gently where she's been and doesn't press for details when she tells him she has had her own bachelor party.

Evie will wonder about that night and about Claude, wonder for years if they would have had sex whether she'd given in or not. Because she's not sure that she did. She wonders how far he would have gone. How big was that side of him. Stark in the moonlight, that edge to his face, that of an animal taking what hasn't been offered. She'd never seen it before because until then she'd never been anything but willing.

After Tommy is born she often thinks of that face.

PADDLING, IN HER GUT she understands there are two tides pulling still. Bloodied by Claude, she opted for the decent. And she wonders aloud if maybe her present journey is a pilgrimage to *before*. These waters do feel sacred, there's no other word. She tells Peter this place is her church. Its breeze holds the mysteries. Its altar is that horizon. Its incense is her fear. Its prayer is — what? Is her simple yearning. Its ritual is this paddle through chaos. She loves this church. She digs in, paddles with belief. These creatures popping up out of the sea and angling down from the sky — are teachers and priests. But this means that the high priest, sent to her in the spirit of auspicious witlessness (it's a religion that pulls pranks to deflate itself) is Peter Gore. She doesn't tell him this part.

But, seriously, he's here for a reason. It's a religion so wild that everything counts.

In any case, she has been warming to him. Quirks and all. Watching a man who is helpless and in a position of learning — which sums up Peter Gore in a kayak — you can clearly see the child. Seeing the child, you see the blameless roots of the man.

She notices her hands on the paddle. They look stubby and young. Has anybody been seeing her as a child?

"Are you still in touch with Gail?" she asks, grabbing for the normal.

Peter is thrown. He was ready to hear more about Claude, and Roy, and her sacred journey, which she assumed he was taking seriously until he dubbed it the Kayakopelian Marine Church of Eve, Feminist. But there's nothing more for her to tell him, there really isn't.

"We occasionally *communicate*." His paddling finds its stumbling rhythm again.

"When was the last time you spoke with her?"

"As a matter of fact I phoned from Victoria. From the hospital."

"Your bladder thing?"

"My gall bladder attack, yes."

His paddling ceases each time he talks. Evelyn quits too. They turn in a slow circle but drift in the right direction. The sea is aware as it bears them steadily north.

"And wasn't this in the middle of the night?"

"Well, what *are* ex-wives for?"

"You moaned into her ear?"

"I gave her receiver a proper thrashing."

"She taught high school too?"

"Now she teaches the school *board*. How to behave themselves."

"She didn't want the golden handshake."

"It was hardly a golden handshake. They let me go early with *half* my pension. It was at best a *bronze* sort of handshake. *Tin*. I'm wearing my estate on my *back*. It's true."

Always edgy about money, as if she were on the verge of asking for some.

"I envy people who have a career they enjoy."

"I *enjoyed* teaching. It's more a case of Gail not having a *book* to write."

She lets this arrogance pass and assumes that, through the years, poor Gail heard a lot about this book. Perhaps not 'poor' Gail. Peter's book could possibly be good. He could write a good book if he relaxed and let himself be funny in it.

"So your break-up was friendly?"

For this one Peter looks about, finds the highest distant mountain peak and stares at it. He scratches his temple, which erects a pillar of greasy hair.

"Breaking-up lasted ten years, so it was *everything*. It was friendly. Angry. Depressing." He pauses, sighs. "*Complex. Boring.*"

"Gotcha." She knows the boring complexities of sharing a lair. "So there wasn't any 'one big thing'?"

"There wasn't, no." Peter has said this too quickly. He actually changes the subject. "But what a day this has turned out to be! This is pretty much paradise, wouldn't you say?"

She wouldn't. The sun is tyrannical. It feels dangerous now. Hair hot to the roots.

"You should put your hat back on, Peter."

He doesn't, so she smacks her paddle and shoots a deft spray of water up his back. Peter gulps breath, laughing, expecting more, a child. They laugh in unison for maybe the first time. Black against the maroon material, the water forms an almost perfect exclamation mark, and then it widens out, losing its surprise.

ROY CAN PLAY a little. He has quirks she does enjoy. Sometimes he toys with mild machismo, which is fun because he's anything but and knows it. Curly's is a sports bar in Toronto that, aside from its Three Stooges motif, serves the hottest wings anywhere. So hot that when they're on the table you can feel the spice-heat on your face. Ordering them from the kitchen the waiter shouts "soo*ee*," the pig-call. Roy, aided by one lite beer and then water, methodically eats them all, chewing slowly, explaining that he is deliberately relaxing all the muscles of his face.

For years, apropos of nothing, Roy has looked at her with mischief and asked, "Curly's night?" As if he is seeking naughtiness and she might not grant it. But she does. They make the drive, and seat themselves at one of the big screens, because it's what people do here. Roy takes little interest; Evie watches if it's baseball. She likes the detail, the pitcher's teasing pace. Watching her watching, Roy might joke about tight uniforms. The tables are formica; napkin-wrapped cutlery is clunked down with their wings. Medium combo for her, large suicide for him. He says thank you. His high voice sounds higher in here; from around a corner he could be mistaken for a woman.

What Evie hates about Curly's night lately is the creeping subtext. Roy as a spying king. Ever since the Oakville plant began making only Windstar vans — in fact all the Windstars in the world — Roy will point to the ubiquitous vehicles and joke, "Our wheat." Arriving at Curly's, after pointing out some "wheat" in the parking lot, Roy is on the lookout for anyone recognizing him. In Oakville, Roy venturing out is Roy meeting his public, but in Toronto he is incognito in the larger kingdom. He really does seem to consider himself incognito. When he speaks to the waitress with a partial smile and glint in his eye, as if he has a secret he might or might not share with her, Evie is nauseated. She can't tell him this. It's so subtle it's almost not there. It's doing nobody harm. But Evie wishes she could tell him that, when he feels secretly important talking to the waitress, it is nothing but clear to her that the important person in the exchange is the waitress. She is bringing people food. What is *he* doing?

"Soooee."

Peter jerks in the bow and Evelyn sees she's said this aloud. He turns halfway, showing her his ear and cheek, and begins to ask, "Was that some kind of —"

He sees the eagle too. It's as if it's been called. About twenty feet off the water it pumps its wings strongly, its body heaving up and down. Flying past, it tilts its head to give them one good stare, then continues on, its shushing of wings loud in this church.

Gore mumbles something. Bitch. Or witch. Evelyn doubts she is meant to hear.

She does enjoy that she and Peter attract coincidence, however meaningless. Certain people seem to, more than others. She and Claude did — she remembers Claude remarking on it. She can't remember any examples at the moment. Maybe Claude said that to all the girls.

MID-AFTERNOON, Peter is tired and any humour has left him. She sees him wince but he's keeping his toe to himself. They both hear the explosive gusts and then spy the biggest fin. They instantly stop stroking. The pod of killer whales is maybe one hundred yards away.

"*Good god*," says Peter, six inches taller in his seat.

"What luck." Tiny rip-tide wavelets slap-slap-slap the hull as if urging her on.

"What do you think?" His paddle is poised mid-air. It could flail in reverse.

"*Yes*."

Working together, which only means not working against each other, they turn and aim at what seems to be the whales' direction. Evelyn counts five, then six. Because they are rolling, diving, shifting position, it's hard to tell but there are at least eight.

"There's *three* of them!" shouts Peter. "No! *Four*! *There's four*!"

They pull hard in a decent rhythm. The pod is moving but Evelyn thinks this angle of approach should get them close. Their sheen is black laquer that curves the sun. Even from here she can hear the muscular weight of their breathing. They have boundless vitality, they feel *eager*, and they're huge. Something she's heard strikes her: when they speak amongst themselves it's a hundred times faster than human speech, and they're speaking about an approaching kayak right now.

"I *think*," Peter announces, breathing hard, "we should stop. Right... about... *here*."

They are fifty yards distant and the whales are, if anything, moving away. In the bow, Peter has stopped paddling.

"They won't tip us," Evelyn says just loud enough for him to hear. One of the whales sports an extremely tall dorsal fin. The dominant male.

"Now — *No, stop*. Now how the *hell* do you know they 'won't tip us'?"

"They see us. They don't want to hurt themselves on a boat."

"I'm sorry but how do you *know that*. And *please stop paddling*." He doesn't turn to look at her. "Stop paddling please."

"Claude knew." Evelyn is breathing hard with effort. "Natives know. People kayak, with orcas. All the time. I read it." In the library, in Victoria, after Claude mumbled about their son's single passion.

"Woah. Close enough. Stop. *Evelyn*." They are perhaps thirty yards from the back-most whales and Peter almost lifts himself out of his seat to clamber back to her.

Evelyn stops. She's counted nine. Two are so small they are obviously children, perhaps even newborns. Calf, is the word. She sees how they roll and breathe in tandem with each other. They rise more often than the adults, two breaths to their one. She has also noticed how one of them always lifts its tail right out of the water and then gives a little downward air-slap with it, like a cute wave goodbye.

"Look at that *little* one!" Peter has seen it too. Still sitting extremely stiffly and half out of his seat, he can't not watch them. "That is unbearably *cute* that little guy!"

The whales move away at a fair clip now. Evelyn feels sick. She might even vomit. The young one with its mid-air flap is having trouble keeping up. It's limping, in effect.

"That's *so* sweet." Gore is chuckling now. He settles in and takes up his paddle. "We should try to stay with them!" He starts stroking. Then looks back at her.

But Evelyn has stopped paddling. She can't watch them anymore. In particular can't watch the little spastic. She has no clue if she's seeing genetics or pollution, or even if there's a difference. Nerve-damage, the stutter-step future of mammals and humans. She feels she's had a hand in it.

"Typical. The *one* day I leave my harpoon at home."

The buck-toothed Brit smile is clear in Peter's voice.

"Or rope — I *could* have done with a water-ski."

IT HAS FALLEN cool tonight. The current of Juan de Fuca comes right up here, direct from the open Pacific, an ocean so big that summer can't warm it and winter doesn't cool it. She sits close so the fire is hot on her face. She likes the whisky. Peter Gore isn't an alcoholic after all. In fact he's timid with it, is startled that she can knock it back like this. She doesn't tell him it's been years. She wants to drink tonight because, with the heat on her face, it's a time machine. She has felt exactly this glow in the stomach and exactly this heat on her face, on beaches identical to this one.

And Roy is pissing her off, pulling her back. She can pretend it's only her guilt that she feels and not Roy's pain, but of course they are the same thing.

Roy sometimes looks over the rims of his glasses at her. He's still religious but doesn't know it, and this has bugged her because religious people can never be wrong. Whenever he gets sanctimonious, or quotes the Bible — to make moral as opposed to religious points — she calls him Mister Bible-thumper and he'll blush and gently laugh. There's no armor over that spot and she feels cruel.

Roy is unaware that he has a new religion. *Organization*. It's his belief in what politics can do and the view is heaven-like. The only commandment is that government must organize fairly. If a thing's well-organized, the "fairly" is assumed.

Peter Gore has found a big dry log and has dropped it on the fire and it has caught. He sits across from her, one shoe off, gripping his toe and rocking. His face is lit orange, demonic. He has given up on her tonight and is talking to himself.

Evelyn's face is hurting-hot. She takes a gulp and a similar fire burns her throat.

Roy, you can organize everyone and everything, all your buildings and water supply and homeless shelters and carpool lanes but you can't organize away the fear, Roy. Hospital rooms are organized, and drugs organize the living hell out of dying brains there, and thank god for that, but a drugged brain or a hospital ward or a fair city is just a small floating chip on the ocean of immortal fear. We're afraid of *what comes next*. Especially what comes *last*. Everyone is. Petrified. It dooms us. Sorry Mister Bible-thumper, but original sin is *fear*.

Roy's wrong. That's why his fences and newer curbs and sewers and lipstick and ice-cube makers and Nike democracy is bullshit. The *wheel* was bullshit, all the wheel did was help fear move us a little faster. Roy-oy is wrong-ong.

This fire in the stomach, and on the face, is not bullshit. Fire ravages the organization of wood. Shouts its glory with heat. Fire is a picture of our fear. Is fear's cartoon.

EVELYN ROLLS FAST onto her elbows, eyes wide. She hears noises, she forgets where she is. Her head aches. She's in a tent, Peter Gore's tent, yes, pitched poorly, on a slope. It's just past dawn. She remembers cups of whisky.

She has on all the clothes she owns and is wrapped in her blanket. Last night was so cold. Beside her, Peter's shiny black sleeping bag is empty. She can smell its plastic material. She hears it's Peter outside, mumbling and peeing in the near bushes. Through the tent fly she sees him limp into view. Last night he couldn't walk on the toe. Either his gout is getting better, or — she hopes not — he has taken another Demerol. He is in his underwear, little beige bikinis. He goes to water's edge, mumbling. He seems to be considering a swim.

The first time you see someone naked, someone you've seen only in clothes, it's somewhat hallucinogenic. Exposed flesh looks amplified and alien. Even the face is changed, overwhelmed by the big whiteness beneath it. Peter has narrow shoulders, a boy's chest, wide hips. A sizable pouch of beige underwear makes her glance away. There's a patch of quite-black hair around his navel and cousin-like tufts around both nipples. Peter's leg hair is scant, as if rubbed off by pants. His legs, though, are long and fine.

He takes his glasses off and balances them on a branch. With naked face he looks even more vulnerable. He moves like he doesn't own his body. It's like he's too aware of it, puzzled that he has a body at all.

Last night comes back to her. They set up on this less-than-choice sloping rock. She remembers Peter sitting cross-legged, rocking himself, cursing his toe. He gave in and took a Demerol. He got animated after that, and she drank whisky herself because, well, sober, his coming lunacy might not be entertaining. She didn't hold him accountable for his babble, some of which was directed affectionately at her. It began to rain. She got some food into him, got him giggling into his bag, and he was snoring so fast she thought he was still clowning. By then the rain had found its heft and there were no overhanging branches for her tarp ropes and — he was already asleep. It wasn't a bad feeling to curl up beside Peter's sleeping body. She got the sense that, even asleep, he liked it too.

Peter has taken his paddle and stands with it, ankle-deep in the water. She knows he knows she is awake and watching him.

"*Right* then, *ocean*." He lifts his paddle in front of him ritualistically. "Ready for your *scheduled beating*?"

THEY PACK UP and shove off. Peter is chemically boyish and cheerful. Evelyn worries that he's eaten nothing. He's a slack monkey. Empty as a husk. She doesn't want to hear the monkey words in his brain. Demerol does help him roll with his paddling. She doesn't like his sudden laughter, or his lurches to point out things that may or may not be there. "It's Caddy!" is his favorite.

"So how is your toe today?" she asks.

Gore considers the matter for long enough to make Evelyn wonder if he's heard.

"It's a … It's a more … It's a more *distant* agony." Gore thinks again. "It's just as big, but I'm not connected to it. I don't know *who's* … in agony." He giggles softly. "Some *guy*."

"Yikes."

"The bad news is that it's also in my ankle now too."

"Okay, there's a town not that far from here. I think maybe around that point. We could—"

"*That* point?"

Peter jabs a finger at a rock outcrop no more than fifty yards away. He looks so hopeful, she feels sorry for him.

"No, that one. That far one. The one sort of blue-grey in the mist."

"Oh."

"If we go hard we should reach it before the stores close."

"*It has a store?*"

"It's a town. I'm thinking a doctor and then a drugstore. For your toe."

"*There would be a restaurant.*"

Peter falls to a steady paddle, occasionally twitching with effort or dreams, it's hard to say. Evelyn paddles steadily too, wishing she didn't know a town was up ahead, or that its name was Chemainus. Twenty-five years ago she was in a pub there and dared go into the Men's room where Claude had written naughty love notes on the wall. She remembered how long-haired men turned, unsurprised, smiling from their urinals.

Can her will hold, or will she let Peter Gore take her to a restaurant?

One thing about Peter Gore on Demerol: it turns her the opposite direction, makes her only practical. Practical and steady and certain as rock. "Right, then. It's *time*. Would you like to hear the *worst story in the world*?" Peter waits, tantalized with himself. He takes her silence as assent. "I heard this from a *friend*, who knew this *fellow* who knew the fellow it *happened* to. So it's maybe *slightly* urban-mythic but lets say *not*."

"I don't like the smell of this already."

"Actually it *is* about bathing. This guy has a *bath*. While *in* the bath he—masturbates."

His thrill in saying the word. Last night was some of the same talk and Peter's forgotten.

"It *does* happen. The fellow's forty and has a wife, but it *does* happen. He also has a fifteen-year-old *daughter* who, some *several* months after said bath, announces that she is *pregnant*. She *also* claims to be a virgin still. *Claims* in fact to have never, in her terms, 'even fooled *around*.' Her mother naturally doesn't believe her. Her *father*, for some reason, does."

Eve smells where this is going.

"He *does* because he recalls the shame he felt after masturbating in the bath, especially as said daughter had a bath not an hour afterwards. Seems there was this textured bath mat, where *whatever* can lodge in and *survive* and *wiggle-while-waiting* and what have you."

"...Ow..."

"*Indeed*. Mother, very *religious*, won't *allow* talk of abortion. Father, *too* horrified to say a word, *mysteriously* refuses mother's demand that daughter undergo a paternity test—"

"They don't do paternity tests on a fetus."

"*Something*, then. Mother suspects father of rape and daughter of collusion. By the time father *admits* to his little wank, the family is in ruins and here in an urban, non-Ozark family we have a baby boy whose *father* is his *grand*father and a girl whose *brother* is her *son*."

Evelyn says nothing. Maybe things like this do happen. And maybe Peter does remember last night. His anecdote is a weird rejoinder to her own paternity-mess that she described. Fine. She won't bother to explain that, despite her mess, and despite Tommy's wildness resembling his biological father's, she still doesn't buy into the thought that paternity equals destiny. It would have been easy to blame Tommy's soul on Claude. But she couldn't *see* it. Tommy, unfortunately, was his own man. Was in a class of his own. That first look he gave her—before he reluctantly sucked, and slept—that first look stopped her heart. No mean feat, her heart being so ripe with first-born rapture. His eyes, with fluent pre-language, quickly checked her out and told her to fuck off.

"What do you think, Peter. Would it be an even better story if a fourteen-year-old boy dillies himself in the bath and impregnates his forty-year-old mother?"

Gore pictures it, does an exaggerated squirm. "That's just sort of..."

"Or he's twelve, it's his very first dilly, and his mother's fifty? She has breast cancer?"

"*You win.*" His hand up asks that she stop. He adds, "Now we're into Greek *drama.*"

Last night when he called her a witch he seemed serious, though with Peter you can never tell. Funny, but she sees him similarly. A grizzled, prescient elf. She senses that he sees through her and he isn't impressed. Why is it we confer wizardry on the English? Something about the mists of their olde island. Their affinity with moles and toads. They kneel in their garden shooing faeries. The way they talk is literally charming. Even the dullest tea-biddy with her pinky out—if she had cause she'd cast that spell and your life would be a stinking bruise.

Shut up. Peter Gore lolls ahead of her. Her muscles are pushing him to a drugstore. Why aren't these facts enough? Why her need to babble silently on and on, to distract herself from the gloss of these kelp bulbs, or that submerged rock spotted with purple sea stars? Above, a gull mews... exotic melancholy. How can she be bored with any of this *long enough to have a single thought*? Let alone a train of nonsense that sees Peter Gore as a wizard?

She loves a bumper-sticker she saw in Victoria: *My Second Car is a Broom*. She loves what she read later in the library (research inspired by the bumper-sticker), how the myth of the flying broomstick came from witches' use of drugs. They learned that hallucinogenic but poisonous herbs could more safely be rubbed into mucous membranes. They soaked a stick of wood in a lysergic brew and, doffing their medieval knickers, straddled it to take psychoactive and maybe also sexual flight—without leaving the room.

She pictures Peter Gore naked, riding a drug-soaked broomstick, a magic dildo. Though visually lunatic it is not a ridiculous stretch—he is English, playing up there in the bow, goofy on Demerol.

As if answering this last thought Peter giggles, and when she asks him what's so funny he says, his accent not so charming, "This *black* paint scrapes right *off*. This *black* boat's actually *white*."

Evelyn sees his elbow working, hears the scritching of a fingernail.

"*Don't scrape the paint*." Oh, she hates that voice. She hasn't heard it in a while.

"'Kay," Peter chirps, his fingernail scritching away.

AT THE CHEMAINUS government dock an old Native fellow with a cane knows everything: there's no clinic, but a drugstore closes in ten minutes. It's a five minute walk. Evelyn repeats this to Peter Gore as he sits hunched in the kayak, gripping a dock cleat, barely hanging on, forlorn at her insistence that they won't be staying in a hotel. Low clouds fly overhead — he is in and out of the sun but too imbecilic to blink as he gazes wistfully at the waterfront buildings of Chemainus. Low and grey — though some have murals painted on their brick sides — they remind Evelyn of the fifties, of the phrase "five and dime." Peter is seeing the skyline of San Francisco.

Only after the police car above them rolls away does she remember the boat they sit in is stolen and worth a few thousand dollars. She hates being back among people and complications. She might smell the smell here. Her stomach clenches.

Holding a hand up, without looking at her, he lets her help extract him from the boat. Evelyn sees what he's scraped in the black paint in front of his cockpit: about the size of a peach, a bright white love heart.

"Peter?"

"Hmm?"

"Please don't scrape the paint off."

"Didn't mean to," he says.

A befuddled stork, Peter limps off up the ramp. Evelyn stays behind to guard their things. The notion of "drugstore" has unsteadied her. Seven years of anti-depressants. Various prescriptions, the effects of each forcing her unawares into a different-shaped room, the walls of which she couldn't quite see. Each new room blocked certain moods and a certain kind of sight.

Kayak tied securely, wet stuff spread on the dock to dry, Evelyn catches her breath and wonders how she feels now. Not feels. Is. Her body is strong, she can see new muscles in her arms. Her lungs go deeper. She can sleep anywhere. All this feels like *mental* health. She is not as scrambled as she was in Victoria, then on Sidney Spit. She wasn't *wrong* then, she still agrees with what she did and didn't do, but she was confused, no doubt about that. For instance, her thoughts now last longer. She can think in paragraphs.

PETER THUDS DOWN the ramp, still limping but cheerful again. He has forgotten to buy the bag of apples and oranges she requested. Evelyn makes her scurvy joke again and Peter startles at this and wants to go back for lemons but there is no time. Evelyn has only to mention the cop car and he obediently picks up his paddle.

Truth is, she needs to move. She is glad they have escaped town without buying food or filling water containers. She has to pee and is glad she didn't. She tells Peter they will stop at the first good place and he is a sad child made happy. She wants to find a small beach, build a fire and smell its smoke, stare into its changing apricot, orange, feel its heat.

They leave Chemainus harbour. One good thing about kayaks is that wildlife carries on as if you were a bumpy log floating past. Just overhead, a seagull drops a clam, trying to break it open. It splashes into the water beside the bald, car-size rock that was its target.

"Missed," says Evelyn.

Gore digests what he's seen.

"Well *look* at that. I believe he was *aiming* at that rock."

"He was."

"He's using the planet as a *tool*."

"They don't usually have to aim. In town they use parking lots."

"No, these *sea*gulls are using the earth's *protuberances* as *tools*. They are using the *earth's warts* as their *dining implements*."

"I think it would be good for both of us if you didn't talk for a while."

"Right. Fine. I will *stop*. Then, in an *hour*, I will open my mouth and *you will receive your scheduled beating*."

"You took another Demerol."

"The pills the druggist had didn't work."

"It was *fifteen minutes*."

Gore ignores her and begins some childishly earnest paddling, as if he suddenly knew where he was headed and why.

The sun is dipping behind Vancouver Island. A deeply-enriched evening light shines on all she sees. Shoreline green glows luminescent, beach boulders reflect the sun almost painfully; the sky is thunderously blue; the kayak's black paint gains an interesting, a more noble depth. Even Peter is beautiful: the sunward side of his face glows in a hundred colours of hair and freckle and a changeable sea of skin. It's bright for this time of evening. This time of year, she could paddle till very late and still read the *Mustang* label on Peter's lifejacket. She could still do her nails. She could read the lines of her palm. She wonders if it's possible to teach oneself palmistry. Well, the first palm reader did exactly that.

"Evelyn?"

Somehow, they have rounded the point and she can no longer see Chemainus. She's aware that Gore has not been stroking. Paddle balanced in front of him, he's rifling the pages of a book. She can smell that the book is new, its chemical waft.

"Evelyn?"

"What."

"Do you want to hear about your son, Tom?"

"What — what do you mean?"

"I have some information. Do you want to hear it?"

"What do you mean?" She won't yell at him.

"I picked this up at the drugstore," he says. He hoists the book over his head so she can see it. "A good one. *Lost Utopias*. Island history." He clears his throat. "Did you know, that '*Sointula*,' the place you think your son is, is Finnish for '*harmony*'?"

"I didn't know that," Evelyn says softly.

She is no longer proud of her mental health. She no longer wants to think in paragraphs. How is it possible she's forgotten where she's going? How is it possible she's forgotten Tommy? And forgotten what — who — is in her pocket?

It's clear to her now that to stop seeing, and start thinking, is to lose one's mind. Even while knowing this, and even while scared by it, she watches herself enter a paragraph where she meets Tommy again. She has paddled a long way. She is as old as she is now, but Tommy looks closer to fifteen than twenty-five. The paragraph, the daydream, doesn't know what face to give him. They are on a wooden dock, not unlike the one they've just left. They shyly but deliberately search each other's eyes for evidence of love and they both find some, it looks like shy lit candles, and the empty space between them is warmed, and they hug. Hugging, they both relax and feel each others' chests empty out on a breath of peace.

"Mother, I want to marry," said Mink.—"Who is it?" —"Oh! It is this Kelp!"—"Nonsense!" said Mother. —"I like her because she has long hair."—"Then go!"—Then Mink married Kelp. He embraced her. "Go down on ground! Go down on ground! Go down on ground!" he said.—"We shall do so by and by," said Kelp, "when the ebb-tide is half."—"Let us do it now."—"You are a funny fellow," said Kelp. "And I pity you, for you will soon be out of breath."

— FRANZ BOAS, *KWAKIUTL TALES*

OUTER CHEMAINUS BAY

GORE WAS STARTLED to find *Lost Utopias* in a drugstore, in a small town. Unbelievable, really. Of all the books he'd read on the region it was perhaps his favorite and, since he'd had to order it from a small press, he'd considered it rather rare. But here it was on a tourist rack at the check out, alongside *How To Catch Salmon*, *Haunted BC*, and *Island Backpacking*. He refuses to let this cheapen the book for him. He thinks it was *this* book, this one in his hand, that solidified his theory, made him nod once and declare "Right then," and commence this journey at all. The cover is rather garish, though, a glossy green and yellow shout. Well, perhaps that's the Demerol shouting.

He thinks he knows some parts by heart.

He puts down the paddle, wiggles some ease into his bum bones and up his spine. Eve has demanded to hear about Sointula. Positioning the book the correct distance from his face he begins to read aloud the chapter called "The Search for Harmony." He is more than happy to divulge something of her Tom to her.

"'European pioneers typically arrived on the West Coast completely unprepared for a wilderness the likes of which they had never seen.'"

Demerol or not, he feels deliciously *ripe* as he reads. Gliding on a thrilling mirror, propelled from behind by a mad woman he might be mad about. He holds the book up like a schoolboy and reads from it just loud enough for her to hear. The scene is breathlessly pristine.

He will remember, for the writing of his own book, that the sea which bears him up is the welling quivering tear of the planet. To his left a bank of trees drifts by, teasing one cheek, while the expanse of sea to his right calms the other cheek. Above, low orange sunset clouds ruffle his hair.

He is pleased to review this story of Sointula. It embodies his own book's main thrust, the idea that here is the spot on the globe where people fled as far as possible and could go no further. What kind of place would that be? What kind of people would result? Would a visitor find massed cranky folks, bitter to have woken from a dream? Emily Carr, that unlikely woman who traveled alone in the late-1800s to paint remote Indian villages, wrote that Vancouver Island was *another big step west past the wild west.* Gore likes that. Emily, exactly what is *past wild*?

He reads: "'... and thus, in 1901, over one hundred Finns preceded Kurikka to their new home on Malcolm Island, off Vancouver Island's northern tip. They arrived with a cow, but lacked grassland on which it could feed. They had seed, but there was no place to sow it. One can imagine those first settlers timid on the beach, appraising their home for the first time. Perhaps there were moans of disbelief. For their new paradise was continuously treed, and the smallest of these trees was bigger than anything in Europe. Typically the trees were giants — Douglas Firs, western red cedars, Sitka Spruce — around which two men could not come close to joining hands. And typically these hands were those of artists, or school teachers, Marxists, hands which had never held an ax.'"

"Kurrika?"

"Their charismatic socialist *leader*. These people moved to Malcolm Island without even having *seen* it."

"I thought it was called Sointula. Harmony."

"That's what they named the village. It *meant* —" Gore flips back a page. "'Harmony among people and with nature that houses them.' They built private little shanties and all ate in this big building.

'Food taken in common represented the equality of all citizens.' Every night it was potatoes and salted raw salmon. The women wore long dresses even when they spaded turnips in the muck." Gore finds himself giggling under his breath.

"That's not a bad diet, really, except for some greens."

"Want to hear some more?" Adding, "About Tom?"

Evelyn doesn't answer, which means yes. While she paddles along, Gore skims silently, searching for good parts. Kurrika turned out to be a hopeless dreamer. His schemes to build a lumber industry landed the colony in ruin. He traveled south to civilization and returned not with seeds and tools, but new musical instruments, which he would proudly unwrap on the dock at the feet of the breathless hungry colonists. A handsome bachelor, Kurrika tried to have marriage banned, arguing that men, and in particular women, should in no way be owned. His theory sounded fine in that utopian sort of way, but it soon became clear that Kurrika — who had clean fingernails because his job was to think and write all day — was getting luckier than anyone else.

Eventually Evelyn asks, "What happened to them?"

"It fell apart. They always fall apart. There was this settlement of Danes on Cape Scott that fell apart because their goats were picked off by cougars. Imagine, it's funny, a bunch of —"

"What happened to Sointula?"

"— a bunch of *Danes* move to *Canada* and get driven out by *lions*. Actually, the north part of the island where we're headed *swarms* with them, with *lions*. And there was another utopia set up by this fellow who called himself Brother Twelve who attracted filthy rich people from New York and whatnot to bring their money and come live in little huts surrounding his much *bigger* hut. They say there's still followers there. Old and bent, and practicing black magic. They speak to *no one*. De Courcey Island."

"That's just up there." Evelyn sticks her paddle very near Gore's face, deliberately he thinks, indicating the far distance. "A couple days away."

"*Really*. Maybe we'll find the *gold*. He made off with a boat full of gold *bullion*, and they found the boat crashed on the beach, but no *gold* and no Brother *Twelve*. The gold is just *waiting* for us. *Paddle*."

Eve's pace doesn't change. She's not in a joking mood. She rarely is. He could help her in that. He could get her laughing. He pictures them finding the gold, and melting it down, using a contraption involving a grand beach fire and conveyor belt of cedar bark and clamshells, and he will fashion a gold helmet and boots for her, and great broad shoulder-pads and wrist shields and codpiece for him and — he really should eat something soon. He also realizes he's been dwelling on the cigar tube in Evelyn's shorts pocket. He can't see it but it's there. The grit and dust of Claude's sad ashes must be an insistent nugget of gold, because why in hell else carry it?

"I sort of like that," Eve is saying now. "Tom being up there. A place called Harmony."

Gore grunts a hollow agreement. *Sointula*. He doesn't tell her that, given the tragic fire, and financial scandals, and in general the evil weather and gnashing teeth and futile, back-breaking labour that came to characterize Sointula, its name could now be used in no way but the *ironic*. The Finns that stayed — about two hundred — settled into socialist poverty, fishing. In the late sixties a second smash of utopians moved up from urban America, barging in on the Finns and bringing their acid and alfalfa sprouts and naked dances under solstice moons, whereupon Sointula enjoyed several more fires, and more than one shooting. Harmony.

Gore picks up his head and eyes the beautifully gliding world with suspicion. Nature looks harmonious enough if you don't add people to it. Harmonious, that is, if the jurisdiction of that word includes a bear ripping apart a skunk in a frenzy of spilled stench and roaring.

"So you think he might be happier there," Gore says, apropos only of keeping his ironies to himself.

"Hmmm. Dealing drugs in the city and getting attacked, or studying whales in a wilderness setting..."

Gore can forgive her sarcasm. Oh, these failed private utopias that are families. He does not understand parenthood but he has often witnessed its glue. For instance, that stickiness in Victoria during the sad whale watching excursion, that American father and his daughter — at least one assumes she was his daughter. He in his Canadian-flag tourist toque, and dangling binoculars and camera; she with her tongue stud and cynical slouch, bored out of spite. Gore heard her called Angel, that most hopeful of parental labels. She did perk up when whales were sighted but slouched anew at the onset of Dad's public remarks. "Dang," he announced to the whole boat, "these are majestic creatures." So loud with his cliches. Once, sounding just like Bill Clinton, "Come ta Papa, big guy, ah need a foe-toe." Snapping pictures one-handed, he had his other arm around her shoulders in a *Isn't this magical, the two of us here?* trap. Rejecting quality time, Angel edged away, keeping Dad off-balance, straining their glue.

Watching them made Gore glad to be childless. Hearing Eve darkmumble on about her nasty Tom, he is doubly-glad. He recoils from her family. He doesn't want to tell Eve, but Roy sickens him. Kind, pious people, especially kind, pious Americans, are slyly noxious, they remind him of adult singers of children's songs, none of whom he ever encounters without twistings of stomach. Sure, they get down on all fours to kid-level and engage in ways Gore hopelessly can not, but the question is — why? Something twisty going on in all that happy googoo. How could any parent resist attacking a fellow adult who with big smiles and American primary colours had warping hold of their children's minds? *Stealing their utopian glue.*

"Peter?"

Pious politicians — they were *just* like that. Especially *Canadians.* Sickening goody-goodies. Or maybe it was just his name. *Roy.*

"Peter?"

"What."

Her paddle calms. She stops sending splash-drops to his neck.

"How are you?"

"What do you *mean.*"

"You're tilting way over to the side. Can't you feel that? You've been tilted like that for five or ten minutes."

"I'm not 'tilted'."

"Jesus."

"I'm 'resting'."

"It really looks like it hurts."

He refuses to straighten up for another minute or so, and then he straightens only gradually. As he does so, the witch gives him another tidbit to chew on.

"There's this idea about men around your age who get seriously ill," she begins, and Gore knows this will be bad. "Basically it's that men who run out of life challenges *make* themselves sick so they'll have a new challenge: survival."

She says it's something she's read, but Gore is certain she's staring right through his back and organs and is telling him what she sees.

He refuses to entertain her notion. But wonders if it could be true. No, it could not. He's writing a book. Which is proving a *challenge*. There is no other word for it. A huge and *healthy* challenge if ever there was. And Eve is a challenge as well. As is this paddling, from a tilt. The witch is only wrong.

THEY ARE TRYING to find a place to stop and rest and have lunch.

"There?" asks Gore, pointing to another break in the steep rock bank, a wisp of beach. He has a kink in his neck from looking always left.

"There's probably people," Evelyn says again.

And they paddle. They've been keeping to the Vancouver Island shoreline (which is hard not to think of as the mainland) as opposed to the outer islands (Galiano and Valdez, Eve reluctantly informs him), which have plenty of deserted beach but no fresh water. The Vancouver Island shore has streams and rivers but is populated to the point that any place beachable has long housed a home or two, if not a small subdivision, and Eve appears loathe to mix with the public.

It strikes Gore that she doesn't want to stop because she's actually in a hurry to see her son Tom and might not know this herself. Into the silence he ventures, "You really want to get up there and see him, don't you?"

Eve doesn't answer, save for a stutter in her paddling, which is answer enough.

Labouring north to cuddle her only child. He feels a sad warmth not just for Tom but for himself as well. Only-children unite. Gail was one, and on this subject they sometimes bowed their heads over a glass of wine and commiserated, perhaps seeking a scapegoat for their relationship's failings. It's their parents' fault, of course. Gore pictures the polite hushed dinner table of his childhood, no booming Italian conversations in hot stained undershirts. Parents who stop at one do a rather dribbly job of carrying on the family name, thrusting an awkward genetic waif out into the competition, unprepared due to a lack of sibling battery. As families, threesomes are sickly of stature, a wobbly triangle. Sickly family, prone to imbalance, if not craziness and —

"Evelyn. Tell me. You aren't an only child by any chance, are you?"

"Yes. Why?"

"No reason." Though of course the witch knows.

At times they can see the Island Highway, the sun reflecting off the distant cars and trucks travelling north just like them. They go so much faster they automatically make Gore yearn to be with them, make him want to call out, climb in the back with the happy kids clutching their cold Cokes, going somewhere great. They belong to a modern world he has for some reason relinquished. Worse, their speed creates the illusion that he is moving backwards — maybe this is no illusion in some currents — and that he is the innocent flailing dupe of someone's satire.

"Keep us steady a minute."

Gore obeys by rote, holding his paddle in front of him like a highwire artist. He feels her maneuvers in his own hips and adjusts for them. He hears the period of concentration and then the tinkling in the mason jar. He tries not to let himself be excited by this again;

he knows it's also the intimacy, the trust, that arouses him. Despite years of marriage, he has never been this close to a woman peeing. Gail not only kicked him out, she always locked the door. Gail loved that the bathroom fan was loud.

He hears the final punctuation of tinkles, a stuttering of commas so like his own — well, why wouldn't those muscles be the same? Then the pouring over the side, the rinsing of the jar, the re-maneuvers to up the knickers and settle herself, the chirped, "Thanks," and a fresh digging in of her paddle that actually puts his head back with acceleration. He lets it fall completely back and stay that way, with his arms still up to walk the wire, until she barks at him to resume paddling. At which point he promises himself that he will now officially stop taking Demerol. It has killed his pain but now his heart is a yo-yo made of jelly, weeping on the way down and laughing on the way up. The drug has no more meaning than that.

Her peeing has enlivened him in more ways than one. Now he has to pee too and he can't do it in the boat. As he has all along, he uses clumsiness as his excuse. It's time for the mid-day break anyway and with minimal grumbling she drops him off near an auspicious creek-mouth. His chores include the water jug to fill, and a fire to make for the ling cod she says she will jig from the nearby kelp. She has promised him it is not all seafood he mustn't eat, just sardines and shellfish. He doesn't really care anymore. He's got drugs enough to combat any disease he decides to *challenge* himself with, and at this point he's hungry enough to eat whatever foolishly strays near his face.

He limps up twenty feet of nameless beach. He not only has to pee: he feels, with not a little apprehension, that it's also time for the daily hunch. He hates it. Hates it enough to stop eating, for good. Refuse to feed the top hole and the bottom hole will cease to be of concern. He loves biology but hates participating, hates this one function particularly.

He taps the last of the toilet paper flattened in his pocket, takes a breath, scans the wall of forest and wonders where he can get most hidden. From the brambles of his brain he hears a voice he hasn't heard for a decade at least: his late father, asking his wry yet booming, "*Do Gores shit in the woods?*" His father's English toilet humour tended to the upper class, that is, secretly cruder than the other classes. He could be a funny man. As funny as his mother was not. He pictures Mum's response to Dad's pun: she shuts her eyes tightly and flaps both hands at the air in front of her face. His father likely didn't have a very full sex life either. Though Peter doesn't want to know in any case.

His father had his elegant side. In fact he sometimes looked on the verge of wearing an ascot. Peter hears his father repeat his pun in a way that demands an answer, "*Do* Gores shit in the woods?" Then his father assumes his most ascotian manner to answer himself with soft, Oxonian disgust: "No."

Father, unfortunately we do. It is one of the dangers of hitching one's wagon to an earth mother's star. Gore steps up through the hedge of salal and in past the first stand of trees. He finds a small clearing, stands, and gazes around. All is cool and quiet. He unzips, pulls down, and startles to sudden hearty laughter, off in the woods. The laughter is quite distant but the timing is impeccable. Gore dips his head to the god of comic coincidence.

It is now, this second, that Peter Gore allows himself to admit that he hates wilderness. It's fine for briefly visiting but hell if one has to exist in it, to make do. Or do-do. At least the campsites had outhouses. The first day in the wilderness with Eve he'd merely held it in, pretending it would go away. It didn't, and the next day was more insistent, and he tried sitting off the edge of a log. There were spiders in the bark grooves and he discovered that you have to sit so far off the edge you can't not fall back into your mess. He squatted desperately with pants at ankles and narrowly missed an Armageddon on his pants and socks. So today he decides to get completely naked.

Humming, pretending he's not in hell, Gore hangs his clothing from tree limbs, even his shirt. He drapes and arranges it like ornaments, delaying. When reality finally insists, he whimpers and falls into position. He can see himself through the eyes of all the people, including Eve, who are of course watching him: squatting on all fours, knees cocked near his ears, he is a hellish white amphibian, a splayed, trembling frog-monster looking fearfully around, doing his nasty as fast as possible, making his noises and stink.

But you really do feel marvelous after such ordeals are over. Empty and fresh, Gore dresses leisurely, as if it's a beautifully showered morning and all his lessons are planned. He whistles while covering his mess with leaves and sticks and then exits the forest with little hurry. He wonders which bird is making that delightful noise. Or is that a chipmunk?

JUST LIKE GAIL, Eve can get mad at him so quickly. All he's done is offer the boys some whisky.

He had the fire going nicely (he had to use the rest of the toilet paper but he hasn't yet told Eve) and was at the creek filling the water jug, a long process as it was shallow and he had to hand-fill it with a cup. The jug was half-full when he heard a horrified, "Holy shit! *Sorry*!"

Around a bend twenty feet upstream stood a young fellow of perhaps sixteen, peeing in the creek. It took Gore a few seconds to understand that the boy was apologizing for in effect peeing in their drinking water. The boy came running at him now, hissing and sputtering.

"Jeez, *man*, didn't *see* you there." He had on a backwards ball cap and the baggiest trousers Gore had ever seen, with several inches of boxer shorts visible at the waist. He wore what Gore termed a muscle-shirt, and this lad wore it for good reason. On some of the larger muscles were tattoos.

"It's truly no problem."

"*Jeez* didn't *see* ya." The wheezing lad was almost upon him and it looked frighteningly like the boy might want to shake his hand or give him something.

"It's a simple case of my pouring *this* out," and Gore began to do so, "*wait* for your particular 'segment of stream' to pass by, and then *refill* it."

The lad stopped, stared at him, then bent double with pent hissing laughter. He found everything quite hilarious. He gulped and hooted. Talking was not easy for him, and he reminded Gore of students who occupied the back row of his classroom. It dawned on him that this boy was stupendously stoned. At this point, two of the boy's colleagues appeared out of the bushes, and Gore found himself helplessly asking, "Would you fellows care for some *whisky*?"

He wonders now if he didn't offer it out of fear, perhaps in the spirit of his predecessors giving beads and mirrors to armed Natives who emerged suddenly from the woods. Or was his a genuine author's interest in island youth? In any case it seems he and Eve have beached at their "party place." The five of them sit around Gore's fire and Eve is aggressively monosyllabic. (To his dismay he finds her sexier angry. He did not want it to be this way.) The boys have declined his offer of fried ling cod but not his offer of whisky. They pass his bottle back and forth like it's some kind of race. A joint comes lit out of nowhere and Gore witnesses more workmanlike efficiency. When they are well into the meat of the bottle the boys are no different for it — and Gore sees that he is gulping at least his share. He hasn't asked Eve if she wants any because, well, look at her face.

Getting to know them is slow going, though the boys do loosen up and act less weird, their early attempts at conversation having been incomprehensible. Lots of hissing laughter and staring at him and Evelyn, as if the two of them were exotic entertainment. Gore has heard that the BC marijuana is famously strong. Indeed, it feels so — in the spirit of cultural anthropology he has had two deep puffs and his heart has begun to lope sideways and his skull to pressurize from within. These lads here don't make him miss his job but they do kindle a certain nostalgia. Boys of this sort sometimes liked him, that wry minority who not only got his humour (hard for Americans) but understood that he played the role of teacher just as they did the role of student. He had to tell them to quieten down and they had to obey, but despite these clanging rules one could still enjoy the civilizing spice of irony.

"So, where you *kayaking* to?" asks Jamie, the one with the tattooed muscles. Even this question cracks them up and Gore has to wait for more wheezes to subside.

"Sointula."

None of the boys has heard of it. They start listing places they have heard of. Gore pretends to listen but takes note of the other two. One, whose name appears to be Ring, looks very possibly mean. He sits too straight, too ready, a posture of taking offense in advance. His hair is the most tightly kinked Gore has seen, like sprung felt; so tight it looks packed full of dust, though of course it couldn't be. Ring listens with a sneer and coughs out disagreements. The other, whose name Gore instantly forgot, appears stupid and ashamed to say much, even to his friends. Skinny, he sits slouched with elbows on knees, head falling forward between his shoulders like a cartoon vulture. He nods slowly in constant accord with whatever gets said.

"So, you lads from *around* here?"

Ring is, and No-name is. Jamie came from Toronto two years ago. They look dismissive of this line of questioning.

"And do *any* of you feel an itch to *leave*?"

The three don't know what to make of this and decide he is criticizing their rural life. They rise in defense of their turf, admitting there aren't any jobs but just look at the place. Ring nods sharply out at the hazy distant islands, says, "I mean this is fuckin' paradise. The Valley's okay, man. Where *you* from?"

Gore peers around him. "Valley?"

Jamie says, "Cowichan Valley, man."

Gore doesn't care for the silence that befalls the beach fire circle. He doesn't care for the disjointedness of the marijuana, or his own faintly nagging *Jeopardy* voice announcing that Cowichan means "the warm place." Eve tells them — he thinks rather clumsily — that "Peter is writing a book," her tone suggesting that this is why he asks silly questions. The boys' interest is tweaked, though Gore understands that they must keep their cool at all costs and not show genuine interest.

"What is — what's it — about?" ventures No-name. Now Gore sees that No-name is only dysfunctionally stoned rather than stupid and ashamed.

"It's about —" Gore stops, shrugs and spreads his hands, palms out. "This."

"This?" asks Jamie.

Gore nods rapidly.

"This eternal moment?" Jamie asks. He snickers and his friends follow suit. Gore sees Jamie anew. He notes that two of his tattoos are calligraphies of Asian characters.

"He's writing a travel book," says Eve, again trying to save the day, but with inadequate information. The book is so much more than that. He wonders whether to explain it further. His descriptive powers may not be up to snuff. He may have just slurred. He will suffer Eve's modest description. Though he does feel rather betrayed.

"A 'travel book' that will scatter gore and rage on every page," he says eye-to-eye with Jamie, to give him a little taste.

"Sick," Jamie says, nodding.

Gore is jostled by this word. It brings to mind a TV show, a snowy mountain, *sick* jumps and crashes, boys in toques and nose rings, cooly talking in code.

"You're *snowboarders*," Gore tells the three friends.

They stare at him, not comprehending. No-name appears concerned, like he might in fact be a snowboarder but all this time didn't know.

"Your use of the word 'sick'," he tells Jamie, and Jamie simply squints, not helping at all. "'*Sick*' used as a, used as a, as a, as a *word* which ..." What is it exactly? As an "opposite" is not quite it, though it's in the ballpark. "As a, as a, as a, as a — As a word which — As an indication of, of, of — Ah, of, of —" This is okay, he is smiling now and the fellows are too. "An indication of, of, of, of, of—" This is fun. "Of, of, of, of—Of ah, of ah, of ah, of ah ah ah ah ah, *ah ah ah ah*—"

"Stop it."

It's Eve who pops his bubble and Gore is disappointed with her. It's a kind of cowardice. There was no telling how wide and high his bubble might have grown. The lads had seemed willing.

Eve walks a plate of fish to him and presents it in such a way that he has no choice in the matter. Fine. He accepts the protein. Indeed he should eat. He has had his share of whisky and the bottle is empty. The fish under his chin steams up a cooked smell that warms and opens the pores of his face. He takes one bite and quickly another, and it's really very good, this ling cod, and he watches in surprise how fast he eats it all down. It's good indeed, the best fish he's ever had. He peers over the rim of fry-pan to see if there's more, but that's it for the ling. He spots Eve watching him. Bewitching him. He bravely meets her eye.

"*Let's* hope this fish doesn't swim straight to my toe."

By way of explanation he tells the lads he probably shouldn't have eaten that fish because this evil sorceress here is trying to poison him. He lapses into a western accent, which he always does passably well, to tell them his goddamn gout 'n' gall bladder lets him eat only beans 'n' whisky. The kids look vaguely startled, so he announces even more forcefully:

"I'm doin' the rim on beans 'n' whisky." And repeats it, with a tuneful little change, "Doin' the rim on beans 'n' whisky, yes *sir*." He sings it again louder, and is about to continue when Eve interrupts him.

"You're scaring all the ghosts away." She turns to the boys. "And so are you."

She sounds sincere, and sad, almost pleading. The three young men, restless, glance at each other.

Jamie asks Gore, "Got any more to drink, my man?"

Gore reaches for his pack.

"*No*," says Eve. "We don't."

She stares hard at Gore. One of them, Ring, laughs *Whoa!*

"Well, lads." Gore smiles, his tone of voice a wink. "Seems we're fresh out."

The boys get up. Eve begins to knock stuff together by way of packing. She tosses the fry-pan at Gore's feet and says it needs scrubbing out with sand. She hands the empty whisky bottle to Jamie and asks him to please dispose of it properly.

It dawns on Gore that she might be overly sensitive to drunken teenagers, given the history of her Tom. Otherwise, Gore finds that he's smiling. He doesn't mind being told what to do. It feels somewhat nostalgic. It is a groove he can settle into. Switch off the will and enjoy the scenery. Most of all, he likes the way she put it. *We don't.* We. He can feel this word in his warmest middle.

"Hey, no," Jamie is saying, eyes lit. He takes the bottle from her and peers into its neck. "We'll write a note." He and his cronies grow a bit animated with this plan, properly excited, as kids should be, and they float opening lines. No-name suggests, "No one's in now, please leave a message." Ring offers, "If you have touched this paper it is already too late for you." They enjoy a round of wit about lowest-tech terrorism, real-bad-cold-in-a-bottle. And look at this, Eve is smiling too. Gore decides he's glad to have encountered them. They are decent young men out in nature and not lying slack-jawed on the couch, faces flickering idiot-box blue.

Gail often watched TV in the dark, lying on her back. Her face bathed in the sad light of what has become the new hearth-fire. Gore thinks he may have had this thought as far back as when he was first planning this trip. When he would watch Gail watch TV.

The boys leave, not seeing his wave. Eve finishes burying their fire and walks toward him. It is a charged moment. For one, she is wearing her shorts, in the front pocket of which is her cigar tube, and it looks shockingly like a penis. For another, he thinks that, from the angle of her approach and the soft way she meets his eye, they might be about to hug. He brings his hands up half way. She simply passes him. He cannot tell if she noticed his hands.

"Evelyn?"

"Yes?"

"I'd like to sit in the back this afternoon."

"Sure you're up to it?"

He scans the water, notes the light chop which will make a bit of noise on the hull and bounce them a tiniest bit. His plan is to sit in back and masturbate. It is scheduled and it is his right.

"Yes."

FIGHTING GULLS BRING him round. Early evening. He wasn't exactly asleep. He finds himself sitting in the back, paddling feebly. For as long as he can remember, Evelyn has been commanding him, "Left. ... No, *left*." Demerol won't allow him the telltale pain but he is hung-over from the afternoon's whisky. And it seems the druggist's pills have kicked in because his toe and ankle hardly exist. In his brain, several places generate thoughts, all making noise at the same time and all of them suspect. He remembers little of this morning, or yesterday, and registers only what's in front of his face. Why's he in the back? Oh yes. Oh my. Right. He's greatly happy it had proven too tight to get the hand in there. Could've been a disaster, Eve learning she was in a kayak with a monster.

These gulls are nasty loud creatures. Come to think of it, maybe *they've* been generating his thoughts. A broad-chested bully has driven off the lesser gulls with screams and pecks while their fish-spine prize coyly sinks away. All for naught. Naught for all. Joni Mitchell would write a song about gulls fighting as a spine-dinner sinks. Or maybe she wouldn't. In any case she was from around here, said one of the chapters in his book which had finally put him to sleep, or whatever that state was. Gore realizes the sinking spine is Eve's — that is, the remains of the lunch-fish she must have secreted away. He finds he is starving. Why didn't he buy something back in Chemainus? Somehow he'd had time to pop in and buy those two fresh bottles of Irish...

He realizes he's been typing with his toes. His feet are bare; he must have just thrown his shoes into the kayak somewhere; with his toes he can feel his computer and he has been typing. Reams of excellent stuff.

About utopias, about mean-Tommy, dead-Claude (rhymes with toad) and a Brother Thirteen, who no one's heard of yet because he is just this week going to debut in bursts in glory from the deep forest. He typed longest about his own private utopia, which involved a magnificent log house he chopped together himself. The huge main room enjoyed floor-to-ceiling windows such that nature spilled in and in spilled out. An ingenious curving aqueduct of hollowed cedar logs rerouted a stream right through the kitchen. The rear of the house perched at the edge of a cliff and a bathroom (full of vases each clutching a dozen pink roses) stuck right out over the chasm. Into a glorious bench (carved with celtic knot designs) he'd cut a perfect smooth hole that fell away to odourless nowhere. The sleeping loft had a view eagles envied, so much so that eagles joined them. 'Them' being he and Eve.

Of course he couldn't have been typing. His computer is snapped shut like a big square clam and, however close they feel to his brain at the moment, his toes are only toes. But he should have been typing. He *should be typing*. A question from the computer as it broods under his feet: *Why didn't you recharge me at Chemainus?*

"Evelyn?"

She doesn't respond. He knows from the patience in her stroke that she heard him and is saving energy by simply waiting for his question.

"Is there another little town up here somewhere? Before Nanaimo?"

"Ladysmith."

"How far?"

"Maybe a day. Depending on whether you paddle too."

"Fine. But could I interest you in a *motel* room for a night? My treat?"

Eve waits for a time. Then says, "You're getting soft so soon."

"No. I want to plug in my computer. And I can get someone to show me the charger. I really, *really* need to get this book going." Gore hears his voice on the verge of a whimper. It is perhaps actually sincere.

"I'm not going to stay in a motel but you can."

His balloon of dirty romance deflates but he will not let go of the fresh-charged computer.

"But where will — Will you leave me there then? And continue on?" He hopes his voice communicates to her that he would prefer she didn't.

"I'll find a nook somewhere. I'm in no hurry."

"You mean you'll wait for me?"

Sweet Eve says, "I'll wait for you, Peter," mockingly, hers the windswept voice of the fiancée sending her G.I. off to war. Yet she apparently means it: she will wait for him, and this is enough to inflate, in Gore's chest, a balloon of romance that isn't dirty at all.

"Can I use your sleeping bag and tent?" she asks.

"If you want, you can *eat* my sleeping bag and tent."

Gore doesn't know quite what he means by this but, being a madwoman, Eve seems to understand.

"Okay," Evelyn says. "Describe that sky."

"I'm sorry?"

"Describe the sky to me."

She has flicked her head casually to her left, towards what Gore now sees is a very large and rather splendid sunset over the mountains. He hadn't noticed. Eve has delivered a challenge of sorts. All this babbling about his book.

"It's —"

Wait now. It's too easy to fall into the paintbox cliches, the *expected*-gorgeous, which is no doubt the witch's little game. How can he best describe that growing wall of pink and orange? It is certainly looming. It is certainly *tall*. Can you call a sunset 'tall'? He's never heard a sunset described as 'tall' before, so the image is fresh, but fresh doesn't necessary mean good. 'Looming' suggests a cynicism he doesn't feel. This sunset is really very pretty, really quite noble and majestic. These cliched words keep knocking at the insides of his teeth. Can he synthesize, come up with —

"I have it," Gore declares.

Eve responds with a surprised look, as if she's forgotten her own challenge.

"It's a royal French sky."

"What?"

"You are looking at a regal, 15th Century, French *sky*."

"Okay."

"It is. It's a sky we simply don't get anymore. It's a Louie-the-14th neon-ballet *massacre*."

"Well, you know," Eve says quietly, "actually it's the kind of sunset they never used to get here. It's actually a contemporary sky."

Gore knows what she's on about, that sunsets are newly prettier thanks to pollution hanging its stinging lens on the horizon, through which yellow light now shines orange.

"Yes, but it *looks* like Louie-the-14th grandeur."

"I guess so," Eve says, still quiet. "Sad, though."

"*Pretty*-sad."

"We're miles from industry, even *cars*, and the entire sky is still full of shit."

"Maybe industry will come up with *really* wild shit and every sunset will be *rainbow*."

"I guess it's good that you can laugh at it."

"Of *course* it's good."

She doesn't have a rejoinder and Gore lets his victory hover as they cut steadily through the water. He can tell she's deep in her own thoughts now, is staring into a world he can't see, and this is the Eve that makes him the most nervous.

The wind has come up, rippling and making the water fall instantly dark. He sees that half of the sunset's grandeur had been its doubling, its inverse twin lying mirrored on a calm sea.

"Maybe I am in a bit of a hurry. To get to him."

"To Tom. Well, yes. One would think you *would* be."

She doesn't speak for a time but she works her shoulders in such a way that he knows more is coming. Such strong shoulders, not at all unsexy. It occurs to Gore that, in the days they've been together, Eve — Evelyn — has grown steadily stronger. And strongly steady.

Saner.

"I don't know if the number ten is important, really," she begins. "What do you think?"

"As opposed to two or eight?"

"If I get there by his birthday on August 10th it'll be the tenth anniversary of him leaving home. Ten years to the day since I've seen him. 'Course I don't know if numbers *mean* anything. If they're significant. And I'm not even sure of what date it is now. But, I don't know, August 10th might be ... nice."

"He ran away on his *birthday*?"

It takes another sequence of silent steady paddling for her to answer.

"It was sort of a last straw. He was so wild. He was often very mean. Sometimes I would even think the word 'evil.' I learned about sociopaths. That's probably what he is."

"Really."

"I was trying anything. To get to him. Get to his heart. Make him care about something. Even make him *react*. I was failing. Life was hell. So I chose — in a fit of significant numbers, I chose his sixteenth birthday to tell him who his birth father was."

Eve sits still in the bow. It's lovely to be able to watch her for once. From behind like this, his eyes can be all over her. Her cheeks are smooth. Her hair bounces.

"How did he react? I mean —" Gore is careful with his voice, "— other than the 'running away from home' part."

"Just sat there. His back to me, like always. I knew it might make him hate me even more. Maybe —" Evelyn shakes her head. "Maybe I was even trying to pay him back."

"That's understandable."

"But you know what?"

"What."

"After he'd gone — I knew instantly when he was gone — I felt a kind of thanks. In the air."

"I see."

"No, it's hard to explain. But I think I gave him something to do. He could go and find out now where he came from. What blood. What ... wild animal."

Gore does enjoy sitting behind her. Though he requires a lesson in *efficient* steering. While Eve talks he fancies he can see the emotions coming off her into the surrounding air, another of Demerol's little side-shows. They are briefly-coloured and arc in the manner of questions. The wind is gusting now, rather disturbingly, and it blows her emotions away as fast as they arise. He can't see the phallic bulge in her shorts pocket, but many of her emotions gather there and it is clear to him that the bulge in her pocket is his main rival. Quite frankly, Claude is beginning to piss him off, Claude with his accent, honking loudly, nature's gallic aphorist: *Zee eegull, ees not really bald, but whitely feathered.* Poor Eve closes her naive eyes and gently opens her adoring mouth. *Zuh squid, has ink, yet lacks a — how you say — a pen.*

Gore realizes he hates Claude because Claude is shaped like a penis and is pressing her without pause.

He doesn't like the back seat after all. He can't steer and this really is quite the wind building up. He has to say something particularly sparkling to make her turn around — and in his present condition this is very hit or miss. For he loves her face — its sincerety, its innocence, the slightly feline eyes. Every witch's face being, of course, her primary spell.

It's an interesting sky. Fighting itself. Low clouds blow one way and higher clouds another. This wind has become a bona fide nautical problem. It's impossible to steer. Eve is looking around with surprise and concern, searching not just the foulblowing maw of the deathdark horizon, but the shoreline of the nearest island. It's blowing suddenly even harder. Now he has to shout to be heard and it's really very alarming. It is the first time he has seen this kind of worry in her eyes.

"*There?*"

"*Yes!*"

He tries to turn them. The water is black and loud and smells cold, it smells angry. He can't hear what Eve is shouting. He tries to turn them, his arms are bursting, his paddle misses water and he clubs her on the back of the head, not too hard, but it makes her stop and turn around and gaze at him steadily in the thrash and bounce, just fixes him with those gleaming eyes while the rest of the world blows and tosses. The witch is smiling. She cups her hand to the back of her head and there's no question he clubbed her a good one.

Mount Waddington, one of the grandest snow-capped peaks on the coast, sits at the head of Knight Inlet and is a majestic sight from Malcolm Island. But with the mountains of Knight Inlet corralling any clouds in the region, and the prevailing westerlies funneling these clouds to the inlet's head, the peak of Mount Waddington is visible, on average, only five or six days a year. No doubt exaggerating, some locals proudly claim never to have seen it. But one can imagine the Sointula Finns, in their darkest times, cursing that mythical mountain and this grey place they now called their home. Though they were ardent socialists, and to a man Godless, they perhaps felt forsaken by that mountain, as by God, until on those rare cloudless days when Mount Waddington appeared, and they could be believers again.

— DON COTTER, *LOST UTOPIAS*

BERE POINT, MALCOLM ISLAND

SOMETIMES THE ORCA arrive at night, so sometimes Tommy Poole stays here till morning, like he's doing now. Out beside his beach fire he won't sleep except unintentionally, sitting up. He told Cal that once he woke falling sideways to the gravel and he scraped his wrist catching himself. Because the whales might see it he keeps only a small fire, and no fire at all when it's warm, and he's told Cal he thinks he was once sniffed by a cougar. Either that or he was dreaming, something he says he doesn't do and isn't sure he ever did. "Not very well, anyway," was how he said it, making Cal smile fearfully, with her mouth only, not knowing if it was a joke.

Now, almost dawn, maybe to test if she's still awake beside him on this log, he says to Cal, "Not many people think of whales at night."

Though it sounds boastful, Cal knows he's only being factual. He has said to her before: "It's not like they go to sleep on the bottom of the ocean. They're always somewhere. Coming up, breathing. It's what *they're* stuck with."

Cal suspects he's secretly ambitious about his night photography. Though he never talks about it. But at night he sometimes positions himself on a special skinny log closer to water's edge, where at high tide his feet get wet and he won't even care. His "boss lady" told Cal that his night photos had been admired by research centers around the province, and one in California. There was even talk of an arty show in a gallery, or even a book, and that a magazine might buy some if he'd switch to colour. Not that Tom will talk about it. He doesn't even know where he got his camera, which has zippy-fast rewind like a fashion photographer's and a zoom lens that brings the whales closer. He says he has no idea where he got it, or even why. She's seen him stare at it when he picks it up.

She's seen some of the pictures. The flash creates the most eerie effects. The surprise of sleek black fins just arrived out of the deep night. In the flash, the ocean water looks dark and terrifying, a place of drownings. Sometimes it's just their heads poking up with wide open little eyes staring into the camera. They are like human eyes, knowing. But ugly, because their bodies are so big, it's like a human eye transplanted into a wall. One picture shows a whale almost half out of the water up the gravel, other fins out there slicing around, watching their friend (who Cal would swear is grinning) in a dare. She doesn't like the general mood of these pictures. The whales look impatient, or like they're caught holding a secret meeting, something humans weren't meant to see. They don't look evil but they don't look good. She doesn't know what feeling she gets from them. She thinks of magic, and doom, the mood some drugs catch you up in.

Some pictures show a thrashing scene — tails, heads, black, white, splashes. A "rub party" Tom calls those times. Sitting beside him on the log now, her bones hurting, Cal realizes that she doesn't even know why whales come here to this beach, this bank of underwater gravel, why they rub themselves on it in the first place. She thinks he told her it's lice or dead skin or itch, or maybe he said it's all three, or that no one knows which one it is. In any case they use this beach like a giant loofa brush.

It must be four in the morning. It's like some *Survivor* episode, just the two of them left standing, only no million bucks at the end of all the rain and dirt and bark and torture. She wants to go back to the tent but she's afraid to walk it alone. She won't ask him again. "Nothing's gonna get you," he'll say, not kindly. He won't smile and he won't budge. He can be an asshole this way, expecting everyone to be a loner just because he's one himself. The strong silent type — she doesn't know if any of this is brain damage because she didn't know him before the damage was done. She's heard things from people who did. Totally odd how a bullet in the head, if it doesn't kill you or make you a complete retard, can just change your personality. But they actually say he's nicer now. Or less angry. Which is hard to believe. Because even the way he sits beside her vaguely scares her: cross-legged, never moving, eyes half-closed. A blanket around his shoulders and a ball cap pulled low — he says that this way, when it starts to rain, he doesn't have to move an inch. He reminds her of the old duster where Clint Eastwood pretends to be asleep wearing a Mexican sombrero. You get too close and he suddenly looks up, he's been awake after all, waiting for you, and he shoots you, a little black cigarette unlit in his mouth. She's glad Tom doesn't smoke. Most every man she's slept with smokes. No matter how much you like them, they stink.

Maybe he's learned to sleep like a killer whale.

She's stuck it out gamely, sitting up all night. Though they slept as long as they could this morning in preparation for this, it's been hard and she's been short with him. She knows she's hit the danger zone whenever he clamps the headphones on her to shut her up. It's hard to stay awake wearing the phones — it sounds just like the kind of ocean you get when in a bathroom you put a pink conch to your ear, but this is both ears, an instant forced zone-out and before you know it you're nodding.

Actually the headphones are a bit of a relief, to tell the truth. She hates the bickering, and not just about the drug run and his part in it. Also she sort of lost her diaphragm "somewhere" and arrived without it, and aside from the implied infidelity it's also led to unprotected sex three times now. He doesn't trust her in this (the unprotected sex part, not the infidelity — he doesn't seem to even consider that) and he has been more crisp with her than usual. She knows he hates, hates, the idea of children. So severe is his hate that she can't even ask him why. Not that she wants any, at least not now. But.

She was aware of Tom Poole only peripherally before he was shot and Marie left him, but she'd heard plenty, mostly that he was the kind of asshole you just don't get involved with. In fact his name had come up more than once in the ongoing discussion she had with a girlfriend, whose psychiatrist or something had told her about assholes like Tom Poole: when a guy doesn't give a shit about anything, there is the threat that this includes you, and this is just the sort of challenge some girls rise to. Time after time. It's a syndrome.

But when she met him — it was during his convalescing, some of which time he spent at the Vancouver Aquarium by the whale pool — to her he seemed almost kindly. Or "patient" might be the word. She was fascinated that first day, her tagging along with him and a few of his friends after he insisted, despite all the Free Willy jokes, that he had to go to the aquarium again. He looked so content just to sit there and watch the two killer whales and one dolphin circle around their pool. It was like they were his entertainment while his head healed. Or more that — was this her imagination? — their circling helped him heal. That was another thing about Tommy. Around him, her imagination got colourful in ways it usually didn't do.

One of the first things she remembers thinking about him is that he sort of reminded her of Brad Pitt, as good looking as that, but a Brad Pitt who never smiled and was quieter. After they were together a few times she even told him this. He pretended to ignore her but of course he liked it. All guys like him do. And the glint in his eyes honestly sort of did, and still does, remind her of Brad Pitt.

At the aquarium they whispered business and she saw that Tommy didn't care about any of it. Friends talked over and around his bandaged head. She knew these Vancouver Island people, all getting rich off BC bud. They were almost a gang. Not in the sense of violence, but more because they worked together and had some of the same contacts down south. Some of the best deals. Which had its awful side too because it got the attention of the real gangs, or at least the Vietnamese, who operated like a gang, or a family, it was never clear to her. In any case they were violent and people just assumed it was the Vietnamese who got Tommy. Though Tommy, on the rare times he spoke of it, said it wasn't the Vietnamese, or he said "Who gives a shit," or he said — she'd heard this from him once — that he "deserved it," and he said this smiling, like it was all a game. But McKay told her it was the Vietnamese and that he knew this to be true.

From all the rumours she'd heard, it seems he *had* treated the whole thing like a game, especially the beet juice thing. After the rip-off (most rumours agreed Tommy ripped *someone* off, extremely big time) he'd gone to Tofino with Marie to hide from the bad guys, painting half his face each morning with beet juice, a big birthmark disguise. It sounded ridiculous to Cal, but some guys' sense of humour did get pretty out there when things got dangerous, she'd seen this before with more than one boyfriend. And all was fine except that in Tofino he wasn't really hiding at all, he was the loud and weird birthmark-man who was still doing deals, and then — according to McKay — he started playing with the birthmark, teasing people by painting it differently some days, first on one side of the face and then the other, and then even little designs. He was probably just bored. And then he was shot. In the two-inch article in the back pages of the *Vancouver Sun*, they used the words "botched gangland killing." As for Cal, she had her own suspicions about Marie, who got herself instantly out of not only Tofino but also Vancouver Island and was now — she'd heard — living in Florida, and living well.

IT WAS GOOD in the tent, but out here it feels like stress. They aren't her fault, these long silences. She just doesn't feel smart enough to offer observations about nature and whatever, so she asks questions. Some about the drug run. Why shouldn't she? She's concerned. McKay came up with the plan, asking Tommy if he could hear boats with the headphones, Tommy saying sure, and it evolved from there. Cal was in the bar with them when the whole idea came down. Since then, Mckay made the big calls and now an actual ship is coming from some secret country loaded with some secret drug — she heard it was coke — and doing the drop at Malcolm Island here at this point only because Tommy had a passion for whales and had a hydrophone and was camped here anyway. She does not think he is getting enough money for it, not getting his fair share. Though all he's doing is acting as a lookout for Coast Guard boats, risk is risk. From what little he's grunted to her, she knows he'll be doing only this: he listens for engines, he keeps a bonfire lit if it's clear, he puts it out if it's not — which sounds to her like cowboys and Indians, considering they live in the age of satellites and cell phones. He's ignored her questions. And some were good ones, like, What happens if some campers — this is possible — happen to be somewhere on the beach and happen to have a big fire going? He shrugged that one off. And, Are you going to hang around even when they unload, even when you don't have to, when it's the most dangerous time? It's like he can't be bothered telling her. Like he can't be bothered even thinking about it. The biggest question — what if he just *forgets* about it? — she doesn't dare ask. Even though in her opinion this is exactly the question somebody should be asking.

Here he is putting himself in danger of jail, or even getting shot again, and he agreed to less money. Unbelievable. "I don't give a shit," was his response to her money question. This answer scared her, not because she wants the money for herself but because she can imagine him not giving a shit to the point that he might not even bother collecting it or, if he did, sticking it in a bag and forgetting where it was. Or tossing it into the wind like some sort of Buddhist. And he is more likely to do that sort of thing if she makes a stink. When you rile him he makes doubly sure he proves his point. Even if he doesn't have one.

Most of all, she's afraid his plans hold nothing more than sitting on this cold beach for the rest of his life, waiting for whales to come. No, *actually* most of all she is afraid that she doesn't know her boyfriend, doesn't know Tommy Poole, never has, never will.

Anyway, the whole thing is going down in a week or two. She's glad she's leaving tomorrow. She pictures it again, says the words like a mantra of freedom: catch the Sointula ferry to Port MacNeil, four hour drive to Naniamo. She feels the winding road taking her closer to a Starbucks and then a bath and a video, maybe *Shakespeare in Love* again. She realizes now that one reason she likes *Shakespeare in*

Love so much is because everything was so dirty back then too, and watching it makes her feel clean. Gweneth Paltrow cleaning her teeth with that old stick.

So one more night of this. She loves him but. He says it's beautiful here but it really isn't. It feels angry. At night, there's nothing. *Nothing.* Hong Kong is beautiful at night. Vancouver is beautiful at night from the Grouse Mountain gondola. Here it's cold and grey. *Summer?* Apparently there's this giant snow-covered mountain across the water that no one ever sees. It's ridiculous here. Most of all she can't, won't, shit in the woods again. She's not a fucking bear. It's disgusting and she won't. What kind of person could live like this, and what kind of boyfriend wouldn't have fixed the place up for her a little. A ratty little tent, that smells. When she first asked him about where to go to the bathroom he just pointed at the forest-in-general, thanks a lot. He doesn't even have any dishes. And he smells, beyond the kind of natural, expected smell that she will tolerate.

A long bath, some microwaved burritos with melted cheese and the salsa with the black beans in it, and a salad, with some oil and lemon dressing...

It's Cal who hears them on the headphones. She knows these squeaks, has heard them on tapes he's played for her. But these are so loud and sudden out of the black silence clamping her head, these are so thrilling, it's all real and happening now and it sounds like huge whales are two feet away. She says, "Tommy?" He has seen her sit up straight and he's already moving. He grabs the headphones off her, puts them on and presses one speaker tight to his head. Hearing them, he lifts the pot of water he has ready, pours it, embers hiss, smoke pounds up thick white, a big billowing ghost, and now they are in darkness. They are sitting on a log only ten feet from the water and the gravel bank that whales are coming to rub themselves on.

There is just enough moon coming through the clouds. She hears him unsnap his camera bag, the click of the lens cap, another click and the flash whines — high-pitched as a whale voice — as it powers up.

"Sometimes," he tells her, in a fever and whispering though he's said the orcas are about a mile away, "when you sit this close you get wet from them blowing." He says this as if it is a good thing.

She rearranges the blanket on her shoulders as he checks something on the tape recorder. And suddenly she hears the first one breathe. They have swum their mile, they have come so fast out of the distant night.

Cal can barely see the dorsals in the dim moonlight. She finds most dramatic their explosive breathing — *PPHWAAHH* — which is so loud it troubles her at first. Each breath is a held one, and when released it reminds her of that first big one during teeth-gritting sex, coming. It sounds *just* like that.

It also startles her to smell their breath. And yes, she does feel their fishy breath-mist on her face.

She watches Tommy as much as she does the whales. Watches Tommy watch, his face red from the light of the fire's embers. She sees now the truth of one rumour: barred from the aquarium, he came here.

PPHWAAHH

He isn't watching her back. He's snapping pictures. He's sitting more still, more strong than she's ever seen him. He's trying to time his shots, trying so hard to anticipate a whale surfacing to breathe. Sometimes the flash lights up a totally empty field of water and he swears.

PPHWAAHH

They are so fast. So is Tommy. He's totally in synch with them now. Look at his face. He doesn't even know she's here. There's something in his face she's never seen before. He adores these whales. He loves them.

PPHWAAHH

She decides not to come here to see him again. She decides not to see him again at all.

Guardian spirits were also recognized by many First Nations. They were believed to bestow power during vision quests. Vision quests were usually carried out in solitude by most males and some females after puberty. During the quest, a guardian spirit would manifest itself to the individual and bestow powers that would protect the person and enhance his or her actions.

— ROBERT J. MUCKLE,
THE FIRST NATIONS OF BRITISH COLUMBIA

STUART CHANNEL

NEVER HAS EVELYN SEEN a squall come up like this. It's really blowing when they make for the shore of Thetis, the wind so loud she can't hear Peter's noise. Rain whips her skin; hair blows from her scalp as if pulled by hands. The waves are high and break on shore. When they hit the gravel beach broadside, the fibreglass crunches and bangs, and she winces for her kayak.

Peter flies out and begins to hyperventilate, and yell. Severely frightened, he's angry at the wind. She gets him to help tip the boat, spill the water and drag it up the bank. While dragging she sees, in front of Peter's cockpit, scraped in the paint beside the love-heart, inch-high white letters: SOINTULA OR BUST.

She isn't sure, but they probably just escaped a close call. They do need spray skirts to keep water out. The kayak was half sunk. More than once Peter almost rolled them. He bashed her on the head! She finds she's smiling. They get the kayak stashed in the high tide logs and she waits for Peter to quieten down. He's asking fast questions. Where, what, how.

She saw the house from the water and maybe was vaguely aiming for it. About fifty yards down the beach from them, it's a modern cedar and glass. She takes Peter's hand and walks him toward it. Floor-to-ceiling windows of what must be the living room face into the storm.

Up in the carport she knows that no one's been here in weeks, though she doesn't know how she knows this. It's a dead feeling in the cement under her feet. She can also tell no one's coming tonight, though she might be wrong in this. The kitchen door window sports a "Beware of Dog" sign and a "Community Watch" sticker. She can tell there's no dog. The signs feel like simple fear, a last resort because no other house can see or be seen. She picks a chunk of firewood off the carport stack. Dripping forlornly at her side, Peter barely has time to draw an alarmed breath before she smashes it through the door's window.

She reaches down and feels for the doorknob and she's in. What she notices is the air. It is cold yet rich — so silent it's sentient. It was just like this with Claude. A different island, a different summer house, but the air was just like this. The oxygen of thieves. Not much is needed to breathe.

Peter won't come in at first but when he does she tells him not to turn on any lights. You never know and it's best to take no chances. She finds a coal oil lamp and a box of wooden matches and gets the lamp lit, keeping the wick low, the flame small. She can't remember ever using one of these but she must have.

"Eve, please. This is *very* stupid."

"Evelyn."

She finds a piece of junk mail on the kitchen counter. An R. and L. Bonneville live here. It's good to know the names of your hosts.

"If a car comes, but it won't, it'll come slowly down the drive and we'll see it and we'll run into the woods. Where we'll spend a really shitty wet night."

Peter points to the glass on the floor. "This is *official* break and enter."

"Sweep it up. We can leave them twenty bucks for a piece of glass. I don't see any problem at all. We were caught in a storm."

"Well, true. We were indeed in a storm."

With Claude there had been no storm. Their going ashore had felt like whim. They merely beached the speedboat, hiked a bit and came upon the house, an older cottagy affair. It was an island not reachable by ferry and there would be no cars coming down any driveways to surprise you. Claude explained that the house belonged to a friend of his who'd long been inviting him to use it. From the way he said, "Forgot to get da key," then booted the padlock two, three, four times before breaking it off the door altogether, she couldn't tell if this was the house of a friend or not. His smile said that maybe it was, and maybe it wasn't.

The air inside — cold, rich, forbidden. She and Claude made love instantly, on the kitchen's mousy floor, and then again, on the musky couch. And then, she remembers, again, her kneeling and hanging onto the edge of the bathtub. Through the alchemy of this kind of use, the house became their knowing accomplice.

SHE WAITS UNTIL he is asleep. Tonight there was no horny posturing. The Bonnevilles had the power turned off and, though he moaned about a hot shower, there was no argument from Peter when she said they should take nothing more than shelter. He was exhausted and simply moved the oil lamp into one of the bedrooms. She remained in the living room, sitting quietly as the storm buffeted the glass. Hearing while not feeling its roar was comforting.

She can hear Peter snoring lightly, helplessly. She tallies his Demerol that morning, the mid-day drinking with those boys, all the paddling, then his panic and struggles in the wind.

She's known all along that if it happens at all it has to happen like this. When he doesn't expect it. When he doesn't want it so much. Some men, you just know not to give victory to because they will bloom obnoxious with it.

There are other reasons it has to happen this way, though she doesn't have words for them.

Peter's lamp flickers orange on the side table. Beside the lamp, his glasses are in a sock. In this dim light, eyes closed, mouth slightly parted, he looks years younger. His beard, which he washed at the sink and smoothed down with his hand, is a pelt. She steps out of her clothes, feels his warmth as she raises his blankets and climbs in beside him. She kisses his ear as she snakes her hand under to write her invitation on his chest. He wakes but doesn't move. She can see his eyes staring straight up. He looks more afraid than anything. She hums wordlessly in his ear and begins to move against his leg. She shushes the mumbled questions. He seems worried, even apologetic, for what is about to happen, and she can picture him with Gail. She supports herself over his face, kisses him lightly, then deeper. His tongue rises to meet hers. Everything is as simple as can be.

Except, she stops. She pulls away from this chest, from this leg, this beard surrounding this mouth, feeling them now for the first time. It's as if, before this second, she'd only been imagining them.

"I'm sorry."

"What?"

"Peter, I can't. I'm sorry."

"Ah." Several deep breaths. "Right. Okay."

She's been a hunter ever since she smashed the door. The inside cool and dark. She doesn't know if she stopped because he didn't feel like Claude or because he didn't feel like Roy. Peter's difference didn't feel bad. She just isn't ready for that difference.

"Are you all right?"

"I'm fine. I'm fine I'm fine I'm fine."

"Sorry."

"No. Really, I'm —" He pauses as if to check that he's telling the truth. "— Fine."

"It's just that —"

"You have complications and I understand." He has never looked more awake and alert. He is vibrant beside her. His eyes are liquid and kind.

She will let it rest at this. She won't feel bad, or good, for Peter Gore. She keeps her body straight and a careful inch away from his. Peter clears his throat.

"If anything I enjoy this. I enjoy being woken up and *rejected* at the brink. This *prolonged arousal*? It's Taoist, isn't it? This particular torture?"

"Sorry, you're right." She taps his chest with a finger and makes to leave.

Peter gently grabs an arm.

"Stay. I'm —" He finds her eyes in the dim light. "I'm being funny. Let me be funny."

She settles back, feeling her nakedness anew, its power. Peter is hurt and needs some upper hand. "Be funny," she whispers.

When he has settled, like a lover she deftly and at her leisure picks a pine needle from his hair above his ear, then strokes his beard with her fingers. His face — she never imagined touching a man with a face like this. It's not that it isn't symmetrical. Maybe 'proportion' is the word. Is it eyes too small, or forehead too big for them? From the feel of it, not very much chin under that beard. If his face were a building, his forehead would collapse into and crush the rest of it.

"This is *far* better. We can have our first intimate conversation. If we had actually gone and done it I'd've long ago rolled off and begun snoring." He chuckles at himself. "Rolled off *already* snoring."

She wants to tell him that it is hard for her too. How kissing a new, fresh mouth was just too bizarre, something she hasn't done since Roy. Two-and-a-half decades since her mouth had felt surprising new lips, a foreign mouth which went right down inside a person, a man. It's amazing teenagers can do that and not really understand the immensity of what they're doing.

"Do you really roll off and snore?"

"As I recall, yes." Peter perks up and climbs onto an elbow to look at her. "Actually all men do. Some pretend not to. Cuddling is a *disguise*. It's snoring with arms."

Evelyn sees, feels Claude in their broken-in cabin. Once, twice. Thrice. She whispers: "Male biology."

He clears his throat. "Actually, it's very true."

Evelyn gets onto an elbow herself, cups a hand at the lamp's top and blows it out. "What, you're all pigs 'by nature'?"

"It's quite, quite true. Look at baboons."

Evelyn smells the oily smoke on her hand. She lies back. "We're not baboons." Moonlight glows in the room. The storm is over.

Peter rises higher on his elbow. "Well. They show why we're still a certain way. Women, for instance, have multiple orgasms, correct?" Peter pauses, feigns bitterness in saying, "At *times*."

She says only, "So?"

"Men *don't*. We hit *one* home run and pass out. But *women* are, in theory, still up to bat. They are aroused and in theory eager for another male of the species. As per usual it's all about fertility. Bill's wigglers might not be up to the task but, hold on now, here come Bob's. Baboons still demonstrate this particular—"

"Women want to be gang-banged?"

"A million years ago this was the case, yes. Only I suspect it was less a gang-bang than it was a deep-breathing female roaming about the *cavern*, leaving a string of slobs *snoring* in her wake. It was stalking, serial, female, *rumpy*-pumpy." Peter starts to giggle.

"You're a grotesque man." But she is smiling too.

"Well it's a grotesque and spooky *business*, isn't it?"

Peter, leaning over her, has found the courage to remove what might be bits of grass from her hair. Touching Peter Gore hadn't been simple after all. She'd touched a big awkward boy happy in his good luck; she'd touched an old man worried he couldn't do what a lover must; she'd touched a rote creature, stiffening helplessly in what we call pleasure.

"Was your Gail a baboon to you?"

Peter's hand pauses in its work. "Not to my knowledge. No."

"Were you?"

Peter settles again, puts his hands behind his head, sighs. "Not to my knowledge ... no."

"Will it be cruel if I stay here?"

Peter is silent a moment. "It will be fine."

She moves into Peter's side, snuggling into pockets of animal warmth.

He says, "Actually, I'm almost asleep. No offence."

He does sound very tired again.

"None taken."

"In truth ... no ape my age can ... manage anything more than ... a few vigorous ... *kisses* ... per night."

He puts an arm around her shoulders and under her head for a pillow.

"Fact I'm about to ... plummet off the ... planet."

She can smell his underarm and though strong it is not an altogether bad smell. Claude sometimes smelled like this, rawly human. Roy, he always has something sprayed on. But there, so does she.

They don't speak further and through the skylight she can see bright, bright stars — she realizes she has been looking at them for some time. She decides not to think of Roy. Though he is part of the equation tonight. Symbolically she has just cut their physical bond. Or at least hacked into it pretty deeply. If she goes back to him now it will be because she wants to, not because she is still attached. Maybe — deep-breathing — she has just left him, she is travelling back into the depths of an old cave.

She won't feel bad for Roy tonight.

Look at these stars. Present yet distant. How is it that stars can be far too much and far too little?

Like this betrayal of stars, Roy's betrayal was passive.

AFTER HER VOLUNTEERING days were over, the one job Roy got for her she soon quit, angry with him.

She enjoyed being receptionist/clerk at the municipal art gallery. If there was bitterness about how she got the job she didn't hear it. Best of all she was invited to join the committee, which, though she suspected Roy had a hand in this too (he was honourary chair), meant she had a say in what got exhibited. The contemporary Ojibwa show, marvelous, and she had lunch with two of the artists. The lesser-known Group of Seven works, so-so, even her amateur eye saw why they were lesser-known. The Roderick Haig-Brown exhibit — it made her ache for British Columbia, and the display of antique fishing gear sparked glimpses of Claude's hands.

"The Changing Face of China" was a fine enough show. Artful black-and-white photos of China's regions and peoples, portraits of gap-toothed old men and curious children. It was mostly "happy" in tone, and smacked of gentle propaganda. The show had moved west from the Maritimes with no controversy at all. Only when the picketing began did Evie examine the display more carefully.

The three Asian women were there one morning when she arrived to unlock and she assumed them eager patrons. She said good morning and they nodded back heavily accented hellos. They didn't follow her in. The morning's attendance was extremely low but Evie took no notice. It was lunch before she saw them still on the steps, holding small placards. One wore traditional clothing which, from her days as a west coast hippie, Evie recognized as Tibetan. The three looked roughly her age, fortyish, though one was so weather-beaten it was hard to tell.

She got to know them over the days that followed. One, Annie Paltro, spoke English. Evie got to know the offending pictures too: five photos of smiling Tibetans, captioned below with, "The changing face of the Tibetan Autonomous Region, Southwest China." The smiles were a big lie, said Annie, as was calling Tibet part of China. It was thievery of an entire country. Made testy by her ignorance, Annie filled Evie in on the relocations, the torture, the sterilization of women, the genocide.

"North America stands like this," said Annie, holding her arms out in welcome, "because China is a big marketplace." She tilted her head and looked Evie in the eye. "How rich you need to be?"

But they stayed on friendly terms. Odd how they made her see her small city anew. Something about them simply sitting there contrasted with the cars zipping by. Windstars were not wheat. The women chatted and laughed with visitors — some of whom turned away and some of whom didn't. For people who were protesting the death of their native land they seemed rather cheerful. They struck Evie as being happy to be where they were, on these steps. There was no where else they wanted to be, whereas the very nature of southern

Ontario was to work to be something else. Evie felt nostalgic for their attitude. It was an attitude she had once shared, but had lost as easily as youth itself.

One day the women arrived in traditional dress, burned incense in a bronze bowl and chanted — an ugly guttural, exotic as could be. It sounded not at all emotional, which she assumed most prayer to be, but rather like the bone-deep urges of animals. Pre-language. Evie noted the sheen of tears on all three faces. The background to their little stage was the asphalt carpark that filled up each morning and emptied each afternoon, and beyond that the towering Ford smokestacks, their belchings a hackneyed symbol of progress worthy of China itself, and wouldn't *we* love to sell our vans to China. Across the street sprawled Lake Ontario, "cobalt blue "— joked Roy in a dig at rival, industrial Hamilton —"because of the cobalt." Across the street lay an exclusive marina where posh sailboats rarely moved from their slips because their owners were too busy making money to sail them.

How had Evie ever settled into this place?

In any event, the Tibetans wanted only to be on the gallery steps. Their aim wasn't to close the show, which would have left them no stage. They wanted to educate people. Roy, who could have put an end to them with a court order, was fine with this. He even came down one day to meet them and give them City of Oakville pins — some Latin over acorns and a key, backed by a cobalt lake — which the women politely fastened over their hearts.

Roy's betrayal came three days after he gave them the pins. The local paper's story about the protesting Tibetans had caught the eye of the *Toronto Star*, then the *Globe and Mail*. One complication, noted the story, was a "Team Ontario" trade junket to China, planned for later that year, that was to include not only the province's hungry businessmen but also its honorable Mayors.

Roy did warn Evie in advance that he was preparing the court order and that she should say goodbye to her friends. She was too angry to get clear Roy's plaintive, pressure-from-above explanation. It angered her further when, after the three women were led off by cops, Roy tried to twist it into a kindness, pointing out that, with the newspapers vilifying him, the Tibetans were publicized anew, furthering their cause. Evie told him he was warped by politics. She added that sometimes life offered simple decisions. And then she made one of her own. She left her job the morning the Tibetans left the steps.

It may have been coincidence that the anti-depressants started soon after, for this art gallery betrayal was one in a subtle string. Maybe because in this case Roy's failure was so clear to her, Tibetans became a symbol of his crossing over to some other side. She knew it wasn't fair, but whenever she saw another picture of the Dalai Lama's charming, fruitful smile, she saw him to be Roy's opposite. It was as if Roy had dimmed. It may have been the drugs, but he began to look and sound more distant to her. As did the walls of her house. As did the streets, trees and waterfront of Oakville, its ambiance hollowing out in such a way to suggest that it had never been.

STAYING IN THE KAYAK, bobbing in boat wake, she watches Peter limp away, up the red-railed ramp of the Ladysmith government dock. He has tucked her note in his pocket. When she handed it to him a few moments ago he looked puzzled until he unfolded it and saw what it was. And chirped, "A love note!"

The paper was from a frozen fish sticks carton she found on the beach in an old fire pit in front of their glass house, its irony alone making her save it. The charcoal she sharpened — no small source of pride — with a chipped shell, as the People here would have done. Had they had writing. But who knows what leisurely fireside art they did with charcoal — on cedar planks, faces, bare backs. Bum cheeks. Stuff that didn't end up in museums.

Dirtying her fingers in charcoal, she wrote the plan in big black letters:

> AT THE DOCK, NOON TOMORROW, IF YOU WANT, I'LL BE THERE WAITING. IF I WANT.

She grips the dock cleat while she watches Peter. Hot air rises off the wood, rich with creosote and rotten bait, the small mussels kids use to fish for shiners. The cracks between planks are full of their broken black shells, and crimped fishing line, and the odd rusted hook, and tiny crab legs cooked pink by the sun. Because of this dock, did Ladysmith kids watch less TV than Oakville kids? She likes this feature of the west coast: every town has its government dock, red-railed so you can see it, always free to use. They stank of bait and gas, because people did use them.

Peter waves boyishly before he disappears behind a building. His smile is hard to read: he wants to be with her but he can't wait to sleep in a motel. He smiles like he might never see her again and she might be off with his sleeping bag and tent. His smile claims that all he's ever needed is this small bag of clothes under one arm, computer under the other.

No. He is simply smiling, and she is seeing possibilities that are only her own. Her thoughts are churning. The water is too. There is nothing that isn't moving. The dock's wood grain moves very slowly but it moves. The hot breeze blows and it's almost like the wood has tender, invisible fur, which moves.

She's surprised by the tug in her depths at seeing him go. He has kept her focused. Having to be a mother is enough to sober anybody. Maybe he's what she needed. Though everything moves, she feels fine. No spaghetti brain, anyway. Her will is stronger than ever. Even if she doesn't know what to do with it now. Last night has confused her a bit.

She pushes off from the float and a horn sounds behind her. She was "parked" against a sign that reads *Water Taxi Only*. A huge empty float with nothing but room, and here is a water taxi honking at her. She can only scowl absurdity at the smoked-windshield.

She back-paddles out of the way then aims for the harbour-mouth. About to dig in, she hears laughter and swearing. The water taxi has not yet tied up when out leap two men in their late twenties, dressed identically in blue hospital gowns that tie at the back. One is barefoot, the other in dirty white socks. The one with socks looks beaten up, or maybe it was a car accident. Black eyes, stitches on a cheek. The other man looks undamaged. Their white-underweared bums and bare backs stick out of their gowns. Most visible of all is that neither man gives a shit about anything. They stride up the ramp, laughing and talking, gesturing violently. The water taxi driver leaps out after them to tie to the dock and he calls, "I'll be needing that money," but neither man so much as glances back. One briefly smiles at the driver's silliness.

They have obviously simply left, or even escaped from, an institution. Not a wallet between them, not a key for house or car, or quarter for the phone. They look dangerous. She feels — she feels a sour hollowing in the gut, a feeling she hasn't felt for some years, of what it's like to be in Tom's physical presence. She watches them disappear behind the same building Peter did. The gut-sense of being in her son's territory doesn't fade.

She paddles away, knowing him again. His touch, his skin. His baby-skin. Feeling what that's like. Feeling his recoil. He resents her breast first and foremost. She watches him latch on despite himself, his little body's hunger forcing him to. His body and mind at odds, he won't look at her breast or at her. Sucking, he looks away. She is tortured with words she's read in a mothering book: *enjoy how they stare up at you, eye to eye ... the love flowing back and forth ... it's now that you bond, for life.* Getting his fill, he sucks mechanically, he is a fleshy pump, jaw working, functional. In some moods, she understands he is a parasite. Shows of public breastfeeding she watches hungrily, sees how Mom and baby do indeed avidly *stare*, a sweet mind-meld. Other babies give Mom the stare even if Mom is giving them a *bottle*. Of *apple* juice.

Full, Tommy either falls asleep or shoves himself off her breast as it drips, abandoned. She is willing and eager to breastfeed him till he is two, but he weans himself at four months.

Older, Tommy is aware of her and Roy's *duty*. New clothes, treats, or special outings spark in him a weariness that thanks are expected. That's what parents do, they provide, and any emotion connected to the exchange sours his face, leads to eruptions of sarcasm. One

Christmas, unwrapping that beloved smurf gun, Tommy can't hide his embarrassment at being excited. He longs only to take his gun and leave the living room. Which he does, sassing a sarcastic singsong *tha-anks* from the hall. He is six.

SHE NEEDS THIS BIG rock a mile out in the middle of the strait. It has called to her and, paddling hard, she approaches needfully. A wake hisses off her stern; she is so much faster with Peter gone. She lurches forward with every dig. Her shoulders feel almost comically bigger.

Since spotting this island yesterday she has pictured herself camping on it, occupying its smooth dome. It looked an acre in size, shaped like the head of a bald man submerged to the eyebrows.

The island proves tinier than it seemed from a distance, the circumference of a large house. But bald, and white at the top and down one side with a wash of bird droppings, which looks dry but which she can smell as she approaches.

She bumps her black beak into a cushion of barnacles. To pull the kayak to safety she has to scrape its glossy hull up harsh rock. She winces, feels for it. Not because a rough hull will slow her down, and not because she assumes the owners will still be getting their boat back, but because the boat is obviously a warm-blooded creature that deserves more respect.

Evelyn climbs the stinky peak to scan her domain. She wonders if the People ever came here. Why would they? Unless to do what she's doing now, which is... nothing. So of course they did. They came to sit and think. They came to pout, and blame. They came to menstruate in peace, or as violently as they wanted.

Surrounded by moving water, a hard dome of rock. No shade. No shelter from wind. No wood, so no fire. She will sit in whatever the sky does.

Aside from rock there is nothing except for a single triangular patch of sand the size of a desk top. A few breaks in the rock allow for scattered tufts of bald man's hair, Scotch broom. Where an ear would be, a blackberry vine arcs out like a five-armed octopus. She finds three near-ripe berries. It's the closest she has come to sugar in a while, since Peter Gore's granola bars, days and days ago.

She mounts the peak again to see if she saw what she thought she saw. There it is, a white feather, jabbed upright into the triangle of sand. It's as grand a feather as those in the front of a war bonnet. It is likely from a gull. Or, tail feathers of bald eagles are white. She stands beside it and it tickles half-way up her calf. She plucks it from the sand. It must have been Claude who told her that eagle feathers are found stuck this way. So heavily quilled that, instead of a downy waft to earth, it falls like a spiraling arrow and sticks in. Looking like a child stuck it. Evelyn has the feather in both hands and she gazes up. Did such a large feather fall from a bird in mid-flight? What kind of air-battle was fought over this tiny island, what were the chances of the feather arrowing down to this single crotch of sand? It makes more sense that a child stuck it here.

Other than dig out her shade hat, because the sun is hot and falling hard, she decides not to unpack or set up yet. It's good just to wander her rock, to learn it. She senses a knowing place but also a fun place. She is allowed to whoop and she does. There is a delicious absence of ghosts. No perfume, and no Ford Windstars. No men. She is alone at last.

Or, no, she's clambering on top of a head, a real head. The bald guy doesn't mind, he enjoys her pitter-patter. He enjoys the sun on top, because under that black water his face is so cold. She can't see his shoulders. Deeper than that, his body so cold and white, she doesn't want to think about. Evelyn warns him before she jumps off a ledge, before she plucks some scotch broom, ow. He has a sense of humour like hers.

Evelyn hears Claude's mumble about Tommy's injury, how he needed "a fuckin *head*-shave, *ow*," so Tommy must have had a bad cut on his head. Now this bald head becomes Tommy's. Her feet fall more carefully. Now it's depressing. It's Tommy's bald little head, he's nursing, he's tender, she's standing on his tender head in her hard, gritty shoes.

She makes it Roy's head. Roy was bald once, he had his head shaved in public for a cancer drive and he forgot to tell her. She came in from groceries and there he was bent over his desk. He said hello and didn't see her wide eyes and he had completely forgotten.

Evelyn gives his head a test stomp and Roy feels right, Roy doesn't mind. She can dance her little songs on Roy, knock some down into his brain.

ROY IS SO KIND. Evie wonders if he's just naive, in that way many American men seem naive, like earnest boy scouts. He and she have had innumerable coffees in the SUB, have not slept together yet though are heading in that direction, when she asks Roy the girly question, theatrically coy so that they both have an out. "So what do you like me for, my body or my mind?" Roy answers in a way that will mark him for her forever, as well as boost her regard, maybe her love. He says, "Jeez, you know I sort of get the two mixed up."

Most men would have in essence ignored her and said, hopeful, "body." Or, throwing a different set of dice, "mind." Unoriginal cowards would say "both." Intellectual bores would interrogate her simplistic question. But here's Roy gently chiding her Platonic dualism while apologizing and making himself look the dumb one.

More than once Evie will see him gracefully undermine that Toronto penchant for labeling men by what car they drive. Someone will say, "*You* know, the guy with the mint Beemer," and Roy will shake his head and admit, "Jeez, you know I can never remember people's cars." It isn't patronizing. Roy is actually apologetic. She suspects it was once deliberate but has sunk in to become his kind habit. He is that kind. People generally don't see it.

A year into their marriage, and he is so kind with Tommy. She's been waiting to see, because she *knows*. It is amazing that Roy takes to Tommy, because he must know too. Roy is so kind that paternity just doesn't matter to him. In fact, it makes him love Tommy more. That is Roy summed up. Roy is that kind of man.

Evie sits on the bird-washed rock and remembers the urgent message from Roy to call him at work. She calls City Hall, asks for the Mayor's Office, something she does many times a month but on this day feels the absurdity conjoined with urgency. She is put briefly on hold, and then Roy is talking to her, excited.

"It's not as bad as it sounds but — Tommy is a psychopath." At first Evie thinks he's joking. She actually laughs nervously at her husband's perversity.

He isn't joking. Tommy has been diagnosed *ex camera*. That is, not in person, but from Evie's and Roy's descriptions of their son's behavior. Because Tommy, fourteen, refused to see any more doctors. Which is just as well. He is ingeniously uncooperative with anyone they bribe him to visit. Displaying what is no doubt a symptom of his disease, Tom can too easily turn on the charm and pull the wool. Evie pictures him, eyes splendid with awareness, saying easily, "I'm a rebellious teenager and they're strict parents. How many of me have you seen today?" Getting the doctor to laugh.

The description of a psychopath — no fear of consequences and no apparent guilt — feels to Evie like a description of Tommy's face. She watches him peacefully asleep and wonders. When he laughs at her or tells Roy to fuck himself, she can now see *symptoms*. When Evie first heard this diagnosis she cried, half from relief. Not just that Tommy had a clear condition, shared by others, but also that he was blameless. *Tommy has a disease*. She can hate the disease and not Tommy. And not Claude. And not herself. Because she is made blameless too.

Relief fades when she discovers that no one knows what to do with a psychopath. It fades further when she learns that the words 'psychopath' and 'relief' simply aren't in the same language. And: she's *given birth to a psychopath*. To think these words. To see the images: bug-eyed family killer. Anthony Perkins coming through the shower curtain. Man in the attic licking the neck of his dead mother. Psychopaths burst the limits of the thinkable as if it's their job.

Of course Tommy isn't like that at all, any of that. He is the opposite of bug-eyed. He is brilliantly but calmly selfish. Evie takes to the term "sociopath," which she learns is the gentler name for the same condition. Maybe it helps that Hitchcock hadn't used it in a title.

Kind Roy's comfortings often take the God route: He was given to us. As a challenge. A burden, through which we will gain strength and wisdom. Certainly, thinks Evie, but what about Tommy? What does he gain, merciful Father? So she chooses science. With it, she solves the puzzle, one she doesn't share with Roy since it excludes him. She can so clearly see Claude's part in the equation that is Tom. Viola: a hawk-nosed boy who cares about no one, least of all himself.

Still, Tommy didn't ask to be made this way. In the eyes of neither God nor science is it Tommy's fault. But as the years grate on, Evie finds she can't feel sorry for him. He just doesn't seem to be in much pain, even while he causes it. She decides Tommy is a textbook sociopath. She also decides that in cases like his, it is best to turn away from the sociopath himself and instead study his swath, for here is where sympathy needs to fall.

WHOEVER'S BALD HEAD this is, her dancing doesn't last. She finds herself at the water's lip. She sits. If she straightens her legs her feet get wet. This is just the place to see Caddy; it feels like his haunt. She watches the water, the endless ripples, lets her eyes spangle with the infinite mirrors diminishing in distance.

She can no longer smell the bird droppings up behind her. A wind has risen from the southeast, blowing the stink away. She turns and stares at the dome of rock, and sees now why the whitewash falls only on one side. It is the kind of story Claude would read in nature, as he instructed her with his blackboard of waves, bones, approaching clouds. The story Evelyn reads goes: this southeast wind is the prevailing winter wind, and the birds who roost here are winter birds. Facing into the wind, they have historically had their shit blown to the northwest. This is why the island is painted so. The white is the calcium of digested fish bones.

Evelyn reads this island-story with pride. It is now that the ghost makes its appearance. It's Claude, of course. He pokes her shoulder. *Ow.* She turns to catch the smirk on his face but misses it. He's poked her for a reason. *Took it out on him, eh?*

She feels him fade to gone. He was never really there, but inside her. The poke came from inside. There's no contradiction. Her hair rises on her neck. Is she possessed? What would that feel like? Someone taking you over without you knowing. It happened at the hospital, at the room-sucking moment of death, a silence so fierce that of course something unknowable has to be happening. He must have leapt to her, the one in the room still breathing. Why wouldn't he?

Evelyn enjoys the creep of ghostly cold up her spine. It rises right out of the ground.

The plan had been to save it for Tommy, but why not? She has no real plans and doesn't want any that come to her. This wind seems just right for it. She clambers to kneeling and pulls the cigar tube from her pocket. She untwists the white plastic stopper. Sniffing, she smells unsmoked cigar.

Evelyn pours dead Claude into her palm. "Ashes" is not the word, is not even close. She squeezes, feels the grit of what must be granules of bone. Bone meal.

She opens her fist, flattens her palm, exposes the grey heap. The "ashes" are so heavy the breeze takes only the tiniest. She raises her hand higher, a gust meets it and a bit more is blown into the northwest. When she's given the wind ample time to take what it will, she changes this plan too and carefully pours the rest of Claude back into his tube. Tommy will get some after all.

Took it out on him, eh?

He says many things, much of it mumbling word-salad, sometimes in French. But sometimes his eyes are open and when he speaks to her he knows it. With one thing he says, he watches to see her reaction. She pretends not to hear. Because she really doesn't hear it. Do you actually hear something you don't understand?

Took it out on him, eh?

He watches her when he says something else, too. This time she does hear. He says it with affection. He says it more than once. Its truth dawns on him and his ramblings cease and his eyes brighten. His voice softens as his mouth shapes a thought he wants to keep alive.

He bought me a house …

Claude knows what this means. He is sharing amazement with her.

Bought me a house …

Tommy never did anything for anybody unless there was something bigger in it for him. Why did he buy Claude a house? How is it possible that such a son purchased a house for such a father? Does a sociopath buy a house for a father *because* he abandoned him and never made contact? Does it take such a great insult to get through to such a son? Does it take such a gift to get through to such a father?

Does it change what she thinks of Tommy?

"*He bought me* a house …"

The wind in her ears is distracting, confusing. In the distance is the growing clutch of lights, Ladysmith. She can blot the town out with a finger. She needs to ask Claude about Tommy. Tommy is alive to her now in ways he wasn't before and she needs to know.

She tried to forget the endless fights and she sees she has succeeded. Maybe too well. No, she can still see Tom's eyes, his angry eyes. At his desk, impatient and threatening, he spins around. All she's asked is, "What are you reading?" Asks it twice, three times. He spins and thrusts the book in her face and withdraws it just as fast, too fast to read the title. The anger in those eyes, anger not just at her. Hair, shoulders, shivering with it as he sits.

She gazes into water opaque with waves. If anger doesn't say a person's in pain, what does? A person in pain wants something that isn't there. What wasn't there for Tommy? Why did this plain logic escape her back then, in the thick of battle? Do sociopaths desire greatly and suffer constantly? It isn't what the books said.

What did he want? What did Tommy want?

When the storm comes, it surprises her. It's one she hasn't seen coming — it's inside her. She has merely taken one long, deep breath, let it out, and for whatever reason sees that girl bitten at the armpit by the dog. Here is her face, the little girl's eyes, mouth, gaping wide. Unable to scream. A sharp sound deep under flesh, a crunch and squeak, the dog's teeth on bone. The dog snorts a breath through its nostrils.

Evelyn doesn't know what is happening. She has a piece of driftwood, the size of a doll, worn so smooth it feels warm, which she lodges in the pit of her belly and folds herself over, rocking on it while she gasps and heaves with sobs.

But, no, she is crying for Claude, for losing him. And now for losing him again. She is crying for those pills of hers, for letting her ignore her life. She is crying for good Roy, too. She is crying for last night with Peter, how it woke her up from her dream of being young. But she's crying for Tommy, Tommy most of all. For not seeing him for so long and for seeing him soon.

Heaving, moaning. Sometimes her teeth clamp and grit, it's too painful to make sound. She might rip apart, she might burn. She plunges her feet into the water but this doesn't stop it. She knows this is the first time she has truly cried. After Claude's hospital, on the beach, it was nerves, it was smell, it was no pills. It was nothing like this. She cries for all she's forgotten, for everything that's gone and is no longer possible to feel, which includes the little girl and Claude and Roy and Tommy because *she forgot to cry in the first place*. What she cries for now is as deep as the death-cold sea.

The southeast wind brings its rain, as her island-story said it would. The wind blows hard, pushes both the tears and the rain to the northwest, across her cheeks and into her ears and hair, until she no longer knows if she's crying.

EVELYN HAS SETTLED. Drained. She feels no peace but she thinks it's in the vicinity, it's here on this little island. Maybe it *is* this island, peace in the rock itself, peace she can't feel because she isn't rock.

But an outside storm has come to stay and it's upon her. It's cold and there's no time and it's dark. She stumbles dragging stuff to the triangle of sand — the one flat spot on the island. Climbs into Peter's sleeping bag and pulls his tent around her as a second sheath. She can smell him faintly on both. Evelyn has touched Peter's nylon tent everywhere so now it leaks and before sleep comes she is wet through. Her body warms the water some, but she is a big dank sponge.

The wind begins to howl. Maybe she read the island wrong, maybe the bird whitewash coats only one side because the other side, the side she is lying on, gets beaten clean by waves during storms. If she gets beaten clean with icy water, how long till hypothermia? Maybe the kayak will be blasted away, maybe she will be stranded.

She breathes to calm herself. She doesn't really care in any case. She reads more: the sand she lies on is free of driftwood and seaweed and is long dry. She can hear that the waves bash some distance below. She will not be getting washed away tonight. The wind's howling begins to soothe her, because she can't quite feel it, snug in her warming sponge, clam-like and actually sweating in her layers of nylon. It is an odd kind of bath.

SHE WAKES SURROUNDED by calm water and a high tide too close to where she lies. The feather she planted back in the sand blew away in the night. She climbs out of her wet cocoon and strips naked, does some quick toe-touches. Though it's summer, it is too cold for this. Two seals tread water barely twenty feet away, watching. They make her feel her nakedness. Maybe she has taken their bed. Maybe they are trying to decide if they can take it back, what kind of fight she'll put up. They seem to be discussing this telepathically as they stare at her.

The day is overcast and cool. Neither tent nor sleeping bag will dry in this. She still has her old blanket stuffed in the kayak, for tonight, but she decides to go into Ladysmith, as her note said she would, to see if Peter shows. Of course he will. She drags the bag and tent and crams it into Peter's empty hole. She opens a can of sardines and chews, eyeing the seals, almost daring them. But she falls to wondering if she should be going in to Ladysmith at all. In the air is the notion of her *giving in*.

She is fidgety as she launches the kayak, gravity and her impatience scraping it even harder on the way down to the grey water.

She hasn't been bored since leaving Oakville. So here's another watershed of some sort: Boredom. Maybe she's back to normal. Normal does seem to include basic boredom. She begins to stroke forcefully, to put distance between her and these thoughts. She is not falling back into Oakville-Evie. This paddling isn't her cleaning the kitchen counter-top. This kayak isn't her glass of zinfandel and News at Six. This hard breathing isn't her yoga class, His Worship doing the cobra beside her, hissing so only she hears. This vista doesn't include smoke pouring out from Ford's three stacks.

She's going back to Ladysmith to see Peter Gore. It doesn't mean she's going back to Oakville to see Roy.

No more thoughts. Tired of thoughts. Paddling to Ladysmith means exercise, that's all it means. It doesn't mean even that. Dig in. Listen to the wake gurgle, boil. Wind, drying her hair. She is making her own wind, she is boiling water. Shoulders, wider than the kayak, *ow.*

Dig, in. Dig, in. Dig, in.

PETER IS NOT at the dock. Well, good for him. Evelyn asks a kid fishing what the time is, and the kid doesn't know. She asks what's his guess but he moves away from her. A pleasure boater happens along; it's eleven. She casts off and paddles the length of Ladysmith's waterfront, then back. It is a typical older waterfront town, typical in that from the start its shore was given over to commerce and is ugly. Most of the town lies up the hill.

She's never out of sight of the dock as she paddles. She returns to it, waits, not getting out of the kayak (but not parked in the water taxi's spot) until it must be twelve. Still no Peter. On a whim she sells the crab trap bungied to the deck to a loitering elderly Asian man for ten dollars, who tells her, happy as can be, that this same model costs forty-nine dollars at Canadian Tire. Evelyn hopes that Peter will like this gesture, this getting rid of one source of his gout.

She isn't surprised that she misses him but she is surprised that she misses him this much.

She pictures him in his rented room, writing at last. He'll be happier doing what he came here to do. He may not admit his life's failures but they're written on his sad face. Failure isn't in his vocabulary but it's in his shoulders' slump. She doesn't want to bother him; she'll just check in with him and encourage him further and have him hang the sleeping bag up to dry. Tonight she can set the tent up properly so it's not touching anything, and she has her dry blanket. With her ten dollars, maybe she'll get a nice little piece of meat somewhere, for some reason a lean flank steak appeals, and fresh vegetables. Maybe a pear for dessert. And find some wood. With this money and wood she can have a banquet on top of her bald-headed friend out there.

It's weird climbing out of the kayak — a black sheath of safety, hard like a beetle's shell. It's like she is the exposed guts, lifting themselves out.

Evelyn aims up a street. Her feet aren't used to walking on a smooth, hard surface and her jello-legs make her laugh out loud. It's no city, it's probably more village than town, but here are people striding past with purpose; there are smells, and cars. Even a small, quiet car is a farting violation. The sky patiently contains it nonetheless, as it does her. How patient for the sky to continue doing what it does, invisibly swaddling all. She doubts any Tibetans live here.

She skirts a gas station, watches an older woman at the self-serve fail to figure out the pump. Nervous, like she's on stage, the woman regards the hose as if it were a broken thing and keeps looking up to glare at the teenager inside at the till, who perhaps sees her but continues to chat with what might be his girlfriend. As human dilemmas go it's tiny, but Evelyn feels an edgy nausea bloom, one she can't shake as she continues her search for Peter.

She startles as a motorcycle *blats* across the street. Family-crammed, a new red Windstar rolls by and she thinks, *not wheat.*

Two girls in the van stare at her. Both laugh without speaking to each other. Evelyn is curious as to why. She has clothes on. She isn't hopping like a frog.

She walks two main streets and counts two motels and one hotel, which is old and sports a facade on its third floor, wild-west style. Its ground floor is a positively dangerous-looking bar, at the front of which sit six muscular, gleaming motorcycles. Peter will be at one of the motels.

Violent conflict was pervasive among groups of the Northwest Coast. Fighting could occur in many contexts, and conflicts between different kinship groups occupying the same winter village or between members of different winter villages of the same nation were not uncommon. Organized war expeditions occurred throughout the Northwest Coast, with the capture of slaves or revenge the primary motivations. Typically a group attacked at dawn, using the element of surprise.

— ROBERT J. MUCKLE,
THE FIRST NATIONS OF BRITISH COLUMBIA

LADYSMITH

ODD NAME FOR A TOWN. Tackling the steep hill to the main part of it, Gore goes into trudge mode. He lends his feet just enough awareness so they won't trip him. He turns vision in, dips memory's toe into a dim pool of research. Ladysmith. Yes, Ladysmith was the invention of a Mr. Dunsmuir, who named his burg after a Boer War massacre-town. Yes, and the streets are named after the English generals who perpetrated said massacre. That's right, and Dunsmuir built his town here because its deep little port could ship coal from his Nanaimo mines. The desperate Finnish and Chinese workers had to construct a quick shanty-town on wages already insufficient for them to feed their families. People actually starved here. This was 1900, and maybe this sort of thing was more typical than notorious.

But here on this violent island up this steep hill is a cruel town whose very name honours racial warfare a world away, and yes — Gore's pool of fact clarifies now — it was these same Ladysmith Finns who got fed up with their boss's noble greed and sought independence and harmony north in Sointula. Meanwhile, Dunsmuir was made an English lord.

They likely also got fed up with this hill. Gore is only halfway up and breathing hard. No more booze. Get off these pills. He stops to rest, staring at his feet. No, one wastes one's time staring at one's feet when in beautiful British Columbia.

Gore spins around to regard the view and — his breath catches at the level of his heart — there, a black sliver being paddled out of the bay. He brings his hand up to his pocket, and her note, the words that promise tomorrow.

THE MOTELS LOOK identical. Their lobbies even smell rather pleasantly the same. Or perhaps it's simply that neither one smells of tidal muck and seaweed.

Peter Gore chooses the SeaBreeze over Motel 6 because the Seabreeze is more expensive. He doesn't know why they charge more but trusts he will enjoy the extras even if he never learns what they are. Maybe it will be softer sheets or a better quality squeeze-packet of shampoo. It doesn't matter, all will be wonderful and heaven knows he's earned it.

Clothes are discarded, the shower is first. Nothing could be better than this shower. Arms up like rabbit-ears, he maneuvers to get the hot blast to scratch his back. Then pivots with a grin to let it violate his beard, flattening and spreading the hairs as if they were multiple legs and all their crotches sweet pits of itch. He moans and groans and laughs his way into a shout and laughs some more. The water sluicing off him into the tub is a yellow-brown, and to watch it disappear down the drain is to watch the banishment of all cares.

He would have liked, loved, to masturbate, as is his shower-habit. But he feels tenderly protective, still, of last night. Last night. What a surprise, Eve coming to his bed. Then a double surprise. Surprise, thy name is woman. No: woman thy name is *typical*. Let down your desire for one moment and don't you know but a witch will jump you. Give desire its natural manly rise and the witch flies away on her illogical stick. It's not fair. It's as unfair as *life*. There is something so cruelly *Buddhist* in this particular life-formula, this one that withholds everything unless you no longer want it.

No, it is he who is being unfair. She came to him needfully. Tremulous in the dark, afraid. Waking him with an understandable plea. They had survived a storm together. A deadly Pacific gale.

(*Gale!* The word dawns on him only now: he had survived a Gail. Wonderful to think of Gail as the embodiment of nature cruel and inchoate, a nature at its *least reasonable*.) But he and Eve did, in effect, save each other's life. *He* saved *her* life. Of course she's going to come to him, to celebrate life, to bring to his bed the spark that lights life's brightest candle, oooo.

Gore scrubs, using the washcloth like an abrasive spoon, digging into various fissures, no longer moaning but grimacing. With an abrupt chuckle he remembers his paddle-accident in the storm. You might say, in a big western accent: bonk her on the head and she'll come on back for more.

Then, in the middle of things, she decides to remember she's married.

Well. Anyway, there is something a bit odious about sex when it rouses you out of sleep and commands you, puppet-like, to perform its ritual movements. Unlike a casual wank, sex with another is so personal. Eye contact. Sounds. Breath. Silent dance of cooperation, challenging. And — and let's be honest, but Eve needed a bit of a showering off herself.

Despite his criticisms, he sees that revisiting last night has him half-aroused. He bats at it with his washcloth to chasten it, shame it. Save it for later.

He recalls that wonderful magazine cartoon, genius in a single panel, pinned over a urinal in that Victoria tavern. While dead, spent, used-up salmon drift past from upstream, a lone salmon hangs out of the current tucked in behind a rock, eyeing his dead comrades with trepidation. The caption reads, "Maybe I'll just stay here and masturbate."

But, save it for later. Because later holds promise. Later will bring the best images from last night, which were — *come* on now, *time* to admit it — rather fine. His first near-sex in, what, close to a *decade*? Eve proved exceedingly sweet while offering the juicy apple of herself. Even if she did keep her eyes open throughout. Even if she did leap away when bitten.

But she proved even better looking than he's been imagining. *Wondrous* pale curves of breast and hip rising out from the shadows of their criminal lair. Oh, dear. Her whispered commands, her breathing, her breathing that tripped into laughter. For that first minute, Eve was uninhibited. All that paddling seems to have left her rather in shape. Their elderly sex, had it occured, would *not* have been that of two spent salmon carcasses thumping together. No, there was something sleek, something eagerly *teenage* about her body and her appetite. Made him feel a bit the young bucking buck himself. She is indeed the sorceress.

Later.

Gore doesn't remember turning off the taps or exiting the shower, but now finds himself toweling violently off. Later. Because now it is time to plug in his computer. Because *now* is a plump apple whose juice is a river of words. Flowing to the ocean of his book.

LYING ON THE BED with pillows propping his back, empty pizza box frisbeed to the corner of the room, Gore sips cola through a straw and watches two ancient sitcoms in a row — Three's Company and Hogan's Heroes. His laptop sits plugged in beside the TV and Gore sends it occasional approving glances.

At first the power-light glowed a disastrous red. When some minutes later it switched to green, it prodded him like a cosmic traffic light, a muse mutely mouthing, *go.*

His plan was that watching bad TV would be a further muse. He knows the trick, it's one of contrast: just as the shittiest manure gives rise to the most vigorous plants, so this excretory tube-literature would seed profundities.

He wakes from a second cat nap and still there are no profundities gathered at tongue-tip. He strides swearing to his machine, sits at it and pops a button to open his first blank page, then shoots out of his seat to spend a frustrating hour striding the room waiting for the sentence. There should be at least a sentence: he can feel the entirety of Vancouver Island in his being, in his stomach. He feels its swelling and spicy isolation. The maxim, "No man is an island," floats in to nudge him and of course it rings false because, encased in skin, clearly every man *is* one. Islandness is the primary human experience. Vancouver Island is not just a separate landmass but an isolated spirit, a personality of its own. In effect, a kind of man.

Gore chews, swallows and digests this. According to the map, here in Ladysmith he is standing somewhere on this man's left calf. Gore begins typing. But the sentence that devirginizes his machine and now sits shyly screen-top, "Vancouver Island is a big unfriendly man," doesn't quite make it. Gonzo, perhaps, but one doesn't want to begin one's book with a sentence that might tax one's readers.

Gore inaugurates the delete button.

At this juncture a new idea, *way* outside the box of his plans, one both hellishly crushing yet deliriously grand, makes him rise slowly, almost ritualistically from his chair. He hums deep within his chest, the sound rising in pitch and tremolo to become the sound of a dove's pure white release from its cage. The idea is this: maybe *The Rim* is the kind of book that should be written *after* all the research is done. That is, finish the trip then start the writing. *No* — says a voice, and Gore feels a dove rudely shoved backwards into the cage — *that's a cop-out, a trap*. Looking into the mirror, Gore shakes his head at his sad eyes and sits back down.

He hates thinking about it, hates even admitting it, but Gail wrote a book. He hopes — no he prays — that this is not why he is writing one too. It can't be. Because it wasn't much of a book. It was thin, and only a text book, on the theory and practice of unassisted classroom learning. Even her explaining it almost put him to sleep. Yet he recalls how, nightly, she would turn an oddly blank smile his way and then step briskly into the den and shut the door, whereupon an *instant* — as if writing a book were no different than wiping the dishes — sound of typing ensued, and at a speedy if not positively chirpy pace. Gail's book got finished and published and more than a few institutions actually adopted it as curriculum. She neither lorded it over him nor tried to write another one.

Gore looks in the mirror and promises his concerned face that while Gail's book may have coincided with her feeling too tired for sex (indeed, with the last time they ever had sex) and while her book may have seeded his idea to write one of his own (in fact, it's around this time that he began his research) her book is not *why* he's writing his. See, hers was only a text book.

Memories of her hateful typing bring him to his initial inspiration, the one he keeps forgetting. His book needs neither ideas nor beauty. It doesn't need descriptions of majestic mountains or interviews with frustrated old men from the sea or with dirt-hippies whose utopias have died. It doesn't need a pod of pretty orcus porcus bubbling by, or coho salmon leaping prismatic in the sun or a stately geriatric cedar dribbling in the deep dark woods.

What it needs is, simply, the quotidian truth. Of this yeasty motel room. Of those three lads trampling out from their working-class forest to pee in his water and drink his whisky. The truth of this pizza, the medium meat-lovers special that is dangerously refusing to digest. The truth of freshly healed gout. The truth of sinews detaching from shoulder-bones at the *thought* of paddling more. The truth that you do get used to sleeping on the ground. The truth of the criminal thrill of smashing into a stranger's very home. The truth of bedding an attractive but spooky witch, surrounded by — if one believes said witch — a houseful of interuptus ghosts.

In other words he must write down the truth of each Gorey day. The truth of having discarded his dirty underwear one by one at campsites and beaches, a kind of marking his path with foul bread crumbs no bird would eat. The truth of what he has now named his "Jesus Pizza," because rather than digesting it seems to be multiplying. He needs a walk, and one whisky. So: time seek the truth of that seediest of seedy hotels he passed this morning, the Harleys parked out front, some bikers drinking in their favorite bar at ten.

Bikers gave Dr. Thompson his start, too.

IN A BAR BATHROOM Gore watches a younger fellow check himself thoroughly in the mirror. The man preens, appears to want to kiss what he sees, tamping briefly and ineffectually at his curls like a woman. It occurs to Gore how he's never cared that much for his appearance, perhaps knowing from day one that he didn't have much appearance to begin with, knowing that 'looks' was not to be one of his weapons. Still, he'd always cared enough to make sure that, leaving a bathroom, there was no major condiment on his shirt, nothing too obvious in a nostril. But today he is not even that fastidious. Nor would he be if he had an actual woman out in the bar waiting to be impressed. Neither ketchup nor snot would concern him tonight. No. And so it strikes Gore that there are likely only a handful of states of mind so free, so unheeding of mirrors, so nonchalant about being personally hideous. One, you don't care what you look like if you have one minute to live. Two, you don't care what you look like for the first five seconds after you've learned you've won millions of dollars. And, three, you don't care what you look like if you are high on Demerol.

Gore pops another of the little white pills. When one is in a place called Ladysmith and one's kayak isn't tied up at the saloon door because one's girlfriend has made off with it, one really shouldn't be concerned with one's appearance. Also, the more he takes, the sooner they will be gone and he can he healthy and normal again. Anyway, Ray and Bishop definitely don't care what he looks like, and they are waiting for him. It's probably already his turn.

It seems human nature dictates that one has to, occasionally, take *some*thing seriously in life. Which explains not only hockey fans and geode collectors but also why Ray and Bishop are concentrating on their darts. By their own admission they are new to it. Here it is three in the afternoon and judging from their posture and pace they have nothing whatsoever of import to fill the rest of their day. Though it doesn't help, they take long meditative aim with their shots. In fact they are meditative in how they sip their beers, nibble their nachos, pick nacho-bits from their beards, amble up to pluck darts from the board or, in Bishop's case, wall. Both motorcyclists wear cut-off jean jackets. While Ray sports a longsleeved undershirt, Bishop's flabbering armpits are bare, and his wafted odor is apparently the incense of his biker religion.

Both an indistinct thirty-fivish, Ray and Bishop are decent enough fellows but they are, after all, bikers, and Gore is careful to let them each win a game. In Bishop's case this calls for Gore's dance of precise near-misses and feigned anger. *Damn*! How-could-I-miss-fucking-*again*! Bishop is hulkingly huge and lacks a main front tooth and one senses that him losing *your* teeth for you might be the day's entertainment should darts begin to pale. The two-bucks-a-game stake clearly doesn't matter to them; it's a pride thing. In fact, when Bishop finally does "win," he ignores his four dollars and simply stands there, at a loss as to what to do next. He eventually drains his mug then announces that he's "goin' outside." Bishop stares down at Ray until Ray pays attention and then Bishop performs a little head-flick. Ray rises and is halfway out the bar before he stops, turns and aims a similar head-flick at Gore. On his own way out, catching sight of himself in the wall-mirror behind the bar, Gore shouts *when-in-Rome* to himself, though his lips don't move. Demerol or not, he feels more wary than adventurous. He has also had three whiskys but they don't seem to have penetrated the linoleum base of the pizza as yet.

"Know what?" Bishop asks sagely of Ray. "That blows, man."

Sitting against the hood of an SUV neither man owns, Ray and Bishop are discussing a friend's bad luck. They actually say "shitty karma," but they seem to mean luck. The day the friend learned he had no visiting rights to his kid, he got "gooned" — drunk — and then "dropped" — had an accident with — his bike. The friend is in hospital in Nanaimo.

Not a breath of a thought in his head, Bishop watches his boot tap the asphalt, and soon forgets to do even that. Ray reminds him what they came out here to do. If these two are Abbot and Costello, Ray is definitely Abbot.

The blend of furtive and casual as they pass a smouldering tube here in the parking lot, standing half-hidden in cars, reminds Gore of sharing a fag at recess amongst the pines at Land's End. Both Ray and Bishop wear their "colours" — the jean jackets emblazoned on the back with JOKERS MC over a grinning skull — which are just like school uniforms, the only difference being that, unlike English schoolboys, these two lads *want* to wear theirs. Which makes them rather the great big sissies, doesn't it? Gore has had but a small puff and is embarking on a much larger one while swallowing giggles produced by dangerous thoughts.

"Hey: that *fuckin'* blows," reaffirms Bishop. "I mean, Nanaimo General? It's fuckin' *summer*."

In truth Gore is bored. The one revelation about biker culture came to him almost immediately upon entering it: Bikers are bikers because they are stupid. Well, actually they can be quite smart, in the way Ray is smart (Gore witnessed him in an argument about coriander, then heard him dispense statistics about Atlantic salmon disease in fish farms), but they were bikers so they were *stupid*. They seemed exotic to him for about five minutes before they felt only familiar. These men were still living the emotional fridge-and-tit-groping lives of fourteen-year-old boys, and Gore had suffered two decades with that breed.

The joint is done. Bishop taps his boot in a rhythm he can't keep. Gore wonders how dangerous it would be to ask probing questions and gain further insights, but the real question is: why bother?

"Fuckin' blows *big* time. How's his bike?" asks Bishop.

"Totalled. Totalled *big* time."

"Worse than Rick's?"

"*That wasn't fucking Rick's*. That was *never fucking Rick's*." Ray flings up cupped hands like an exasperated Italian and looks to heaven for relief. "*Fuck!*"

"Well *fuck off*, you know what I fuckin *mean*." Bishop is whining and it's clear who the top dog is. Gore is careful not to look at Bishop until he settles.

The only edge to them is their danger and Gore thinks he has that one covered. They like you if you are confident and funny but not if you are too confident or too funny. His one joke during the dart game—"You Canadian lads are half as English as me, which maybe explains why you're twice as bad at darts"—made them glance at each other in a way that told Gore he teetered at a threshold.

It dawns on Gore that sharing this illegal smoke with them has freed him of suspicions that he may be police, and he wants to ask them whether they are, as it were, warrior barons of the drug trade, the bikers of Quebec being famously that. What better way to get them talking than to let them talk highly of themselves ("highly" of themselves yet another pun they'd miss). But what way in?

"Fellows, I don't mean to get personal but—"

The way Ray and Bishop rise so instantly alert to this makes Gore stammer.

"Well, I mean, I'm travelling with my lady-friend, this lady I'm presently *with*, and she's looking for her *son*, you see. Turns out he was into a little *dealing*—that is, I suspect rather a *lot* of dealing—and, um." The joint has frozen one part of his brain and he has to relocate in another. "Well, it seems that about a year ago he was, ah, felled during some kind of 'business transaction.' So to speak. Anyway, you lads seem to be rather *worldly* if you know what I mean, and, so, I was curious to know if you might *know* him."

Ray and Bishop are staring at him and it isn't fun. They don't look to be on the verge of saying anything.

"I mean, *lads*. I'm *not* a cop." Gore feels his chin quiver in a chuckle so lame he wonders now if he isn't a cop after all.

Ray snorts, a clear articulation of, "Of course you're not, look at you."

"Don't know what you're asking, man," Ray says evenly.

"Please, it's not a big deal, I was just—"

"I mean, you haven't told us the dude's *name*."

"What's his name, man?" echoes Bishop, though you could tell he hadn't till now realized what had been lacking. His tone suggests Gore was withholding the name on purpose.

But Gore sees that both men are very interested.

"Ah. It's—" Gore begins to giggle, and then to laugh with great, stuck, farting and choking sounds. Ray and Bishop wait professionally, with patient smiles, until he hisses, "*Tommy!*" Whereupon he begins to laugh anew.

He does eventually tell them that all he knows is that his name is Tommy or Tom.

"Your lady's looking, like, for his *body*?" Bishop shakes his head wisely and adds, "Never going to find it man."

"No no no. He's not *dead*."

"You said he was hit," says Ray, and both men are suspicious again.

"He was *beaten*. I think badly *beaten*. He's some kind of whale researcher. He's way up in a place called Sointula." Gore tosses this off cheerfully, pleased to have solved the miscommunication. He realizes his error, his lie, too late. He's just told them his lady is searching for her lost son and also that she knows exactly where he is.

But neither Ray nor Bishop have cottoned on. Both are brow-knit and thinking.

"Nope, don't know a dealer named Tommy," says Bishop.

"Not a badly *beaten* Tommy," jokes Ray, mimicking Gore's accent.

"Nope," laughs Bishop.

"That blows, though. Lookin' for him."

"Blows big time."

"*Big* time."

"Never find him."

"Fuck's wrong with you?" Ray raps Gore on the shin with his boot because Gore is bent over himself in pain.

"*Jesus*," hisses Peter Gore. "*Pizza*."

IT IS THE NATURE OF Demerol that a sense of "day" or "night" doesn't arise except that light falls differently in the eye. It's the same with "asleep" or "awake." Events in one state might be more implausible than the events in the other, but in neither state is there much to get excited about. Which is why, as a drug, it works. And which is why Gore, being fresh out of it, is in agony. Why, why did he waste it on his gout, on a nagging little digit? His entire abdomen is swollen and on fire. This is at least as bad as the attack that forced him to the hospital in Victoria.

He has made his decision and he must live with it. In the biker tavern he saw himself impaled on either of two nasty horns. One, he could enter the nearest hospital and have an emergency operation, and lose not only an organ but also Eve, who would be at the dock tomorrow but not the next day too, or the next. She would paddle away, rebuffed and proud. Face it man, she would not wait. (How much could one expect from a woman who abandoned a family?) Two, the second horn, he could ride out the fire-breathing bladder with calculated doses of whisky and marijuana, the latter being touted in all the newspapers these days as the latest cure for chronic pain.

He has been riding it out. Since closing down the bar and returning to his motel room he has had five or six scalding showers, which seem to help if only by directing his attention from deep-body agony to surface-skin agony. Who knows what helps and what doesn't. The whisky seemed best, but he has none of it left either.

He laughed at this thought while drunk, but he can't laugh at it now: he came to the motel desperate to write and to sleep and he has done neither. He has done neither in spades. Life is conspiring, of that there is no doubt. A man works hard, he plans, he takes early retirement on a shoestring, he moves dutifully from east to west — all to live his passion. Yet he is not allowed to write, or sleep. He is not allowed comfort of any kind. He is not allowed even to eat. How can any of this be? Maybe this journey is his personal dark night of the soul, maybe something good, if not grand, will come of it. It can't get any worse.

Well, no, it could. He still might get beaten up tonight. It must be two-thirty or three in the morning. He punches the TV remote buttons without having to look at them, gets the station with its little clock print-out along the bottom. Ten to three. He's eyed the time ever since deciding he had reason to worry that Bishop and whoever else might be paying him a visit. He tells himself it would've happened already if it was going to at all. It would've happened when the bars closed and they've been closed a good amount of time now. Though maybe they have a secret bar, maybe they could still be on their way. Maybe they've finished guzzling rum and stomping rats at the city dump and are even now hopping their bikes and spraying gravel on their way to get here. He is certain he let slip where he was staying.

Gore tries once more to make clear what happened. It was a slap. A vigorous slap, Bishop hitting him on the neck. Question one, was it intended for his shoulder — friendly — or his face — hostile, extremely hostile. (That Bishop *intended* to hit his neck is too weird to consider. No one hits necks. Though you never know about bikers, stoned bikers, bikers on this strange island, bikers trapped in a forested bell jar, neck-hitters.) Question two, what had Gore said to earn him such a slap? This question is harder to answer than the first. He had gotten himself quite medicinally drunk and there were hours of activity in that bar which are now very dim. He knows he spent lots of money. He knows he visited the parking lot for more BC bud, which he began lamely to call "my buddy." He knows he played more darts and met more bikers. He recalls being generally ignored, or tolerated. He listened to drunken stories and babbled a few of his own. He recalls little blurts, brown-neon moments, for instance when he stood and announced, "Who here *won't* be incinerated by the janitors of hell?" If he'd said that, it means he could have said virtually anything. He doesn't remember yacking about his book or taking notes on napkins, yet napkins he found crammed in his pocket are inscribed with the barely legible, *Everything is alive and edible,* and, *Women at sea men on land.* So, the question remains: what did he say to make Bishop swat his neck?

His neck still stings. He decides he'd rather be killed than beaten up.

He's been playing a little game. His shoes are off, he strides his room, scuffing his feet violently, then he touches the door-knob, *snap*. Scuff scuff scuff *snap*. It's something to do while he paces and groans and watches all-night TV. Sometimes he succeeds in seeing his pain to be no different than a laugh track that's gotten stuck.

Hogan's Heroes. Look at the funny wicked wily Nazi. Look at the bumbling fat sergeant. Both are rather thoroughly loveable. Both are dead now in real life. Both could make him cry.

Gore paces to the bathroom again. He catches a glimpse in the wall-to-wall mirror and looks quickly away. One of the motel perks he hasn't noticed until now is the second mirror, a small round one on a telescopic arm, bolted to the wall. Woman, they name is vanity-mirror. Gore gropes and fiddles, getting it to stretch until it extends behind his head, the back of which he can now see more clearly than he has ever wanted to. Women are so pathetically vain, to have to see the backs of their heads. Who would want to see the back of their head? He cannot imagine Eve using this mirror. Though perhaps she checked the back of her head in her old life, perhaps she checked it routinely. Well of course she did.

It takes Gore several brow-knit seconds for the notion to trickle in that, wait, it's *men* who are vain. They are vain because they *don't* check the backs of their heads. Women want to see the backs of their heads because they're *scared*. What else explains a need to see behind you? At this need men snort, vain as can be, unconcerned that the back of their hair might be stiff with baby goat saliva from their visit to the petting zoo.

Eve is scared. Of course she is. Gore searches for an image of her, finds one, focuses it, studies it. She is sitting on a stump, chin up and pointed in the direction of her fantasy. She is stubborn, she will stare at something the rest of us can't see, something that isn't even there, and she will declare it to be an immovable rock. She is clearly paralyzed, she is clearly scared of that nasty son of hers. She doesn't want to see him at all, but why doesn't she admit it? She needs comforting. She is camped alone, somewhere — somewhere *out there*. He can hear the wind. He can hear rain. *God* it is blowing out there. What is he doing sitting vain in a motel room? He discovers he feels physically torn. It's as though his body now feels the outdoors to be its true home, stormy or not. He has Eve to thank for this, for immersing him in something so primal. He should be out there cuddling her in that shrill and big-eyed night. Who has abandoned whom?

He could get quite weepy with thoughts of Eve tonight, out in that storm, but he won't let himself. Though he will look after her more carefully, more tenderly from now on.

Snap. Scuff scuff. He finds himself standing in front of the TV again. Another reason to feebly weep: his stomach pain seems to be subsiding. Maybe? Is it? Hallelujah? He laughs weakly, hopelessly, seeing himself in the wall mirror beside the TV. He should stop this looking in mirrors because he is scaring himself. He looks so, so old. And weak. Look at him laughing weakly, that *old* guy. The fat 'n' jolly sergeant is chuckling too, but unadvisedly, for he is about to be upbraided by Colonel Klink.

His stomach pain is not subsiding. Maybe a little. He is so *tired*, if that's even the word for it anymore. He has just passed out in a chair, his moan waking him up. Maybe he could try lying down again, on the bed. Miracle of miracles, he has a *bed*. The sheets are cool.

IT IS DAY AGAIN. He hears traffic outside, people must be going to work. He thinks he has, in fact, slept some. Light streams in the windows. The computer sits in shadows, fully charged. His stomach *is* better. He is not even hungover; all that pain *smiles* at so a puny a thing as a headache trying to poke through.

At last there are no excuses. An excellent day to begin.

Gore walks to the bathroom with the little glass coffee pot, fills it at the sink, pours it into the coffee machine's back, presses the button. Its little eye glows red not four feet from his computer's eye glowing green. He stands patiently, pleasantly. Sure enough, the machine starts heating and hissing and dripping. He closes his eyes, opens them. And now he has a coffee. He sips, slightly burning his lip tips, but the numb blood of his lips keep him safe from this too.

He finds his hand on the TV remote. He picks it up, his thumb already pressing the chief button. He drops it on the bed as if it were hot. He swears, picks it up again. Just the *time*, the *weather* channel. No, *Jesus*, he can see the weather outside, it's a fair day. He drops it on the bed. He moves to the window and parts the curtains to confirm: yes, it is a fair day.

Hmm, breakfast? Could he, should he write on an empty stomach? He should definitely go out and — What is he *thinking*?

Maybe he can't write. Simply can't. Maybe he belongs to that group of people who should write, who would be brilliant at it, who have the soul-intent and the good ideas and the proper tools, but when they sit down they — can't. No reasons, they just can't.

Thank God he isn't one of those people.

He sits at the writing desk, carefully not looking at the computer. He picks up the phone. He lets the black plastic warm against his ear. He knows Gail's number by heart and punches it in. Well of *course* she's not home. The thought of speaking a message leaves him more forlorn than is bearable. She's at work in the corporate outskirts of Detroit, school-boarding from an office, nary a student to be seen, like him a teacher who has left the students behind. He could get her work number from directory assistance but any chatting with her at work would be stilted, brief, blunt. Plus there is the possibility of him whimpering or, worse, declaring love. Long pained sighs, for sure. Gail would be abrupt and who could blame her.

He only wants to tell her how the writing's going. And he also wants to tell her he is no longer lonely. He wants to tell her about Eve.

Eve, Eve is the reason he does not write. Eve on her witless, witchy way north, her kayakical journey to her heart of darkness named Tom. Chasing her Annie Dillard moments, she is clearly, at the root of herself, terrified. But keeping him in line with matronly threats, with her woodsman lore. And also with the harlot's tease, yes she does, she can't hide it. That night, naked and exposed, soft as eviscera within the carapace of blankets. Crawling over him wordlessly, with hunger. Hunger bigger than both of them, irresistible, Darwinian, wicked.

Pain has ebbed, underwear has peaked. Later has arrived.

But wait — why fall to this habit? Eve is superb fantasy but she is more than that. She is down at the dock. She almost slept with him. It was a first date. A woman like Evelyn Poole does not just lie down and let you take it. They will work with her concerns and then she will sleep with him. He *has* seen the gates. He *has* a lover. *He has a lover.*

Flicking fingertips as one sprays water on a flaring barbeque, he snaps his underwear-pole a good one. It stuns his poor friend for a moment, long enough for him to pull on his jeans, which he does with some reluctance. Old habits die hard, and Gore notes more than one sad pun in that.

Hardness is everywhere. He'd almost forgotten that the morning's most recent, most powerful dream involved them having actual sex. It took place in the impossible confines of the kayak and while battling another storm. She is whimpering and he is seductive. Then an odd segment, him taking that morbid cigar tube from her pocket and trying to, well, insert it. He laughs gently at the image now, but at the time it was an angry act: you want Claude back? *Here*. It was high-kinky as she grew accepting of it, and he pushed, and then she was girly and coy, and the dream got up-close and icky rather than sexy, all rather technically graphic like the surgery one flicks past on the operation station, and soon the dream shifted such that there was cod jigging and flourescent bait involved.

He has been angry with a cigar tube. Amazing — he is already jealous of her. How absurd is he? Well, and how human. And shouldn't he be getting himself down to the dock? He stares at her love note, spread beside his pillow, its charcoal reduced to smudge.

Gore laughs again. He is, for this rare moment, almost fond of himself, and he discovers in this fondness what he must do to salvage his book, and this trip. It's been literally right in front of his face. He has Eve to thank for this as well. Eve with her romantically etched note, her pen of charcoal pinched from the fire.

Gore unplugs the computer rather violently, noting with grim satisfaction that this is the last time he will have to suffer the stupidity of that white screen, and the lunatic glare of that green light. *Go*. Sure, right. *You* go.

GORE RETURNS TO his room with a bag containing an apple, five little scribblers, a dozen unsharpened pencils and an envelope holding eleven-hundred dollars in cash. Standing in the open door to his room he sniffs its air as if adjudging the nature of the beast who lives here; he grabs a chair to prop the door ajar. Then he empties the bag on the bed. He figures the apple is a safe bet but isn't ready to risk it just yet. His guts are empty and painless and, compared to last night, feel oddly like they're not even there.

He knows he got ripped off. A pawn shop was not the place to sell a state-of-the-art computer but there was no other place in town that dealt in used technology. The mousey guy behind the counter said as much with his smile and shrug. When Gore explained that a three-thousand-dollar American computer was a five-thousand-dollar Canadian computer, the man smiled wider and shrugged higher, followed by his one pretense at bargaining: a grand leap from one thousand to eleven-hundred.

Gore returns from the bathroom with a shower cap, which he lays on the bed. Into it, as into a nest, he deposits the wad of cash. Then wraps it up double and squeezes it all together and stuffs it into his pocket. One cannot be too careful. A kayak is a virtual submarine and their world is a wet one. Waves and spray and Eve's playful splashings-from-behind. And they are due for more rain. They will paddle through said rain and perhaps storms, *bring it on*, and they will huddle in his tent and, between warm and spooky bouts with her, he will write his book.

He misses her dearly. It's overtime to get himself to the dock. In fact he's quite late. He won't even entertain the notion that she didn't come for him. He has only to remember her face as they kissed. The way she watched and assessed him, the look in her eyes spookily close to love.

He packs his scant things. Clean shirts he pulls down from the bath curtain bar. He hums while he tidies the towels (one of which he keeps). He misses his lover. This notion, these words, make him warm. He notes his erection but observes it with cheerful interest, much as he would a sunrise, because an erection pointed at another — so to speak — is a delightfully novel and warming thing. When you're happy it's so easy and right to be kind. He places the remote control on top of the TV for the next renter's use. He picks up his room key to drop at the desk.

About to leave the room, Gore turns and stares long at the phone. When will there be another one? While he is looking after her, others remain worried. It's the right thing to do. Of course it is. A good deed. One can't have enough good deeds.

It takes but seconds with directory assistance, then he simply asks for the Mayor's Office. A secretary with a universal voice answers and she tells Gore that the Mayor does not take personal calls but if he were to leave his name and number and briefly state the nature of his enquiry, the Mayor's Office would issue a —

"I'm phoning with information about his wife Evelyn."

He is put on hold and a rather oddly high-pitched, breathless voice comes on almost at once and asks, "Hello? You have news? About Evie Poole?"

In none of Eve's stories did Roy sound like this. Roy sounded like a professor, like a news anchorman. Not squeaky.

"Hello?"

"Yes, hello. Is this Roy? Roy Poole?"

"Is she alright?"

"*Ab*solutely fine. *Rest* assured." Gore clears his throat. He'd garbled that 'assured' as though he were drunk. He doesn't feel drunk. He doesn't know what he feels like.

"Where is she? Can I talk to her?"

"She's out in her kayak I'm afraid so, no, not at the moment. And — and I think it would be *best* if *she* called *you*. That is, I'm not sure she'd *like* it if — if I just stuck her on the *phone* to you without her *permission*. I mean, if she were even here. And, um, well." Calm down. "And to be honest with you she isn't aware of what I'm doing! That is, I didn't ask her anything *about* this."

"Could I ask who I'm speaking to, please?"

"Pleased to meet you, yes. My name is *Peter* Gore." Why is it so hard to communicate to this politician that he is being done a favour?

"And Evie's alright? How do you know her? And where is she?"

"I'm her good friend and we are travelling together."

"Will you please tell me where? Can I call her?"

"*I'm* not at liberty to divulge where she is, as I said."

"Can you please get her to call?"

"I'll try my best. I *can* tell you that she is on her way to see Tommy, who's apparently —" Gore hears himself chuckle, "— apparently still hard at it up north with his whales."

Roy Poole says nothing and Gore is not liking any of this. What seemed a good idea is a bad reality. It's like he has shocked awake an unknown animal and he holds it by a thin electric tail. He can hear the Mayor's anger and desperation coming through his tail-wire. Gore thought that he and Roy would be having an earnest conversation about the ins and outs of a woman named Eve. Truth be told, Gore had wanted to ask him a few questions.

"You're saying you're calling me without her knowledge."

"Yes. I thought it best."

"Is she well? Is she *able* to —"

"No no. She's well." Goodness, was she? He makes himself chuckle respectfully. "Though, you know *her*. She can be somewhat the spooky little —"

"She's upset with me? Is that what you're saying?"

"No no no. Well, I mean, perhaps. I really don't know."

"Then why is —"

"You see, I thought you might be *worried*, and I *just* wanted to let you know *she's fine*."

Roy says nothing for a moment, and then, "Well. That's good then, I suppose."

"And — and that she is in *good* hands."

The silence in the receiver deepens, as though the animal has been pacing in its lair and now it has stopped to listen. Indeed Mayor Poole sounds newly confused, so much so that his famous kindness accents what he says. "Well, I don't understand what's going on, but it sounds like I should be thanking you."

"No thanks *necessary*, truly. I just wanted to *reassure* you."

"Well, thank you."

"For nothing. Seriously. She's fine." Gore pauses. "She's quite a woman."

"And she doesn't want to call me. Am I to understand that?"

"She's — she's suffered a death. It is my considered opinion that she will call you when she is ready. In the meantime, well... And she's — she's a bit of a *spook*, you have to admit." Here Gore chuckles encouragingly, wanting to nudge the same out of Roy but to no avail. "Still I'll — I'll try to pry a phone call out of her, yes."

"I sincerely appreciate this."

"It's no problem. Though — of course — we are not often near phones."

"And you say she's well."

"She is, yes. Lots of outdoor activity. The picture of health." He hollows saying this. He sees her talking to herself and to people who aren't there. He sees her poking her scab. That spin of hers. Though it is true that she hasn't been doing much of that lately. "But you know I wish I could say the same for myself. Actually I was up all night with a *gall* bladder attack."

"I'm sorry to hear that. I hope it's better?"

"It's still a bit tender. And I'm, *I'm* a little cloudy." He pauses here, shaking his head at himself. Mouth open, he waits in the silence. That there could be a silence between him and Roy Poole! "I have to say, it's *odd* talking to you. I've heard so much about you and, and here you are!" Gore shakes his head at himself again. Shut. Up.

"She's going to see Tom."

"That's right, yes."

"Well, that is good news. That's wonderful. I have to say it's about time."

"I have to *agree*. It's been, what, ten years? Since they've communicated?"

"Communicated?" Roy laughs falsely. "It's been a lot longer than that."

"I see."

"She hasn't been emotionally well. I should tell you that. I'm glad she's doing as well as you say."

"She's quite *sparky* really."

"Evie... Evie has a way of absenting herself. From what isn't working out. She can withdraw *absolutely*. She did it to Tommy and now she's doing it to me." He pauses, and it's almost as if Gore can hear the depth and complexity of the man's thought. "Sorry to get this personal but I have a feeling you've already been filled in on our family history."

"I have." He feels too powerful now, and sorry for Roy Poole, who doesn't know that his wife is carrying Tommy's father in her pocket.

"But it's a good, good thing, her going to Tommy. Please encourage her for me, will you?"

"I'll do my best to see that a reunion takes *place*."

"And you give my boy my best, will you? He's been through a lot." Now it is Roy Poole's turn to clear his throat. Roy has begun to sound a little weepy. There will be no joking about his wife. "Can I ask you — Peter? — can I ask you to pass on a message for me?"

"Of course."

"Please — Peter — tell her I love her and I will come in a heartbeat if —"

Gore smashes the receiver down, because wouldn't you know but the coy witch herself chooses *now* to poke her head in the chair-propped motel door, smiling happily at him. His hand pressing hard on the phone, as if to keep Roy Poole down, he stares at her. Evie Poole, in the flesh. Those eyes, eyes afire. Hair tied back severely. She looks fierce. It's like he has been talking to Roy about somebody else entirely.

Her head tilts now, like a quizzical dog's. He feels his mouth quiver as it smiles. The witch is pretending not to know what she has caught him at.

SOINTULA

With everything up for grabs to the first-comer, like the man I had seen stuffing his freezer with cod, the abundance of the coast is fast disappearing. For the commercial fisherman, the struggle to survive has put a grim face on what was once an attractive way to make a living. There have been ugly confrontations on the beaches between rival gangs of clam diggers. "Creek robbers" seine illegally in remote estuaries, extinguishing remnant races of salmon in a single set of their nets.

— MICHAEL POOLE, *RAGGED ISLANDS*

PORT MACNEIL

MCKAY DRIVES ANGRY onto the Malcolm Island ferry. He rides across angry and disembarks angry, and is pissed off tooling through the weird little village of Sointula, weird because the cars drive like they still seem to think they're buggies, and people just walk anywhere, sometimes in the middle of the fucking road. Famously there are no cops on the island (another reason he chose here) but on the cement retaining wall those hand-painted words — "Place of Harmony" — he doesn't believe for a second.

He's mad at Tom Poole, but maybe part of his anger has to do with this place to begin with, he can admit this. In fact, McKay's interested in places and what they can do to your mind. He loved hearing about the Indians on this coast and how for thousands of years there were plenty of places they just would not go. Which explains how lots of times, entering a new valley or balancing up on a ridge, even along the highway in your car, you could suddenly just feel the shits. The place could even be sunny, didn't matter. You could be with your best friend and a cold one in your hand and best dope in your brain and yikes, it's like a black veil gets pulled.

Almost the whole road up to the north Island is like that. From Campbell River to Port MacNeil, along an endless logging road that got paved not too long ago, it's a string of dark haunted pockets that make you feel the shits. You wouldn't be surprised to hear about a race of cannibals living scattered about. Absolutely without question there were hermits around, hermits no one's even aware of, hermits so twisted you couldn't describe them. And let's not get into Tom Poole, here.

McKay's mood lightens as he leaves the spooky village and his big tires attack the gravel road and he enters forest. The practical Finns built their roads straight and they blast through as the crow flies, some nice little hills to fly over. By the time he reaches the little dirt parking lot at the trail head he isn't angry at all. He does like his hit of nature and it's been a while. The size of these trees. Nothing man-made as far as the eye can see. Ravens croaking as soon as you open the car door. The ocean crashing nicely just over that bank, that clump of salal. He knows it's salal because down-island he's seen the Chinese women picking it to sell to florist shops as background greenery. And smell the air. They say you can smell the Queen Charlottes from here, but that would be impossible. One true thing is that just across the water to the mainland, maybe twenty minutes in a cartop boat, is major *grizzly* territory. Tommy has assured him with a smile that they don't swim to this particular beach. Thank you very much. Whenever McKay asks the bastard about bears and cougars he smirks like the bastard he is and says, "Dogs 'n' cats?"

McKay checks his watch. So where is Tom Poole? And what exactly did Tom Poole *tell* her? What does Cal *know?* Anger rising again, McKay locks his car (which he knows is absurd even while he does it), and starts down the trail. The guy might have forgotten. The guy might not even own a watch.

The trail falls instantly dark under its canopy of trees and McKay isn't wild about being here. He likes nature but not this much nature — last time he visited they partied at Tom's campsite not far from right here and McKay came face to face with a fucking cougar. He'd asked a guy on the ferry about black bears, was told the island hadn't seen a bear, "not in years, though they do swim," and wouldn't you know but that very night a hiker told them he'd seen a "mother-fuckin' bear this high at the shoulder," a mile away and heading here toward Bere Point. "Ha ha," the hiker had added, "Bere Point." That had been scary enough, Tom and him — mostly him — having to make sure that food scraps were buried and that there was no prawn butter or barbeque sauce spilled on your pants before you went to sleep. They kept the fire high and had a few beers before hitting the tent, and in an adult version of scaring the shit out of each other with ghost stories they traded newspaper accounts of bears dragging people screaming from their tents in the night. Going to take his final pee, flashlight in hand, McKay poked out onto the beach, zipper down, swinging the flashlight hither and yon looking for the gleam of bear eyes. He saw eyes alright, twenty feet away at most, but instead of bear eyes he caught in his beam a holy fucking jumbo cougar. The lion was calm and just staring back at him, or at the flashlight beam probably, and the look on its face was as detached and crazy as any cat's. McKay backed away, never not aiming his light at it, and when he half tripped backwards over a root the cougar leapt off in the other direction, two hundred pounds airborne and utterly silent, and McKay instantly found himself in the tent, unable to talk. When he finally did get the words out, Tom Poole laughed mildly, his unconcern a lot like the cougar's. He was snoring a minute later.

One thing, it was the first time McKay had seen Tom laugh since he'd been shot. Though Tom Poole always did laugh at the strangest stuff. You don't want to go out in public and see a heavy movie with that man.

McKay really doesn't want to walk the whole way in. The walking gets way harder. Some juvenile delinquents had been paid to lay wood chips, and cedar planks over mud holes, but apparently the project money dried up after a hundred yards. Now the trail is even darker and getting swampy, with skunk cabbage patches to the left and right (he's heard bears eat the stuff), and dense underbrush hanging with moss and tendrils. A *Lord of the Rings* place, not Hobbit-like but Golum-like. If he meets a cougar here it will talk to him in Mandarin fucking Chinese as it paralyzes him and then eats him. McKay's anger sparks. Tom Poole missing the appointment at the trail head is more evidence that the man can not be relied on. And when a guy's unreliability affects other people, most of all McKay himself, it is time to do something about it. It is not too late, not quite. The boat is less than a week away.

Stepping quicker, McKay rounds a giant rotten stump and there is Tom Poole in the path. It's almost like he's been eavesdropping on McKay's thoughts because he's already looking at McKay with no surprise. Tom's just standing there holding a long stick. His face is filthy, and the backs of his hands are almost black. He says a simple "hi" then turns back to what he is doing, which is poking his stick into a pool of muddy water and studying it.

"I don't think this place drains," he says, so softly that McKay has to get him to repeat it.

"Is that right?"

"It's been sunny two days now, and look." Tom strikes the puddle with his stick, splashing mud onto his pants. "I think the trail has sort of wrecked things."

McKay is now nervous. What he is seeing here is more evidence.

TOM POOLE SITS in the car like he's never been in one before. He keeps a hand on the door handle and sits rigidly so his head doesn't bob on the bouncy dirt road. The opposite of relaxed. Nor has he commented on the vehicle, a Toyota SUV with the works — air, moon roof, killer CD — but McKay is still feeling a tad sheepish about the unit himself after his girlfriend gave him shit for buying a muscle-bound offroad polluter when all he really ever did was tool around the city.

So another reason to come up and see Tom Poole is to get free and take the vehicle off-road, though this gravel strip isn't exactly that. Anyway, the immediate idea is to treat Tom Poole to a burger. Have a visit but mainly find out what the hell's going on, what he told Cal. Here's a guy who never did give a shit, and now he's brain-damaged on top of it. Maybe they should all just go right now and knock on the prison door and ask for the corner suite.

There's a burger shack on the main fishing dock, makes huge honking burgers with tomatoes and cukes and hippie sprouts and gobs of sauce flying out all over your hands and they take an hour to make but they're really good. The only other place they could go in this weird little village is its one spectacularly depressing bar, called The Tank, which hides in the basement of a sort of tiny hotel, and though right on the waterfront it has no windows. It's the kind of place that would make an alcoholic hate himself just for being there and drink six times as much, hard booze, bang bang bang, might as well step in front of a bus. McKay has had only scant beer for almost ten years now and he is proud, you could say desperately proud, of his discipline. In any event, he wants one of those big burgers.

McKay stands at the open window and comments to both Tom and the girl working there how much they've fancied up the menu. Neither responds. They appear to know each other. But of course they would, this being one of those tiny pinchy places where everyone knows everything about everybody. About sixteen, the girl looks like a librarian-to-be except for her little nose-ring, which is a simple ball of green jade — an awful choice, he wants to tell her, because you really shouldn't have a thing that colour, that size, positioned that close to a nostril. He feels vaguely sorry for kids stuck in remote spots like this, because despite TV they really do grow up style-challenged. After the girl assures him it's "really good," he orders the Greek burger, and Tom Poole goes for the Sexy Finn, which is an oyster burger with melted "Malcolm Island gruyere cheese" and which, though he keeps it to himself, McKay thinks is enough to gag a maggot. Tom Poole orders "extra cukes" on it.

So it's going to be cukes, oysters and cheese. You can't help but picture that oyster burger in those dirty hands. The guy looks like a fucking coal miner.

Rotten luck but some weather's blowing in and rain spray hits them before the clouds are even overhead. They take a seat in the shelter made for such occurrences. It's a rough log frame with stapled plastic sheets housing two picnic tables. Due to the day's sun, inside it's hot and smells like a cedar sauna.

McKay wants to get right to it so they don't spoil their meal.

"Okay. Tom. Listen up. About our little transaction that's not even a week from now. I have some worries."

Tom Poole's reading a newspaper, which the date says is only days old but is already yellowed and wavy. He picks his head up and meets McKay's eyes for the first time today and it is, for a moment, unnerving. McKay speaks quickly, clearly.

"You and Cal broke up, right?"

Tom smiles. "What she tells me."

"Okay, I know her a bit, right? I mean I *like* her, but you have to admit she has a bit of a mouth on her, right? Gets a bit loud when she drinks? I mean she's *funny* and everything, but."

Tom Poole just waits.

"Okay, I have one big question. Tell me what you told Cal because Cal's in the bar now with every Tom, Dick and Harry and she's blabbing everything to everybody, so I need to know what it is these guys are hearing."

Tom Poole's expression doesn't change at all. Perhaps he's digesting what he's been told. His eyes fall back to the newspaper but he's not reading it. McKay pictures Cal in the bar two nights ago, a dead-cute reckless maniac, necking with not one but two guys at the same fucking table. Bouncing off Tom Poole with a vengeance. She must have loved him. What did Tom do to her?

"Hey, I didn't mean anything with the Tom and Dick thing. But I know you guys are finished, and she's a hot number, and I figured it would be no surprise, you know, that she's —"

"I couldn't give a fuck."

"About —?"

"Cal."

"Okay. Good. Now we need to get straight what she's saying. We can assume — we *should* assume — that everything you told her is now public knowledge." McKay tucks his head down into Tom Poole's field of vision and gets the man to look at him again. "Okay, I know I'm being very blunt here. But this is a big serious deal we have going on here and it's only six fucking days away. So talk to me please."

Tom Poole goes deeply silent. Brow knit, he turns and gazes off over his shoulder.

"Think I have time for a shower?"

"Ah — sorry?"

"They take their time here with the food. Think I have time for a shower?" Tom Poole points his chin across the parking lot to a new trailer. Under the WASHROOMS sign is a smaller one advertising hot showers, two minutes for two dollars.

"It's for pleasure boaters."

McKay detects the hint of wry in Poole's manner, watches him rise and begin his slow limp across the parking lot. McKay smiles, though he's just been told to fuck off. He's always surprised to learn that Tommy Poole is as tough as ever, and still a bit scary, handgun-lobotomy or not. McKay likes that one. Handgun-lobotomy. Apparently the twisty bastard came up with that one himself.

SOMETHING ABOUT OYSTERS and cheese still disgusts him, but at least Tom Poole's face is clean as he eats it. His own Greek burger is good, some of that feta cheese, and olive slices, and green peppers instead of lettuce. Good sauce, the white garlicy Greek stuff.

The back of one of Tom's hands isn't clean, though, and McKay doesn't look at it because it makes him sad. It's the good hand that isn't clean, because of course it would have been the lame hand trying to scrub the damn thing.

"You didn't tell her anything."

"Nothing."

"Okay, Tom, now I'm calling you on that because I *know* I heard her tell fucking Terry that she's pissed off at you not getting enough money out of the deal. I mean, I heard her say, 'Tommy's not getting enough money out of the deal.'" She had also added, "the fucking loser," and laughed like the cruelest bitch, but McKay kindly leaves that out and stares at Tom Poole.

"Whales."

"Sorry?"

"I don't get paid for the whales. For my research. Don't get paid a thing."

"Oh, so—"

McKay sits back and regards Tom Poole. One side of the man's mouth is affected by his injury and it hangs a bit, doesn't do much of the work forming words, and wet food has a hard time staying in, especially when he's eating and talking at the same time. It's awful to watch the guy take a bite of bread and oyster and then hear the crunch of cucumber, jesus. Plus he got the girl to squeeze a lemon over the whole mess, so there's all kinds of stuff coming out that Mckay's trying not to look at.

It's almost impossible to consider that this guy is being slick and deceptive with you, though that might be the case. It's also impossible not to feel sorry for him, the limp, the hand crimped up like that, and way he's gone all slow in general. Looking like he's thinking deep thoughts, when that might not be what's going on at all. He was just so *fast* before. On top of everything. Maybe he still is.

It's the not-giving-a-shit side that worries McKay. He doesn't know the whole story, but the guy across from him not giving a fuck for his gorgeous ex-girlfriend is the same guy who ripped off someone big to buy his wild French dad a house, and who had a chance to pay it back but didn't bother. Wouldn't sell the house he gave his dad because, as he put it to McKay almost rhetorically, "Claude's never had his own place." Instead, owing all this money, he leaves town, but starts doing deals and just paints his face with fucking beet juice. Fine, it did look like one of those birthmarks, but Tom goes and plays around with it, changes it every few days, paints funny drawings—according to Marie, one was an X's and O's game—the guy does have the wickedest sense of humor. Some people called it a death wish, but McKay thinks it's Tom Poole's sense of humour that got him shot. That, and not even considering putting his old man out on the street. Old French guy who laughs a lot and can pour gallons into himself and play jumbo African bongos like a speed machine. Tommy told McKay once, shaking his head fondly, that his dad's favorite drug was Ecstacy, like a teenager.

"Okay. Tom? Fine. But look. I also heard Cal talking about the hydrophone. Why would she talk about the hydrophone?"

"She liked listening to it."

"I know, but she was talking about the hydrophone and boats, *ships*, how *you* can identify *the boats and ships and anybody out there*." McKay has to calm himself down. He knows Tom Poole doesn't respond well to anger. "So. Okay. Why would she talk about that?"

"Because I can."

"Because you can?"

"Because I can identify the boats and ships and anybody out there. Why wouldn't she say that? It's interesting. Especially in a bar with a bunch of boring assholes."

McKay knows he's being included in this bunch and doesn't know what to ask next. He knows what he heard in the bar. He saw the shine in her eyes, saw the bland bragging expression, how you don't act excited at all, how you pretend to be bored as you drop tidbits about the biggest baddest stuff.

"You know, *Tom*." McKay pauses, only half-believing what he's about to say. "It's not even cops I'm worried about. They're the last thing I'm worried about. There were no cops in the bar with Cal. There were no people in the bar who would hear stuff and then go and *tell* any cops. I'm not fucking *worried* about that. I'm worried about the same guys who shot you. There were guys in that bar who maybe if they heard about our deal going down might brag about knowing about it, just like Cal was doing, and *they* tell someone, and *they* tell someone, and before you know it there's more than just us waiting for that ship to come in." He meets Tom's eye for this last part. "I don't want some Vietnamese guy showing up at your tent."

"They weren't Vietnamese."

McKay rolls his eyes and looks away. He's heard this before. Tom Poole not knowing who they were, but knowing who they weren't.

"Anyway, you can see why I'm worried."

McKay hopes Tom can't sense him lying, because his real worries are much bigger than Tom Poole at his tent. What he hasn't told Tom

Poole is how big this deal is really, and how right Cal was in complaining that Tom should be making more. When the big boat comes, not only are they off-loading coke, two tons of it, but on-loading BC bud, two tons of it. Straight pound-for-pound deal, no money at all. Imagine growing dope so good it's ounce for ounce as desirable as coke. BC should be proud of itself, it really should. Their unloaded dope truck, now a coke truck, would get back on the ferry and just keep on going until Montreal, unload the candy there. It might be going on to New York but he doesn't know and because his money is coming from Montreal. The money is big, big, big, and all McKay has to do now is wait for the five untraceable installments into five banks. He can retire, though it's not the word he likes to use. But the deal is so sweet: he doesn't even have to watch the guys hump the bags on and off a boat, he did none of the actual growing, he'll do none of the travel, he won't even have to touch it. He doesn't even have to *be* here. He made a bunch of phone calls and two visits; McKay is for the first time a pure businessman. The only downside, which makes the whole thing double-dangerous, is that all the stuff will be here, in one place at one time. Coke and pot, everything. If the cops or bad guys come and grab it, he will have dangerous farmers chasing him on two continents. Mommy.

Tom just shrugs again and this time there's a little smile to go with it. McKay feels defeated. The doubts he ferried over haven't lessened at all. Tom Poole has given him nothing. It's never not been this way with Tom Poole. McKay's known this guy for a decade but he hasn't known him at all. Tom gets himself shot, and now McKay knows him even less.

And so, though McKay doesn't really need to be here, he decides again to stay. Just in case. He was right in bringing his sleeping bag, his cooler, extra clothes. Sleep in the back of his vehicle beside the stupid sawed-off .22. He's hidden it back there more out of embarrassment than anything. Not that he'd ever have to use it, except maybe to scare somebody off, but a .22. Though a .22 was big enough to take out Tommy, wasn't it? This one's a semi-automatic, which, sawed off, is a poor man's Uzi. Fast as you can pull the trigger. Maybe he should hike deep into the bush and try it out, get in some target practice, shoot an antler off a deer. And try out Doug's stupid 'silencer,' which was really embarrassing but which Doug said actually worked — an empty 2-litre plastic pop bottle with a hole in the base. You just duct-tape the bottle-neck to the muzzle, said Doug, and you can hardly hear it from one hundred feet away. Doug has to be full of shit and all it will do is screw up your aim. But then again, Doug did know how to saw the barrel off a rifle. And it'll be fun to try it out.

Basically he'll hang around, see who gets off the ferry each day, wait around until his ship comes in and his deal gets done. Maybe do some aimless hiking, check out some properties, see what retirement's like.

Accommodating anywhere from one to several people, most sweatlodges were rounded structures with a pole framework overlaid with earth or mats. Much like in a modern day sauna or steambath, water was poured over hot rocks to create high humidity and heat inside the structure. In addition to their hygienic value, sweatbaths were commonly thought to enhance the effectiveness of plant medicines and to provide spiritual cleansing.

— ROBERT J. MUCKLE,
THE FIRST NATIONS OF BRITISH COLUMBIA

TRINCOMALI CHANNEL

EVELYN DOESN'T WANT TO press. Peter was so embarrassed to be caught at the phone. It's touching, that he's still attached to Gail. After a divorce. After *time*. So that expression is wrong — time has nothing to do with healing. Time has only to do with washing over you and over you until the memories fade to white and die into little bleached feathers. Healing and forgetting are different. Healing stands on sturdy legs, it's compact, it's rosy and plump and loyal, full of eager blood. Forgetting lounges like a Suess dog, mauve and long-haired and bony, staring into a hand-mirror, blinking long eyelashes, thinking candy thoughts…

So it's touching that Peter cannot forget Gail. He sits in front, paddling too hard and with no sense of where they are heading. He jokes about Ladysmith and how he rogered their biggest blokes at darts and left town with a bag of money. He thanked her for inspiring him to sell his computer. Packing the kayak, he showed her his pile of scribblers and rattled a cellophane bag of yellow pencils. He tells her that at long last his book is going swimmingly. He declares that finally he is enjoying his "new job." He describes a gall-bladder attack "so ferocious it's left me willing to never eat again." He says it's great to be back together, that he missed her. Peter appears sober and undrugged but very tired and she is worried for him. It looks like in one night he's lost ten pounds and hasn't slept. He's manic but not sarcastic with her.

The rain is mostly mist and the afternoon continues warm. As long, low Valdez Island comes into view, Peter continues talking too much. The weather, their speed, his book. All falsely cheerful.

"I missed you," he says again.

She will go to the heart of it. "You were talking to Gail, weren't you?"

Peter guffaws. Then sits unmoving. His head lifts in a tight little spasm, then tilts like a puppy's, where it stays.

"It's okay to call Gail."

"I didn't call Gail."

"It's okay to feel a little guilty."

"... Um..."

"About the other night."

"Well I don't. *No* guilt. None." He turns so that his beard and ear come into view. "Do *you* feel guilty about it?"

"No."

"You don't regret it then?"

She hesitates, knows that her answer, whatever it is, will sound as loud as a shout to him. What is her answer? She leaves it at another, "No."

"Well then, why don't we *carry on*. With what we almost *accomplished*."

"Because... we're in a kayak?"

"Doing it in a kayak is *actually* a dream of mine."

"Peter, I'm glad you called Gail, you don't have to pretend that—"

"My dream of *extreme marine rumpy-pumpy*."

Evelyn can't help smiling. He's laughing at himself and his voice has fallen to weak and weasely. Just enjoy the man. They are joined at the hips, sharing this plastic torpedo.

Enjoy him. He's *here*, he's as alive as anything around her, he's as present as that logged-off mountain, as the fibreglass cold on her calves. If it's not him, it's the slap of waves on the hull. His noise is no different than a tricky wind. He blows her thoughts to unforeseen places. He helps her to see farther ahead, and farther back.

It dawns on her that Peter doesn't feel guilty about the other night after all. She sees now that he called Gail to brag.

ANKLE DEEP, EVELYN HUMS doing the dishes in the falling light. Shreds of rock-cod skin she has flicked to the side, and already tiny crabs are all over it, turning it into themselves. On their way to it, a few crawl over her toes. The "dishes" are two forks, a knife and two plastic plates, and "doing" means rubbing sand into them, rinsing them in small breaking waves and dropping them up on the moss bank till morning.

The vista west includes a golden wall of sunset. She thinks those lights up Vancouver Island's coast must be Nanaimo. A colossal mill sits near it, bellowing a white tumble of cotton that rides the sea for miles, rising high enough to be graced at the top with gold. She thinks of a pun bad enough to be worthy of Peter Gore: pollution can be breath-taking.

Peter cleaned and cooked the rock cod tonight, which is why she is on dishes. The fish was ragged from uncertain butchering and cooked dry, but it was a first for Peter. (His gall bladder must truly be a worry because he regarded the fish on his fork as trouble and ate next to nothing.) Otherwise the evening has felt smooth and good, the domestic details of boat and campsite and food joining in a rhythm that feels like life moving, synchronized, maybe even on a benevolent path. Clockmakers must have been secretly joyous. What clocks did the People here have? They had totems, reminding them of their family story. They had neat racks of smoking salmon strips; they had the season of huckleberries preceding the season of blackberries. They knew what day the herring came to spawn and coat the shore with eggs and milt. The People had tides, every day, what a blessing these tides…

Evelyn wanders down the beach a ways and finds a boulder to pee behind. Valdez Island has almost no people on it, she sees but one light more than a mile off; she's shy only of Peter. Not shy, but something has changed. She feels the warm evening on her legs, imagines herself taking a quick hygienic dip, takes a second longer to feel that her underbody has been considering sex all along, all day. Not an urge. More like a possibility, an opening. A tang of salt at the rim.

Evelyn pees, shivering at the start. She doesn't want to swim. She pulls up her shorts. Maybe she should suggest they swim together. Two kids in the moonlight. And it might be fun to drink a little. Whisky and a skinny dip. Isn't she the perverse one though? A week of tsking Peter's whisky-mongering and here she is wanting a drink on the first day she's known Peter to have none.

She can't see the exact path to their clearing but she knows the spot in a general sense and she cuts up through the salal. It tickles her skin, knees, thighs. Itch and sting and tease. What would it feel like — she laughs aloud at this and actually feels a buzz in the groin — how would it feel to doff her shorts and walk wide-legged naked through these waist-high twigs, probes, leaves?

Or, run. Nature as feathery vibrator. Has a woman ever done that? Has a woman on this island ever done it? On this shoreline? Through this patch of salal?

The north star is just coming through, insistent as a needle, as she climbs to their clearing, which is already dark except for their fire. Peter has stoked the fire tall and he hunkers behind it, staring at her as she nears. His hair is as wild as always but his face in the pulsing yellow is slack, serious, the face of someone who is determined, against all good judgement, to tell someone he loves them.

"Evelyn?"

"Did the dishes, dear." She will keep it light.

"No, Evelyn, I just want —" he begins. "Well, it's not a big deal so I shouldn't *make* it a big deal. But I *feel* lousy for not telling you earlier, which in retrospect has now *made* it a big deal, *makes* it a big deal but — And *also* in retrospect I really should have asked your permission, but —" Peter pokes a stick into the fire, toppling a large balanced chunk, causing a bouquet of orange sparks to lift curling almost to the treetops. His face, momentarily white, is red again. "I can *also* say I don't regret doing it. But I do admit I am a little, ah, concerned about your reaction."

He tells her about Roy.

EVELYN'S REACTION CONCERNS her as well. She stands, spins and walks from the campsite. Head up, shoulders back, her anger wide and cool and clear.

She doesn't know why she is angry. Or exactly what she feels. Sitting on the beach surrounded once more by quiet, she isn't in a rage at all. Maybe frightened about what happens next. Mostly, Peter's call has brought Oakville right here to Valdez Island. Oakville has jumped three thousand miles and landed. In her. She feels like her Oakville self. Roy might as well be standing behind a tree. Concerned for her, ready any second to speak. Roy might touch her. It feels like he could.

Evelyn hates having two worlds, this double vision, her whole body a bad lens. Both places are too clear and they push and overlap, mixing flu-like right behind her eyes, making her want to throw up. She has to keep breathing deeply, formally.

Sometimes she has to stand and walk. She catches herself pivoting on one foot, changing direction in the sand. *Ow*, Peter has really blown it. She lets herself get angry again. She stares at Nanaimo's lights, and at the mill smoke, lit up in a way that makes her think, *Zorro's spangled hat*, though it doesn't look like a hat at all.

When after an hour she returns to bark at him, he is only quiet and sorry for himself. He retreats into the tent. She sits by the fire and watches it die down. She hugs her knees until all that's left of the fire is black coals with scattered orange mouths, catacombs. It's late and she might be able to sleep. She gathers her blankets and steps into the tent, feels to find room beside him in the dark. There's no way he's asleep.

"You phoned him to tell him about us."

"Evelyn it *isn't possible* that I would for a moment —"

"You called to tell him."

"I truly truly didn't."

"Did you call it 'rumpy-pumpy'?"

"Jesus."

"Did he laugh?"

"He had no reason to laugh. He expressed his concern for you."

"I mean what the were you *thinking*?"

"Well surely — Evelyn, surely your loved ones are worried. I wanted to reassure them. Because they're no doubt *worried*. He *was* worried. And now perhaps he's not. *Quite* as worried."

"You told him. I can't believe it."

"Why would I tell him? We didn't *do* anything."

"Yes we did."

"We — we *necked*."

"And you told him."

"No I didn't."

"You didn't. Why did you hang up like that? Why were you so scared?"

"I can honestly say that I didn't. You — you startled me. And, and *c'mon*. Admittedly I was going behind your *back*. To do *good*." In the dark, in his sleeping bag, Peter thrashes once, indignantly. "Get real, *please*. As a former husband my*self* I knew he must be going crazy. *Forgive* me for putting him at ease." A triumphant pause. "Roy says *hello* by the way."

Evelyn hears the name with her whole body. Overlapping lenses. Selves. She shakes her head violently. Peter waits, gets nothing from her so he bullies on.

"I thought you still *felt* for the man. And he sounded like a decent fellow."

"He's none of your business."

At this Peter falls timid again, so she knows she is right in saying it.

"What did you tell him about us. Your exact words."

"*I* don't know."

"What."

"I said we were travelling together."

"Yes?"

"Because you want to find Tom."

"Yes?"

"That's it."

"No it isn't."

"Well, I told him not to worry."

"Because why."

"Because she's in — because you're in — good hands."

"I *knew* it."

"*Sorry*? What?"

"You told him. I knew it."

"What?"

"Ownership."

"Ownership?"

Evelyn doesn't answer. Peter knows. He persists and asks "what?" once more but there's weakness, guilt in it.

She feels better. Oakville flies back east where it belongs. Roy is back there, brooding in his sleep, brooding now for a different reason, maybe a reason easier for him to understand.

She feels good enough to let herself drift. She feels Peter bruised and alert beside her, his strategies filling the tent. She feels him finally settle on one.

"I'm *sorry* if I meddled in your affairs. But nothing like the other night has happened to me for years and years." A perfect pause. "I'm sorry if it wasn't as special for you."

After a minute, he finds another.

"*You* became my business so *he* became my business."

A minute later, another.

"I can't eat anything, I'm bloody *starving*, and I get confused."

Ten, twenty minutes go by, and she is more asleep than waiting. The last one does come.

"Nothing like you has ever happened to me."

Against this Evelyn has nothing. She breathes steadily and ushers her senses through the thin fabric of tent, out into the trees. She can see them, both from inside the tent and out.

Did the woman who lived here, who lay in the dark on this same patch of ground, did she have these problems? Evelyn wants no more thoughts. Hitting Peter Gore would be simplest. Her counterpart of a thousand years ago would have hit him. As his possession, she would be safe to hit him. Evelyn has never minded a man's ownership. As long as it has nothing to do with her.

She wishes for a strong wind tonight. If there were loud wind and waves, howling and simply pounding over and over them, none of this would be a problem.

FOR TWO DAYS and nights she finds she is still wide and cool with him. It's just the way it is; she neither wants this nor doesn't want this. It is their tide. They strike a rhythm in their paddling and in their work. It is natural that Peter is also made angry by her. He is silent and grim and at one point accuses her of inconsistency, and Evelyn accuses him of logic, and though both accusations sound reasonable enough, neither grows less angry.

A strict and simple goal of north fuels them both. Their kayak bow is as insistent as a hunting beak. Always finding north, very like the point of a compass. They don't need to talk because it is a simple life and they know what needs to be done. Silently they know to take turns jigging or gutting or cooking or finding driftwood. They don't resist accidental fun, as when Evelyn steers them into the wake of a gull-chased fishboat, which they follow awhile, a ball of gulls over them, until splat, splat, white gobs hit them and they squeal like kids and paddle off to safety. They sleep in the same small tent because they spend the day in the same small boat. In neither place do they touch. Once, sometime in the night, in a fit of loose bravery Peter does reach out to cup her shoulder and squeeze. After a minute of nothing back from her, no clue for or against, he withdraws his hand, performing a contented sigh to suggest that everything has gone according to his desires.

The second afternoon of their silence they skirt a lovely shallow bay on what Evelyn regretfully knows to be De Courcey Island. She remembers Peter's interest in the mystic fraud Brother Twelve, whose main colony and gold-hoarding happened here. He would want to know this for his book. Though he hasn't been writing, not that she can see. Maybe he writes in the ghostlight.

They aim for a flat bit of sand. It looks like a deliciously spirited little island. The air in the shadows between trees suggests paisley. Twenty feet from shore she digs in and they pick up speed. Peter tenses in his seat. Her crotch tickles as their underbelly scrunches into the sand.

"This is De Courcey," she says, simply. "Brother Twelve?"

Peter looks into the trees with new interest. He surveys the beach left, then right, then looks to the trees again.

"I doubt we'll find pentagrams in the sand," she adds, regretting it as she does.

Peter ignores her and climbs out nimbly — that is, nimbly compared to before. He turns and watches her. He doesn't help steady the boat for her, a first.

"I know it's De Courcey. Maps show a stream near the southwest, which is where we are standing. I was looking for this stream because De Courcey has almost no water." He turns away from her and gazes once more into the forest.

"You knew this was De Courcey?"

"Yes. And the last two nights was Valdez."

Evelyn points at a big land mass due north and a lesser island at its left.

"What are those?"

"That," he says, "would be Gabriola." He flicks his face at the small one. "So that would be Mudge. All that smoke comes from the mill on the outskirts of Nanaimo."

"You bought another map."

"No." Peter settles into a smugness that looks very English. "*Respecting* your decision to be map-free, I studied a chart on the wall of the Ladysmith tavern, and while waiting for my turns at darts, *memorized* it." Not even looking at it, he points to the south tip of Gabriola. "There will be a Dengen *Bay* right over there if you are interested in a sheltered anchorage."

Peter stretches his limbs dramatically, groaning and grunting. Evelyn sees that his shoulders have grown visibly bigger. They are almost of normal size. His paunch has long gone. She notes in his beard the grey currents coursing down from his sideburns like glacial-silt creeks flowing into a darker sea.

Peter pats a clean blond log.

"Let's sit. I have a *question*."

In a gesture almost of disobedience, Evelyn stretches leisurely before sitting. She takes off her wet shoes and socks, she wiggles her feet and plunges their mild smell into the sand. She looks up at Peter and waits. She doesn't tell him how many people have sat on this log.

"This has been fun," Peter begins. "But I'm *wondering* what your plans are. Your *actual plans*. That is, I'm wondering if you *have* 'actual plans'."

"I've told you my plans."

"On your way to see Tommy? Those plans?"

"Yes —"

"In time for his *birth*day, August 10th?"

Peter's manner reminds her of the night they first met, on Saltspring Island. Brusque, self-certain, outraged at details and not knowing how funny it all looks.

"That would be nice. But —"

"Ah. 'That would be nice.'" Peter snorts almost inaudibly and looks away from her.

"What?"

"Bullshit, Evelyn."

Evelyn doesn't want this. Her plans are tonight's dinner. She's hungry. Her plans are to conserve water until tomorrow. She knows, she's known all along, that they have just enough water for two people, for one night. These are plans so the body can make its way forward.

"And you're 'on vacation.' Right."

"Well, I am." She says this tunefully and smiles. "So are you."

Peter ignores this. He actually digs his heels in, punching them into the sand, first left then right. He persists in his hurt and pompous performance.

"I don't know how you stand with *arithmetic*, but during my studies of the tavern map, I learned several things. Granted I was quaffing endless great mugs of *beer* while pursuing these equations, but I think I was clear enough on the first point, which is that, Vancouver Island is a rather *large place*."

Peter puts a quick hand up in case a retort is forthcoming, though none is.

"Next I memorized the south of the island, and all the little sister-ugly islands we've been sleeping on during our time together. Before I got completely soused, I arrived at a formula that might interest you. The time we've traveled in our ten days together — It has been ten days, correct?"

"I have no idea."

"Ten days. In ten days we've traveled maybe forty nautical miles. North, as the crow flies. Now, it might *seem* like we've traveled farther, because in truth we bloody well *have*. Here." Peter plucks up a bleached-white stick and with it pokes two holes a foot apart in the sand. "This, apparently, is your idea of the quickest route between two points." With the stick Peter slashes sand in zigs and zags that go nowhere near the two holes. The zigs become violent thrashings and sand flies and Peter ends it all with a baritone bellowed, "FUCK."

He puts up his hand again. She isn't sure if he has seen her smile.

"The next calculation is vital. You want to celebrate your son Tommy's birthday with him. Fine. Fine display of *fondness*. His birthday is in seven days, and do you know what that means?"

"A week?"

Peter ignores her. "By my humble calculation, at your present rate of speed — whether I'm with you or not, which is another matter we should get to — you will arrive at Sointula sometime a little more than a year from now."

Evelyn shrugs, says almost in sing-song, "Oh well, then."

"I'm serious. This isn't even taking into account Johnstone Straight's hundred mile *impersonation* of water. It is in fact a chute for storms, tidal rapids, ten-foot waves. It's *legendary*. It has steep banks with no place to haul up a boat let alone camp. It took the barest research to see that you have thought *none* of this out."

"I never said I did."

Peter is eyeing her warily. Evelyn can see that he wants to call her crazy but is probably afraid this will insult her or make her crazier. Or maybe he is finally tiring of her, coming to the conclusion that she's no bargain. How long should a man indulge a woman who makes demands, is "inconsistent," and yet doesn't put out? She sympathizes.

But he attacks.

"You don't want to go see your son at all. Your husband told me that first you abandoned your son, just as now you are abandoning him. *Those* were his words. And I'd have to —"

"He said that?"

"— say the proof was in the pudding. Yes. He said that. Okay, not exactly that. But it's exactly what he *meant*."

"He said I abandoned Tommy?"

"It wasn't the word he used, but..."

Now Peter has looked her in the face and is stammering for what he sees in it. She tries as best she can to relax every small muscle to make her face blank.

"So what do you want from me, Peter?"

Peter appears not to have expected this. She's glad to disturb his act, his route. Look at his face. It's like she's just turned a log over. Pale moss and fresh dirt.

"I suppose I —" Peter begins. He thinks, turns fully to face her, holds her eye. "I don't want to be ignored."

Evelyn can answer honestly. She nods. "I won't ignore you."

"And you know? I suppose — I suppose actually I do want a *plan*."

Evelyn is already shaking her head. She smiles, hoping he will understand. But he doesn't.

"You *see*, Evelyn, I — I'm *really* very bad at — at this kind of *chaos*."

THAT NIGHT, in the tent, she won't be sexual with him and he is furious. They have retired early, and perhaps this was Evelyn's mistake;

perhaps he thought they were going to bed early for that reason. Evelyn's reason had to do with their lack of water. They'd found no source of it, and their searching in the heat had parched them, and all they could have was two careful sips apiece, saving what amounted to one sip each in the morning, at which time they would have to set out quickly. She thinks his anger might partly have to do with thirst too — if his body is anything like hers he is feeling a muscular tug, sour and threatening, from all his cells. She remembers how thirst can grow quickly frightening.

Sex itself would have been easy, would probably be pleasant. In the tent, which had felt so cozy until this fight, she can't explain her refusal to him. Because she has not explained it to herself. She has no words for what she feels tonight. It's something like, sex feels more like his plan than mine. That's one reason.

Another has nothing to do with Peter. It has to do with her feeling so weak she could die, she could vanish in a breath. She feels good but, underneath, so fragile, fragile as balanced water. She is strong only so long as she does exactly what she wants. Nothing else. Moment to moment, exactly what she wants. She needs to stay on this delicate path in order to keep up her strength, and she needs this strength to keep going. The going has to do with keeping free of Oakville but most of all with moving north to Tommy.

Why does a mother meander in going to her boy? Maybe because she needs to gather strength. Strength to be hated by a boy like that, now to be hated by a man like that. Strength to put her nose into the backyard mess of her past, her past a boneyard of angry dogs. The dogs, while maybe not waiting for her, are *ready* for her.

She supposes she wants to apologize to Tommy. No, she knows she does. Even though she tried her best. Even though she was, is, nothing but loving. Abandoned him? It wasn't she who left.

No, she wants to apologize for his life itself. For giving it to him, for bringing him here at all, to this hard earth, laying him on this bloody anvil of a planet, everywhere these hammers. Giving life to Tommy was like delivering up a sacrifice. Children like Tommy have no business being here because they don't have a chance, not at all. They are bundles of hopeful nerves in a land of fire and slaps. Tommy understood none of it, never did, he had no chance. Of course she couldn't have known this, and though her fault was only that of a conduit, and not even a willing one, she can still apologize, still love him, and that is why she has to go see him now and why she has to be strong. And to say no to anything *extra*.

But Peter's furious and storms out thirsty into the dusk, saying not a word. "Sorry" is all she said to him and the only truth she is capable of. But he no doubt heard in these words their echo in nights to come. She has no idea if he has heard right. She feels guilty only because, here she is, a replacement for Gail, the refuser. Peter will not know that he has put her here, has fashioned her in Gail's image. The patterns we fall into, who knows why. Some enjoy a string of kind loves, others a string of violence. Others, like her, enjoy a pattern of no pattern at all.

THE CANDLES ARE LIT. Evie and Roy enter the dining room singing Happy Birthday. Funny, Evie thinks, how only a few years ago she felt grim singing this song to this sarcastic boy, but now she feels almost goofy. There really is no other way to survive it. Sing over-loud with tremolo. *Forget* him. He no longer scowls or sneers. He cares too little now for that. Today he blows out all sixteen candles with no effort.

The cake is cut, Tom going along with what has become the corny family tradition of holding high the knife and feigning a samurai attack for the first cut. Even Evie has to be a samurai on her birthdays. It is Roy who demands these minimal traditions, these birthday parties, cakes and presents. Tom sometimes misses his parents' days but they are happy he has made it to, and stayed civil at, his own.

He wolfs two pieces of the lemon cake and leaves. Roy finishes his cake as well, makes his noise of satisfaction, something like "*mm-hmm*," thanks Evie and heads to his den, the somber gist of tricky phone calls already on his face. Evie rinses the dishes and stacks them in the dishwasher, then knocks at Tom's bedroom door. He allows her in with a low "What."

She has her plan. Tom is at his desk hunkered over the car stereo, Roy's present to him. She is about to give him hers. It looks like he's already destroyed the stereo; the desk top is a scatter of metal pieces and screwdrivers and wire. Tom had often declared that he would have a car "the same week" he turned sixteen. Apparently he had a particular car in mind, and it lacked a stereo, because a car stereo was all he wanted for his birthday. Neither she nor Roy have asked him where the money for the car was coming from.

"I have a present for you."

"What."

"I'm going to tell you where you come from."

Her delivery, low-key to clash with the apocalyptic statement, works. Tommy puts a tool down and turns in his chair to face her. Evie feels she could as well have said, I'm going to tell you why you are the way you are. He's already smiling.

She doubts he's ever heard the name Claude Longpre within the walls of this house but he's not surprised by it, or by the news. Not surprised in the normal sense. Pleased, perhaps. Entertained. He smiles mildly.

Tommy is never surprised. He is *never* surprised. He can be bothered by something, he can be pleased, or angry, but he is never surprised. Gifts, report cards, threats, loud noises, the best or worst news — he fields with a knowing, almost condescending look. It is intimidating. Odd in anyone, let alone a boy raised in the suburbs. Odder still, it is the most noble thing about him, something he has that kings and presidents probably don't. She has no idea if this noble trait, this *awareness*, is a mark of a sociopath.

Nor does she know if the state of never being surprised isn't simply a sad and lonely predicament.

He bends back to his wires, picks up a hot soldering gun, still smiling. Clearly, so she can hear the quotation marks, Tommy says, "Dad's not 'dad.'"

"Wrong. Your father's always been your father. Even if he's not your biological —"

"He know?"

"I think — Tom, I haven't been as blunt with him as I've just been with you. I thought that, at your age, it was your right to —"

"Other dad know?"

"No, Claude doesn't. He knows you exist but not that he had any, you know, connection, any —"

"Function at the junction."

He may even have said "at your" junction. She ignores this. Tommy tells her with possible sincerity that he's always wondered where his nose came from. She answers his questions about Claude's background, his general looks and personality. Tommy nods when she calls Claude "fiery" and "utterly independent."

"Where's he now?"

"Probably still in Victoria."

The next morning, when she finds her credit card, leather suitcase, and Tom's newest clothes gone, she tries to remember if she gave him any other hints as to Claude's whereabouts. Had she also said, "Still probably working on the waterfront"? She can't remember. She's worried, but not sick.

And apparently, on his way out in the morning, Tommy did some last damage. Roy has always been an early riser and it seems they have had an encounter. The look Roy gives her articulates plainly enough that further talk is not necessary.

IT'S WINDLESS, so it isn't a hard morning's paddle. Thirsty or not. As they gain the southeast tip of Gabriola Island near the mouth of what Peter informs her again is Dengen Bay, they spy a rather grand dock extruding from a treed, sandless shore. They head for it without comment, no consultation needed. When they get even a bit off course, Peter side-paddles peevishly, splashing her a little, until they're perfectly targeted once more. He's been brusque all morning. She can feel his thoughts. A cactus in the bow.

The dock's wood is newly cut, raw, unweathered. She can smell it, the powerfully resinous spirit of newly dead trees. The dock is boatless.

An older main house and a string of brand new cabins front a lawn, their backs to the trees. A carved wooden sign at the head of an empty parking area reads *Endless Love G & M Ranch*. When they bump the dock Evelyn ties a cord around a cleat bolted there for more significant boats, while Peter lurches trying to get right out, banging the same knee several times but refusing to swear.

"Not lying in the dirt all night and starving to death all day," Peter mumbles to the dock wood. He doesn't look at her and walks away. She finds her legs and joins him, barely keeps up as he climbs the ramp and heads across the incongruous lawn to the main house with a little "Office" sign above a side door. A large white clucking chicken races to pass in front of him and barely makes it. Peter pushes right in, dings a bell on the counter, dings it again.

Evelyn steps back out and goes to the hose she spotted beside the door. She lets the water flow for a few moments, washes the nozzle with her hand, puts her mouth to it and tries not to gulp. Well water, it tastes of sulphur as well as plastic hose. She drinks just enough for now and rejoins Peter, who dings again.

Breathing more heavily than the walk from the kayak would account for, Peter mush-mushes a stuffed shower cap on the counter an inch from the bell.

When the woman comes to check them into their cabin-with-hot-tub, Peter signs without asking a price and otherwise pays no attention to the woman, who has eyed them both with some suspicion. They both do need a wash and a change. Evelyn eyes her back. She is oddly striking, both ugly and beautiful: a near-albino with white-blonde hair and an angular, one-of-a-kind face. Evelyn decides that had she been alive in the era of portraits, she would have been a famous painting.

Peter hasn't registered her face at all; instead he stares at what appears to be the woman's side-business, maybe the "ranch" part of it, which is free-range chickens. Another carved wooden sign on the wall, also new, spells it out simply: Eggs, Chicks, Layers, Uncooked, Cooked. One red word, ORGANIC, sits like a crown over all the other words. Under the sign is a freezer, and beside that, a glass oven with four chickens turning on spits.

"How much for one of those?" Peter has been pointing and stabbing with a finger for some time before he says this. His finger aims at a huge skewered bird rotating coyly, the sun through the window basting its sheen of fat in delirious light.

"That one, please. To *go*," says Peter. "And, and a glass of water?"

Peter side-steps along the counter to be closer to his chicken. Something in his manner causes the woman to meet Evelyn's eye. Evelyn smiles; the woman understands. Peter has his chicken wrapped in metallic paper and string and handed over, along with a styrofoam cup of water. He disappears quietly out the door, leaving his shower cap on the counter.

Evelyn finishes up the business, supplying, for some reason, a false address. She uses D'Arcy Street. She counts out the cash for one night and pockets Peter's wad of bills. Glenda—for they've exchanged names and have had a friendly minute—leads her to cabin number four, which she describes as the least private. Glenda explains that they are lucky to have it, since the resort will fill up this evening. They walk through the middle of the lawn, passing Peter Gore hunched at the lone picnic table, at work on his dripping chicken. The empty cup lies on the grass beside his feet. He's being good with noise, but his face is already a mess. A long tear of golden fat beads unnoticed on his elbow.

HOT TUBS, THEY truly are perfect. Though they're better in winter. She has one at home in Oakville.

In fact, when the realtor pointed it out to them, sexily-hidden on a sundeck of its own, it made Evie decide she wanted this house. Not so much for the tub as for the concern with which Roy was staring. She could read in his face: does a mayor, *should* a mayor, have one of those?

Roy kept his luxury item hidden from visitors like he would have a weakness for scotch. Only on special occasions, like anniversaries or blizzards, would he don his bathrobe and announce an imminent soaking. It fell upon Evie to see that it got lots of use. Out of the same perversity that made her want Roy to own one, she took to inviting all and any guest in, no matter the social occasion. Other mayors, Roy's own council, the blue-rinse members of this board and that. She maintained a large assortment of swim suits and towels for this purpose and noted Roy's peevish relief whenever her invitations were turned down, as they usually were. But sometimes total strangers took the plunge — like that tiny Mr. Tobiko, the Mayor of Kobe, one of Oakville's sister cities, during a lovely December snowfall.

Her head resting on the fragrant cedar rim, she doesn't care that her house in Oakville has one. No over-lap affects her vision. That hot tub is there and this one is very much here.

But Claude hated them too, singling them out as the pinnacle of yuppie crap. She doesn't care. Maybe he's also why she bought her Oakville hot-tub house. Who cares. Hissing hot bubbles rough her up from all directions. People melt and moan here, people have babies here — the same babies conceived here. This heat, these impossible bubbles.

Wispy Glenda smiles and waves as she walks by with a load of towels for the neighbouring cabin. Evelyn is naked but doesn't care because Glenda doesn't care. Her resort exists with just this spirit in mind. The hot tub is exposed, sunken into the cabin's front deck, with no fence between it and the fronting path, the lawn, the dock, or the stretch of salt water and Vancouver Island. With no walls, it feels like one's nakedness goes on forever. It is really quite the spot.

Maeve cruises past as well, waves and smiles too. When Evelyn met Maeve an hour ago, her look was as suspicious as Glenda's had been and it became clear to Evelyn that Glenda and Maeve were lovers, were the G and the M of the Endless Love Ranch. Maeve, a friendly, beer-drinking type, an Aussie, is squat, dark, butch — Glenda's opposite.

She can imagine the two of them writing the Ranch's glossy brochure, which is very funny. A water-warped copy lay beside her head until she realized she could smell its harsh chemistry. Now it lies where she tossed it. One of the phrases that sticks with her goes, "Here at G & M we encourage hard-core explosions of inner self." Another, encouraging nakedness while mocking corporate notions of female beauty, says, "A waist is a terrible thing to mind." The brochure promotes the healing aspect of the place, but also the partying. It doesn't out and out say "lesbian" anywhere, nor does it say that men are not welcome, but its repeated use of "women" and "their relationships" is fairly plain. No wonder the assessing looks given her and Peter. But Glenda and Maeve are friendly and fine, the mood here good. The surrounding forest approves of this particular scar.

Except that Peter is still groaning in the shower. The gall bladder attack came on swiftly, only an hour after the chicken. He has paced, he's gulped water, he's been in and out of the shower. She's fetched aspirin for him. Some time ago he announced hoarsely through the window that "This one is going to be a bad one." Then, only a few minutes ago, "This is worst one I've had."

Evelyn looks to her left. Peter's white, white feet are beside her face, so close that she has to pull her head back to see them clearly. They are pruney from the shower. A water drip from his shorts lands cold on her forehead.

"I think…I really *think* I might be dying."

Evelyn looks up. His face is upside-down but she can see it is red and very pinched.

"Are you serious?"

"I don't know. This is really really bad. It's not even *plateauing* yet. It *doesn't* come and go." His voice catches in a sob. "It. Never. Goes. *Away.*"

Peter begins circumambulating the hot tub, head goosed forward, hands held like scoops over his stomach to cradle his pain. A stricken monk.

"The aspirin didn't work?"

"Didn't work."

"How many —"

"*All* of them. *Eight.*"

Evelyn asks, "What does a gall bladder do, anyway? Exactly."

As if the pain he clings to hoists him up and makes him lighter, Peter pads daintily, making no sound when he steps. Evelyn knows what a gall bladder is but her question gives him something to do. He steps in rhythm to his words.

"When we eat fat, we need something special to digest it. Bile digests it. Bile is made by the liver. It is stored in the gall bladder. Which is connected to the liver. When we eat fat, the gall bladder senses this. It squirts bile into the stomach. So the fat can be digested. The gall bladder is a muscle."

"And a gall bladder attack. What is happening to you, now?"

"Some people make gall stones. No one knows why. The stones collect in the gall bladder. They can't get out the little hole. Sometimes, in the middle of a squirt, one gets stuck. The bladder keeps trying. To squirt. It goes into spasm. It doesn't stop." Peter doesn't speak for a few steps. "That is the attack."

"The worst that can ultimately happen?"

"Become infected and burst and kill you."

"How long would that take from the start of an attack?"

Peter hesitates. "A few days."

"So you're not dying."

The padding resumes behind her head. "Not quite yet."

"In the meantime, what can be done?"

"Nothing. Except pain killers. Or an emergency operation. Neither of which..."

"Why don't you get into the tub with me?"

"I have to keep moving."

"You can move in the tub."

He begins to climb down the stairs.

"Take off your shorts."

"No. Why?"

"It's just weird if you don't. And I've seen you naked. C'mon it's a hot tub."

Peter steps to the bench and supports himself on it with a hand. He remove his shorts. Faced with his naked body once more, Evelyn sees again how he's not in touch with it, doesn't quite own it. For however long he's in it — seventy, eighty years — he will be a renter.

He climbs into the tub and Evelyn takes his hand before he can pass by. She guides him in front of her, has him sit on the deepest bench, down between her knees. Palming his forehead, she draws his head back so it presses between her breasts.

"Try to relax," she says.

Peter moans in agreement, a moan equally full of pain and hungry for pleasure, a moan that grows louder and is so long and drawn out and pathetic that they both laugh at the end of it.

Then Evelyn's hand begins to move on him in such a way that its destination becomes obvious.

"THE CLINIC ISN'T open till Monday," Maeve tells Evelyn. Australians have such fun accents. *Cleen*eek.

"When's ... When's Monday?" That sounds wildly stupid. "I mean what day is it? Today."

Awareness of a sort in Maeve's eyes. She smiles with a corner of her mouth. "It's Friday," she says. "Friday evening." Froy-dye eevnin.

Back in the cabin, Peter is prostrate and moaning non-stop. The bottle of wine she procured for him has only made him moan louder. Evelyn has come to the office in search of other possibilities. Maeve is asking her just how bad it is when Glenda comes in from setting up some guests. Evelyn describes Peter to them.

Glenda perks up and grows stern. Her cheek bones protrude. Her nose sharpens. Her wispy hair is made for flight.

"It's getting worse?"

"Seems to be."

"Then this is serious."

Glenda tells Evelyn about the excellent emergency helicopter service to Nanaimo General.

"Holy cow."

"We've had to use it before."

"A helicopter."

"Should I call?" Glenda has removed a cell phone from her pocket.

"Maybe we should ask Peter."

As though to get her point across to a dreamy child, Glenda lowers her head and tilts it forward to say to Evelyn, "I really don't think we leave it up to him."

Or, apparently, to Evelyn.

IT COMES LIKE violence unimaginable. Hovering, the helicopter is a constant explosion. The *exhaust*. Hanging over the lawn, hanging above the trees, it roars in extremes Evelyn's senses cannot take in. She feels it can kill them all, *is* killing them all. It lands, yet keeps its motor going, keeps doing damage. The forest is shocked and its hidden people are long gone, had seen it coming.

She can't walk with Peter to the helicopter door though she knows he wants her to. A paramedic has run out to do that job in any case. On his way, craddling his stomach, held by an arm, Peter looks so like a little boy, hunched, limping, frightened under the slicing blades. Through his pain he finds the strength to turn and kiss his hand and blow it to her. Evelyn is surprised how easily the kiss reaches her through the rock-hard noise and chaos. And how it settles her and warms her through. She blows him one back but he has already been guided into the side mouth of the smoking grinding machine, and not three seconds pass before it howls triumph and leaps into the sky.

Has she seen Peter for the last time? That's what it feels like. That's what it feels like though it doesn't feel like it's time. She feels that in seeing him climb into the helicopter she was seeing him fail at his book, and his life. When he sums up, what will he see? She loves that he has the heart to rage and laugh.

SHE IS BACK in her hot tub. It has grown fully dark. The helicopter has come and gone, as has Peter Gore, but it has taken a good hour for the shrieking noise and its diabolical wind to stop savaging her, to stop rasping her bones. She has to force her jaws apart and breathe.

She sits and lets the noises, the pictures, fade. Peter Gore isn't here. The heat, the jetting bubbles, the glass of wine, are here. As are the couples, all women, who pass in front of her on the path. Some look at her and lightly wave. Some look at her and don't.

She hears voices from the cabins, from other hot tubs. What at first she thought was crying is someone's wheezy eccentric laughter. Stars cluster above her and she wishes she knew how to turn off the underwater light that has come on automatically. It not only obscures the stars, it turns the water a green that has nothing to do with real water. She thinks she sees a tiny rope of Peter's sperm drift in front of her. It glows with milk's phosphorescence, weakly hinting at blue. It looks like the fetus of a dragon. Swept away in a roil, it gently arches its back.

She can hear him here in the tub, asking her, "Why now?" He is joking, but mostly forlorn. Here she is giving him what he's wanted for days and days.

It's easy to stop his words. She doesn't answer at all. She doesn't tell him that her hand is on his penis now because she is tired of him being in agony. Or that it's best when a man doesn't expect it, doesn't take it for granted. Or that she's stroking him now because there is no longer any good reason for her not to be. She doesn't tell him he is a see-through teenager and doomed always to be this way. She doesn't tell him her hand is on him because all of this is her fault. It's her fault for getting in a kayak with a lonely and failing man. It's her fault for going to that park with Claude in the first place and for having Tommy, at all. She's doing this with her hand because so many hard questions are bathing her in bubbles. She is surrounded by a circular wall of questions. North to my son? Back to my good mayor? The absence of answers, Peter, is why she lived on the streets, for days sitting on benches and in the dirt, because to move is to choose, is to pretend answers. Then on a beach a dog biting deep into a girl's armpit made her get into a little boat and go. The dog wasn't on a leash and nor are any of the other reasons. All of this is why she's in a hot tub with his penis in her hand.

"MIND IF I JOIN YOU?" *Moynd eef oy join yah?* It's Maeve, in a robe, standing above her.

"No."

"Adding a bit of salt and pepper are we?" Maeve asks. *Peppah.*

Evelyn smiles and says nothing. She doesn't think Claude ever made it to the tropics. She taps a bit more of Claude's ashes into the lovely, warm, turquoise water. Maeve assumes he's some kind of bath salts. Evelyn recaps the cigar tube and rolls it back towards her jeans.

Evelyn decides not to tell Maeve about the ghostly little dragon fetus either. She doesn't think it's a concern. What if Maeve knew who she was really bathing with? With the weird residue of two absent men. And what would Glenda think if Maeve turned up pregnant and stammering? And wouldn't all of it be a story Peter Gore would love to tell.

"I'm sure he'll be alright."

Maeve has doffed her clothes at tub side and is toeing her bulky way in.

"Peter. Yes."

Evelyn notices the woman's leg, a gnarly bump just under the left knee, the size and shape of — of an extra kneecap. Maeve sees her staring. The injury, Maeve tells her, ended her field hockey career.

"*This far*," she adds, pinching thumb to forefinger, "from making the national side." *Thees fah.*

Maeve enjoys describing the grisly details of the break. She saw her own bone. Evelyn wants to tell her that she, too, is comfortable with blood, but she thinks it will sound somehow forward. Maeve is less entertaining in her story of recovery. Evelyn only half-listens now, insulting Maeve by listening harder to her own thoughts about Tommy and his similar leg. Actually, yes — it was Tommy's joke that he had "an extra kneecap."

Evelyn has forgotten so much. Is it age? Is it the years of medication? Are anti-depressants in truth just anti-memory? Or maybe it's understandable to forget a boy's broken leg when it gets outshone by a larger, more solar injury, one as bright and vast as all of Tommy's waking hours.

It isn't so hard to remember that Tommy was eleven and a star athlete when he fell off the school roof. "Star athlete" maybe didn't apply quite yet, for most of the games and races he won were unstructured schoolyard events. But his body was lithe and perfect and he was unnaturally fast. School sports day was Tommy Poole's day: he won everything. Anything to do with speed and agility, he won. Evie didn't care for the boy's brand of happiness at winning. It was cocksure and belittling of everyone he beat. How many times did he come home red-faced, bragging, still breathing hard? Winning races wasn't enough: he'd also race home to tell her.

What she's almost forgotten, or forgotten until tonight, was how sad Tommy had been after the accident. There was the expected sadness, at the news he'd be wearing his cast for another month, at the news that the first pin hadn't worked and that there had to be another operation. There was the longer, greyer sadness after the failed attempts at running. His look of accusation because his encouraging parents had lied to him. Then a sadness stubborn and ever-lasting — sadness that appeared to shape the growing bones of his brow and the set of his jaw — at being reminded that, though he no longer had a limp when he ran, he now had an extra kneecap and was no longer the fastest boy in the world. There was that week of missed school, that joke-that-wasn't, about suicide.

Evelyn realizes she'd forgotten one very simple thing: there was a point when Tommy's young life went wrong, when it took away what he reveled in, erased what he loved.

The other thing she remembers tonight is not as simple. Maeve has since left; her half-beer is on the deck; Evelyn hopes she doesn't feel too insulted. The other thing she remembers is the argument. A hot, herky-jerky argument, the kind you *try* to forget, and she had succeeded. Imagine, her and Tommy in the back of the ambulance, arguing on the way to the hospital, Tommy so mad at her he's stopped crying. It's a bloody-splinter-of-an-argument and Evelyn doesn't like pulling it out now. It would have been unresolvable at the best of times. It has to do with why he was up on the school roof to begin with.

The school had a policy (or a mean janitor, according to Tommy) about removing the balls and frisbees and other tossed stuff (bullies would send kids' new sneakers up there) from the roof only once every September, and once every June. (It was a roof which needed a long ladder to scale. The kid-method involved an impossibly sheer wall.) By May lots of balls were "roofed"and plenty of games didn't get played because of it. The night before breaking his leg, Tommy bragged to Evie that he had a plan to makes lots of money: he was going to get the roofed balls and shoes and sell them back to everyone. That was his story. It's what he told her. She forbade him, as required by her, and he disobeyed, as required by him.

But in the ambulance, when in her worry and anger she yelled at him why, *why* did he go up there, and he said that he did it in order to give the balls back, she didn't believe the word "give" and accused him of lying.

"*I was going to* give *them back.*"

"*Last night you told me you were going to sell them.*"

"*I was going to* give *them.*" Now he was raging in his tears. She was so good at giving him reasons to rage.

They didn't speak of it again. Ever. She laid it all out to Roy but Roy didn't bring it up either though it was right up his ethical alley, how greed injures everyone including the greedy. What she didn't tell Roy was what she heard a kid say to another kid at the scene, before the ambulance took Tommy in and hauled them both away. It was the barest snatch of gossip from a ring of young gawkers. What Evelyn heard a kid say was, "... Poole said he was going to liberate the balls and ..." *Liberate* — it was a word the kid wouldn't know. It was exactly a word Tommy would use.

In the heat of the tub, in the roil of bubbles, Evelyn has her head back and wishes she could see the stars. Stars sometimes can feel like advice. She remembers the other possibility, one she entertained back then for only a moment before rejecting it. What if Tommy had truly intended to kick the balls and shoes off the roof, *liberating* them, a Robin Hood giving the cheering crowds their possessions back? And that he had lied only to *her*, saying that he was going to sell them. Why would he lie about this? She didn't, doesn't, know, but she feels now that he was, that this was the case. Was it because that's what adults did — they made money — and Tommy was showing how adult he could be?

Or was it just his need to irritate her?

Or, more accurately, was it — and this is the one version she won't think about, the one that had her by the throat from the start, so much so that she wouldn't answer Maeve's several concerned questions — was it just a dutiful son feeding a mother's dark version of him?

Tommy was going to liberate the balls.

Tom Poole bought his old man a house.

Your husband — um — said *you* abandoned *Tommy*.

Deer was paddling along. His son Fawn was sitting in the bow of the canoe. It was foggy. It was the fall of the year. Then Fawn spoke to his father. "Stop!" Fawn said. "There is the sound of warriors." Fawn heard the sound of paddles. "No, child," said his father. "It is only whistling in the nose, child. You hear the whistling in my nose."

— FRANZ BOAS, *KWAKIUTL TALES*

NANAIMO GENERAL

"LET'S START AT THE *top* then."

To punctuate his decision, Gore gives his new map a rattle. And finds it amusing that maps have a rattle all their own. Which, depending on how violently shaken, can sound merely — Gore searches for the word — *rousing,* or, especially if one doesn't know what lies ahead — *dreadful*, like the stagy thunder crackling from the wings of a Victorian play.

"Excuse me? Did you ask for something?"

The young nurse stands at the foot of his bed, bearing a tray which presumably isn't his or she would have put it down. Her smile is on the verge of beaming. He is starting to hate this.

"No. Go."

He figures he can get away with being "humorously honest" for not much longer. It's the pose of the cranky English eccentric and it's tiring him. One by one the nurses have been coming in to enjoy it. He's trying to forgive the hospital staff for being so easily entertained, what with their daily Sisyphean slog up the mountain of frightened whiners.

Tonight's honesty is residual. The full-blown version began with the sodium pentothol, a part of general anaesthetic that also happens to be the infamous "truth serum," circa the second war. Gore doesn't remember the first truths he spoke during his muddy coming-to in the recovery room. What he does remember isn't pretty. Two rows of beds filled with immobile lumps emerging from various depths of post-operative idiocy, all compelled because of that damn drug to *vocalize,* be it a showy snore or the blurt of an inappropriate truth. The god of comedy has built itself a cruel and hideous stage here. One man, thirty-ish, sporting a Dracula-Suess contraption of body-tubes, spoke in a language that sounded like astrology, saying how, according to this squared planet and that steady horizon line, he knew all along that today he would not die. Another man, Gore's own age, was weepy about his daughter coming down from Campbell River to drive him home. A woman kept waking up to swear briefly and colourfully for no reason and then fall back asleep, wakefulness but a vent for welling scorn.

The worst recollection of all is of the cluster of nurses and doctors at Gore's own bedside, come there to beam at him while — *damn* it — he performed his high school Latin.

He is glad he hardly remembers. He does vaguely recall being boastful about it — that is, adopting a *smug, childish tone* while conjugating perfect lists of verbs. Why would anyone, drugged or not, do such a thing? And damn the staff for shamelessly taking advantage of his cheap sideshow lunacy. He recalls rising to another invitation, too, with cruel clarity can hear himself rattling off facts about Vancouver Island, stuff like, "Did you *know* that next to Newfoundland, which was its own nation until 1949, this island *right here* is the biggest North American island, not counting those Baffin-size chunks up there under the mostly-ice," sounding like some smarmy *fan* of this place that was *their* place, not his place at all.

But that's quite something, isn't it? The human mind? He hasn't uttered a word of Latin since —

Oh god. He remembers more — oh *god* — he remembers finishing *amore* and launching into a little ditty to the tune of *Volare*. He was being very much the rake. He may have *winked. And he may have said* handjob.

Oh, and he recalls saying proudly, "She won't let me call her Eve." And, fondly, "She's a nasty little spook."

Gore wills himself to remember no more. In case will isn't enough, he taps his stapled incision, shouts once, then settles into the distraction of some groaning. Another nurse happens by, smiling an open ocean of concern, and he refuses her.

IN THE DEEP OF NIGHT, though it looks like day, Gore tells an old roughed-up Canadian doctor that the nurses' policies are confusing. Or — he points into the shy man's face accusingly — perhaps *confused*. When the man pleads that he is only the night janitor, Gore persists with his complaint anyway, making it a dry run or rehearsal, his complaint being that, when he asked one nurse for a map, she went out and bought him one, this beautiful map of Vancouver Island. But another nurse wouldn't wash his clothes, and *look* at them. Gore points to the closed closet door but the man won't go and see for himself. Maybe it's up to the nurses themselves, says the man, but he's not convincing. Nor is he trying very hard. He does try to leave with his bag of garbage. Gore verges on telling him how much his baggy face resembles a cartoon bloodhound's but he doesn't, he sees no point. He does tell the janitor's back that they are giving him too much of this morphine for clear *thinking*, though come to *think* of it, it might be time for more.

HE WAKES AND, apropos of another thing minutely remembered, he accosts another doctor who this time happens to be a doctor. The doctor is very tall, and thin, and looks almost shy, and not very tough at all.

In a spasm of responsible clarity he asks this doctor what would happen if, after years of taking them, someone just went off antidepressants, cold turkey. The doctor moves to check the chart at the foot of his bed and Gore interrupts him, saying, "Not me."

He'd forgotten, but it's what Eve told him. Just the once. Back on that first morning, before he joined her on her journey. Before he got in her boat. She had tucked it into an extremely long sentence, one that apologized for her condition, for her tremulous state of mind, a sentence revealing that her friend had just died, that she lived in Ontario with one of its mayors, that her son had run away, that after many years she'd just gone off her pills, anti-depressants, that she'd been sleeping on beaches, and much more.

The doctor pauses, puts his hand to his face, rubs the skin around his mouth. Hmmm. After muttering the professional qualifiers, how it depends on which one and how many and this and that, the doctor raises an eyebrow, which in turn drags a lid up and bares one eyeball, suggesting concern and wonder. He meets Gore's eye and smiles the oddest little smile to say, "*Any*thing could happen."

While maybe not explained, Eve is excused. Gore slides back to sleep.

USUALLY HE SLEEPS and wakes for no reason. Muted ceiling-lights tell him it is night. There isn't much to think about. Actually the morphine takes care of that for him, helping the most trivial inner babble keep him interested in himself. He's been told he'll be staying an extra few days because he is at high risk of infection. Another rough Canadian doctor came to lecture him about leaving it so long. This doctor complained about a gall bladder so swollen he'd had to "dissect it in your body cavity and pull it out piece by piece." Someone else comes to tell him he is suffering from exhaustion, and that he is borderline malnourished. His white blood cell count reveals something else, as do his liver enzymes. He is disappointed in himself for being a biology teacher and not knowing what liver enzymes quite do. Enzymes interact with substances in a violent way, in that they are involved with breaking things down. But where did this violence take place? The liver itself? In bile that flows to the stomach? Through the gall bladder, which he now lacks? He needs another map, one of the body and its inner islands and streams.

He has journeyed west to Vancouver Island and here on its shores left an organ.

"Can't sleep either?"

This from the next bed over. Man of about sixty, American, retired and moved here. Cancer biopsy. Lymph nodes removed from armpit. Always cheerful. Gore recalls they've had conversations.

"I guess I can't." How did the man know? Oh. "Have I been, ah, talking out loud?"

"Not a problem. I can't sleep either."

"I've been talking to myself?"

"Well, you've been reminding yourself that you lost an organ." The man — that's right, his name is Lawrence — laughs helpfully, as he does to explain the humour in most of what he says. "I would too if I lost one. Can't be very nice." A moment's respect. "Gall bladder, right?"

"Yes."

"Well, if you needed it I don't think they would have taken it." The helpful laugh.

"One would hope not."

Gore has turned to Lawrence and sees his roommate propped up, eating, smiling. One can tell he is forced to wield the spoon with the hand he doesn't normally use; something gravy-like has fallen down his front, and what looks like beet juice is all over his chin. Lawrence is a big old dying baby.

All this horror drones to resemble fatigue and Gore almost slides into sleep. On morphine, sleep happens at random and isn't as delicious as it is normally. Another sad note is that here he is in a bed at last and he doesn't care. What a waste. He is just beginning to visualize that distant, stupendous waste lying across a short span of water: Eve, and a hot tub, and a cabin, and its double bed, ever only used as a single. Eve being generally sweet, and usually naked. He can almost care about that.

"How big is a gall bladder?"

"A lemon."

"What does it do, anyway?"

Gore gives Lawrence an abbreviated, slurred version. He is sliding off somewhere fast. He could be mistaken but he thinks he has heard Eve's voice, Eve talking to him, whining actually, about her Tom, saying she is surrounded by evidence that she has been a shitty shitty shitty mother. Gore wants to answer her, calm her, say to her, *from my observations I'd conclude that your pain is bloody well self-manufactured, so get it done,* only he cannot begin to say the words, and what is he thinking in any case?

"So where is your bile going now?"

He doesn't know nor care but wishes he could rouse himself enough to say something funny like *my eyes* or *my immortal soul*, but he has slid to a babyish zone of pre-speech and doesn't answer. Lawrence talks anyway. Gore lets himself be further rocked and comforted by the older man's night-time tale of cancer, and ironic retirement timing, and distraught wife, and butchered armpit. In hearing all of this again, Gore realizes from his simple underwater zone that he would cry if only the morphine would let him, and not just for Lawrence.

OF COURSE YOU'RE going to be sad after an operation, especially your first. Of *course* you are. You are going to have bout after bout of this: You feel like a helpless little boy who is all alone. And then you suffer the harsh leap into sudden old age. You see your white, eroded body. You understand this may be your first operation but it won't be your last. You are not a lonely little boy you are a lonely old man — where did your life go? What have you done with it? Not even morphine can sugar the view of your middling career, your descent-of-a-marriage. Your phantom of a book. You understand that you have always known that your new career at this age is folly; at best it will be a hobby, but one less productive than tending meagre flowerbeds and knocking back weeds with your cane. You have learned nothing because there is nothing to learn. You *are* nothing. You are not even this sadness or this fear. After death you will be even less. And now of course even your sense of humour feels like death, because it's been death's humour all along. Naturally you want to phone Gail, and naturally you won't. Or *can't*. You measure the strength of *won't* against *can't*, and for all the time it takes to declare *won't* as the victor, it's taken this long to understand that while the call might be welcomed and pleasant, in the end it will do nothing but shock this emptiness even wider and make you feel dangerously worse.

A WOMAN HE'S NEVER seen is tugging him girlishly by the arm, waking him up. There's something for you, there's something *for* you, she says. She's one of these heavily-rouged volunteers he's been eyeing warily for days, avoiding their dreaded help until now. She's looming, not smiling, rigidly insistent that he must wake and acknowledge his package. In this place of emergencies, it is the closest she can come to participating in one.

"It's special *delivery*," she says.

"Okay."

"It's for you," she adds. "Are you awake?"

"Didn't *you* get anything?"

She doesn't get his Christmas-present joke, but nobody here gets anything he says to them. Canadians have a talent for incomprehension, for the *bovine*, that rivals even the Scottish. Or it might be him. He remembers deciding last night to quit morphine today, his *scheduled relief*, not just because he is bored by it but also because it lets him be irritable without guilt. It also lets him say whatever he wants, regardless of whether it has anything to do with communication.

"Thank you," he tells her. He rests the package on his chest and lets his head fall back. He can see her hovering, wanting a look-see while he opens his present, and he wishes he didn't want her to go away.

"It's from Gabriola Island."

Gore sits up at this news. Until now it hadn't occurred to him to consider who it might be from. How many people even know he is here? Jesus. He begins tearing at the courier envelope and the woman settles in to watch and to help if need be.

"Do you need a box-cutter?"

The package comes open and out falls his stuffed shower cap, not much smaller than he remembered it. A dozen pencils clatter onto his lap like pick-up sticks. One of them has been sharpened — by the look of it, with a knife or, perhaps, broken clamshell. His scribblers, still virgin, wrapped in cellophane. And a letter, written with the one sharpened pencil. He knows all of this instantly, because he knows her to the bone.

The woman smiles at Gore enjoying his present.

"Can I get them to bring you some breakfast?"

"Please. And thank you very much."

First Gore reads the letter, and then he counts his money.

DIRECT SUNLIGHT ON HIS near wall says it's late afternoon. Across from him, Lawrence's curtain is drawn but he can hear every word of a touchingly intimate, indeed life-and-death conversation Lawrence and his wife are conducting. Lawrence's wife cries softly, almost tunefully, in a way Gore sees must be comforting to her body. He spoons his chocolate pudding, remembering the glories of a hot tub. A woman's magic, giving him a brief minute of peace. It was a quite remarkable time. He'd felt nothing like it before. On a purely body level there was the contrast between such pain and such pleasure. That part was weird enough, watching pain and pleasure do handstands for his attention. Spice was added by there being no fence — people happened along the path not ten feet away. The locus of activity was submerged but her lithely pistoning arm and his big red face were not. He probably looked like a giant bearded strawberry. He probably looked like a hobo happy as he suffered a fatal heart attack.

He remembers in the middle of the action asking Evelyn, "Why?" He remembers even more clearly her not answering him, not in words anyway, her hand suddenly finding more graceful energy and climbing another rung on the ladder of wonderful. Which was a kind of answer, surely, a because-I'm-trying-to-make-you-feel-better gesture. But he'd meant more with his question, much more.

Each time he rereads her letter it supplies him with yet more questions to ask. He plucks it off his side table and unfolds it smooth. As revealing as the words themselves are the manner in which they were written. When Eve wrote him that small note in charcoal, the crude capital letters were rather cute, rather creative and fun. Here, the child-like capitals are mildly alarming. What do they say about her mood? Was she sitting? Was she standing and in a hurry? Was this her idea of a joke?

Gore reads the letter for the fifth or sixth time:

> HERE'S YOUR STUFF. YOUR CLOTHES WERE FILTHY SO I BURNED THEM ON THE BEACH. HOPE THE OPERATION WENT WELL. I KNOW YOU UNDERSTAND WHY I CAN'T VISIT—LAST TIME I VISITED SOMEONE IN HOSPITAL HE DIED. SERIOUSLY, IT THREW ME. THE SMELL. CAN'T DO IT. ANYWAY BY THE TIME YOU GET THIS I'M PROBABLY OFF TO SEE TOMMY. I STOLE BUS FARE FROM YOU, AND PAID FOR ANOTHER NIGHT AT GLENDA AND MAEVE'S. THANKS. I MISS YOU. YOU HAVE NO MORE EXCUSES NOW NOT TO WRITE "THE RIM." WHICH, AS YOU SEE, I'VE STARTED FOR YOU.
>
> LOVE, YOUR FIRST MATE,
>
> *Evelyn*

Slashing straight through morphine, the salutation and lovely signature have aroused Gore yet again. He watches it gently nudge the weight of not just a gown but also a sheet and a blanket, which he regards as something of a miracle. He puts his head back and drifts momentarily in sweetness.

At first the last sentence had him puzzled. Then he happened to see through the cellophane wrap that one of the virgin scribblers was not virgin after all. Written in finely-flowing pencil, no crude capitals now, was the sentence: *It was a dark and stormy storm*. The cellophane had been scotch-taped closed.

He felt slightly insulted — not because he thought his talent was being ridiculed but more that she could treat his ambitions blithely.

Then he paused, stared at her sentence, and came to see it as a fairly decent, almost literary in-joke. It occurred to him that there was something casually brilliant about this dumbing down of the dumb. It occurred to him further that Eve had captured — perfectly — not only his own style but also his intention.

It *was* a good beginning to his book. Any book is a vain thing, so what better opening than something so self-effacing it circled back and kissed itself on the tricky lips? Plus it was a good beginning to a first chapter, which would be *in medias res*, a mid-storm account of their battle with Neptune's blow off Valdez Island. Of *course* you start with some action, and then you recount.

Thank you, my witch.

The rest of the letter Gore finds equally interesting. He is dying to see her but he isn't sad she's not visiting him here. He is fed up with the wonky angle their relationship took, her the hearty captain and him the damaged weakling. He has only now graduated from the bed pan to a limping shuffle to the toilet, where bending to sit is accomplished with a full-body wince and some real tears. And though he finds her rather frank, she is right about the smell. The hospital's and his. He might as well still be at sea: his hair is slick as tin foil and his body out-and-out stinks. His skin *feels* smelly, and not with honest body odour but hard-edged and unpronounceable toxins. The topper is this tube 'n' bag which extrudes from just beneath his rib cage. He still finds himself staring at it in horror — an actual plastic tube is stuck inside his actual body, into his guts no less, and it functions as a drainpipe for a dribble of foul brown fluid. Oh, excuse me, Eve, quit fondling me please, the nurse has just come to change my brown *bag* if you don't mind.

But, most of all, most of her letter melts, drifts, fades away, to leave only the hot, polished diamonds: I miss you. First mate. Love.

And, of course, instructions as to where he will find her.

THEY SAY HE'S BORDERLINE infected so it takes an absurd amount of haggling to get himself discharged early. Which is odd when you consider that so much of medicine is inexact, is guess work. What's a few days? But once some doctor's opinion becomes a signature it apparently becomes hospital law, because Gore must sign a stack of lawsuit waivers and release forms and submit to several rough Canadian lectures before they will pull out his tube and show him the door. He has to promise to return to have his stitches out, and Gore nods earnestly. A doctor he's never seen before brings him a vial of antibiotics — giant ugly mauve things. Standing there and rattling it (and Gore thinks, *witch doctor*), as a final rebuke the doctor tsk-tsks and shakes his head, telling him this drug is far more effective given intravenously.

Gore is actually itchy under the skin from having accepted no morphine since last night.

Because he and Lawrence are both leaving today, the mood in the room is almost celebratory, less we-have-serious-disease and more we-are-feeling-better. A young doctor comes so that both he and Lawrence can have their drainage tubes taken out. As Lawrence's curtain is pulled they bond with a quick wink. Gore has second thoughts when he hears, behind Lawrence's curtain, the doctor's soft, "This will be uncomfortable," followed by a pitiful gasp, followed by the nurse's, "He's fainted."

Gore is worried about his own de-tubing and prepares himself. The doctor and nurse enter; his curtain is swept closed. He hears Lawrence mutter to himself, then laugh in amazement at how bad that had been, at how pain can be that painful. Gore himself tells the doctor, "This will be uncomfortable." Absurdly, Eve's face appears before him and he is glad she is not a witness to this. The doctor pulls, the plastic bar sticks, clotted deeply in his guts. A bond breaks then it comes out instantly; Gore doesn't faint because the pain is far too alert for that; it is pain bright as the sun; incredibly, the plastic bar is *ribbed*, it jump-bumps its way out, ribbed not for his pleasure but for the devil's delight. He makes noises but hears none of them.

The smiling nurse bandages his tube-hole and he is free to go. He dresses slowly, limps to the bathroom and washes his face. He checks the mirror but briefly, a confirming glance. Lawrence, sitting on the bed, waiting for his wife to come and get him, asks, laughing, "You still itchy under the skin?"

Afraid Lawrence might offer to scratch him, Gore says no. Gore also declines an invitation to come this very night to dinner. He thanks the older man, tells him he has someone he really must see.

He is slim and trim, slimmer than ever, and trim in more ways than one: a surprise greets him at the front desk where he stops to settle his bill. In truth he almost walked right past, and maybe should have. But he didn't and he learns that, while his U.S. insurance will reimburse him, for now he owes a staggering amount of cash. He meekly counts out the amount, in hundreds and then twenties. His wad is so reduced it is no longer a wad and needs no shower cap to contain it.

He gets through the glass doors. Limps out onto the street, into the sun, *discharged*. It is the right word. The building behind him is clean and bold and he has dribbled out of it, a thin and ugly issue.

He gets directions to the bus depot — six or seven blocks — and begins his long limp there. Unlike the morphine, the pain-pills he's on — he didn't ask what they were — allow his wound to stand out blazing at its mouth, like it's painted with fire lipstick. Walking is easier with hand held up like so, with a geriatric shuffle-limp. God knows what he must look like. But he's actually slim and in shape, thanks to her. His clothes are still dirty, and now wet, for the rain's coming down pretty good. Thank goodness her courier envelope is this plasticky stuff.

He finally does get a good view of himself in a storefront window, and he can't stop himself laughing, despite the pain and threat of ripped stitches. He's a bum. A shrubbie. He began his journey to Vancouver Island with state-of-the-art equipment and state-of-the-art intentions. Now he has neither. His clothes are mostly dirt, his only money flutters loose in the empty breeze of a pocket. His only luggage is a courier's envelope full of paper and pencils.

He passes shirt stores and shoe stores and whatever other stores selling conventional self esteem. He goes into none of them because his one shirt is fine. Also, he knows neither what a ticket to Sointula costs nor when the next bus might leave. For all he knows, there's one a week. For all he knows, Eve has been there, had her fill of mean Tom and is already planning her escape. *Any*thing might happen. He can schedule no delay. And — he highly doubts the feeling is drug's residue — he has this gut sense that a bus is leaving soon, is leaving now, and he will just make it if he doesn't dawdle. The timing just feels right. Coincidence — Eve told him that he and she share coincidence.

Not share, *create*. When he sort of runs, and points sideways, one shoulder leading the way, the limp becomes a little hop and paradoxically doesn't hurt so much.

A PAYPHONE HANGS OFF a concrete wall. The sight of it actually stops him mid-limp. A car honk gets him going again. But he could call Gail. The phone is a lifeline. He could simply call her. He could get money sent. Words of sympathy. Or, if he were honest, he could tell her his plans and she would hear the finality in his voice. But he doesn't call. Because it's true: he no longer has any need of her. The him-and-Gail saga began with his pursuit of her. As pursuits go it was typical, except that he persisted, he kept on when other men would have dropped the chase. He tailed her, and badgered her, and finally she laughed and gave in and married him — but he never really quite caught her, did he? As he walks past this payphone, he feels this to be truly the end of him-and-Gail. He is truly moving on. He's now gone as far as he can, west. The trick is to keep moving once you hit the western wall. It might be a cinderblock wall, painted pale green, and you don't let yourself be seduced by any phones hanging off of it. You have to keep walking, you have to turn either south or north. Peter Gore has just turned north.

He feels so clean, so clean and light. Clean as a bird, light as a whistle. He spots the ticket booth. The sign over it says — perfect — *Destinations*.

It's a good thing he didn't stop to buy a shirt. At the ticket booth he learns that his remaining money has barely bought him a bus ticket to

Port MacNeil and a walk-on ticket for the ferry across to Sointula. One way, what the hell. Damn all maps and plans, wasn't this the instruction of his guiding witch? The timing isn't so coincidental after all, seeing as there are two buses a day and he has two hours to kill until the next one. In any case, he'll get to Sointula the day before her son's birthday. In a place that small — it's a dot no bigger than Sombrio Beach's — everyone will know everyone else's business and Tom Poole shouldn't be hard to find. And one assumes, one *must* assume, she'll still be there. He won't be interrupting anything, he doesn't think. Evelyn will have had her brief and good reunion. Consoling Tom through his father's death, Evelyn will feel, will be, needed. They will find their little harmony. And then it will be time for her to look for something else.

To get some northern tongues flapping, and perhaps for nostalgia's sake, and maybe even for fun, Gore retraces a block back to a liquor store and buys a bottle of whisky. Then limps into a thicket in an adjoining city parkette and has himself a few sobering sips. Doing so, he feels for the first time somewhat the professional drinker. He notes that none of the empty bottles at his feet are as high-end a brand as his. Not that he feels flush. All the money he has left in his pocket might buy him a hamburger in Sointula.

HE SEES THAT long-haul buses are now taller at the sides and all smoked glass and stylish, but he recognizes the deep reek of the bathroom Detol. And good lord, there are screens hanging off the luggage rack and it seems that once out of Nanaimo they will be watching an in-flight movie. Gore chooses a seat midway down the aisle. He turns and questions his bus-mate, an old woman occupying the window seat. She looks Native; there will be stories; he checks his courier bag for his scribblers and trusts that the one sharpened pencil is still there. A voice over an intercom tell him to prepare himself for a six-hour drive. There will be three rest stops. He asks the woman if she has done this trip before and if she has ever seen a cougar from the bus. She looks at him blankly so he asks if perhaps she has seen a bear. A cute, pie-faced old woman, her skin olive-smooth and babyish, she gives him a concerned once-over. It is a perusal so *dramatic* with disdain and sympathy both that he feels something of a character, and recalls a name from an in-flight movie from the past: Ratso Rizzo.

The woman says, "You see bears only if they're around, eh?"

"Around? Where?"

"If they're standin' out there by the road, you'll see them, eh? If they're back there in the trees, you don't see them."

"Ah. Of course. But the cougars. Your north island has the highest *density* of cougars in the world. And the most aggressive *strain*. Tell me about cougars. Or do you call them mountain lions?"

"We call 'em cats."

"And from the bus, do you ever see them?"

"Even if they're sittin' on the bus, you won't see them." The woman is watching him sagely.

"Do you mean me, personally, or — ?"

"No!" The woman's pie-face rises without a wrinkle into a sweet smile.

The movie is about young — very young, aren't those people teenagers? — romance. Despite some plot twists it is predictable. It assumes the viewer is interested in youth, and in what has been rehashed a million times, and is still called love. Gore wishes he had something to read. He wishes he had some fresh morphine in him to make none of this matter. The pie-faced woman beside him appears to be enjoying the movie. She laughs at almost everything.

OUT THE WINDOW it is so dark it might as well be night, and sometimes Gore forgets it isn't. There is always a wall of rock or a strobe of uniform trees, the tops of which are in cloud, or perhaps this is fog. Sometimes he sleeps. Sometimes a fevered voice arises unbidden to supply him with facts, such as: four hundred million years ago, this Vancouver Island was located south of the equator and ever since it has been moving north at seven centimetres a year. Eighty million years ago it lay beside California. It's still moving north. So, on this speeding bus, Gore understands he's going even faster than it seems.

Beside him the pie-faced woman tries to read, this woman whose culture, Gore remembers, watching her, was the most complex ever to flourish without resorting — resorting — to agriculture. Her people, then, would be hunter-gatherers.

Their shoulders are an inch apart. He looks closely at the impossibly smooth skin of her face, which is soft as bubble that is in no danger of popping. No worry lines, not even crow's feet. Her eyes alone betray the decades of gravity. She is wearing a ski jacket, done up, while in his shirt he feels rather too hot. He supposes he has a fever — well, yes, the way his eyes burn round their rims he can feel that he does have a fever, and his incision throbs a fiery heartbeat, but all of this must be par for the course after an operation, and days of morphine.

"Have you ever heard of Cougar Annie?"

"No. Who's Cougar Annie?" The old woman speaks slowly and doesn't look at him. He loves the husky rasp of her voice. She appears able to read and talk at the same time. She's reading a thin romance novel, its cover cheesy with rippling muscles and perfect curves, and two faces as asexual as TV news anchors.

"She lived on the west coast of the island in the thirties and forties and grew immense flower beds and shot dozens of cougars."

"I like her," she says, smiling sweetly but still reading. "What island she live on?"

"This one. Vancouver Island."

"This isn't an island."

She's told him she lives in Alert Bay, which Gore knows is on Cormorant Island, which is only half the size of the one he's going to, Malcolm Island, whose width you can hike. So Vancouver Island wouldn't seem like an island, no. Do the inland Irish feel like they live on an island?

"But you don't get cougars on the smaller islands. Like Malcolm. Isn't that right?"

"You get 'em. They like to swim, eh? Friend of mine chased one once in his boat and hit it with a paddle. Drowned it. Drove in circles around it, kept poppin' it." The woman chuckles fondly. "Did doughnuts around it, eh?"

"Why do you hate cats so much?"

"I dunno. You don't look so good. You should rest, I think."

She says this looking pestered. In fact she rattles her book when she says it. He doesn't want to leave her in peace though. She is the first Native who has spoken to him, aside from the snarky comedians in the bar in Victoria.

"I *am* resting. Compared to what I've been doing, this bus is a big brass bed."

She doesn't ask what he's been doing.

"So. Cougars. You hate them."

In the middle of a blink she decides to keep her eyes closed. "They're crazy. Shoot 'em."

"How do you know they're crazy?"

"Haven't you ever looked in their eyes?" The old woman looks in Gore's eyes and he is startled by her timing.

"I — Well, I've never seen a cougar. Like I said."

"I mean a cat. You never seen a cat?"

"Oh, a *house* cat."

"They're crazy."

"I suppose." Gore yawns and keeps his mouth clamped to hide it.

"They hallucinate."

"It does seem so, now that you mention —"

"Shoot 'em, what they good for?"

"Cougars, yes. But by that, that *logic*, what is *anything* good for?"

She is studying him now and she may have said, "Lots of stuff," or he may have filled it in for her. He so loves her voice. He thinks he can get it right, on the page. Though there's no need at the moment. He knows he will hear it in nights to come.

"You going to Malcolm?" she asks, the first time she's initiated a topic. It's humorous to think that she may be making sure he's not coming with her to Alert Bay. He nods and smiles.

"What you going to Malcolm for?"

"It seems I'm — well, it seems I'm getting married."

The old woman is still looking at him and appears not to believe him, even though it isn't quite a lie. Only the words are a lie. What they mean isn't. He loves, loves the feeling they have given him. He thinks he might go to sleep on them, might take the wise woman's advice.

"You gonna need a jacket, I think," she tells him now, from the pages of her book.

He is fading back into this seat. The bus blankets him with its dark beige noise. The old woman thinks he needs a jacket to get married in. She is so sweet that he wonders if she might not be ominous. A seductress, a siren, a raven. Carlos Castaneda — he who blazed the obliquest of trails for the contemporary travel book — would portray such tricksters wearing just such a ski jacket and reading just such a novel. It's a romantic notion, one to lose consciousness to. And her friend, good god, killed a mountain lion with a paddle. Her people called them ghost cats. In bars, and you gotta like this one, they call lonely women 'cougars.' Women on the hunt. Women Eve's age. Now, that is one woman on the hunt. What might her quarry be …

At one point he wakes with his hot head resting lightly on the trickster's shoulder.

Many tribes carried much residual anger against European settlers, and for good reason, but this was not always the case. Proximity often led to friendships, to intermarriage, to commercial opportunities for both sides, and to general helping. Natives typically felt sorry for the white settlers who they saw flounder and eventually fail. Perhaps one cannot blame them for keeping quiet as they watched settlers building a cabin against a hillside that never saw the sun, or choosing for their settlement an empty cove that was empty for good reason, so full was it of dark spirit that not even the hungry hunted there.

— DON COTTER, *LOST UTOPIAS*

BERE POINT

HE'S BEEN STARING ALL night at black water. It's almost as if the brightening world taps him on the shoulder to get him to turn and look at its sunrise. He sees a case of scenery really overdoing it. The bank of towering clouds is so tall and pink and obvious he has to laugh at it. *With* it. Having it come into his eyes, he feels pink, he has to laugh.

Up all night again, he's going to have to nap today. He had that hunch there would be whales — transients — but there weren't. He had "that feeling." He should know by now that they *always* surprise you, and "that feeling" should be a sign of *no* whales coming. But of course if he felt his feeling and stayed away strategically, then they would come, guaranteed.

He knows you can't fool surprise. You just have to do the time.

THE SUN IS ALMOST high and the pink cloud bank is elsewhere being another shape and colour. It's hot and he's sweating and this itself is a surprise. It rains here so much that when the sun comes out it's a sudden and a sheer heat. Only when this happens does he remember it's summer.

Tom removes all of his clothes. He thought he had underwear on but, look at that, he doesn't. He sprawls on his back on two old logs stuck in the sand lying tight together, their centre groove a nice hollow for his spine. Wood so smooth and today so warm it's *inviting*. An expression is true sometimes. This wood is more inviting than a woman because there is nothing extra involved. He opens his legs to the heat. He's known this feeling but doesn't know when or where he's been like this, legs cracked open under the sun. Not many places can you. Big fleshy funflower. He can feel breeze there on his balls even though there isn't any. It makes him a little horny. But he cuts this avenue off. He doesn't want to change what has been a laughing pink morning. And people do come by here, Sointula picnickers, tourist hikers. He doesn't want to be a tourist attraction, however fun it would be to give them a souvenir, a conversation piece to take back to Calgary. Fellas, we were hikin' this little beach in the middle-of-nowheres and here's this fellah pullin' his pud. Naked as an egg. Not kidding. Handsome fellow, though, so we got the camera out. Here, pass these around. Don't he remind you of Brad Pitt?

He shouldn't stay naked long anyway. The sun on his palest places doesn't feel all that great. It's already harsh, already feels like damage. But he wants to soak some in and keep it. It's like he hasn't been warm, not really, since before. The bullet did something to the part of him that understands heat. Weakened a main nerve, something along those lines. He feels cool all the time, like thin paper. It feels borderline unhealthy. He doesn't think it was like this before.

He goes and gets his blanket from under the plastic sheet. Snugging on the headphones, he unravels extra cord so he can return to the smooth logs. Wrapping himself in the heavy blanket, he sits. He settles himself. He feels his whole shape, slouching, like a wise old Indian. When he genuinely relaxes and slows his breathing down, and slows it some more — he's getting good at this — the white noise from the headphones slows too and breaks apart into all its specks — it's the aural equivalent of watching a wide white tabletop slowly come apart into moving bits. You can focus on individuals or find patterns. The word "fractals" comes to him and he knows he used to know it and that it would apply somewhere here. He pictures a paisley shirt that was probably a friend's.

He stares down past his knees at nothing. He has already begun a heavy sweat. He likes it, it's the old way of getting clean, even though in the long run it is a waste of drinking water. He will probably nap this way, sweating, showered by this particulate noise from the sea.

AT THE SOUND of the prop of a crew-boat, a few miles away underwater, Tom's instantly awake and alert and looking around fast, thinking of McKay's deal and the ship. He wonders what day it is. But that's right, it will come at night. And not even tonight. Tomorrow night. Unless he slept round the clock, the thought of which rouses a nervous smile. It is a possibility, a comic possibility. He'll light a big fire tonight just in case. A practice run if nothing else.

What is he worried about? There's pot so there'll be a truck, and if there's a pot truck there'll be guys to carry it, so he'll know it's time when some guys arrive with a truck. They'll walk out to him and ask how he's doing. He'll probably know one or two of them. Not that he'll remember their names. You call guys like that "Mate." They like that better than "Buddy." Probably because guys secretly want to be Australian. Claude says everybody wants to be French, and he's not even joking when he says it. He should call old Claude some day, get him up here. Cal could drive him. He wonders when Cal's planning to come up next.

It was a good nap. It looks like afternoon. He's still half in his blanket, on the sand against the log, out of the direct sun. He can't remember moving. And he's naked. He does remember hearing dolphins, but doesn't know if he dreamed them. They sound like birds, comedy-birds that know computers and whistle about them in fast code. Whales and dolphins would get more respect if they had deep voices.

Dolphin dreams, whale dreams, underwater shapes so fast you can't identify them. He often dreams of fast things, and of moving fast. Maybe because he's slow now. People tell him he talks slower than before. And the getting around part, well.

Tom takes a last slug of water from his thermos then stands to pee. He really should eat something today, because he feels on the weak, sick side of hunger. He thinks he has some cans of tuna left in the box. He sits down. He leaves the phones off, though. The breeze is warm and it feels good on the face and in the hair. He settles his eyes on the horizon line, watches below it for that sudden stab of black.

Why aren't the transients coming? It's late in the season. Though with transients there really is no season. Still he's craving that big, black fin, one with a notch in back like a bottle-opener on a knife blade. A huge male. Boss-lady told him to be on the look-out for it. Whale-types have named it Kamoo or something but he will wait and see it and then name it himself. He gets a kick out of naming them spontaneously, foolishly. One he's named Elvis. He hopes when it does come it hangs around so he can get to know it a bit, and it can get to know him. He'd love a night visit, get some good close-up shots. The camera is loaded and wound and lying under the plastic next to the recorder. He sees he has it pointed at the ocean already, like girly hope.

He likes transients best though he's seen them only three times, and two of those from a distance. There's no comparison really, like a Lambourgini to a Mazda Miata. They say you can't tell by looking, but he can. They are just different. You can't see it but you can. Their black shines deeper, the shine goes *in*, simple as that.

Residents stay in family groups, follow migratory routes, trail the salmon runs. They eat only fish. Transients travel mostly alone, follow no patterns, hunt the shoreline. They eat only meat. Seals, otters, sea lions, dolphins, other whales. If a beach is sloped enough so they'll fall back off it, they'll jump right onto dry land to rip into a pack of sleeping seals.

If you listen to the Inuit, transients eat humans. Imagine something like that coming out of the water at you. It would be like being attacked by God.

It is one of his clearest memories, first reading about transients. He sort of remembers the hospital room and the decent view of Vancouver lit up at night. Despite the flourescent ceiling always partially on. He slept, read, sucked juice through a straw. The little TV on its Canada-Arm. The juice always watery. The jello always too sweet — he could feel the burn of sugar though he couldn't taste it. Once he had vodka in his pineapple juice, he doesn't remember who did that for him. He doesn't remember who visited. Marie probably did. Maybe not. But McKay and a few others. He didn't know Cal then. Claude came by, a couple of strange and ugly friends along, making a big excursion out of it. Claude all hopped up and excited because it was his first time off Vancouver Island in a hundred years. He came back the next day after a night on the town and now Claude's head was bandaged too — just gauze over an eye and nothing to compare with his own big brain bandage, but they had a little laugh about that one, about coincidence.

He has some pretty clear memories of before, of Victoria. He remembers Claude's place easily, can see the mid-morning sun coming through the glass patio doors into his basement suite. That whole wall was basically a window onto the back yard. And the backyard was cool too, being so private due to the tall hedges. He can remember having sex out there on the lawn. That would've been Marie. He remembers Claude snoring, you could hear the old maniac snoring right through the floor, so loud he might as well have been yelling. Snoring any time of day or night. He'd never seen a guy that age party like that. Thing about Claude, though, is that he could party hard yet never turn into an idiot. Always had his wits about him no matter how much damage he challenged himself with. In this, Claude reminded Tom of himself. Also, Claude could be fucking funny. That visit to the hospital in Vancouver, one friend told Tom that Claude had bashed his head on purpose so he could have a head bandage too. The guy might have made that up, but Tom does remember the Hawaiian turkey: Thanksgiving, Claude dug a pit in his new backyard and buried two turkeys with hot stones. Though they were forgotten in the heat of battle and got left there until the next morning and had to be hosed off, lots of the meat was perfectly done and almost tasted good.

He has some still earlier memories but they make no sense in the way they come from nowhere and lead nowhere. Back in Oakville. What's probably his bedroom. Sometimes fucking, and he wishes he had more of those. Usually it's faces, snatches of talk, a fight. School spectacularly boring, except for biology. He remembers shoes under desks. And sitting at the TV, fast with the remote, watching three shows at once, getting yelled at for doing that. Evie, Roy. He can't find their faces. But there's an ambulance ride with Evie. Her voice plus the siren, here she is yelling at him in an ambulance. Her white emergency-face. What's she doing with him in an ambulance? It wasn't when he was shot. He also remembers her in a jeans store at the mall, him dashing out laughing, pregnant with balled up shirts under his shirt, it's a joke, they're pink and green and too small, but he's way too fast for the security guy, a twerp with glasses, and of course Evie drags him back in, no sense of the larger picture. He remembers the concession girl at the Vancouver aquarium, her smile that was instant love, and a smooth smooth neck. He remembers wooden salt-and-pepper shakers in the dining room, clearly as if they were here now, a yellow wood that didn't match the table.

What he misses most is taste and smell. He *thinks* he misses it most, but because he can't remember what good taste is like, not exactly, he can't tell how much he misses it. He thinks that the way food feels is a clue. Carrot-crunch or bread-soft or meat-tear. Anyway, texture keeps food interesting. Sometimes he likes to suck a lemon because it makes his whole face freak out, even up into his ears. Cucumber, he likes cucumber — it's not supposed to have much taste but he can crunch it and feel a sort of taste up his nose, a gas taste. Also he can taste blood, getting from it some of the animal's mood — a grungy dead fear. Not that you get many opportunities to taste blood except in a rare steak. Raw salmon is different again, "tastes" different, fresh muscle that doesn't quite know it's dead. It can be crisp as cucumber. The Indians around here would let it rot, maybe so they could taste it more. Sometimes they'd bury it till it turned to satanic jelly, eat it then. Or kimchee, Koreans throwing a bunch of peppers and garlic and cabbage into a hole and digging it up a year later and blasting their heads off. People really do get bored. He should get some. He could probably taste, or at least feel, kimchee.

THE CELL PHONE RINGS, under the plastic sheet. He doesn't move until it stops ringing. It's probably Boss-Lady, who has this system where she lets it ring three times then hangs up and phones five minutes later. This is to give him time for a more leisurely gimp-limp to the phone.

Walking to the plastic sheet, for some reason he hears her soft, insistent voice say, "Back to normal." She means with whales. Back to normal. She says it often. Lots of people seem to believe in that. Back-to-normal is such a baby-faced lie. Back-to-normal is wishful thinking they don't even teach in kindergarten anymore. Boss-Lady calls occasionally with news about what's happening to orcas, like down in Puget Sound near Seattle, where they're dropping like flies. It's been two years now since a calf has survived past a half-year. You expect that in the States, it's why they're rich. Here the trees have all been logged too but the water couldn't look any cleaner. Probably because there are no fish left to fuck in it, ta boom. But Boss-Lady is upset. Not totally convinced of doom, she allows herself these dreams of back-to-normal. Her voice sometimes shakes as she keeps him informed. When he started here she filled him in on more history than he needed to know. He likes the more insane stories, the best one being the giant machine gun a fishermen's group installed on a bluff near Campbell River, whose one purpose was to shoot killer whales because they ate so many salmon. This was decades ago and it never hit anything, but still. Fishermen all had deer rifles at the ready, and back then Seaworld had trouble capturing any orcas from around here without visible bullet holes.

The last time Tom lifted up the hair over his left ear and looked in a mirror, his own hole had gone more skin-tone than red. Tiny, healed-over anus pucker. They say it came from a medium distance, and could even have been a stray. Tom knew accidentally-on-purpose when he saw it. He was glad he couldn't answer their very first question, Who shot you? He can't remember what he said to the second, Why would anyone want to? He should have said someone thought he was a squirrel. A .22, for christ sakes.

It's easy to see the thrill in shooting a whale, especially from a small boat — a kayak! — but how dumb were these fishermen? Until Europeans came, any October you could walk across any river on teeming salmon backs. Your net comes up empty, you blame killer whales? Killer whales, who have always lived here with the teeming salmon? It gets funnier: the transients were full of bullet holes too. Here were whales genetically not able to eat salmon. Here were fishermen killing the only predator of the real salmon-eater, seals.

His cell rings again. It's in his hand.

"Hi."

"It's me, Catherine."

"Yeah." He knows she wants some small talk. It should be clear by now that he won't do that, but he gives her a bit. "It's a nice day here."

"Well good, here too. Actually I'm down in Telegraph Cove. I'm so close I was thinking I'd visit. It's been a while and we have things to discuss. Next year, for one. And I can take your data, of course, and save you a trip in to the post office. Though I know you like —"

"The thing is —"

"Yes?"

"Thing is, it's not the best time."

"Well, Tom, I'm thinking that it really has been a while. I meet with all the others in-field three, four times more frequently than —"

"Girlfriend's coming up."

"Oh."

"Cal. My girlfriend. Ladyfriend. You know: *friend*." Tom makes himself laugh for her. In saying Cal's name, he wishes she really were coming.

"Yes, I've met her. And I know she won't get in the way."

"Oooo I hope she *does*." He laughs again.

"Okay, Tom, another time then." She sounds peeved.

"Next year?" This is a funny one, catching him by surprise too. He did want to talk about next year, but it comes out like a joke. She ignores it.

"How's it going in general?"

"It's ... back to normal." She misses this also. "It's slowing down."

"As it should. Any transients?"

"I wish."

"Well, next week then. Though it's getting pretty late in the season."

"It's pretty late." How late is it? "How late is it?"

"Today is August ninth."

"So tomorrow's August tenth." Boss-Lady doesn't laugh at this little thingie either. But saying August tenth stirs something in him.

"No K57 pod? Sub-pod?" she persists.

"No."

"Hear any pods around the corner, heading for Robson?"

"No. Just, y'know, big drug ships cruising around."

"Indeed."

They speak for a minute longer, and Tom hopes he didn't just sort of hang up on her. In jerky conversations it can be hard to tell. She wanted to come. And he can tell she "likes him." Well, who wouldn't, etcetera. He should learn to limp with both legs so they all would.

He would've liked to discuss transients with her, though, to discuss next year even, weird as that seems, him having no idea of this fall even, of where he will go once it gets colder, though it'll probably be down to Claude's. But he had to tell her not to come, had to act up a bit and scare her off because the deal is going down tonight, next night, whenever. Cal will know. He should call her, get her up here for a night. But they've had a fight of some sort, haven't they, yes. Anyway, tonight, he has to keep a big fire going, the all-clear. Has to keep listening on the headphones, which he wants to anyway. He'd rather be thigh-to-thigh under the blanket with Cal, watching for whales, not a nervous ship of tough guys humping dope up and down a beach. He wonders if McKay remembered to tell them to bring packsacks or wheelbarrows for the trail. If not, he can hear them swearing at McKay already. Maybe he'll ask nicely and get one of them to accidentally tear a bale and toss him some spillage. He could use a toot of something. He wonders if they'll be getting more money than him, but who gives a. He forgets how much McKay is giving him. Maybe he could build a little cabin here, back in the woods out of the wind. He's thought about this before. Buy himself his own house. But small. Tight. Warm. This room he lives in now is too big, too cold, lacks a roof, and those stars can get to you.

He wonders if any of this land is for sale, if it's even owned. Maybe he heard that one of the Finnish families still owns lots of it. Would they sell a bit, let someone build a house here? A shack? Something small and tight. A wood stove. Take some trees down in front so he could see them blow, see them approach, have a telescope sitting in the one big window. He could open and close the window like an observatory roof. Sit in a big stuffed chair. A generator for lights, for charging the hydrophone batteries. Headphones on, sit there for ever. He could get McKay and someone to hump in a big easy chair for him. Maybe get old Claude up here, have another little house warming.

No. Even if buried in an insulated shed, wouldn't a generator thud deep into the ground, travel along roots to under the beach, resonate in massive deep boulders, turning them into big woofers thudding out to sea? Would they feel invited by some thudding machine? They sure don't swim up to the hippies who play their spirit flute while sticking a special toe in the water. Orca are curious, and they might stay and teach you a few things, but in the end they really, really don't care about you.

HE NAPS AGAIN then heads off for firewood. The search keeps getting harder, longer. The easy wood got grabbed first and fires get steadily harder to build. The odd storm tosses some new stuff his way but it's not till winter that the howlers hit and load up the beach again.

Firewood. He scans the distant tide-line and aims for a jumble of root balls that might be hiding some sticks. It's not a good walking beach. Stones the size of fists. Smooth, which is why the orca rub here, but lousy for walking. Especially if you're lousy at walking to begin with.

But you need firewood. It took an ancient guy from Sointula (he still had a funny Finnish accent, meaning he might have been a child of some of the originals) to tell him one night about cedar, even wet cedar, being best for getting a fire going. Cedar burns up, poof, so it's useless other than to get the thing going. Like some partiers he's known. Alder's best for the long haul but if it's green forget it. Fir is your standard good firewood, and it's fir he looks for now. It looks like he'll be doing some long dragging of outsize logs. He has to remember, next time someone comes around, to get them to pitch in and make a wood run. Firewood and shitting, these are the two main problems you get staying in one spot. You consume and you shit. You have to walk farther to do both. He's like a city unto himself. He'll have to hire trucks to bring his wood in from northern lands and haul his dumps off to poor countries. But it's a telling fact that he's changed this beach single-handedly.

What did the Indians around here do? Did they live in stink? Shivering? Not likely.

Catherine MacLeod and him should talk about next year. Maybe next year there will even be some money in it. Maybe he should call her back. But, money, that's right, he's getting lots of money from McKay. How much? Cal might know.

He is surprised by the sunset forming up. He stops to watch it. He had no idea of the time. These beams of purple-gold will build. It feels like he can almost understand them, these beams, their purpose and direction as they swell and brighten, and their glory makes him a little nervous in the stomach.

It will be one of those huge, God-overseeing-the-fall-of-civilization sunsets. The kind that makes you sad but also makes you feel part of the loop.

The meaning of the name "Sointula" was most cruelly felt the morning after the fire. Their one grand building was burnt to the ground. It was the centrepiece, the spirit, of the settlement. Eleven people, mostly children, burned alive. Reduced to ashes, as if they too had never been. One can imagine the heap of smoldering ruin, the human wailing and shouts of disbelief, the pain of burns, the dumb fatigue, the witless clouds scudding ignorantly overhead, a people's past and future smashed like glass — was there ever a morning less harmonious than this?

— DON COTTER, *LOST UTOPIAS*

GABRIOLA ISLAND

AS ON OTHER MORNINGS, Glenda brings orange juice "on the house." Evelyn has to reassure her that, no, she hasn't spent the night here in the tub. Glenda doesn't stay and politely chat. She treats Evelyn more like a friend now, meaning she can ignore her and get right to her gardening.

Evelyn lifts her orange juice and studies it in its plain glass. The fact of orange. Of colour at all. The sun can't quite get through it. It's easy to see that every colour is just a different style of muddying. Colour might be more earnest than frivolous, but it's still just something extra.

An eagle, a young flash-in-the-pan she's named Dennis, circles above her. He exudes an ambition to go international. Conspiring from their favorite cedar snag, ravens call and try to trick him. She's learned eagles aren't very smart. Glenda's chickens range behind the house in a treed field, loosely fenced, and the eagles see them but can't quite figure it out. Apparently bald eagles often starve to death. Nature has given them this grand persona but not the brains to back it up, so it's a ruse they're stuck with. It makes her see other birds differently, those robins as plump Swiss-in-aprons for instance, and those crows as loud marxists, black-on-purpose, and she's heard the magic thrum of hummingbirds but hasn't glimpsed them. She still sees the hummer she burnt back on Sidney Spit, but the shock feels like a muddy dream now. A flash of ruby, a coincidence that lacks any weight.

She wonders if it's time to leave here because she's forgetting to breathe. It's happened five or six times since yesterday and it just happened again now. Sitting in the hot tub, thinking densely, her lungs surprise her by drawing in a big, necessary one. It puts her head back and throws her chest out. It happens completely without her doing. It's a long loud pull and the air is sweeter than water when she's thirsty.

Under this blue August sky in a hot tub on Gabriola Island's Endless Love Ranch, she's forgetting to breathe. You don't get any more relaxed than that. Perhaps it's time to go.

What's keeping her?

She's stayed on here longer than her note to Peter said she would, but she refuses to agree with what Peter said, that she hasn't wanted to see Tommy all along. It's not that simple. Yes, she's afraid. But she's afraid of every direction on the map. She hasn't been much afraid in this hot tub. Though maybe she should be: her thoughts have been thickening, and now she's forgetting to breathe.

She's checked the bus schedule, so it's not like she's avoided it completely. She can leave Nanaimo in the morning and make Sointula late the same afternoon. Tomorrow is Tommy's birthday. If she actually does it — gets up early, ferries over, buys a ticket, sits all day on the bus — the reunion might go as she sometimes imagines it. Tom, on your sixteenth birthday I told you who your father was. Now, on your birthday ten years later I can tell you that he's dead.

She is afraid to imagine his face.

Eve has considered paddling across to Nanaimo to see Peter.

Evie has considered simply paddling back, south, retracing her steps, which includes the flight back east.

Evelyn climbs out and grabs a towel, notes her toes' talc-white dead skin. Since turning the temperature down she's been able to soak for hours at a time. She's never been so clean. She doesn't smell the chlorine anymore. Maybe her body has absorbed it all and a skunk can't smell its own.

A breeze off the sea hits her, it's cold, and she climbs back in to continue her soak.

She's gotten to know the three other resident eagles besides dumb Dennis; she thinks she's seen a porpoise jump way out there but it could have been a big salmon closer in. Claude would watch the water like this. He'd watch alertly, but he'd see what wasn't there. Scanning a calm sea, he'd say, "Boy, last year this time she was blowin' tru here like you wouldn' believe." He'd be stiff with the memory of being out there in the danger. Or, gazing out, "The coho'll be forty, fifty mile north about now, eh?" Always tuned to adventures distant. Looking for that next drink even with a full glass in his hand.

She's become such a fixture here on her deck that guests stopped waving to her from the path by Sunday and now — Wednesday? Thursday? — the guests are gone. No one but Maeve and Glenda and herself. Tonight they are having her to dinner in the main house and invited another to make it four. It's something she'd rather not do. The fourth is some kind of whale researcher woman they've asked because Evelyn has mentioned Tommy's job, and her own journey. She imagines Maeve and Glenda planning this guaranteed ice-breaker while they discussed the menu and the music and the napkins. She's been there a thousand times.

She'd rather just sit here in her stew.

THIS AFTERNOON she needs to pursue her memory of the dark little man, the psychiatrist, Christopher his name was. What did he say in the end? What was his verdict? It's on the tip of her tongue and she suspects it's sticking there because it's not pleasant and most of her doesn't want to remember. But it's her duty to remember. Going off these drugs has given her back so much and it remains her duty to get it all.

Maven of coincidence, Maeve triggered this memory too, though this time not with her second knee cap. She had just climbed into the tub and said what she said, and memory-seeking Evelyn did not speak to her — but Maeve no longer takes these silences personally. A social creature, Maeve has been joining her daily for a soak since the weekend guests departed. They're naked together but there's been no question of touching or anything. Evelyn has not to her knowledge been alone with a lesbian before, certainly never while undressed, and though the shock of nudity has worn off she enjoys treating it as a dangerous event. But Maeve is simply Australian, a buddy who doesn't like doing things solo, and Glenda doesn't like hot tubs. Glenda in a hot tub would be like a dry feather poking up out of the stew. Maeve is a potato. Evelyn a carrot. Or an onion. A glass onion.

This afternoon Evelyn's reverie was broken with Maeve's naked calf beside her face and an announcement that, "This tub's quite the psychiatrist." This was a not unskillful thing to say to someone who'd been spending hours in one, her gaze unfocused, forgetting to talk and sometimes to breathe.

"I had both at once, once," Evelyn found herself answering, not explaining the joke, remembering even as she said it the small, dark Christopher, his voice, the evening under the stars, Roy leaving them tactfully alone. The memories came full-blown and she turned away from Maeve to help them come. She could clearly see him take his steam-fogged glasses off, could see how he squinted to see her. So much of his job, she understood, must have to do with interpreting the many faces of pain.

It's easy to remember him speaking. He calls her "Dear," getting away with it because of his Scottish accent and cute ugliness. When Christopher arrived for dinner equipped with a bathing suit she suspected that the evening was all Roy's doing, but no matter.

Christopher tells her he had until recently been a psychiatrist but left "all the neurotics behind for that giant neurotic — civil service." He works at "social planning," which Evie, who's had drinks on top of her meds, says sounds sinister. When Christopher waggles his eyebrows just right, he and Evie launch into a good hot tub relationship, talking as fast as heat like this allows. Soon, apropos of nothing, he asks Evie about Tommy and, again smelling collusion with Roy, she hesitates. She has been down in the dumps and she knows Roy thinks it's about Tommy. And wouldn't you know it but exactly tonight is the fifth anniversary of Tom's flight from the coop, his 21st birthday, with neither cake nor son in sight.

Christopher says this to her next, and with a nearly ironic smile:

"I lost a daughter to cancer a few years ago. I understand you lost your son."

"I don't know what Roy's told you. He's still alive."

"But he left home extremely early."

"Some kids do."

"One thing Roy did pass on was that you never mention him. As if he *were* dead."

"That's not true." Is it? No. Roy has his own version. Possibly she never mentions Tommy to Roy. She mentions him to herself more than enough. "Not true at all."

"Well, let me ask you a question about him then. Just tell me if it's none of my business, Dear, but—"

"No, I miss talking to shrinks about Tommy. Better him than me." She smiles at her quip. She knows where this is going. She knows Christopher's question about Tommy will be about her and nothing but her.

"Okay: tell me what you think he's doing right this minute." He watches her face. "Yes, it's a game. Describe what he's doing. Describe it in technocolour."

"All right. He's in BC. Where it's, what, six-thirty. Six-thirty on a Friday night. So he's probably almost drunk, and probably stoned too."

"Not 'probably.' Is or isn't. You're there, Dear."

"Okay, is. Is getting drunk and is already stoned."

"On what."

Evie has closed her eyes to see Tommy.

"He's had three imported beer. He's had three Beck's beer. Before that he had two big lines of cocaine very neatly centered on his second-hand glass coffee table and he's getting ready to have two more."

"What's he been doing during this time?"

"There's music going. Harsh and jangly music. Angry music. It's loud but not too loud, not loud enough to get him evicted from this apartment too. He's had warnings. He's tired of moving."

"Good. Is he perhaps dancing to it?"

"He's on the phone. He's trying to round up some friends for the night. Maybe a girlfriend. Actually he's been phoning all sorts of people, seeing what they have in mind. It's his twenty-first birthday tonight — actually." She glances at Christopher, who doesn't look surprised by this. "He's talking fast, sipping a beer. Hanging up a lot — he has this way of hanging up where he doesn't put the receiver down but stands there talking with his finger ready on the button and when he's done with them he presses it." She shows him how fast the finger stabs down. "He never takes the receiver off his ear."

"Will he think of you, even once, this evening?"

At this Evie snorts. Then offers, "Yes, actually. He'll come home when he's tired everyone out, it will be getting light out, he'll open the fridge and there'll be nothing there. He'll visualize my leftover lasagna, and my drawer full of clean forks, and my microwave. That's what he thinks of me. It's as close as he ever comes, even when he lived here."

Christopher doesn't comment through any of this nor does he participate when, tired of the one-sided game, Evie invites him to do the same drill with his daughter. He says, simply, "I believe in the word 'terminal.' She's not doing anything at all other than knocking around in here." He taps his head and smiles and they both leave it at that. But he does offer her a summing-up of Tommy. She can tell he knows lots more, from Roy. For certain he has heard Roy's stream of anecdotes.

"I know you had various diagnoses of Tom. And that Tom wasn't there for them, the later ones. But regardless of any of that, you know I really think that sometimes in this business certain labels are used to write off a complex patient. I really do. Just as, in standard medicine, a 'heart condition' is ninety percent of the time reducing what is actually a *life* condition. You catch my drift?"

Evie nods, not liking this already.

"So in all honesty I'd have to say that your Tom doesn't sound like a psychopath at —"

"Sociopath."

"Same thing, Dear —"

No. One horrifies her. The other only declares that Tom's destiny is not a warmly human one.

"— Clinically the same thing. Anyway — But it's really hot in here now, isn't it?"

It's like autism, another born-with condition Evie's almost relieved to learn about. There are many conditions beyond a parent's reach.

Christopher hoists his small body out of the tub. He stands on the second step, water to mid-calf, steam tumbling off him into the cold night. Such a smoldering little man should be comical, but it makes all the more ominous and memorable what he says next. And, yes, it has been a set-up all along, and Evie is getting angry.

"Roy tells me you and Tom had quite the ongoing thing together, and that you were very demanding of him."

"*Roy* said I was 'demanding of him'?"

"Actually he said you were 'hard on him.'"

"I was hard on *him*?"

"Anyway." He's smiling, though his eyes are dire. "I've always thought it a mistake to write someone off with a label. Because, case in point, from what I've heard of Tom, he sounds to me like he was — now here comes an exotic clinical term for you — he was extremely pissed off." Something in Evie's look makes him stumble. "Not at you, necessarily. At the world. Please. I'm not for a second ascribing blame here."

"I was hard on *him*?"

Evelyn has just said this again, aloud, years later in her hot tub at the G &M Endless Love Ranch. Maeve has turned to her, eyebrows up, perhaps thinking she means Peter Gore. She looks ready to join this conversation if Evelyn wishes to include her, which she doesn't. She will continue the memory, which keeps coming, and which is probably mostly true, and which she senses will get worse. Because Christopher did say more.

What he says next about Tommy is, "It sounds to me like he was depressed."

No, what he said exactly is, "He sounds to me extremely and clinically depressed."

"Depressed."

"But even *that* word, Dear, I would caution you not to rely on as a label. Not that—" Here Christopher makes himself chuckle, "—*You* would see anything easy in the word." Of course the man knows her history, and her recently more potent prescriptions.

Seeing something in her face, Christopher looks suddenly self-conscious in his little body. Turning his head, he searches the night over his shoulder, though without his glasses he can see nothing.

The water jets are now somehow much louder and Evie thinks they sound pissed off themselves. She tries to keep her voice from shaking.

"Depressed."

"Mmm-hmm. Yes."

"Jeez. Just like me."

He doesn't appear to register her sarcasm. "Sure. Yes. Though generally speaking you don't seem all that angry."

"No."

"At least, it doesn't exactly show."

She waits, meets his eye, makes sure he is actually looking at her.

"I think it might look different in the mother."

This is exactly what she said. She *was* angry. Then and now. At whom, it is hard to say. What she said to herself, over and over, is, *Just like me. Just like me.*

Tom is just like me.

SHE REALLY DOESN'T want to be doing this, knocking on the door to the main house, not a paying guest but a dinner guest. A friend. She would prefer to do her waiting in the hot tub. Meeting new people is the last thing she needs. She needs to remember, to reaquaint with, more of the old. It feels like the evidence is stacking against her. Not that you should believe everything you remember.

She knocks at the main door, metal painted a rose red. She waits for the footsteps or muffled shout. She's been at such doors before. Its red compliments the woven green of the cedars towering just behind the house, but then of course it would. Glenda is a woman of taste, and would have spent time here with colour swatches held up to the trees.

Evelyn resists peering in the glass door of the office just a little farther along, at the phone in there. There where she's lately avoided phoning Roy. She's phoned for bus schedules and, hanging up, it seemed there was not a reason in the world why she shouldn't call Roy. She had to squint and calculate: If she phones him she will have to explain herself. She will have to tell him that she is taking a dead father to his son. That the past she is exploring on her way is not Roy's past. The more she says about any of this, the more distance she will put between them. And there is the matter of Peter Gore, even though that's finished. But to tell Roy it's finished is also to tell him it started, and this would drive Roy even further away and could only hurt. The phone is for bus schedules only.

She knocks on the door again, harder this time. The evening sun coming hot off the red makes her turn and take in another beautiful sunset. The resort faces due west and sunsets over Vancouver Island are the specialty of the house. This one is the best yet. They've all been the best yet. This one is — But why describe it? The night he left, Peter lifted his pained gaze and said the sunset looked like "Hamlet imagining what jewelry the dead Ophelia deserved." Peter was funniest when in agony.

With him gone she has truly begun to relax. She really could stay here. She has figured out that there might be nothing to figure out. Or, another way of seeing it, if you can't decide what to do, why do anything at all? It's so beautiful here. Orange juice, hot tub, sunsets — these are anchor lines. Eagles, ravens and guests angle in and out of her line of vision. It's occurred to her, more than once, that she has been enjoying the absence of men. She doesn't know what has relaxed her more — no men, or the hot tub. A hot tub of no men.

Maeve thuds inside, yelling behind her at Glenda as the door opens with a waft of roast chicken.

"Why didn't ya just come the hell in!" Maeve shouts. She is clearly excited about the dinner party. Life is too quiet for her on this island, Evelyn suspects, especially when the resort empties.

Evelyn's stomach sinks as she enters the house's inner sanctum and it takes her a moment to understand why. This could be the living/dining L of any house in Oakville, including hers. The peekaboo serving window from the kitchen is just like hers, as is the placement of the main windows. The decor is arts-and-crafty, with some Haida prints, but none of it hides the basic house. It feels ominous. She wishes she hadn't come.

Maeve points her to the bulgy cream couch in front of the burl coffee table and asks if she would prefer red, white or beer.

"Red, please."

"Or in a pail all mixed up!" offers Maeve, so smoothly it might be an expression of hers.

Glenda calls from the kitchen that Darlene will be here any time. She adds that it's a twenty-minute bike ride. She emerges with a tray, which she brings to the coffee table. "You'll like her," she says, quietly and not looking at Evelyn, handing her a pewter goblet. Evelyn wonders if this is a blind date. She prays that this Darlene doesn't smell. So far, she has caught a whiff from the deck of one crowded cabin. She hasn't smelled it on either Glenda or Maeve.

Maeve announces, "Dar, is, *bril*liant." Dah, ees, breeyent.

Well, of course she's being paired up. Of course these two women — maybe three — are seeing it this way. Why wouldn't they? The concept entertains her a little. Maybe she'll fall in love, maybe she's already begun her new life and doesn't yet know it, maybe a year from now she'll be married again, married to a woman. Maybe she will stay here after all.

But if romance was ever in the air it isn't for long. It turns out she doesn't like Darlene, who arrives clattering up on a refurbished antique bicycle, its old-fashioned front basket carrying two loaves of fresh-baked bread covered by a checked cloth that looks made for just that purpose. She dismounts so awkwardly it's clear she hardly ever rides it and rides it tonight for show. Hawk-nosed, bright-eyed, dressed expensively, Darlene is perhaps forty. Briefly puffing and fanning her face, she enters smiling with an air of expecting to be congratulated.

The four of them sit and sip wine, and Darlene, sitting erect and staring sightlessly at the coffee table, listens hard as she's being described to Evelyn. Evelyn wants to tell her that she shouldn't be winded, that instead of a showy antique she could buy a good used mountain bike with gears at a yard sale for thirty dollars. Maeve and especially Glenda see Darlene as something of an island hero. She was arrested at Clayaquot. She isn't a whale researcher but the head of an orca protection coalition. She's in other coalitions as well. She's received a death threat, they're all convinced, from a real estate developer here on the island. Listening alertly, Darlene is quick to make minor corrections of dates and place-names, adding the occasional self-deprecating, "Oh, nonsense." To support herself, Darlene teaches sociology at a community college in Nanaimo. Darlene is one of those people who is hard to like but impossible not to admire.

Evelyn cannot touch her wine. First it was the house. Now it's Darlene. The hosts' nodding admiration is too familiar — that hunger over stature and reputation, that adoration of accomplishment. It's vampirish, and all the worse when the blood-filled one enjoys being sucked.

Evelyn knows there's no real reason to hate Dar. She's just tired of feeling lesser. Which isn't Dar's doing. It's Evelyn's doing, it's Evelyn making the fatal comparison. Why compare yourself at all? It's deadly and it's stupid and everyone loses, every time. Since she watched Claude die and learned the mortal equality of everyone, she hasn't felt it, hasn't felt lesser, hasn't let herself fall to that. Why is she doing it now? She's tired of it. She's tired of it because she's felt lesser all her life.

Can she just get up, leave? She wants her hot tub.

Darlene, taking over from Maeve as a conduit of coincidence, turns to Evelyn. "And what do you do with *your* time?"

Evelyn feels herself blush. She mumbles, "Well..." She's wearing the black spandex shorts she stole islands ago and she lightly stabs a spot on her thigh with a finger, this habit no longer producing pain. "I guess I'm doing it."

"Evelyn's kayakin'," says Maeve.

She *will not* care what Darlene thinks of her. If you really don't like someone anyway, why this need to impress? On the tip of her tongue is her list: group home worker, life skills teacher, volunteer for the blind, hospital board, friend of Tibetans.

"Heading where?" Darlene asks.

"I think north."

Maeve helps out again. "Evelyn's on a bit of a walkabout."

Evelyn smiles. "I've been calling it 'vacation.'"

"Well —" Darlene adopts Maeve's accent. "*Good* on ya." Both Glenda and Maeve laugh and Dar listens to their laughter as she did to their description of her.

"Waitin' here for her friend to get better," Maeve adds.

To this Evelyn says nothing and Darlene looks at her, indicating interest with supercilious brow and slight tilt of the head.

"Her friend got real sick their first night here," explains Glenda. Her pale features have begun to redden with the wine. "We had him airlifted out."

"Oh yes, I *heard* about that," Darlene says.

It's clear to Evelyn that the three of them have talked about all of this, and that this conversation is their chance for added morsels.

Maeve says, "He's in Nanaimo General probably wondering where his gall bladder went."

"So that was *your* friend in the helicopter," says Darlene.

"He's not my *friend*," Evelyn hears herself say. Into the predictable silence she explains, "Not my *friend* friend."

"Ah!" Glenda exclaims.

"As in," says Maeve, "not *together* together?"

"Well," says Glenda, "we did wonder about you and Peter."

The way Glenda pronounces his name suggests that she assumes him gay, and that the nature of their relationship is no longer secret. Evelyn says nothing to this. Through the chill of her betrayal she thinks she sees Glenda meet eyes with Darlene, a brief but significant glance.

"But how *is* Peter?" Maeve asks sincerely. Evelyn announces that he's fine and that he just wants out of the hospital. Her betrayal is eased by these and other embellishments she thinks Peter would have enjoyed. She tells them he's looking forward to coming back and eating another one of their chickens, and also that he has a fatal crush on a doctor there. *Another* chicken, she says. *Fatal* crush. Peter would have enjoyed this.

"But I think I'll be doing all the paddling for a while."

The other three laugh politely.

Evelyn now feels as defined as Peter. Well — funny — maybe she *is* how they see her. Or could be. It would be fun in a way to flirt with Darlene. From her pocket, Claude approves, he punches the air and shouts *Yes*! Dar, who is transparent and has no rhythm of her own, who is at her core lonely. Evelyn could do anything she pleased. But she doesn't think cruelty is in her. Not even Claude's unthinking kind.

Sitting in a cloud-of-a-couch, falling into each next sentence, she can still see herself too clearly. She decides that, most of all, she feels not *back* to normal but *more* than normal. To get here, she seems to have skipped normal somewhere along the way.

"What about this view?" Darlene is asking her. She has turned and taken up a pose of gazing serenely out the window. The view is of Evelyn's long hot-tub days.

"It's wonderful," Evelyn answers, joining her in taking things this step further, which is how these things are done.

Darlene is only trying her best, like anyone. Like ghostly Glenda, a gentle cadaverous faerie. Like Maeve, who'd be more happy drinking beer and watching a game on TV, more attuned to it than Roy. She trusts Maeve isn't pregnant with Peter Gore's little sea monster.

The wine is going down well, for Evelyn now too. Encouraged, Maeve rises and goes to fetch a third bottle, an untried wine, made in the from Cowichan Valley from organic grapes. On her way she laughs about organic headaches.

Poor Peter. Evelyn wonders if he will head home now. If he still has a home. He abandoned Spokane. It's easy to see him — feel him — lying in his hospital bed, restless. So many words but no book. Will he give up or will he persist? She does like his main idea, of Vancouver Island being the farthest place west on the planet. A place settled in the name of restlessness, in the name of dissatisfaction. A place where, if you leave, you by definition go *back*. She wonders if he's had second thoughts, if he's decided there's nothing that special about this place that beat him up and put him in the hospital.

Is any place ever more special than any other place? Of course. If asked, young children call a glass of water white, because they have no word yet for clear. Evelyn hardly notices her arm extending her glass to the wine being poured because she can feel through the living room wall, through to the glow of various greens, in past the blackberry scramble to the rough brown stand of cedar, then farther in, to where it's endless dark charm. There are powerful places and this living room isn't one. But not fifty feet away lies unfathomable spirit.

"Thank you. It's very good," she says, after her glass is filled.

She hasn't tasted it yet, it's a new bottle, but nobody says anything. She means the colour of it, and the feel. And that it's good to eat and drink what comes from your own backyard. Which is what the People here did, forever. They never should have reached out for the blankets and the mirrors. Blankets thick with smallpox. Mirrors that made them infinitely weaker.

"Sorry Ev'lin? Ya say ya want a blanket?"

DINNER IS QUITE something and Evelyn eats and eats. Her stomach doesn't take much to fill so she waits before refilling her plate. The others have long stopped, but they don't seem to mind. Glenda's proud that Evelyn likes the food. The chicken, the runner beans, the garlic, herbs and blackberries for the sauce — all come from their property.

"Reggie says the pod's headed north."

Evelyn lifts her attention from her plate. The talk has at last turned to whales. It doesn't feel all that forced. It turns out that Gabriola Island doesn't get many orcas so it's news when there are sightings. Dar's group supports the movement to stop whale watching from boats, to stop harassing resident orcas in particular as they try to live their daily lives in their ancestral habitat. Evelyn wonders what Tom's position would be. What would he say, how would he confront Darlene if he were here at this table? Evie can see him eat, head down, hair falling forward; can see his deft and impatient fork. Like it was yesterday.

"Just imagine it," Darlene instructs. "We're sitting here having our coffee, trying to talk, whatever. And now imagine if we were surrounded by, by *weed*eaters. Or *chain*saws. Right in the room. All around us. *Never* off." Darlene pauses to breathe indignantly. "Imagine *making love* surrounded by all that buzzing of boats. All summer long, every day, *every* day, they are surrounded. It could make you cry." She nods at them by way of explaining that she has.

A whale researcher would have a position on this. Tommy will look ten years older, and his lifestyle may have stressed more years onto that. She tries to imagine him, studious, with a clip-board, having a position on orca-watching tours and backing up his comments with facts — and she can't. He is fifteen, he's said nothing good about the meal and on his clipboard he has written crude slogans about lesbians. He waits for dark, whereupon he will slip outside and borrow someone's speedboat.

Claude would already have left to borrow someone's speedboat.

Evelyn listens to facts about whales, orcas mostly, basic stuff she doesn't know and feels ashamed not knowing. They are actually a species of huge dolphin. Residents, transients. Matriarchal lineage — a fact that perks Glenda up and makes her proud, as if it confirms something she wants confirmed.

Tommy not only knows these details, he is perhaps passionate about them too. It's a Tommy she has no clue about. A scientist. She does remember his bedroom floor and its scatter of mechanical pieces of things he never cleaned up.

"And your son." Darlene turns to her. "Who's he with?"

"I believe he's alone."

"I guess I mean 'working for.' It's probably Cathy, she got ten this year."

"I'm not exactly —" Evelyn pauses.

"It has to be Cathy. Catherine MacLeod. She has a whole scatter of grad students up Robson Bight. Though he could also be with Alexandra, or Paul, though I doubt it. They're, ah, more alternative? Cathy's with UBC. Stable money. The others attract the oddest types. They are *in love* with these animals. Some of them get — Well even *Cathy* gets a little ga-ga, herself. Just a little religious."

"What's wrong with that?" asks Glenda. "Seems like a good religion to me."

"What's wrong is it lets the politicians keep killing them. If you want to save them you can't come off like cranks. If you want to save them you give the man his science, you give the man statistics, and you give it —" Darlene's voice darkens and slows, "— sober, as, hell."

"There's a guy here, near Dengen Bay," Maeve adds, inappropriately jovial, "says he's swum with the buggers naked." She giggles from the gut. "I think there was a full moon and some drugs involved."

"So your son's —?" Darlene has turned to Evelyn again.

"We really haven't been all that much in touch."

"But do you know where he's stationed?"

"Yes. Sointula."

"Sointula." Darlene looks shocked.

"Wow," Maeve declares. "You're goin' all the way to Sointula? We've been there." She indicates Glenda with an oddly formal palm-up gesture. "It rains. Take the boy an extra raincoat."

"We had a wet time," Glenda affirms. "It's a powerful place though. The history."

Darlene has been staring at her hungrily.

"*That's* your boy? On Sointula?"

"That's where he is. Last I —"

"That's him? With Catherine?"

"I don't know who he works for exactly."

"Why, Dar?" asks Maeve. "You know him?"

"Well, I —" Darlene glances to Evelyn as if for permission. "I know *of* him. Cathy and I debrief sometimes and he's, he's —" Again she looks almost pleadingly at Evelyn. "He's an interesting fellow. His name is ..." She aims her face in tip-of-the-tongue posture.

"Tom."

"That's him!"

"Well, isn't this fun!" declares Maeve, who bounces up for another bottle of wine.

"He's doing so remarkably well." Darlene puts a soft hand on Evelyn's wrist.

"Yes."

"I mean, it's *so* remarkable."

"What is?" Glenda asks.

Darlene turns, forthright, to Evelyn. "Evelyn. Do you mind if I tell them? If it's private, please just say. But we're all adults here. And I think what's he's doing is just remarkable."

"Sure." Then Evelyn adds, "Please."

"For one thing he sits up all night to take pictures of them, which I've seen, and they're remarkable." She turns to speak to Maeve, who has just returned. “We’re speaking about Evelyn’s Tom. And I think it’s just so fantastic that he’s so attentive. Given the nature of his injury.”

“What injury is that?” asks Maeve, and all three women turn to Evelyn. Evelyn isn’t responding, so Darlene offers a sad grimace and continues.

“Well, let’s just say he had dealings with undesirables. Evelyn, is it fair to say that?”

“... Yes.”

“And that they caught up to him and, well, tried to kill him, *thought* they’d killed him, shot him in the head, but he survived, though with —”

“Oops, Evelyn’s spilled,” says Glenda. She turns to Maeve. “Get the salt. We need some salt here. Get the whole box.”

Evelyn finds herself simply sitting. Maeve arrives with a box of salt and busies herself on the carpet near Evelyn’s feet while Glenda mops the table-drips with several napkins. Evelyn tries to ask Darlene something.

“Sorry? Evelyn? Describe ...?”

“... His injury.”

“Well, yes,” she says, nodding, speaking to Maeve and Glenda. “He’s made remarkable progress, according to Cathy. She says he looks after himself extremely well. He can’t manage his water, or food, because he’s apparently far from the village, and his walking is very iffy, but he persists and he copes with his disabilities very, very well.” Darlene ends with earnest nods into the middle of the room.

Evelyn is sitting up straight. She has placed her knife and fork diagonally on her plate, achieving this, metal against china, without making a sound. She recalls being proud of her ability to do this.

“How many,” she begins, “about how many whale watchers would there be on Malcolm Island?”

“I assume you mean the official kind? You mean other than the relics chanting and saying prayers to them?” Darlene can be funny after some wine.

“Yes.”

"It would be just Tom."

Claude saying, *He's okay now, the boy's okay, he's up and around now and he's gonna be fine, gonna be fine.* Concern plain on his face, Claude saying all this a little too fast and she can see now that he said it often, to himself. *He's okay, boy's gonna be okay, gonna be okay.*

Evelyn pushes back her chair and moves to an armchair by the livingroom window. They aren't overly troubled by her though they appear to have given up; she hears someone whisper the words "awfully withdrawn." She knows already that she's not going to cry. She's too scared, too hollowed out. It would be too easy to float away if she began to hear her own screams. But she won't. She'll try her best to not let any of them know what Darlene's just done. It's not her fault.

Or is it that she doesn't want them to know she was ignorant of the most basic tragic facts about her only child? Yes, it's that too. Shame rises hot up her spine, until she violently shakes her head. It's not her fault. It's not her fault either.

They soon join her in the living room, agreeing with themselves too loudly that Evelyn's move to comfy chairs is a wise one.

He sometimes shook his head and mumbled, *Hard to even recognize 'im now like that, you don' even recognize 'im*, and Evelyn had thought he was talking about an awful new hairstyle, Claude having taken up the parental role of nag.

What does Tommy look like? Not knowing is somehow the worst of it, is now aching everywhere in her body. Worse still is that she cannot lurch up and simply run to him.

"Oh, look. The moon has come out," says Darlene. "It's a perfect half moon."

"That's not a quarter moon?" asks Maeve.

"It's a perfect half moon."

"Oh, look at those clouds!"

Evelyn tells herself that tonight has changed nothing. Only her knowledge has changed. The damage is long done. There is nothing she can do.

"Those are mackerel clouds," Evelyn tells them. She feels her lips move and jaw work and the right words come out. "Like the markings on a mackerel. Coming in from the west. It means it won't rain tomorrow but the next day."

The evening continues. Binding her panic is the steady weave of voices and gestures, that which is called a dinner party. She talks, it's not hard, and more than once her horror even puts on a smile. It's like a thousand evenings in Oakville. It makes no difference what she says or doesn't say because there is nothing she can do until the morning. Her hot tub would feel even more like delay than this does, and there would be no escaping, not for a second, the words: Tommy has been shot and he has been shot in the head.

Archeologists concur that the ancestry of all First Nations of North, Central, and South America lies in Asia and that the route taken from Asia to the Americas was via a land bridge known of Beringia, the area surrounding what is now the Bering Strait... Archaeologists are certain of two things: that people have occupied this part of the Americas for at least 12,000 years, and perhaps for 20,000 years or more; and that all migrations involved passing through portions of British Columbia.

— ROBERT J. MUCKLE,
THE FIRST NATIONS OF BRITISH COLUMBIA

PORT MACNEIL

IT IS NOTICEABLY COLDER when they disembark at Port MacNeil in the near-dark. You wouldn't call air like this summer air. It's not exactly drizzling, it's more that they are walking into a cloud that's trying to turn itself into rain. The bus terminal is a gas station parking lot. Some passengers scatter to waiting cars, the rest start a group trudge to a ferry dock. Gore said his goodbyes to the old woman as they stepped out of the bus and now here he is walking three feet behind her. Half the group is Native. Some of them murmur in tones so soft it sounds secretive but Gore can tell by the lilt that it's not.

He follows them down a waterfront sidewalk, turns onto a heavily timbered ferry-dock platform and lifts the boarding pass from his shirt pocket though the uniformed ticket woman isn't looking. Instead she's greeting people by name and laughing at something Gore doesn't hear. He doesn't feel well. He's hot and tired and likely sick with something. Maybe it's time for another antibiotic. He feels okay, though, because of the pain pills. Not well but *okay*. With these pills, which he knows are manufactured upon a base, a warm hearth, of opiates, he could get even sicker and still feel okay. He could be on a torture rack, or dead, and feel okay. Not *well*, though, and he doesn't feel like joking around. He wants to get to Sointula, find Eve and Tom, have a good hard curative sleep, and in the morning sip coffee and watch whales. Whereupon he and Eve would continue their odd vacation.

Eight or so vehicles are lined up. Gore stands under a shelter, for it has begun to rain. The old woman doesn't acknowledge him. He wishes he had asked her about residential schools, something real, and now it is too late, and he sees that, like most windows of opportunity, they become clearer once they're shuttered.

Heads turn to the lights of a vessel as it rounds a point of land and approaches in the dusk. The ferry looks shabby and small and lacking in animal comforts. Gore decides not to be depressed though it's become apparent to him that he should be. This little trip will be taking him off Vancouver Island proper and in a north-east direction. East, not west, and this feels not only like backtracking but like a portentous departure from his root inspiration and plan. And of course there are other things: It's near dark, it's raining, he's wounded, tired and broke. His destination is less than clear.

Yet he feels almost rather okay. He knows it's not just the pills keeping despair at bay — it's travel. Travel is only good. It not only broadens, it sharpens. Travel is automatic wakefulness. It is its own *raison d'etre*, its own destination. He's *travelling*. He's only *begun* to travel. He's not only standing on a wood launching pad to the unknown landmass of Malcolm Island, with its historic gemstone, Sointula, he is setting foot on the shore of the limitless island of the rest of his life. What's there to be down about?

Of course included in his travels is the imminent exploration of a woman's vast heart.

It would be so, so nice if she were waiting for him at the other side, but of course there is no way for her to know. Witch or not. Hostess of coincidence or not. Yet he can't help but imagine her at the Sointula dock, cup of cocoa in hand, wearing a nurse's uniform, a golden halo, and a smile the likes of which he's not yet seen on her.

THE WALK-ONS BOARD first. Gore follows the backs of people to the passenger compartment at the ferry's side, a long room of dulled aluminum and old tile, like a public bathroom but with windows and hard benches.

A crude paper sign hangs flapping over the doorless entrance — *No Corks* — and Gore has a delightful moment in that he knows this must be the misspelling of "caulks," which is pronounced sort of like "corks," and which refers to the spiked boots used by loggers whose job is to dance about on logs as they dangerously float, or to walk their lengths as they lie in a pile, like pick-up sticks, after they've been sawn down, that is, *felled*. He stops and checks the linoleum at his feet and, yes, it is well-pocked by these spiked, caulked, or corked boots. He wonders whether this ruined floor is the result of loggers who don't care or can't read, and wonders which is worse. In any case, this is not tourist country. He takes a seat, stares out a window into the black. Cars load, each with a bang. A truck makes the ferry dip. He can hear one car needing a muffler. He recalls reading that Sointula has no resident police and that the people like it that way. The ferry lurches out to sea.

The lurch triggers an automatic realization. He has left his luggage — his courier package holding paper, pencils, both vials of pills and near-full mickey of whisky — in the overhead rack on the bus. He flies half out of his seat, almost ripping his incision. He yelps once and begins to hyperventilate — but stops. Wait. He can get paper anywhere. He can sharpen charcoal sticks on the beach. It's time he stopped drinking anything but water. Pills? He would embrace his pain. He would embrace all that lay in store, in the name of travel. His book now has a new sub-title. It's no longer *around*. It's now *The Rim: A Journey* Beyond *The Last Island*.

Gore sits and simply breathes. Out the window he charts the passage of sparse lights which mean nothing to him. These *side* windows show the houselights boatlights bouylights not of the destination but the passed *by*, the *whatever*, the *beside* the point. He has also noticed that all the people in here are white. Where are the Natives? Are they forced to stay outside? Kept in steerage? This has the makings of a story. It is the duty of *The Rim* to report any minor apartheid. He heaves himself up, grabbing his abdomen and screaming silently, and limps outside.

He stands on what is in effect a travelling parking lot. It's hilariously cold. The wind from the ferry's speed whips his fever away. He stands clasping his shoulders, chin into the wind, casting his regard at the horizon — for there it is, they have rounded a point of land and there is the clutch of lights of what must be Sointula.

"You take this a while."

The pie-faced woman has taken off her ski jacket. It dangles puffy from a fist and she is softly punching his chest with it.

"I couldn't possibly —"

"You said you had an operation." She's punching him a little harder and she looks more angry than anything else.

"Just for a while then. Thank you." When he calls to her back, "I'm going to put you in my book," she waves at him without turning around.

She's a round old thing so the jacket is big enough, except for the arms, which leave almost a foot of forearm showing. The woman had come from the bathroom and she has since climbed back into a car, and now Gore sees where all the Natives went. They're all in cars. The cars of friends. For you can tell which are the Natives' cars. Not because they are all mostly full of friends, and not because they are generally older and more rusty, which they are, but rather because they are all on one side of the ferry deck, pointing backwards. On the front dashes are orange cards reading *Alert Bay*. The other cars, facing forward, have yellow cards, *Sointula*. These cars are a little newer, and for the most part empty.

So Native walk-ons jump into Native cars. White walk-ons go sit in the passenger lounge. It's a noteworthy observation. He has no idea what it means. Which island, for instance, will they go to first, and will that be favoritism or logistics? He's instantly hot and sweating in his ski jacket, but it's too cold out to take it off.

Sointula hasn't gotten closer. Indeed they look to be turning so they must be going to Alert Bay first. He notes people standing behind metal pillars, out of the wind, smoking. Some are drinking beer. Across from where he stands is a distinctive gathering next to two brand-new green SUVs, notable because the vehicles are so hefty and polished while the men are so uniformly small. He looks closer. Because of the black hair and brown skin he'd thought them Native at first, but they are all of them thin, small-boned, high cheeks. Vietnamese, he guesses. Six of them altogether. All are smoking. Their wrists are delicate. Several are stylishly, almost effeminately dressed, what one would have once called slick. Nike stuff, tear-aways, thin gold chains. Two wear sunglasses. All of them have turned to look at him, because he's been staring. None are smiling.

He turns away, shaking his head. He must have been gawking like an idiot. Checking them like he's never seen an Asian, in this land of Asians. Though they do stand out. Compared to the Natives they look arrogant and aggressive.

In his musing Gore remembers and congratulates himself on his theory about Asians finally conquering this land after the initial, ice-age foray had failed. Not that the Natives had failed, exactly. They just weren't very flamboyant, or persistent. Especially now. Compared to the slick second wave, look at them: Generally tending to pudgy. Mumbling to each other in rusted cars turned backwards. Though he is getting rained on and they aren't.

A FOOT TAPS HIS calf and a voice grumbles, "Sointula." Gore jerks up. He's been sleeping slumped on the bench in the passenger compartment, which has emptied out. The ferry worker says without humour how it's lucky he checked or "you would've slept back to Port MacNeil."

Gore limps onto the ferry deck, which is empty too. The cars are already off; he can see the tail lights of the last ones a few blocks away. He has trouble thinking. He couldn't have napped long but it feels like hours. They are in Sointula. They must have stopped at Alert Bay first; the Native cars are gone. He is still wearing Moon-Faced Woman's ski jacket.

He has barely stepped off when the ferry ups its front lip and pulls away from the dock. Gore stands alone, watching it leave. The rain is steady. He whispers to himself, "I'm travelling now," in a tone less adventurous than haunted. He's has seen enough of the town to know he could be in trouble. For one, it's not a town. 'Village' would be a stretch. It is a paved street along the water, two or three blandly soviet-style wooden buildings, unlit, and a surrounding huddle of houses. Not only is there no neon, there are no signs. Clearly, anyone who lives here knows what these buildings are for and who is welcome in them. This ferry ramp is Sointula's middle.

He takes a traveller's breath, walks into it.

From the ramp onto the fronting street he can turn either right, or left. To the right are houses, half with porch lights already turned off. To the left are more houses and what looks almost like a store. He turns left.

At least in this direction the rain is out of his face. He walks a block, two. This town, village, settlement, is so quiet, thick with history that excludes him. But, he's here: here is his destination announced on a cement retaining wall that keeps a bank of earth from falling into the main street. From what looks like a grade-school project, the wall has been painted bright blue, with a scatter of yellow daisies at the borders and a few dolphins leaping out of pointy waves. The bold white lettering says: SOINTULA — "PLACE OF HARMONY."

How this name must have needled the Finns at the depths of their bickering, their fatal fire, their later-day explosions of violence.

A roving car passes him, slowing down for a good look. He smiles for it, his face hunched in between his shoulders. He sees that only one headlight works and, as it rumbles off, neither tail light. A minute later a second vehicle passes, one of the green Vietnamese SUVs. This one doesn't change speed but he smiles for it anyway. He continues walking, his hopes pointed at the light over the entrance to the sort-of-store one more block along. Mostly, he hopes Eve has had a good reunion with her son. He hopes that at least it hasn't gone badly. For certain it will be a rich time for her, no matter how she is received, no matter how opened or closed their hearts are to each other. As for his own part in this, he hopes he will know when to keep his distance and when to approach with a dry shoulder.

But: they've been intimate now, and the sleeping arrangements might be awkward. Grown or not, Tommy is her child after all.

A bell tinkles over the door when he pushes it open. A glass-fronted fridge displays two quarts of milk, one package of cheese, pepperoni sticks, some pop. It appears also to be a hotel lobby and video rental kiosk. Wincing in his reach up, Gore tinkles the door bell with a finger. He waits another minute and still no one comes. He receives a thrill to be staring at the cash register like he is, but the thrill is brief because he knows he never would.

Two doors lead from the room he's in. One, looking like it's been painted by the same children who did the retaining wall, reads "The Tank." Beneath, a martini glass holds a perfectly round olive. Gore turns the doorknob. In dim light he steps down some stairs, and finds himself in a tavern. No one is here either. It does resemble a bar in every way except size, for it is no larger than a large bedroom, which may be what it once was. But it has the requisite wood panel, and a wet bar, and recessed fridge behind it. Three tables and a total of seven chairs. A window has been painted on a wall, and in this window is a sky-blue day, with a rainbow, hummingbirds and those same dolphins that also leap from the retaining wall a few blocks away.

An angry blond woman steps out of what Gore had assumed was a closet. She doesn't sound angry when she asks, "Can I help you?" but her face is one of the angriest he has ever seen. He has a little under five dollars in his pocket. He doesn't want a drink, but nor does he want to anger her further. She looks fifty, like him, and she looks like she used to be very pretty. Maybe that's what she's angry about.

"I was wondering if there was someplace I could get a sandwich?"

The woman turns away. She picks up a wet rag and starts passing it over the bar in a figure eight. It's an unthinking habit, the rote spasm of a caged tiger; he expects there is a figure-eight impression in the formica.

For a moment it seems that she isn't going to answer him. He sees he hasn't let go of the doorknob. After a time she says, "Well," under her breath.

HE WAKES UP to her voice, which is calm enough, though her face, when he gets it in focus, is still angry.

"I thought you were just kidding," she says.

He finds he is sitting in a chair at the table nearest the door.

"Saying you're hungry and smiling and then just sort of sitting hard on the floor."

"Really."

"I thought you were pretending." She drops a glass of water in front of him and wipes her rag beside it. "I know someone like that," she adds, in a way that doesn't release him from suspicion.

"Just had an operation," he says. "I think it's—" he begins, then stops. What he imagines are little pockets of anesthetic moving sluggishly around his whole system, putting him to sleep when they loop through his brain. It really does feel like that, but he can't be bothered to come up with all the words.

"Feeling better?"

"Yes."

"Mary's kitchen is all locked up so there's nothing here I could sell you except beer or a pickled egg. And I don't think you want a beer."

Her face angry as ever, she's pointing at the large jar sitting on a stool behind the bar. The sight brings him back to the worst of teaching. That immense jar of pickled eggs is cousin to any bucket of formaldehyde-and-fetuses you'd care to name. The slightly grey hue of egg is the colour of embalmed piglet.

"Water's fine."

"There's the burger barn."

"Really? Where?"

"You drivin'?"

"Is it far?"

"The corner of Bere Road."

"Sorry?"

"Bere Road."

"Is that away from the ferry dock or towards the ferry dock?"

The woman's face holds on the verge of what might be increased anger, then she tells him, "Away from. Edge of town. Open till nine. Unless Judy went home. It's a Tuesday."

"Excuse me but, do you know a whale researcher out here, in Sointula, or at least on Malcolm Island, named, well, named *Tom*? Tom *Poole*?" Though who knows what last name he might be using.

"I know about the whale-guy. Don't know if that's his name, though."

"Lives by himself? Right on the beach? Watches whales?"

"That's the man."

"And he's, he's—" He doesn't know what to say next. He was about to say "a drug dealer," but that might make her angry indeed.

He's risen and has moved to the door. She's watching him closely, the way he limps, the protective clutch over the liver. Then she says something fantastic.

"He walks just like you."

HUNCHED IN THE RAIN, he's turned left, away from the ferry dock, aiming for the one bright light at the edge of town. He tries to hum a tune but can come up with no song not utterly false. A car passes slowly, then stops, idling. It's the one-light car that's passed and slowed before. When he overtakes it the window comes down and a boy, not remotely sixteen, asks if he wants a ride. Another boy, same age, is his passenger. Gore tells them no thanks, he's just heading up to the Burger Barn. Is it open by the way? The boy says yes and drives off.

As he walks, the incision hurts more and more, and he has a headache now. But he isn't disturbed by the pain. It's basic pain, a kind that revealed itself very early on in the game and though it may get worse there will be no mysteries or surprises with it. What he doesn't like is the fever, which makes him feel bulgingly puffy, like there's far too much face for his skin to contain. He lets his ski jacket fall open at the front. The cold air coming in keeps him moving.

The Burger Barn is lit by a single bulb, shielded at the top with what has to be a First World War helmet. The window slides open at Gore's arrival. Not looking at him, a young woman asks what she can get for him then sits back in her chair, reading.

"What are you reading?" he asks her, cheerily.

"This one." She turns the book's cover his way and shoves it at him as far as her arm will reach. It's Hesse's *Siddhartha*. She must not know how to pronounce it. She is reading again and he examines her. She could be a recent ex-student of his. Late teens, not unattractive, dressed like a hippy of old save for a tiny nostril ring. Malcolm Island must not have changed much since the invasion in the '60s. Odd and perhaps touching how she would adopt the garb as well as the reading material of her parents.

"Have you decided?"

"I'll have one of those burgers, and fries and a Coke, please." He points at the list of fancy-named burgers he can't seem to get in focus.

She tells him the deep fryer is down for the night. She asks if the "Sointula Burger" is what he wants and if Pepsi is okay. She closes the window to commence her burger-making. Gore stands for a moment, insulted, and then raps on the window. He watches her move quickly from a chopping board to the grill and back before opening the window.

"Do you know where I could find a certain whale researcher? Named Tom? He's on the island somewhere. He's young, that is, about twenty-five and he —"

"You know the Whale-Man?" She gives him a half-smile.

"Can you tell me where he's staying?"

She, too, studies him and gives no indication that an answer might be forthcoming. He wonders what it is about these Sointula women.

"I know what beach he's sleeping on, if that's what you mean."

"I guess that's what I mean, yes." He had envisioned some kind of cabin.

"He's been at Bere Point all summer."

"Yes. Can you tell me how to get there?"

She points right past his face.

"Right down this road. Right to the end of it. That's where the trail starts."

"Trail."

"The trail to the beach he's on. Unless he's moved beaches."

"How far are we talking about, altogether. Road plus trail."

"Were you thinking of walking?"

"Yes."

"Tonight?" She brings fingers to her mouth to press back some laughter there.

He takes his burger and Pepsi to a plastic shelter rigged beside the barn proper. Inside it's very cold and he keeps his jacket zipped. He's sweating freely, though, and the inner fabric is sopping. His wrists are freezing. His nose is stuffed so he keeps his mouth open to breathe, making chewing difficult. Plus, the Sointula Burger turns out to be halibut, with lots of sauce and cucumber slices, a few of which fall from his open mouth to his lap. Because of his stuffed nose he can hardly taste it, aside from something lemony. None of this is amusing.

The young woman has told him "it's a skinny island" and it's only four or five miles across to where the trail starts, but she has no idea how far along the beach trail the Whale-Man might be. She says friends of hers have sat at his site and had a beer, and these friends are no hikers, so it's probably not far. But it'll be dark. When she pointed to the outside bulb over his head and said that this was the last light he'd see, his stomach hollowed and all travel courage left him.

He sits with his burger. He stares at the sauce slopped onto a finger and notes that it's yellower than mayonnaise and contains pieces of what appear to be seaweed. He has no appetite for it right now but can tell that this burger is likely very good. He has to put it down with only two bites gone and he hopes she doesn't see him. They'd already survived an embarrassing moment—when paying he'd forgotten about taxes and whatnot, then some of his dropped coins rolled under the Barn itself, and he was almost a dollar short. When he offered his Pepsi back she looked at him in that way of hers and he saw he'd already opened it. In the end she forgave him the shortfall, but wouldn't return his smiles when she closed her window for the last time.

HE STANDS AT the corner of what he's been told is Bere Point Road. Two cars have come along the waterfront but instead of turning his way they continue on to houses farther along. The girl closed up and left the Burger Barn perhaps an hour ago now.

Something of this night reminds him of his first one out in the wilderness, the one he spent buried in cold sand outside Bill and Bob's tent. He's always considered that a night he would one day write about with a light touch, but he doesn't think tonight will ever be seen in fun. This is real wilderness. It has nothing to do with trees. It has to do with an incision, and rain, and wet pavement reflecting nothing because there is no light.

He won't for a moment entertain the possibility that he might not be welcome, though the world which hides and protects Evelyn seems to be telling him otherwise. But her note. Its gentle humour. The word "love," in painstaking charcoal. The hot tub. Evelyn.

He imagines the first hopeful Finns, here in winter, shivering in the rain, like him. Like him, they were educators, artists. Shivering, hungry, trusting in the fundamental goodness of fate, believing in simple hard work and sharing — and so they suffered for their beliefs. Maybe they came to believe in bad luck. Or in non-belief. He can clearly, too clearly, envision a middle-aged man, educated, stooping in the dark rain to work his hand into the icy muck, freezing and chafing his wrist, to come up with a single muddy potato, deformed and shrunken. He holds it up so the rain washes the mud off, while he stares at it, hungry. Also clear, from pictures he saw in books, is the handsome leader Kurrika, he of fancy words and dark-eyed rakishness, tupping the comeliest and most idealistic young things. He sees an old Kurrika falling to the night sand with his Eve, tupping on both of their minds, when the car stops for him. He'd even forgotten to put his thumb out.

It's the same car, with the two boys.

"Judy said you might want a ride out to Bere Point."

They must be bored, these two boys. He is their entertainment for the night, perhaps the week, as evidenced by the way they fire questions at him once he settles himself, steaming, in the back seat. Where from, where to, so how do you know the Whale-Man. Gore chooses the briefest answers, whether true or not. The passenger boy whirls around to show him what he has in his hands, telling the driver boy to turn on the inside light. It's a baby chick, pale-lemon coloured, nested in a wine-stained cloth napkin. The boy says it has a broken leg and he hopes it'll heal. A boar stepped on it.

"Boar? You mean, like, a pig?"

"Well, no, like a boar."

"They have wild boars here?"

The driver pipes up, gently scornful. "His dad grows them in their yard?"

"And one of them stepped on this guy." The boy brings the chick to his face and tenderly kisses it. These boys are no more than thirteen.

The driver, who keeps to no more than ten miles an hour, perhaps to stretch out the entertainment, goes on to explain that one hundred years ago the Norwegians in Bute Inlet brought in a bunch of boars as livestock because they could live in forest. These front-yard boars are their descendants.

"Do you two know any Finns here?" Gore asks.

"We're both," says the driver, with no apparent attitude.

Gore wants to ask other questions as well. For instance, he'd noticed a lack of licence plates on either front or back of the car, but he is too tired to ask what this, and the fact of them driving underage, might say about their island home.

"You want the heat on?" asks the driver.

Gore hears his own breath hissing through his teeth and looks down at himself shivering. They've left the dome light on. His coat looks so awful, climbing his arms like this.

"I'm okay."

The three look out their windows, the single beam illuminating the gravel and potholes. Gore likes these two boys. They're rare, students this polite, this lacking in irony. But they aren't his students, not these two. They're Finns. He recognizes now, in the driver's face, those sleek, almost feline, almost Asian features, that way some Finns look quite native, or aboriginal, some even having slanted eyes, that weirdest nordic race. Yes, and their language, Finnish, he thinks he read that it's a crazy language that has no known linguistic cousin or root, not the Latin or Danish or Russian of any of its neighbours. It's like they just started their own, came up with all their own sounds. Or they walked over the polar ice cap from China — how could they *not* have their own sounds after that? These boys, glowing under the dome light, cooing at the fuzzy peeping lemon, were magical boys. He would be honoured to teach them. He could tell them about their vascular systems, about all the tough and fragile membranes that kept them alive; he'd love to teach them why they glowed like that, tell them about their rods and cones and why a cat's, a cougar's, pupils would narrow to the merest slit in this hard light. And these boys could teach him their language.

"Do you… Do you boys know, ah, *Finnish*?"

The boys glance at each other. It's clear in their shared look that they know lots of Finnish, too much Finnish, and it's a question they've been asked too many times before.

"*Sointula*," they say together, smiling while watching each other say it. It's an in-joke. Perhaps an island cliché. It sounded not at all like Gore would have said it himself, more like a piggish snort through the nose that ended with a quick *tla*, like a flip of a tail.

"Do you like your island, you guys?"

"It's okay," says the driver. "Can get kind of boring here."

The passenger adds, "And you kind of keep expecting it to be *warm*, sometimes."

"Is it a magical place?"

The boys glance at each other, and shrug, and smile. They say they don't know.

"Lots of *coincidences* happen here?"

They say they don't know if more happen here than anywhere else.

THEY DROP GORE at the trail. Headlight pointed briefly at it, the entrance through the trees looks exactly like a cave mouth. At the opposite corner of the dirt clearing, illuminated in the same sweep of light, are the two green Vietnamese SUVs Gore had seen on the ferry. Those guys hadn't looked like campers. And the bastards could have driven him directly here, now couldn't they? He hears one boy wonder to the other who that is, meaning the SUVs, and the other boy doesn't know. The tone of this questioning is alarming, as it suggests not only that strangers are uncommon here, but anyone at all.

They ask him again if he'll be okay. He says he'll be just fine, thanks to them. He has described Eve to them but, no, they haven't see anyone like her around. Which doesn't mean a thing, they assure him. She could definitely be here. The boys can't agree whether Whale-Man is a mile or a mile-and-a-half along the trail before you cut down to the beach. They tell him the trail is in good shape, they both worked on it, and that he should make it okay, he's not going to go off a cliff or anything. If only there were a moon out it'd be no problem.

He stands beside the idling car, unable to remove his hand from the rim of the driver's half-open window. He can hear ocean waves but they are muffled, so there must be trees. He understands how dark it will be once the car leaves. He wonders about asking them if he can have the back seat for the night, once the car's in their driveway. He won't bother anyone at all; he has his coat to sleep in; he'll be gone by morning. He's about to joke that he'll rather enjoy the sound of boars hoofing about to the accompaniment of fleeing chicks, but when he picks up his head to say it, the car pulls away, and then it's around the corner and gone. It pounds potholes and throws gravel, going far faster than ten miles per hour.

The world loses even the echo of light and it is startling. He is blind. He can feel himself, encased in clothes, and skin, hot. He breathes steady as a metronome. There's nothing else going on except the sound of surf, and the wind high up in trees he can't see. As a joke, he tries to see his nose on his face. It's not funny. Nor is it funny that he can't see his feet. His feet are still there, but who knows where they will land. He takes a step.

HE CAN MAKE OUT the faintest shapes, so he probably won't fall into the most glaring ditches or smash against the widest of trees. At times he can see the contour of the trail. Most times he baby-steps blindly, arms thrashing in front of him, hands ready to hit something awful. He's too busy to think. Too busy to be too afraid.

Perhaps a hundred yards along the trail (he knows it could be half or double that) the root (it could be a monster's talon, he can't see it) more or less grabs his ankle and takes him down. It feels like a violent, mean act. It feels intentional. Face down in wood chips, Gore admits he's made a fatal mistake. Even wet, the hair on the back of his neck stands. It's not that it's pitch black and he's alone. It's not that he's broke and sick. It's that he's not wanted here. He's in a place he doesn't understand. It feels like a new world altogether, a vastly unknowable one, one that is ignoring him but *not completely*. It feels like this place understands him with no trouble at all.

He picks himself up and continues. He hurts from the fall. His few remaining dry spots — his incision, for one — are now soaked too. Groaning helps for a time, but soon not. He steps carefully, wills his eyes to descend into his feet, lifts his feet higher. He flaps his hands in front of him, afraid of what he might touch yet afraid because he is touching nothing. He might just wander off into the forest, and suddenly touch the face of an evil clown and then be dragged to the clown bog that lies beyond all imagining. Except that where he walks does still smell like wood chips, it still smells like trail. He still has his smell, he does have something. He has his thoughts as well, like this voice, this quick voice he can turn on to remind him: large stone figures were found on Vancouver Island facing this island here, crude sculptures that predated any known inhabitants, humanoid forms that gestured either a *goodbye*, or a *stay away*.

The wood chips end. The cold air now smells of slugs and rotten wood and the sourness of exposed roots, and threatens with shapes coming alive behind him. A quick grab at his neck. The crashing ocean not too far through the trees sounds detached, merely impersonally dangerous. But he still has sound, he still has sound.

Gore imagines the old rock wall in his backyard in Land's End. The old rock wall that kept the older wilds out. Even as a teenager he felt those wilds to be out of bounds, especially at night. At night they felt inconceivable, as alien to his instincts as the bottom of a river. At night, it was not that he wouldn't go over the wall but that he couldn't, no more than he could fly or find his way into the centre of a stone.

The welcome voice reminds him of the Chinese story of Fusang, which describes the visit of a Buddhist monk to this region in 499 A.D. White historians naturally pooh-pooh this. Captain Juan Perez of Spain was the first European to explore here, in 1774.

He finds himself walking quicker, against his will and breathing far too hard. It appears, yes it appears he's gone over the wall. Why do we assume that going over one's wall will necessarily be a good and courageous thing? Gail, I've gone over my wall. Look at me now. Gail — did I never tell you about my wall? If I did, do you remember? Were you listening? You're right, I'm sorry, you had a wall too and I don't remember yours either. We were busier listening to ourselves than to each other.

Gail, listen to me now — it's not necessary to go over the wall. It's not a very humourous place. There might not be a way back. Can you hear me?

Gore wills himself to stop the moans. He also gets himself to stop walking, to just stop and stand still. He tells himself he is resting for a minute. It's the oddest feeling, to stop right where you are in the middle of total darkness. He whispers, just to prove he's actually here.

"Well. Damn."

That's it: he should be angry.

"*Damn.*"

He realizes he's been lured here, by a witch.

Nonsense, he'll feel better, he'll feel great, when he sees her. He's not going to die. He's just had a halibut burger and a conversation with two friendly young people, and one doesn't die of exposure after either of those things. He could sit down right where he is and wait for daylight. He has a puffy ski jacket on. Only his wrists are cold. It's summer for God's sake.

Then he hears the old Native woman say, *They like to swim, eh?*, about the same time he feels his hair stand violently on end. He doesn't know if one caused the other or if it's simply that he is *being watched and is about to be killed by a cougar*. It's what the Natives say, isn't it, that your hair goes on end when a cougar is watching you? And also that *they hunt at night*. This over-the-wall place is their day-time, is their playground. They can see his neck and his eyelids blink and his hair standing up, yes they can see his fear, they are *reading this jerky panic*, they are *coiling to pounce*, don't fucking *run, jesus, he's fallen, he has the stature of a sick little child, pick off the child, the child who's now lost a shoe, pick off the sick child, cull the stupidest, pick off the weak little* —

He hears pops — poppop, pop, poppop — and breaking glass, from the direction of the parking lot. More little pops, like popping corn, but slower, and now it's *bangs*. Aren't those gun shots? He doesn't have the faintest idea, but it does get him up off the ground again. He tries to walk with one shoe gone and finds he can't, it tips him over, so he kicks off the other shoe. *Of course* he should be shoe-less. Surprises continue, now in the form of little lights up the slope to the left, in the deeper part of the forest. They look like tiny flash-lights held by running people — and look, one has fallen and gone out — and he can hear snapping twigs and the oddest hissing voices, and Gore goes down on a knee and suddenly there is an angry Asian face-to-face with him and he sneers and makes as if to shoot Gore with fingers shaped like a pistol, but this is all impossible, and look, now he's gone and so are the rest of them.

The phantasmagoria progresses with little silent explosions, little suns going off, to the right this time, toward the water, so bright — flash! flash! — that he can see his hands in the dirt, he can see a beach down through the trees.

Gore rises and launches forward and takes no more than ten more steps and — there it is. A beach fire, it's a big one, a bonfire, and it illuminates a path leading down to it. Huge drift logs are scattered, white, around it. The sand glows. It looks like the promise of heaven and, barefoot, Gore descends.

A lone figure stands at the edge of the water. He holds a camera which he slowly lets fall from chest height to stomach. It looks like something fast just happened here. The young man wears black headphones attached to a long cord that runs under a tarp.

Not ten paces from the man's feet the tip of a huge black fin skims into the firelight and just as quickly vanishes. The young man brings the camera up — flash! — waits, then lets it sink back to his waist. He's slow, he missed the shot, and now the fin is gone. It happened so fast that Gore isn't sure he saw a fin at all.

ONE THING ABOUT this young Tom Poole is, he isn't easily surprised. Perhaps he's not capable. He was standing there with his headphones on, staring out at the black water, when Gore tapped him on the shoulder from behind.

What, is all he said. He didn't even turn around.

When Tom went off to make tea, Gore could see how wounded and gimpy he is. Eve didn't mention any of this so maybe it's new. He's handsome but also disturbingly not, like a young Robert Redford who's somehow also old. He's dirty and greasy but his eyes light up and shock you. He moves ludicrously slowly, like one of those fly-catching lizards. And it's not that he's relaxed about any of it, not at all.

Though Gore isn't exactly seeing very clearly. Reaching safety, he's been able to let go a little and as a result his vision sometimes goes double. How's that for relaxed. He has to grip the tea in both hands. Some shakes over the edge onto his fingers but he can't tell if it is hot or cold. It tastes very bitter.

"You say this is Japanese?"

Rather too marvellously, something chooses now to roll out from under the tarp that lay beyond Tom Poole's feet. No doubt it has been nudged in the whale-action, had teetered in the aftermath and a breeze or something has sent it forth. It appears to be a crystal ball, and Gore concludes without surprise that, if Eve is a witch, the son of course is a wizard. The bonfire is made small, and burns upside-down in it. Well done, Master Wizard! Then Gore sees the warp and ripple, and coloured tint, and recognizes it as blown glass. An antique fishing float, the kind you sometimes find on remote beaches. The kind used by...the Japanese.

"Twig."

Gore remembers his question. He sips automatically. He doesn't want anything inside him. He's not exactly in pain but his whole body, especially his feet and face, feels swollen. Hot, or is it cold, all under pressure. His bare feet feel like they are perhaps very cold.

"Did you hear the gunshots?"

"Gunshots."

"Gunshots. And...And..." Gore can't continue. Tom had had headphones on, so of course he wouldn't have heard. And Gore has no clue how to describe the commotion on the trail, or even if there had been a commotion. No, he heard breaking glass. Saw people with lights darting through trees.

Tom stares at him, sees that no more words are forthcoming. He puts on his headphones again, listens for a while, takes them off. For someone who has just been invaded, late at night, miles from anywhere, he has absolutely no curiosity. Not even about his mother. He is as frightening as Eve's stories about him, but in ways Gore hadn't anticipated. After a time he finds himself telling this young Tom the little known fact that "Vancouver Island" was first named "Quadra-and-Vancouver's Island," to commemorate the friendly meetings that took place between the Spanish and English captains, but stops the story short when he understands that, though staring at him, Tom is wearing his headphones and hasn't listened to a word.

God, where is she?

Gore motions for Tom to remove his headphones, and the young man does so.

"Tom, ah, do you, ah, happen to know, time?"

"Know time?" Tom looks pleased at this.

"*The* time."

Tom struggles getting a watch out of his hip pocket and Gore feels bad now for asking.

"Ten after midnight."

"So — happy birthday."

The young man doesn't respond. He is somehow not surprised that Gore knows.

"So she hasn't come *by* yet," Gore says, again, shaking his head, staring into the fire. "*Really* odd. And, *sad*."

"My mother's coming. You're sure about that."

"Well, yes."

"My mommy's coming?" he asks flatly but with an indescribable smile, one that's not part of the conversation.

He sits so still. It's like he's coiled, spring-loaded. But of course he couldn't be.

"You my new daddy?"

Gore is newly unsteady on his log. He briefly eyes Tom who, simply watching the fire, absolutely corrupt in his power, looks twice as large as he should.

SOME TIME LATER, Gore doesn't know how long, after awkward and painful bits of conversation he can hardly abide, this man Tom Poole does something that will cement Gore's view of him forever. In fact, it will make him cry.

What Tom does is stare at Gore for an over-long time, as per usual, but this time taking in Gore's troubles. He apparently is concerned about Gore's bare feet, for he lurches up, limps away, and an endless time later reappears with two dirty T-shirts and a roll of duct tape. Saying nothing at all, except a mumbled something, two words of which Gore makes out to be "fashion statement," Tom kneels in front of Gore. With head humbly down, working hard with one hand and half a hand, Tom wraps one of Gore's cold feet in a T-shirt and begins to secure it with duct tape. Partway into this labour, Gore lets himself understand, and well up, and cry. He's crying for several reasons, he thinks that is indeed the case. Tom Poole just laughs. Both feet take a long time.

They were approaching the beach of the houses of the Ghosts when the Ghosts began to make a loud noise. Then all the Ghost men and women, and also the children of the Ghosts, came out of the houses; and the young men of Property-Maker became dizzy, and their bodies were twisted about. Only two of them were not wrong, those who had washed with urine.

— FRANZ BOAS, *KWAKUITL TALES*

BERE POINT

HE HAD THE PHONES on when the orca came. He was deep into the breath. God's breath, the in-and-out-at-the-same-time. He was imagining the skin of a blue whale as it swam slowly past his face, an inch away, a grey-blue wall moving and moving and moving, the occasional scar or barnacle, then more grey-blue.

When they came, one breached so close that its splash was caught in the light cast by his bonfire. He'd heard nothing, and then in the phones a ka-BOOM when the whale came down. It was like they were holding their own breaths as they came in. To surprise him.

They were transients, a small pod. No big notched-fin male. No calves either, and maybe it was the pod that Boss-Lady talks about so much because it depresses her. No calves equaling the end of the world. Orcas the canaries of the sea. But he thinks he did get some good shots. Two whales spy-hopped beside each other, and he thinks he might have captured that.

Right then he gets a tap on the shoulder.

Shaky little tap on the shoulder. Naturally, at first Tom assumes that tonight is the night and here are the guys with the truck. When he sees the barefoot old goof in the Sally-ann ski jacket he knows it's something different. The guy's right hyped. Tom also realizes that the deal isn't going to happen this way, he's going to get a phone call first. Why wouldn't he? He has a cell phone, they have his number, at least

McKay does. It only makes sense. Maybe even the ship will call. Maybe he'll have one of those, "Over" type radio-calls. He thinks Claude called him from a tug this way once in Victoria. *How ya doin' there Tommy, over. Great, Claude, over*. They're fun. He hopes the ship calls. *The coast is clear, over. Got my eyes peeled, over. Show me the money, over 'n' out*. Cowboy fun here in the middle of nothing.

He needs a stretch. At his tent he fires up the Coleman and gets the Brit some tea, some of the health shit from Cal that tastes like dirty bark. Maybe dirty bark is what it is. Or maybe secretly it's dried human shit, maybe it's peasant revenge. Why wouldn't they? He makes himself a coffee. He plans to sit up all night again, he's had a nap. He's got two reasons for staying up: whales and maybe a ship. And now he has company too. And maybe more company. Maybe a mother. And maybe some guys in trucks. When it rains it pours. Weird huge pod of random people, after spending a summer alone.

Back at the fire the Brit stares at him and asks the time. Tom has no idea but fakes having a watch in his pocket and guesses it's midnight or later.

"So — happy birthday."

It sounds right. In fact, August 10th sounds exactly right. He wonders if this magic-Peter also knows how old he is, because he has for the moment forgotten.

If it's his birthday on top of everything else, this might just be the biggest night of his life.

"Should I blow out the candle?"

The guy's okay, he gets it, he calmly says "Quite" without Tom having to look at the roaring fire in front of their faces. Doesn't smile either. You have to like a Brit when he's dry. The guy's nuts but okay.

But old Peter's also scared of him. Funny though — he never really knows what people are afraid of: him, or his injuries.

"You can't stay here."

The second Tom says this, he realizes it's true. Of course the guy can't stay here. There's a *deal* happening, maybe tonight. What if McKay comes to supervise? He probably won't but if he does he'll go ballistic, finding a doofus in a ski jacket with long white wrists watching coke unload.

"Well, it's your mother I—I *really* was expecting your mother. To *be* here." The guy looks seriously nervous now. He might cry.

Tom keeps a straight face. "Just because *she* lets you sleep with her..."

The guy doesn't like this one. He closes his eyes, a shudder. He might be gay but he's probably just nuts. Arrives here with nothing, all sweaty. Of course he's nuts. Tom wonders where his mother dug him up. Where are his fucking shoes? He wonders if his mother is even on her way.

His mother?

He doesn't want Evie here either. It's for a different reason, one he can find no words for yet.

"It seems I—I have to say I'm in *dire straits*. I mean if you have an extra *some*thing, a *blanket*, a *large towel*, I could just carry on down the beach and—" The guy is laughing but not really. "—And *perhaps* not die."

Tom moves to stoke the fire. It needs a log or two. It's one of those evenings where it gets instantly dark plus instantly cold. He can remember the sun going down but not the world going black. It's a summer's-over feel. He can see his breath. It's only August. In fact it's only his birthday, which he remembers from parties as a hot time of year.

Tom finds himself up and in search of some of the firewood he gathered earlier. He'd dropped it behind some big beach-log where it's hard to see now because tonight's fire is so bright that the shadows are even darker. The guy—Peter—follows him around then performs the pathetic helpful gesture of throwing on a chunk himself, some green alder Tom has been ignoring for weeks and hasn't burned on purpose. Peter limps off for more. Maybe he's planning to curl up by the fire all night. Tom watches him walk, stoop, drag up more alder that will smoke them out of the circle of heat if a wind comes up.

"Hey," Tom says. "We're the same."

"Sorry?"

He points at Peter, who limps to a halt and stands hunched, like he is, with one arm cocked up.

"You're like me in a hundred years."

"Ah, my. Quite," Peter says, smiling. "Well I just had an operation. Had my gall bladder taken out."

Is Evie really coming? Why? Claude too? Was this going to be some sort of, what, *intervention*? Son, we're worried about your isolation habit and we have come to take you home. We have no home either but we are going to take you to it. We have no *we* either but we made you and we are going to take you with us.

"When."

"Sorry? When?"

"When was your operation."

"Ah, a couple days ago. Three ago. Actually —" The guy winces on cue but Tom believes him. "— I think I'm getting — I seem to have become *infected* or —"

"And so you come up here to see my mom?"

The Brit doesn't get this one.

"Yes, but, and — And to see the historical utopia. Sointula. And maybe see some whales. Eve tells me you … You, ah …"

"Eve?"

"Um, Evelyn."

"Do you know what 'Sointula' stands for?"

"Actually yes. I researched the —"

"Feeling all harmonious tonight?"

"Can't — Can't say I do. No. And, and *touché*, I suppose …"

Tom is enjoying this old guy. He has edges.

"What do gall bladders do, anyway?"

"Eat fat."

Tom glances at this man who is really too thin already. He stares and stays with it a while until the Brit starts to get nervous: his eyes shift and his lips purse. His eyes bulge so that when he blinks, his eyelids have to stretch thin.

"Want to listen on the headphones? Might be more tonight. Ever seen orca?"

"Actually, yes. Paid to. In a boat. And then, well — then your mother and I actually chased some." He makes childish little paddling motions. "In our kayak."

Tom points. "Right there they come and rub on the gravel. Totally cool. Listen on the phones."

"Actually it's *cold*. I thought there'd be a *cabin* of some sort. But you say you do have a tent?"

The guy has a sassy side to him that verges on ugly. It makes Tom want to shut up. He'll let this mouse-pounder sleep in his tent tonight but tomorrow there's definitely a deal going down and the guy's got to go.

"You can sleep in the tent. Use my bag."

"Ah — well — really?"

Tom doesn't answer. It feels like he's had a good nap today and he wants to stay up anyway in case of another transient. And keep the fire high. Tonight probably isn't the deal but you never know.

The Brit is already moving. "Really — *thanks*. Can you tell me exactly where it might —"

"So how's Evie?"

"Ah."

Peter sits back down. He looks out to sea, as if he can see it. He reaches to pick up his tea, winces, leaves it where it is.

"She's very *sad* of course and, and *anxious*, but — otherwise very well. Very *fit*. She looks *good*."

"What's she so sad about?"

The guy stiffens at this and goes into a spasm of hiding something he knows. A scared seven-year-old has a better poker-face.

"She's — I don't know, really. I should let her tell you herself."

"So she knows where I am?"

"Well, she told *me*, and here *I* am." Peter closes his eyes again, and shakes his head again, this time violently, and faster. When he gets tired of this he breathes heavily and his mouth gapes open. For the first time, his guard is down and he looks ridiculous. For a while his beard and glasses made him look smart, but it's easy to see through that now.

"So what's your book about."

This catches him by surprise. Tom ignored his earlier babble about it, so now the Brit looks pleased. He smiles and burbles and doesn't know where to start. His mouth opens but his brain doesn't give it anything. Finally, he gives up, shrugs, and raises his hands to indicate everything around him.

"*This*," he says. "*Here*."

Tom lets the high school teacher stay happy with this for a few seconds.

"She looks *good*, eh?" Tom gives the guy a leer to go with it and it works too well. He's never seen a more frazzled man. Eyes looking for a place to hide, trying to jump out of his head. Brain fast as dolphin-talk but it's witless garble. It's true the poor bastard's just had an operation, he's all by himself in the woods with a fever and, the kicker, he's got it bad for Evie.

Who gives a shit what or who Evie does?

"So do you know old Claude, then?"

This gets him too and he can't say anything. Tom decides to ease off. In fact the Brit doesn't look to be good for any more talking tonight. He looks plenty sick, and he's actually sickening to watch, with his white feet all twisted up dead-cold beneath him. Tom, remembering that his cell phone has been up at his tent all this time, and that he'd better go get it and keep it on him, decides to give this big baby a new pair of shoes. He goes to the tent and comes back with some laundry and duct tape (and no cell phone, he'll realize later, snorting at himself), and gets to work fashioning the old guy some derelict sandals. It's crazy night-fun more than anything else — a red shirt, a charcoal shirt, doubled up under the soles and wound round with tape — but in the end it makes the poor guy cry. Maybe he can't take such a comic display of his own poverty. But he keeps the things on.

Tom asks him if he wants to go lie down in the tent and Peter nods in feeble hysteria and then out comes a big breath of relief he almost dies from. Tom actually has to help him up then guide him through the darkness back toward the campsite. He doesn't want to touch him, his skin has a yellow sheen. And that greasy ski jacket, riding up to his elbows.

Tom pinches a sleeve to pull Peter along. He tugs it sideways to turn him. He could do it with his eyes closed, but having to help this guy makes him see the path new and he almost stumbles himself. The Brit goes down twice. Tom can't help laughing. It's the guy's new shoes, but also it's the notion of two guys each dragging a foot, middle of the night in such wilderness, and it's hard to say who's helping who. The Brit is breathing heavy and hoarse, and all sense has long left him. Tom pictures the scene as if from the water, from a whales'-eye-view. You can see the whales just shaking their heads and understanding completely how it is these stooge-people are killing off everything on the planet.

They scuffle into the clearing and stand rickety in front of the tent and Peter declares, "The Empress." He commands Tom to fetch him the charcoal stick lying there in the cold fire pit, and Tom does, mostly because the Brit actually used the word "fetch."

Tom gets the guy into the tent and stands outside it for a time, listening. The Brit's breathing stops.

HE'S BEEN STANDING at the outer verge of trees for quite some time now, he doesn't know how long. It's not drizzling anymore. There are no stars to the south-east, so the wind is pushing more bad weather in. He should get back to his headphones. He's been standing here thinking hard and having memories unlike many he's had since before. Of his mother, of Roy. He feels the knot that is his stomach. It's hard to breathe. He had her face clear for a minute there, but now it's gone.

Is she really coming? Why? Is she coming up with Claude? For some sort of corny — What about Roy? Maybe Roy died and she's free. No, Roy wouldn't die. Maybe Roy finally got elected emperor, maybe he finally kicked her out.

Tom is halfway back to the fire when he stops and wonders why he let the guy crash in his tent. The ship might come tonight. It might be out there now. Jesus Christ. The signal fire is high. Good.

Tom throws another chunk of green alder on the fire when he understands why he hates the thought of Evie coming. It's because she'll be *expecting* this, she'll be *expecting* a signal fire with drugs-on-the-way, won't be at all surprised by the ship when it comes. It's no coincidence, it's like she planned it, it's what mothers like her *do*. He feels this more than knows it. It's more funny than anything else. And the — he's thrown the alder on because the Brit did it and it didn't smoke that badly. It must be because the fire is so big and hot to begin with. He's still learning the world of this beach.

He sits and gets the headphones on and tries to settle in. He can't listen well because he can't stop thinking. He's irritated at the thought of another tap on the shoulder, this time Evie. Or the truck guys. But he really doesn't want Evie coming up here. He'll feel like a kid caught hiding a nickel bag under the bed. He can see Evie clear as day now, yelling at him, in front of the truck guys, for conducting a multi-million dollar international drug deal. Well, not in *my* house, Mister. She's proud, it's exactly what she predicted. Through all this the Brit guy is chasing her around, sweating, babbling into her ear. Roy is at an important meeting. Jesus Christ — Oakville has arrived, Oakville has chased him here to the middle of nothing and now he'll have to leave here too.

Tom jerks off the headphones. He might not hear the cell phone with headphones on. What was he thinking?

No. He's talked to enough people already. He's had enough taps on the shoulder. He sees the headphones in his lap, puts them on, shifts them till they're comfortable, till he can no longer feel them.

He sits up straight — to a faint, faint orca call, whining, curving, left to right behind his head through the rushing ocean specks. Even though a voice shows nothing of size, he feels that it's the big notched-fin male.

But it's gone. Or it never was. He remembers having this before, probably lots of times. It might just be a memory of a call. Or it might just be the sound of him wanting one.

Surely no people wish to share in moments which reveal humankind's basest nature. The history of Europe's contact with North American Natives is strewn with such moments, not the least of which is the opening of the sea chest and the handing over, to some thankful people in a wooden canoe, of several blankets. It will never be known for certain whether the sailors knowingly handed over smallpox, or if they knew that what these blankets carried would travel hundreds of miles in a very few years and open up so much land to settlers. But so it is suspected.

— DON COTTER, *LOST UTOPIAS*

GABRIOLA ISLAND

THERE IS NOTHING SHE can undo. The damage is done. Only her knowledge has changed.

It's barely dawn when she passes in front of the main house, and office. She has her shoes off for quiet, and walking on the lawn she is surprised by the dew flashing clean between her toes. This is a sensation owned by suburbs; a lawn is a peculiar thing around here.

She has a cloth beach-bag and her few clothes fill only a half of it. Claude is in her pocket.

In the office a night light is on. She stops, keeps her feet still in the wet grass. And forgets to breathe. She steps quietly up, turns the knob, the door opens. She's in. She steals a cold cooked chicken in foil. She takes Maeve's good black raincoat off the wall hook, stuffs it into her bag as well. Take an extra raincoat, said Maeve.

There's the phone. In this sharp air of thievery she could easily steal a long distance call to Roy, tell him that she is going, now, to see their son, who has been severely wounded. It takes her only a second to know she won't call.

She recalls Roy in their living room, sees his face as he pivots to wish her luck in Victoria, saying too bad he couldn't free up time to come with her, saying see you in a few days, good-bye. He wears one of his favorite polo shirts, pale green. Roy is one of the few people she knows who makes green look good to wear.

Evelyn leaves the door an inch ajar and heads quietly for the dock, each step lush with cold beads on these soft rich waves of grass. It appears that, until the sun comes, the ocean lives thin and secret on land. For a few hours nothing is thirsty. On her feet the water feels supremely refreshing, feels like joy might, if there was joy.

She doesn't have to look off into the forest to know that no ghosts are up. But maybe there are no ghosts in the woods, never have been, never will be.

SHE HEARS THE WATER taxi's tiny roaring from out of the lights of Nanaimo before she can see it, a little black shadow in the distance. It throttles back a good half mile away, and when it slides against the dock she can hardly hear it at all. This boat seems a part of this place. The seagull on the piling over her head hasn't flown. It might be asleep.

Ten feet away, turned on its side, her kayak is dry. The bottom is scarred, wounds which go deep. The black upper deck is marred to, the scuffs bright white and telling a version of the trip. Much of the back, near her hole, is whitish grey because more paddling there has worn the black away. Near the front, near Peter's hole, she can see the white words "or bust," and there's the love-heart.

Abandoning the boat gives her a feeling she can't name. It's like throwing out certain old jeans. It's like selling that first, that modest, Oakville house. But a kayak's something Glenda and Maeve could use here. She's paid for the first night, has stayed three or four. You could call it a gift, or call it payment.

A thick, soft rope hits Evelyn on the ankle.

"Sorry, Honey. Thought you were ready."

Are they all women here?

"Twenty-five dollars, please." The slight woman, about Evelyn's age, steps down onto the dock and holds a hand out for money. She is wearing a heavy floater coat though the morning is only cool.

"Just one way, please."

"Not round? On the phone last night you —"

"Just one way." On the phone last night Glenda was at her elbow. Glenda thinks she is visiting Peter and then coming back.

"Okay, just the fifteen."

Peter's paddle is lying right where he threw it. Catching the sun's first rays, it looks alive. This shining vision of it rocks her back on her heels, skews her sense of time. It shows her the last few weeks all in one second. She knows that, in no more than a second from now, she will be on a bus out of Nanaimo. Less than a second later she will be seeing Tommy. This shine off the paddle is so slow and wide it shows a life that moves at ridiculous speed.

"Wait. Would the bus to Sointula take a kayak?"

"There's no bus to Sointula. It goes as far as the Port MacNeil ferry."

"Would that bus take a kayak?"

"This kayak?"

"Yes."

"Is it yours?"

"Yes."

"The bus to Port MacNeil takes anything. I've seen a coffin on the bus to Port MacNeil."

The woman charges Evelyn five more dollars to take the kayak aboard. The two women wrestle it on with not much trouble at all.

"Don't want to wake up Maeve and Glenda," the woman says, giving the boat almost no throttle, doing the first hundred yards as quietly as she did coming in.

Watching the water, Evelyn says nothing, though she could shout, could run on the spot, suffering an image of Tommy at six, of him watching her from the shallow end of the Oakville Municipal swimming pool, the bottom half of his face submerged, his eyes bright and taking her in, seeing all there is to see, then, bored, going under.

Nothing in the world has changed. Only her knowledge has changed.

And her plan. Who knows where she'll be sleeping tonight, and after tonight?

Who knows what wilderness, and what weather?

What expression on his face?

As they pick up speed the kayak shifts and rides heavily against her knee, which hurts. She adjusts nothing. It's his twenty-sixth birthday. Will there be scars? Will it be Tommy at all? She sees him again at six. Then at sixteen. What about these ten without her?

IT'S A RELIEF TO have slept on the bus, because last night at Glenda and Maeve's she hadn't at all.

She doesn't hate herself but she deserves none of this kindness. When the bus driver finishes his luggage removal and says his goodbyes, then sees Evelyn standing alone beside her kayak, beached here in the gas-station parking lot, he insists he help her "hump" it down to the water via the government dock. He may have said "hump" in a certain way but her antennae are rusty and she isn't sure. He is round and pink-necked and tight in his skin and looks the type who allows himself anything he can get when he's away from his wife, which is often. She tries not to let him but he grunts "Don't be ridiculous" and picks up one end and waits for her to stuff her bag and paddles and tent and untouched chicken into the two holes before she picks up the other. Not looking at her, holding his end up with one hand, he stands simply waiting — not a tall man but muscular, and you would guess bald under that hat. They hump the kayak across the road and down the sidewalk toward the ferry terminal and government dock, the driver asking the obvious questions and getting the shortest answers.

"So what we got here?" he asks, slowing down but not stopping as they round a corner.

A panic of police cars' flashing lights surround a tight clutch of vehicles and men. Police cars plus ghost cars too, and some of the police aren't in uniform. Two police cars speed off with what appear to be prisoners in the back. At the centre of things are two olive green SUVs which, as she draws closer, Evelyn can see have been riddled with what are probably bullet holes. What's left of the windshield glass is hanging and cloudy, and the side window glass is gone altogether. It seems the two vehicles were stopped as they drove off the ferry from Sointula.

Two more men, handcuffed, are being led to the backseat of a cruiser. One is minutely shoved from behind. He turns and glares and is shoved again. Both the cuffed men are small, thin Asians. They look too well-dressed for around here. Evelyn thinks, *disco*.

The bus driver says, mostly to himself, "I'll be hearing all about this one."

Nearing the approach to the government ramp, which is as close as spectators are being allowed in any case, Evelyn can see bullet holes tinier than she thought bullet holes might be. Two close together make her think of a doll's nostrils.

They take the kayak down the ramp to the dock and then drop it into the water gently. Evelyn is struck by the way it floats, riding light as a flower petal, almost a pose, waiting coyly for her to get in and give it proper weight. The bus driver has tied it up for her and has been trying to show her how to tie the easy-release knot herself.

Wanting to avoid more help she is loathe to ask directions to Malcolm Island but she has to and suffers the driver's smile and jab, jab, jab at the landmass beyond the point. Maybe an hour's paddle, or at most two.

"Sointula is ... Look—" This from a woman stringing laundry on the rails of the sailboat across the dock. "You can almost see the buildings — If you stand and —"

Evelyn asks her if she knows where on the island would be the best place to see whales from shore. At this the woman dives below for helpful maps while the bus driver says he'll go ask a friend who knows for sure and he'll come back and tell her, just you sit tight, but Evelyn can't bear these kindnesses and the bus driver's has turned an unmistakably leering corner in any case. She slips into her stern hole as easily as sitting in a chair and yanks the quick-release knot. She's out of Port MacNeil so fast she can't hear the woman's shouted directions. She waves thanks with a paddle, but that's all the time she can spare.

She'll find him. That's obvious. Clearly, it's the submerged life she can trust more than she can the apparent. There's an underweather and a kind of garden that grows magical linkages between people whether we choose to notice it or not, up here. In the past, she hasn't noticed much. But now it's only obvious. If she's going to hear about him from a hospital bed two hundred miles south, if she's going to hear about him from strangers at a dinner party halfway here, it's obvious she will find him. She will paddle close to Malcolm Island's shore, hugging the beach. She will round a point and there he will be.

She digs in. Her shoulders feel ripe, eager for this. Her stomach is ready. She is otherwise witless.

ONE HUNDRED YARDS OFF the shore of Malcolm Island, and its village of Sointula, which does from this distance look neat and simple and possibly even harmonious, but which she has no desire to visit, Evelyn has to decide left or right. She chooses left, the source of the fresh breeze and the approaching grey weather. It is obviously wilder, so it is where he will be.

It starts to rain and though the coming clouds are broken she pulls on Maeve's black raincoat because this is a steady cold. The coat has a funny hood, rising to a point, a witch's hat without the brim. Pointed black witch in a black and white boat. It's hard to believe it is August 10th. She feels the water with her fingertips and here lies the reason, this icy ocean body that chills all. Its cold is foreign to her fingers. She recalls some of Peter's endless info about this place, how it has its own ecosystem, a wedge of alien weather in the middle of the BC coast. The Queen Charlottes and even southern Alaska are warmer, drier. The water is too cold for oysters to survive.

In her mind she sounds the words "August tenth" and sees a backyard party baked in summer heat. Squealing, sassy seven-year-old boys, trying to win at games by being the loudest. They loved the money in the cake, the little treasures clean inside the wax paper, the small glory of money hidden in food. She feels in her chest the year when the parties stopped. Tommy's choice.

Just ahead, she sees a seal roll, then sees the tail flip and knows it's an otter. Then an otter family, three it looks like. They begin to roll and dive in unison, and the sight looks not unlike pictures she's seen of sea monsters. Of Caddy. The three coils, with a tail at the end. Could sea monsters be that simple? Otters and misjudged distance? Maybe. But Claude was not stupid, never stupid, and he did see something.

Today might be her last day to see Caddy. She puts her fingers in the water again. It feels too cold for Caddy's playground. She thinks of Caddy as warm blooded and a beast who could travel any sea he wished. Why would he choose numbing?

You can see all sorts of things if you let yourself. Can refuse to see all sorts of things too. *He's depressed. Like you.* Amazing if, all along, she had been looking in a kind of mirror. If, all along, she saw in his eyes what he was seeing in hers.

Paddling, most of all she keeps alert to his face, what she can remember of it. It's hard to capture but glimpses come. His face coming in the door after school, looking to the blank TV and not at her. When asked, How was your day?, his face considers her simple, reasonable question before deciding if it deserves an answer, an answer reeking with what he takes to be wit.

What is his new face like? One awful autumn night — she remembers it was windy outside and branches scratched at their aluminum siding and the moon shone bright and evil — she searched for his face on Roy's computer and she is ashamed of this. Not quite a year after he left, it dawned on her to search the internet's basest pornography, and with every click of the mouse she expected to see him in this next picture, part of a group, doing it with a mean grin. Horrified at herself. She surfed strings of photos, glanced at herky-jerky videos, never pausing, just seeking that face, or that bare arm or leg she'd instantly know. There was no telling what Tommy might do for money or for fun. Or for revenge, knowing — of course he'd know — that she was searching, just like this. A foray into a gay site told her he wouldn't be here — it looked too stylish, in some sense too decent.

She stumbled upon a site that apparently specialized in young men with older women — that was all she could take and she had to reach around back and shut the computer down with her eyes closed.

Newly ashamed of herself she paddles northeast along Malcolm's shore. What was she thinking? Hadn't she been paying attention for fifteen years? How could she not have understood that Tommy would never display himself so cheaply? Tom would never wallow on the public side of a camera. He would do the shooting, he would own the company, he would be completely in control.

Like father, like son. The father, who is in her pocket, nods to affirm this, not so much proud as matter-of-fact. This father who lost more and more control, and who now has ridiculously no control over anything any more, least of all what remains of him, a tube of bone-beads and dust.

How much is Tom in control?

Catherine says he is handling his disabilities extremely well.

HARDLY DARING BLINK, she rounds the point, she watches a beach emerge at her right, and, yes, there is the smoke of a beach fire. And what stops her paddling cold is the idea, a new one, but one that has been long percolating, that her voyage to Tommy might not be the end of this, that it might be the start of a longer voyage.

Not that she's there yet. She's knows it's him on the beach, but she isn't there yet. It is now that she imagines the whale. A single whale. She hears wisps of Darlene's lecture about orca, about transients, the meat-eaters, the largest being male, how they hunt alone and come out of the sudden deep to surprise seals and sea lions, take them whole, sometimes coming right out of the water in the speed of their attack. She feels a single whale, not far off, deep. The hair on her nape prickles. She understands she is in a place they favour, and sees too clearly that, from below, her boat is the size and shape of a sea lion. She sees what it looks like to the eyes of a male coming up at great speed.

"Mother, I want to marry," said Mink. —"Who is it?" —"Oh, it's Diorite-Woman." —"Well, then, try again. But will you not be tired if she does not talk?" — "That is what I like." — Then he went to his future wife. Night came, and they lay down. He tried to speak to his wife. "Speak!" —"You're a funny fellow," she said.

— FRANZ BOAS, *KWAKIUTL TALES*

BLUE TENT FADED WHITE

PETER GORE WAKES LYING on his back, loosely clutching a sharpened stick which points straight up. He smells himself and he smells the tent's main inhabitant and apparent equal in odor, Tom. Tom who helped him to this tent and didn't stay, who lurched back into the night.

A night which, as nights go, was indeed quite the beast. He doesn't remember much, mostly that he survived it. He sees his feet are bound in tape and shirts. He can recall slivers of that blind hike in. The rain, the dark unfriendliness of nature and people both. He can still taste burger cucumber. He can remember too clearly the sour, peaking sickness and he can still hear his own feverish bleating. He remembers gun shots and smashing glass and that little guy shooting a finger-gun right in his face, and swirling lights in the forest. Then there was Tom at the fire with his camera and his headphones and the echo of his whales. And Tom's broken body.

And no Tom's mother.

Odd to wake up clutching a stick that you have for some reason aimed at the sky. He sees it has a charcoal tip which is itself rubbed away to almost bare pale wood. He squints, focusing on where the tip points, and sees that sometime in the night he transferred much of the charcoal to the tent's ceiling. That is, he bloody well wrote on the tent. All capital letters, they begin rather carefully, with "SOI." The next is probably an "N" and the rest, which degenerate into energetic slashes, more than likely complete the word SOINTULA. The overall style has an affirming look about it, not unlike a *eureka* gaspingly scritched onto the stone wall of a dungeon, and it ends with — damn — a hole poked straight through the nylon. This was perhaps the decisive and celebratory punctuation.

In fever he seems to have thought he was starting something, and he had even given it a name.

THE PATH FROM the beach up to Tom's camp is thin and tentative, for that is how Tom walks, such that occasional protruding salal leaves have survived many comings and goings. Gore unwraps his feet, and follows it down. He no longer has a fever. Walking kindles the incision over his liver but it feels exactly like a cut should, and no more. Though he is weak from hunger, for some unrelated reason he feels clear and strong.

On the trail, which is centuries of dropped needles and is soft as carpet, he gradually picks his head up. Something demands his attention. What. Now he comprehends that these trees are the largest he's seen, anywhere. They are cedar, red cedar and, yes, western hemlock. Passing either he notes that the two species smell differently from one another. Somehow he knows that the smell is more robust because they are wet but not too wet, and that this also has to do with heat of summer. Indeed, the scent rides into his nostrils on a warm and lush but invisible mist.

The position of the barely discernable sun tells him that it is late afternoon. It isn't raining now but, after a minute, when he reaches the beach and sees Tom and another man, it is.

The man is large and freckled and needs a wash too. He doesn't see Gore's slow and careful approach over the logs until Tom nods toward him, whereupon the man turns quickly and gives Gore a steady glare. He's close to Tom's age and — what is it about this place? — also appears to need sleep.

"So this is Strike Three," says the man, apparently referring to Gore.

"*Good* morning," says Gore, well knowing it isn't but no longer caring about such things. He is still over the wall but it has gotten easier. Indeed, someone has gone and found his shoes for him, and there they are neatly side-by-side on a log.

He arrives, pulls on his shoes, and becomes one of a standing circle of three men around the smouldering fire. It seems there is always a fire going here. Gore notes that Tom is never not positioned to face the ocean, is ever only half-involved in a conversation because it's the ocean he's attending to. This young man who doesn't know that his father is dead.

"You're Strike Three," Tom Poole turns and tells him, smiling, looking almost interested before steadying his gaze back onto the water.

Gore looks at his companions questioningly. Both, like him, are bare-headed in the rain. Neither looks ready to explain.

"Um," is all Gore says. He looks down at his feet and shrugs. He wants food. He has done a quick scan of the site and has seen nothing remotely edible. Though, down by the water's edge, isn't that a dead crab? He wonders how long it's been dead. Or perhaps it's just the molted shell. Eve taught him the difference but he forgets. But, no matter what it is, perhaps if he boiled it into a soup?

The man shakes his head violently now, for no reason. He looks confused, stoned really. Tom, still watching the water, says, "It doesn't matter. Tell him. It's funny."

The man glares at Gore again, shakes his head once more, and says, "You're here to visit his *mother*?"

"Yes." Gore puts out his hand to be shook. "*Peter* Gore."

The man shakes his hand but doesn't introduce himself, until Gore asks, "And you are?" and the man says "McKay" impatiently, tossing his head at this item of no consequence.

"So." McKay begins his story, one he's apparently told Tom already. "So. There's this 'business deal' set up and... Well, a shipment was on its way. Which I just had to, you know, '*cancel*' because... *First* of all, because..."

"God, are you ever out of it," says Tom, glancing at McKay and smiling almost affectionately.

Now McKay explains with a sheepish smile that the cops will likely end up here soon so he either had to throw away his "bag of bud" or smoke it. He lets his eyelids fall halfway down his eyes and does floppy oysters with his lips to illustrate for Gore what he'd chosen. Then the story continues in its halting fashion. Gore ascertains a drug deal, a chatty girlfriend, and a Vietnamese gang that came snooping around. McKay gets animated — he crouches down to show how he hid — when he describes his sawed-off gun and the men getting out of their cars.

"You knew they were off in the woods, right?" asks Tom, clarifying a point for Gore.

"I believe I met one on the trail," says Gore, but he is ignored. He sees too clearly the hateful face of the man who had paused in his flight long enough to pretend to kill him. He'd had a frail wispy mustache.

McKay is nodding. "They all got out. They all went into the woods. In this direction. I followed them a bit to make sure. Then —"

"And first you gave them the note?"

"First I leave a note on the front seat telling them to fuck off and —"

"That's all you wrote on it?"

"That's all I wrote on it. 'Fuck' and 'off.' Then —" McKay's eyes brighten, "— I come racing back, I stand there, and I completely *blow the shit* out of two new Explorers. Right off the lot." He holds an invisible gun in childish arms and pulls a trigger fast, his arms jerking with the recoil. "I take out the glass, I nail each door, each panel, I make *sure* of it, I *hate* those bastards. Gun's got this really mickey-mouse silencer, right? Just an old plastic pop bottle that sort of works for a while and then it just falls off and hangs there and now the gun's loud so I know I have to get the fuck out of here. Then I hit a hubcap I think and one comes zinging back at me, I hear it and *feel the air* go right past my *fucking neck* into the bushes and I think that maybe it's them but I know it isn't yet, so then I go, 'What the fuck are you doing shooting near the *tires* man, you don't want them fucking *staying* here."

McKay's out of breath and shaking his head at himself. He sits on a log and puts his head in his hands, tufts of hair sprouting through his fingers. Gore notes that he has the hair most freckled men have, though darker because it's greasy. McKay moans and asks Tom if he's got any more tea and Tom doesn't seem to hear.

Gore recalls last night's two vehicles in the parking area. He can hear again the pops and glass breaking and then bangs. So here sits a man who imports drugs in quantities that require a ship. Gore doesn't care; there's no heart in it; in his book it will get cursory mention. Nor is he remotely curious why he's been called Strike Three. McKay has brought his head out of his hands to ask Tom in exasperation, "So where should I do it?" and Tom says, "Not here." McKay asks, "Tofino?" and Tom answers, "That's ridiculous." Gore doesn't really listen to any of it, but catches Tom apparently asking for money—"Last night wasn't my fault, I want some money anyway"—and mumbling something about building a cabin. Tom points to the bank of trees, staring at it over-long, ignoring what McKay goes on about next, a waiting boat and trucks and where the hell should he tell them to go.

Nor is there any point asking about Eve. If there has been any word of her, certainly he'd have been told. He knows that she has done one of two things. One, she took that bus, came and took one look at her son and chickened out. Two, she changed her mind and decided to paddle the entire way. He knows Eve didn't fly back to Oakville.

Evelyn. She's right, "Evelyn" is the better name. It's a sound of a rivulet that feeds meadow grasses, and as a name it softens her hard nature. She's probably known this all along, and it's a name she's been trying to live up to.

One half of Tom's mouth manages an impish smile. He seems to have been enjoying McKay's story a second time round, and says, to get McKay going again, "Then you called the police and *told* on them?"

McKay chuckles and shakes his head-in-his-hands, then raises it.

"I call the law. I inform them that drug cartel members are coming off the Sointula ferry in two identical vehicles. Which I describe." McKay smiles immodestly at Tom. "I leave out a certain detail about bullet holes and no glass. I figure the cops might notice this on their own."

"You saw them get on the ferry?" asks Tom.

"They drive onto the ferry. Their collars are up because their vehicles have *no glass*. Did I tell you I threw some dope under the seats? Before I started shooting?"

Tom sort of nods with his eyelids alone. "You used the word 'cartel'?"

McKay shrugs, obviously proud. He's big and a criminal and has just committed vehicular carnage, yet the deference paid to the silent limper is unmistakable.

"You're the cartel," says Tom, a joke too small for a smile even, and now Tom looks bored by the whole affair.

McKay stays down with head in hands until it looks like he might be falling asleep. Tom stoops to place a log strategically on the fire. He has a healthy mound of dry wood at the ready, and Gore understands he's had McKay do some leg-work, despite the heroics and the ruptured business deal.

Gore picks up a stick of wood himself and drops it in the flames but it lands on a bad angle and rolls out onto the surrounding stones. Tom turns his head up to him and his look suggests he is still trying to read Gore but is finding it difficult.

Gore returns his look. "Before I ask you for something to eat," he says, "I want to tell you that last night I poked a hole in the ceiling of your tent."

"No big deal," says Tom. Then he catches himself, remembering. "With your stick?"

"Apparently." Gore does feel bad about it. He sees what a tent means up here.

"Is that what you wanted that stick for?" Tom's half-smile is aflood with irony.

"So it seems." Gore smiles back.

"No big deal," says Tom, the moment over. "Duct tape," he adds, already turned away.

And that seems to be that. Gore turns to scan the water too. He almost says *I've begun*, but doesn't, and in any case his book is still a private and tender growth which might not survive explanation. He only knows he feels good. Almost invisible with weakness and hunger, but good. It feels so good to have survived. Not only last night's black pit but everything that came before: England, a new life, Gail, and Evelyn. Evelyn too. That's right. It is now not crucial that she come. He's over the wall now and he's fine.

Hunger, the simplest of things, persists, and when Tom limps away, Gore hopes he is going off to get some food. He's not. Instead, Tom stops at his tarpaulin and stoops for his binoculars, which he puts to his face. It is painful to see him bring his crooked arm up to badly-thumb the focus.

Gore turns to see what it is Tom has spotted. He squints through his glasses, which he only now notices are still covered in the grime of last night's adventure. But there, a pointy black fin has rounded the point. It's not rolling, not like the killer whales he's seen, but rather has a strangely uniform glide. It appears to have aimed itself, determinedly, straight for them.

"*It's coming this way!*" Gore can't help but hiss, throwing an arm out to point at it, perhaps tearing a stitch.

Tom does not respond at all. His binoculars are down, his face is unreadable, and Gore can't understand why he has gone neither for his headphones nor his camera.

EPILOGUE

Cannibal-at-North-End-of-World and his child had just been turned to ashes. Then Wisest-One took a small mat and fanned the ashes, and the ashes began to fly about. They turned into mosquitoes, and some into horse-flies. Then Wisest-One said, "You shall eat the flesh of later generations." Thus he said to them. Thus the ashes turned into horse-flies and mosquitoes.

— FRANZ BOAS, *KWAKIUTL TALES*

NO MORE THAN a brave day's walk from Sointula, Evelyn Poole comes to Bere Point, and Tom.

Standing up on the gravel watching them is Peter Gore. He has the enlivening feeling that this cool wind on his face is no different than his future. If asked what harmony means to him, Gore might be inclined to say that it lies over a wall and is best not talked about, for it will go away. For her part, Evelyn might claim that harmony is the unheard sound of everyone's desire — it is cacophony really, like an orchestra trying to tune up — but it is stunning, and it is the one thing we share. Her son Tom would not say anything at all, though if he did it might be to say that thoughts about harmony are just thoughts, which die, and so should not be taken seriously.

It's an oddly muted arrival for a mother's reunion with a child after a ten year absence. Perhaps the rain has added to the quiet reserve; the clouds have not broken for them; the sun has not come out. Also they have company, witnesses. Though one of them, the large McKay, has taken in the arrival and mumbled "Strike four" before stepping up onto a fifty-foot white log to take the wooden route back to the parking area and presumably his hidden car, en route to Sointula and away.

Tom Poole and his mother have not hugged. In fact they stand, and then sit, some distance away from each other, about four feet apart, on the log facing the fire. Tom is positioned to view the ocean, and any sign of orca. Though when Peter Gore returns from his task of making and bringing tea, and cups and saucers, he sees that they are sitting slightly closer now, two feet perhaps. Gore, on the other hand, has already had his hug, embracing Evelyn roughly after getting wet to the knees helping her beach the boat. He let her go after what turned out to be a brief hug when it was clear her focus was not him. He does not look hurt by it.

An eagle cruises in low, scattering the gulls that had collected on the emerging mud flats. Tom tells them that this eagle is around pretty much all the time. Gore points to the mud flats and asks Tom, and then Evelyn, if there might not be edible clams on this beach. In answer, Evelyn goes down to the kayak and brings them one of Glenda's cooked chickens. As if confirming a miracle, Gore proclaims, "Which I can now eat!", tapping his shirt over his incision. He rips the bird apart with practiced hands and, with a bearing of fairness, hefts each portion in a little bounce before distributing it onto one of the three saucers.

Even while eating, Tom's mother sits erect; her pointed black hood is still up, which adds to the effect. She is thinner than Tom remembers her to be, though memory is the last thing he trusts. He trusts more the sense that beside him is a person he does not know but at the same time understands deeply, in ways he hasn't caught up with yet but which are beginning to roll and swell in his body. Likewise he is nervous for reasons he can't fathom. There's no doubt that whatever is taking place is new. It hasn't occurred to him that a person can hope to remake herself and partially succeed.

"Have you seen any whales lately besides me?" Evelyn asks Tom, the depth of her voice so familiar to him. The joke is an offshoot of Peter Gore's having gone on and on about the lovely coincidence of her being mistaken for an orca of all things, though of course the mistake had been Gore's alone.

Tom doesn't answer her because he doesn't need to. Instead he asks Gore to lift the tarp to reveal the recording gear while he explains it. He sounds not unlike someone showing another proudly around his house.

Behind them, trotting out of the forest, a small brown dog, with curly fur and a grey beard, senses them, startles, and barks. Humans appear and settle it, and they turn up the beach to continue their hike, two young women and a little girl, perhaps six. None of them have clean hair; they are likely camping somewhere. They don't wave to the group around the fire, not wanting to intrude. The little girl tries skipping in the dense, round gravel but her legs wobble and her feet make lots of noise. She laughs, but doesn't try to get the two women to watch. She looks to be the kind of six-year-old who knows she's on a special outing in a special place, and is keeping herself happy because of it.

It is a new moon and an extreme low tide, which has exposed the spread of mud flat. Beyond that, the water is dead calm. With no breeze, the tidal smell hangs heavy in the air, but it's a smell of logical decay that none of them find fault with. Tom points to the embedded rebar and mike and he explains why it had to be moved. When Gore leaves them and descends the gravel bank to cast the chicken bones into the sea, and then grind some mud and gravel into the plates, Evelyn turns to speak to Tom.

"I hope you don't mind that I came."

Again Tom doesn't answer, this time because he has taken her words literally and there is no understanding them.

"Well," she says, more softly. Tom turns to the sound in her voice and his mother is reaching into her pocket.

She says, "I have some news for you."

PETER GORE HAS gone off to "use the bathroom," wandering grimly and far, and when he returns to the beach he sees them at water's edge. He stays discreetly away because Evelyn's arm is around Tom. With his good arm, Tom waves a cigar tube like a stubby magic wand. A spill of what resembles sand disturbs the water at their feet, and a minor plume of grey dust hangs and drifts back in their faces, causing them to flinch, though Tom's flinch is awkwardly delayed. They softly laugh, a similar, family laugh, as if the ashes have pulled some knowing joke.

Tom tosses the empty tube away, a flick of the wrist absent of any religion. He and Evelyn stand quietly but not for long. It is clear by how they move that a moment is enough.

Then, an incredible thing. Biologist Peter Gore could have thought them monkeys. Evelyn has turned to her son and whispered a question and now she is going through his greasy hair, delicately but swiftly searching in it, her wide eyes inches from his head, her eyes clouding when they find what they find. What's incredible is that he lets her do this. He even inclines his head her way, almost tottering forward.

CREDITS AND ACKNOWLEDGEMENTS

Quotations on pages 55, 87, 239, 265 and 391 are from *The First Nations of British Columbia* by Robert J. Muckle (UBC Press). Reproduced courtesy of UBC Press.

Quotations on pages 9, 31, 107, 291 and 305 are from *Ragged Islands* by Michael Poole (Douglas & McIntyre). Reproduced courtesy of Douglas & McIntyre.

Sections of the novel have appeared, in different form, in *The Fiddlehead*, *Event* and *Hobo*. My thanks to the editors.

Thanks to Lynn Henry, and all the good people at Raincoast. And to my agent, Carolyn Swayze. Thanks also to those who read early sections and versions of this meandering journey: Dede Gaston, Joan Macleod, Aislinn Hunter, Jan Geddes, and my taskmaster, Edythe Crane; also to Mike Matthews, Jay Ruzesky, Bill Stenson and Terrence Young of the Gentleman's Fiction Club. Special thanks to Jack Hodgins, for his care and friendship. Thanks to Dag for the paddle out to Snake Island. And thanks to Troy, the Whale-Man.

ABOUT THE AUTHOR

BILL GASTON is the author of the novels *Bella Combe Journal*, *Tall Lives*, *The Cameraman* and *The Good Body*, and several short story collections, including *Sex is Red* and *Mount Appetite* (Raincoast, 2002), a Giller Prize finalist. His story "The Kite Trick" was featured in *Granta* magazine (Fall 2003). He is the recipient of many accolades and awards, including the inaugural Timothy Findley Award, given by the Writers Trust of Canada to a male writer for a distinguished body of work. Bill Gaston lives in Victoria, British Columbia.

This book has been typeset in Whitman Oldstyle, designed by Kent Lew. It is a thoroughly contemporary serif font with classic, crisp features and a stately structure that draws inspiration from such 20th-century text faces as Caledonia, Electra, and Joanna.